SOUL WARS

More great stories from the Age of Sigmar

Sacrosanct and Other Stories
Various authors

The Red Feast
Gav Thorpe

Rulers of the Dead
Josh Reynolds and *David Annandale*
Contains the novels *Nagash: The Undying King* and *Neferata: Mortarch of Blood*

Soul Wars
Josh Reynolds

The Realmgate Wars: Volume 1
Various authors
Contains the novels *The Gates of Azyr, War Storm, Ghal Maraz, Hammers of Sigmar, Wardens of the Everqueen* and *Black Rift*

The Realmgate Wars: Volume 2
Various authors
Contains the novels *Call of Archaon, Warbeast, Fury of Gork, Bladestorm, Mortarch of Night* and *Lord of Undeath*

Gods and Mortals
Various authors

Scourge of Fate
Robbie MacNiven

• HALLOWED KNIGHTS •
Josh Reynolds
Book 1: Plague Garden
Book 2: Black Pyramid

Hamilcar: Champion of the Gods
David Guymer

Blacktalon: First Mark
Andy Clark

Shadespire: The Mirrored City
Josh Reynolds

Callis & Toll: The Silver Shard
Nick Horth

The Tainted Heart
C L Werner

Overlords of the Iron Dragon
C L Werner

Eight Lamentations: Spear of Shadows
Josh Reynolds

The Red Hours
Evan Dicken

Heart of Winter
Nick Horth

Warqueen
Darius Hinks

The Bone Desert
Robbie MacNiven

Audio Dramas

Realmslayer
David Guymer

Eight Lamentations: War-Claw
Josh Reynolds

Shadespire: The Darkness in the Glass
Various authors

The Palace of Memory and Other Stories
Various authors

The Imprecations of Daemons
Nick Kyme

The Denied
Josh Reynolds

Guns of the Black Eagle
C L Werner

SOUL WARS

JOSH REYNOLDS

To all those who worked to make this book the best it could be.

A BLACK LIBRARY PUBLICATION

First published in 2018.
This edition published in Great Britain in 2019 by
Black Library,
Games Workshop Ltd.,
Willow Road,
Nottingham,
NG7 2WS, UK.

10 9 8 7 6 5 4 3 2 1

Produced by Games Workshop in Nottingham.
Cover illustration by Igor Sid.

A CIP record for this book is available from the British Library.

ISBN 13: 978-1-78496-989-9

Printed and bound by CPI Group (UK) Ltd, Croydon, CR0 4YY

From the maelstrom of a sundered world, the Eight Realms were born. The formless and the divine exploded into life.

Strange, new worlds appeared in the firmament, each one gilded with spirits, gods and men. Noblest of the gods was Sigmar. For years beyond reckoning he illuminated the realms, wreathed in light and majesty as he carved out his reign. His strength was the power of thunder. His wisdom was infinite. Mortal and immortal alike kneeled before his lofty throne. Great empires rose and, for a while, treachery was banished. Sigmar claimed the land and sky as his own and ruled over a glorious age of myth.

But cruelty is tenacious. As had been foreseen, the great alliance of gods and men tore itself apart. Myth and legend crumbled into Chaos. Darkness flooded the realms. Torture, slavery and fear replaced the glory that came before. Sigmar turned his back on the mortal kingdoms, disgusted by their fate. He fixed his gaze instead on the remains of the world he had lost long ago, brooding over its charred core, searching endlessly for a sign of hope. And then, in the dark heat of his rage, he caught a glimpse of something magnificent. He pictured a weapon born of the heavens. A beacon powerful enough to pierce the endless night. An army hewn from everything he had lost.

Sigmar set his artisans to work and for long ages they toiled, striving to harness the power of the stars. As Sigmar's great work neared completion, he turned back to the realms and saw that the dominion of Chaos was almost complete. The hour for vengeance had come. Finally, with lightning blazing across his brow, he stepped forth to unleash his creations.

The Age of Sigmar had begun.

PROLOGUE

AS SURE AS DEATH

The dead thing stumbled slowly across the eternal desert of Shyish. Its bones were baked the colour of a dull bruise by the amethyst sun overhead, and what few pathetic tatters of flesh it retained had become leathery and fragile. Yet the lack of muscle and sinew had proved to be of little impediment in all the slow, countless centuries of its task.

Back and forth. Back and forth. Across burning sands, to the very edge of the Realm of Death, and then back, ten thousand leagues or more. Slowly, but surely.

As sure as death. As certain as the stars.

There was a soul of sorts, in those brown bones. It was a small thing, akin to the last ember of a diminished fire. It had no hopes, no fears, no dreams, no desires. Only purpose. Not a purpose it recognised or understood, for such concepts were beyond such a diminished thing. The directive that provided motive force to its cracked bones had been applied externally, by a will and a mind such as the dead thing could not conceive – and yet recognised all the same.

The master commanded, and it obeyed. The master's voice, like a great, black bell tolling endlessly in the deep, was the limit of its existence. The reverberation of that awful sound shook its bones to their dusty marrow and dragged them on. The master had sheared away all that the dead thing had been and made it into an engine of singular purpose.

The *only* purpose.

Cracked finger bones clutched tight about a single grain of pale, purple sand. The mote rested within a cage of bone and was incalculably heavy despite its size, weighed down with potential. Moments unlived, songs unsung. The dead thing knew none of this, and perhaps would not have cared even if it had.

Instead, it simply trudged on, over dunes and swells of windswept sands. It was not alone in this, for it was merely a single link in a great chain, stretching over distance and through time. A thousand similar husks trudged in its wake, and a thousand more stumbled ahead of it. Twice that number lurched past, going in the opposite direction. Their fleshless feet had worn runnels in the stone beneath the sand, and carved strange new formations in what was once a featureless waste. The silent migration had changed the course of rivers and worn down mountains.

Jackals hunted the chain, having grown used to the sport provided by the unresisting dead. They streaked out of the dunes, yipping and howling, to pluck away some morsel of dangling ligament. The dead thing paid them no mind. It could but dimly perceive them, as brief, bright sparks of soul fire, dancing across the dunes. By the time its sluggish attentions had fixed upon them, they were gone, and new fires beckoned elsewhere.

A carrion bird, one of many, circled overhead. Once, twice, and then it alighted on a sand-scoured clavicle. The bird twitched its narrow head, digging its beak into the hollows and crevices of the dead thing's skull, as generations of its kind had done before it. For wherever the dead went, so too came the birds. Finding nothing of interest, it fluttered away with a skirl in a flurry of loose feathers, leaving the dead thing to its purpose.

On the horizon, a second sun – a black sun – shone. Its corona squirmed like a thing alive, alert to the attentions of the master. As that great voice tolled out, the sun blazed bright with a hazy, bruise-coloured light. When the voice fell silent, the sun shrank, as if receding into some vast distance. But always, its dark light was visible to the dead thing. And always the dead thing followed the light.

It could do nothing else.

All of this its master saw, through its empty eyes and the eyes of the carrion birds and the jackals, as well. All of this, its master knew, for he had willed it so, in dim eternities come and gone. And because he had willed it, it would be done.

For all that lived belonged ultimately to the Undying King.

In every realm, wherever the living met their end, some aspect of Nagash was there. Once, such a menial task would have been undertaken by other, lesser gods. Now, there was only one. Where once there had been many, now there was only Nagash. All were Nagash, and Nagash was all. As it should be, as it must be.

The dead were his. But there were those who sought to deny him his due. Sigmar, God-King of Azyr, was the worst offender. Sigmar the betrayer. Sigmar the deceiver. He had snatched souls on the cusp of death to provide fodder for his celestial armies, imbuing them with a measure of his might and reforging them into new, more powerful beings – the Stormcast

Eternals.

Worse still, he had not been content with the nearly dead, and had scoured the pits of antiquity, gathering the spirits of the long forgotten to forge anew into warriors for his cause. Every soul lost in such a fashion was one less soul that might march in defence of Shyish.

Nagash saw the ploy for what it was, and a part of him admired the efficiency of its execution. Sigmar sought to beggar him and leave him broken and defenceless, easy prey for the howlers in the wastes. But it would not work. Could not work.

His servants had been despatched to the edge of Shyish, where the raw energies of the magics that formed the realm coalesced into granules of amethyst and black grave-sand, heaped in grain by grain. Over the course of aeons, he had gathered the necessary components for his design.

Even when the forces of the Ruinous Powers had invaded the Mortal Realms, he had continued. Even when he had been betrayed by one he called ally, and the armies of Azyr had assaulted his demesnes, he had persevered. Unrelenting. Untiring. Inevitable.

Such was the will of Nagash. As hard as iron, and as eternal as the sands.

CHAPTER ONE

BLACK PYRAMID

NAGASHIZZAR, THE SILENT CITY

At the heart of the Realm of Death, the Undying King waited on his basalt throne.

He sat in silence, counting the moments with a patience that had worn down mountains and dried out seas. Spiders wove their webs across his eyes, and worms burrowed in his bones, but he paid them no mind. Such little lives were beneath the notice of Nagash. His awareness was elsewhere, bent towards the Great Work.

Then, Nagash stiffened, alert. Purple light flared deep in the black sockets of his eyes. The scattered facets of his perceptions contracted. The disparate realms slid away, as all his attentions focused on Shyish and the lands he claimed for his own.

Something was wrong. A flaw in the formulas. Something unforeseen. The air pulsed with raw, primal life. It beat upon the edges of his perceptions like a hot wind. He shrank down further still, peering through the eyes of his servants – the skeletal guardians that patrolled the streets endlessly. He saw… green. Not the green of vegetation, but dark green, the solid green musculature of things that should not be in Nagashizzar. He heard the thunder of rawhide drums and tasted a hot, animal stink on the air.

Something was amiss. *Inconceivable.* And yet it was happening.

Nagash shook off the dust of centuries and forced himself to his feet. The creaking of his bones was like the toppling of trees. Bats and spirits spun in a shrieking typhoon about him as he strode from his silent throne room, shaking the chamber with every step. He was trailed, as ever, by nine heavy tomes, chained to his form. The flabby, fleshy covers of the grimoires writhed and snapped like wild beasts at nearby spirits.

He cast open the great black iron doors, startling those of his servants in the pillared forecourt beyond. That the fleshless lords of his deathrattle legions were gathered here before the doors of his throne room, rather than seeing to their duties, only stoked the fires of his growing anger. 'Arkhan,' he rasped, in a voice like a tomb-wind. 'Attend me.'

'I am here, my king.'

Arkhan the Black, Mortarch of Sacrament and vizier to the Undying King, stepped forwards, surrounded by a gaggle of lesser liches. The wizened, long-dead sorcerers huddled in Arkhan's shadow, as if seeking protection from the god they had served briefly in life and now forever in death. Unlike his subordinates, Arkhan was no withered husk, for all that he lacked any flesh on his dark bones. Clad in robes of rich purple and gold, and wearing war-plate of the same hue, he radiated a power second only to that of his master.

Nagash knew this to be so, for he had made a gift of that power, in days long gone by. Arkhan was the Hand of Death and the castellan of Nagashizzar. He was the vessel through which the will of Nagash was enacted. He had no purpose, save that which Nagash gifted him. 'Speak, my servant. What transpires at the edges of my awareness?'

'Best you see for yourself, my lord. Words cannot do it justice.'

Though Arkhan lacked any expression except a black-toothed rictus, Nagash thought his servant was amused. Arkhan turned and swept out his staff of office, scattering liches and spirits from their path as he led his master to one of the massive balconies that clustered along the tower's length. At his gesture, deathrattle guards, clad in the panoply of long-extinct kingdoms, fell into a protective formation around Nagash. While the Undying King had no particular fear of assassins, he was content to indulge Arkhan's paranoia.

'We appear to have an infestation of vermin, my lord,' Arkhan said, as they stepped onto the balcony. 'Quite persistent vermin, in fact.' Razarak, Arkhan's dread abyssal mount, lay sprawled upon the stones, feasting on a keening spirit. The beast, made from bone and black iron, its body a cage for the skulls of traitors and cowards, gave an interrogative grunt as its master strode past. It fell silent as it caught sight of Nagash, and returned to its repast.

Many-pillared Nagashizzar, the Silent City, spread out before him. It was a thing of cold, beautiful calculus, laid out according to the ancient formulas of the Corpse Geometries. A machine of stone and shadow, intricate in its solidity, comfortable in its predictability.

It was a place of lightless avenues of black stone veined with purple, and empty squares, where dark structures rose in grim reverence to his will. These cyclopean monuments were made from bricks of shadeglass, the vitrified form of the collected grave-sands. Harder than steel and polished smooth, the towering edifices resonated with the winds of death.

Nagashizzar had been made from the first mountain to rise from the eternal seas. There had been another city like it, once, in another time, in another world, and Nagash had ruled it as well. Now all that was left of that grand kingdom were threadbare memories, which fluttered like moths at the edges of his consciousness.

Those memories had taken root here and grown into a silent memorial. Or perhaps a mockery. Even Nagash did not know which it was. Regardless, Nagashizzar was his, as it had always been and always would be. Such was the constancy of his vision.

But now, that vision was being tested.

Nagash detected a familiar scent. The air throbbed with the beat of savage drums and bellowing cries. Muscular, simian shapes, clad in ill-fitting and crudely wrought armour, loped through the dusty streets of Nagashizzar. Orruks. The bestial, primitive children of Gorkamorka.

Below, phalanxes of skeletal warriors assembled in the plazas and wide avenues, seeking to stem the green tide, but to no avail. The orruks shook the ground with the joyful fury of their charge. A roaring Maw-krusha slammed through a pillar, sending chunks of stone hurtling across the plaza. It trampled the dead as it loped through their ranks, and the orruk crouched on its back whooped in satisfaction.

The orruks were the antithesis of the disciplined armies facing them. For them, warfare and play were one and the same, and they approached both with brutal gusto. They brawled with the dead, bellowing nonsensical challenges to the unheeding tomb-legions. There was no objective here, save destruction. Unless…

Nagash turned towards the centre of the city, where the flat expanse of the Black Pyramid towered over the skyline. It was the greatest and grandest of the monuments he'd ordered constructed. Unlike its smaller kin, hundreds of which dotted Shyish, the Black Pyramid was the fulcrum of his efforts. Its apex stretched down into Nekroheim, the underworld below Nagashizzar, while its base sprawled across the city – a colossal structure built upside down at Shyish's heart.

A flicker of unease passed through him as he considered the implications of the sudden assault. It was not a coincidence. It could not be. He looked at Arkhan. 'Where did they come from?'

The Mortarch motioned southwards with his staff. 'Through the Jackal's Eye,' he said. Nagash's gaze sharpened as he followed Arkhan's gesture. The Jackal's Eye was a realmgate, leading to the Ghurish Hinterlands. There were many such dimensional apertures scattered across this region – pathways between Shyish and the other Mortal Realms. They were guarded at all times by his most trusted warriors. Or so he had commanded, a century or more ago. As if privy to his master's thoughts, Arkhan said, 'Whoever let them pass through will be punished, my lord. I will see to it personally.'

'If the orruks are here, then whoever was guarding the gate is no more. The reasons for their failure are of no interest to me.' Nagash considered the problem before him. Then, as was his right as god and king, he passed it to another, one whose entire purpose was to deal with such trivialities.

'Arkhan, see to the disposal of these creatures.' Nagash looked down at his Mortarch. Arkhan met his gaze without flinching. Fear, along with almost everything else, had been burned out of the liche in his millennia of servitude. 'I go to bring the Great Work to its conclusion, before it is undone by this interruption.'

'As you command, my lord.' Arkhan struck the black stones of the balcony with the ferrule of his staff. Razarak heaved itself to its feet with a rustling hiss. The dread abyssal stalked forwards, and Arkhan hauled himself smoothly into the saddle. He caught up the reins and glanced at Nagash. 'I am your servant. As ever.'

Nagash detected something that might have been disdain in Arkhan's flat tones. Of course, such was impossible. The Mortarch was no more capable of defying Nagash than the skeletons trudging through the wastes. And yet, he seemed to, in innumerable small ways. As if there were a flaw in him – or in Nagash himself.

For a moment, the facets of Nagash's being hesitated. Then, as ever, the black machinery that passed for his soul righted itself and continued on. He had been mistaken. There was no defiance. Only loyalty. All were one, in Nagash, and Nagash was all. 'Go,' he said, the stentorian echo of his command causing the air itself to shudder and crack.

With a sharp cry, the Mortarch urged his steed into a loping run. The skeletal monstrosity galloped across the balcony and flung itself into the air. The winds of death wrapped protectively about both rider and steed, carrying them towards the battle.

A moment later, a cyclone of howling, tortured spirits streamed past Nagash and spiralled into the air in pursuit of the Mortarch. He watched as they hurtled upwards and away, a cacophonous fog of murderous spectres, twisted and broken by his will into a shape suited to their task. They had been criminals, murderers and traitors in life, and now, in death, they were bound in stocks and chains, afflicted with terrible hungers that could never be sated. Nagash knew himself to be a just god, whatever else.

He turned away, satisfied. Arkhan would see it done, or be destroyed in the attempt. The Mortarch had been destroyed before and would be again. Always, Nagash resurrected him.

His term of service had no end, for so long as the Undying King required his services.

He cast his gaze back towards the Black Pyramid and let his body crumble to dust and bone. Even as it came apart, his mind was racing through the confines of the pyramid like an ill wind. Its interior was a labyrinth of impeccably placed tunnels and passageways, all polished to a mirror-sheen. These pathways resonated with the energies of the aetheric void that encompassed and permeated the Mortal Realms, invisible and inescapable.

Construction had begun in the depths below Nagashizzar, in the underworld of Nekroheim, the wells from which all other underworlds had sprung. The dead of entire civilisations had surrendered their bones to form the walls and ceiling of the cavernous reaches of the underworld. The vast expanse was lit by a dead sun, the flickering wraith of an ancient orb long since snuffed, stretched upwards from the deepest pit in the underworld. Its sickly radiance cast shrouds of frost and fog wherever it stretched, and an eternal corona of wailing souls orbited it.

Now, that sun churned malignantly, its incandescent heart pierced by a capstone crafted from purest grave-sand. He had placed that capstone himself, with his own hands. Only through his magics, and the fluid nature of Nekroheim, had such a feat of engineering been possible. The Black Pyramid had blossomed from that point, spreading outwards and upwards with glacial certainty.

Once, the black pyramids had been the wellsprings of his power, designed to draw in the souls of the dead, like fish in a net. Most were gone now, reduced to rubble by the rampaging armies of the Ruinous Powers.

But this one eclipsed them all, in both size and purpose. Every element of its construction was bent towards drawing the raw stuff of magic itself, from the edges of Shyish, to its heart. The greatest concentration of those magics which sustained the Realm of Death would be refracted and reflected through the pyramid. Thus would the raw magics be refined into a more useful form. It had been constructed over the course of aeons, assembled by generations of artisans, both alive and dead. And now, it was complete, awaiting only his presence to fulfil its function.

His spirit raced through the passageways, and where he passed, the skeletal servitors scattered throughout them twitched into motion, following their master into the hollow heart of the pyramid. This central chamber spread outwards from the structure's core, from capstone to base, banded by pillared tiers, one for each level of the pyramid.

As Nagash's spirit billowed into the immense chamber like a black cloud, silent overseers, stationed among the pillars, stirred for the first time in centuries. They directed the new arrivals onto the assemblage of walkways and ledges that extended from the tiers towards the hundreds of platforms that clung to the central core of the pyramid.

The core stood in stark contrast to the orderly nature of the rest of the structure. It was a contorted spine of jagged shadeglass, reaching from the interior of the capstone up to a glittering field of amethyst stalactites that spread across the pyramid's base. A web of shimmering strands stretched out from the core in quaquaversal spillage. The core and its calcified web were covered in innumerable facets of varying sizes and shapes, all of which shone with a malevolent energy.

To Nagash, that light was almost blinding. It throbbed with morbid potential, and he felt the Black Pyramid's monstrous hunger almost as keenly as his own. It clawed greedily at his essence, but he resisted its pull with an ease born of long exposure. It feasted on the strength of the realm, battening on the winds of death, as he would feast on it, in his turn.

His deathrattle slaves entered the chamber, and many of the skeletal labourers were ripped from their feet and drawn into a sudden crackling storm of amethyst energies, as Nagash drew their essences into his own. With brisk efficiency, he disassembled the unliving slaves and reassembled them into a new body for himself.

The God of Death flexed a newly fashioned hand, feeling the weight of new bones. Satisfied, he stepped onto the largest of the walkways. Ancient warriors, clad in rusty, age-blackened armour, knelt as he passed through their ranks. Deathrattle champions and lords, the kings and queens of a hundred fleshless fiefdoms, humbled themselves before the one they acknowledged as their god and emperor both. The diminished husks of slaves and artisans abased themselves, grovelling before the master of their destinies. Nagash surveyed the silent ranks and was pleased.

At the urging of the overseers, skeletons trooped across the walkways to the great platforms clinging to the core. Occupying each platform was a millstone-like ring of shadeglass, dotted with turning spokes of bone. These lined the core's length, from top to bottom, one atop the next, rising upwards along the spine. Strange sigils marked the crudely carved circumference of each ring, and these glowed with a pallid radiance.

'The time has come,' Nagash said, as the last of the skeletons assumed its position. The walls of the shaft hummed in time to his words. As one, his servants stiffened, their witch-light gazes fixed upon him. 'Go to your prepared places, and bend yourself against the wheel of progress. Let it turn and time itself be ground between the stones of my will.'

The fleshless shoulders of princes and slaves alike bent to

the spokes of each wheel. As the skeletons pushed against the spokes, the stone rings began to move. A thunderous, grinding growl filled the air. Violet lightning flashed across the facets of the web and sprang outwards, striking the polished walls of the shaft.

A rumble began, far below. It shuddered upwards through the pyramid, shaking it to its upside-down foundations. Loose grave-sand sifted down like dry rain. Nagash, still standing atop the largest walkway, stretched out a talon, gathering together the strands of crackling energy that seared the air. With precise, calculated movements, he looped the shimmering skeins of magic about his forearms, as if they were chains. The skeins flared, burning as he pulled them taut, but he ignored the pain. After all, what was pain to a god?

Facing the core, Nagash gathered more and more of the skeins, and his titanic form became a conductor. Amethyst lightning crawled across him, winnowing into the hollow places and filling him with strength enough to crack the vaults of the heavens. This was not the raw magic that soured the edges of his realm, but a purified form.

He hauled back on the strands of magic he held, lending his strength to that of his servants. As they pushed, he pulled, forcing the great machinery into motion. Around him, the faceted walls began to shift and scrape as slowly, surely, the Black Pyramid began to revolve on its capstone, as he had designed it to do.

The structure rotated faster and faster. The dead sun beneath it flared brightly, as if in panic, and then burst with a cataclysmic scream that shook Nekroheim to its intangible roots. Rivers of cold fire streaked up the sides of the pyramid, flowing towards the base, or else washed across the cavern walls. Nekroheim itself shuddered, as if wounded.

The cavern floor began to churn and shift. Millions of bones clattered as the rotation of the pyramid drew them in its wake. Like some vast, calcified whirlpool, the entirety of the underworld was soon in motion. A storm of bones and tattered spirits, spinning about the ever-turning pyramid.

Within the pyramid's heart, Nagash felt and saw all of this in the polished walls of shadeglass. He saw the streaks of purple light stretching out, flowering into storms of raging elemental fire as they broke through the borders that separated Nekroheim from the other underworlds. The purple light dug into the metaphysical substance of these other realms, hooking them the way a meat-hook might sink into a side of beef. Steadily, they were drawn towards Nekroheim, becoming part of the growing maelstrom.

Nagash threw back his head and bellowed. He felt as if he was on the cusp of dissolution, as if the monstrous energies he sought to manipulate now threatened to rip him asunder. Only his will prevented him from succumbing to the forces he'd unleashed. A lesser god would have dissolved into howling oblivion. He clawed at the storm of magic, drawing more of it into himself, pulling the world-spanning chains tight.

Outside the pyramid, Nekroheim was crumbling. Changing shape. The underworld bent beneath the oscillating structure, bowing up around it. Becoming something new.

The reverberations rippled outwards across Shyish. Through the eyes of his servants, Nagash saw the skies above Nagashizzar turn purple-black. Orruks wailed as their green flesh sloughed from their bones, and they collapsed in on themselves. Billions of skull-faced beetles poured down from the swirling clouds, devouring those greenskins that were still in one piece. Nagash laughed, low, loud and long as the ground beneath Nagashizzar began to buckle and sink. Soon, every realm would feel the echoes of what he did here. Reality would shape itself to accommodate his will.

His laughter ceased as shadeglass cracked and splintered all around him. Something moved within the polished depths. They came slowly, drifting through the dark: vast impressions with no definable shape or form. The air of the chamber stank of hot iron and spoiled blood, of sour meat and strange incenses. He heard the rasp of sharp-edged feathers and the clank of great chains. He felt the flutter of unseen flies, clustering about his skull, and their hum filled the hollows of his form.

Something that might have been a face slipped across the cracked facets. It gibbered soundlessly, but Nagash heard its words nonetheless. It spoke in a voice that only gods could discern, spewing curses. He turned as something that might have been a blade, wreathed in fire, struck another facet. More cracks shivered outwards from the point of impact. Nagash did not flinch. To his left, enormous talons, as of some great bird, scratched at the shadeglass, while opposite them, a flabby paw-shape, filthy and sore-ridden, left streaks of bubbling excrescence along the facets.

Eyes like dying stars fixed him with a glare, and a howl shook Nekroheim to its roots. Great fangs, made from thousands of splintered swords and molten rock, gnashed in elemental fury. Nagash lifted a hand in mocking greeting. 'Hail, old horrors – I see that I have your attention.'

The Ruinous Powers had come like sharks, stirred from the deep places by a storm, as he'd known they would. They came roaring, thrusting the barest edges of their inhuman perceptions into his realm. Was it curiosity that had drawn them so – or fear?

He felt their awareness as a sudden pressure upon him, as if a great weight had fallen on him from all angles. The immensities circled him through the facets of the walls, prowling like beasts held at bay by firelight. 'But you are too late. It is begun.'

Something bellowed, and great claws of brass and fire pressed against the reverse of the shadeglass, cracking it. An avian shadow peered down through the facets of the ceiling, whispering in many voices. The stink of rot and putrification choked the air. Had any of his servants been alive, they might have suffocated from the stench. Voices like the groaning of the earth or the death-screams of stars cursed him and demanded he cease.

He cast his defiance into their teeth. 'Who are you to demand anything of me? I am Nagash. I am eternal. I have walked in the deep places for long enough and have gathered my strength. I will shatter mountains and dry the seas.'

He turned as they circled him, keeping them in sight. 'I shall pull down the sun and cast the earth into the sky. All of time will be set aflame and all impurities in the blood of existence burnt away, by my will and mine alone. There shall be no gods before me, and none after.' He gestured sharply. 'All will be Nagash. Nagash will be all.'

As the echo of his words faded, something laughed. A ghost of a sound, no more substantial than the wind. Nagash paused. Something was wrong. Belatedly, he realised that the Ruinous Powers would not have come, unless there was some amusement to be had. Not the orruks, but something else. Some other flaw in his design.

'What mischief have you wrought?' he intoned. He found it a moment later. Familiar soul-scents, bitter and tarry, wafted on the currents of power flowing through the edifice. Tiny souls, these. Like bits of broken glass. The skaven spoke in hissing, squealing tones as they scuttled through the pyramid, wrapped in cloaks of purest shadow. He did not know by what magics the ratkin had avoided the guardians of this place. Nor did he care. That they were here, now, was the only important thing.

It seemed the orruks were not the only ones who had come seeking the treasures of Nagashizzar. He looked up, into the insubstantial faces of his foes. 'Is this, then, the best you can do? You send vermin to stop me?' The laughter of the Dark Gods continued, growing in volume. Incensed, a part of his consciousness sheared off and slipped into the depths of the pyramid, seeking the origin of the disturbance while the rest of him concentrated on completing the ritual he'd begun.

His penumbral facet swept through the passages and pathways like a cold wind, but moving far more swiftly than any natural gust. He found them in the labyrinthine depths, chipping away at the very foundation stones of the pyramid. Their desire for the vitrified magics was palpable. The skaven had ever been a greedy race.

How long had they been here, pilfering the fruits of his labours? How had they gone unnoticed, until now? As their tools scraped at the bricks of shadeglass, crackles of purple lightning flowed through the walls. The more they collected, the greater the destabilisation became. Nagash watched the arcs of lightning, tracing their routes and calculating the destruction they would wreak.

Somewhere, at the bottom of the deep well of his memories, something stirred, and he had the vaguest impression that all of this had happened before. The pyramid, his triumph, the skaven, it all felt suddenly – awfully – familiar. God though he was, he could not well recall his existence before Sigmar had freed him, though he knew that he had existed. He had always existed. But he could recall only a few scattered moments, frozen in his recollections like insects in amber – instances of pain and frustration, of triumph and treachery. Was that what this was? Had he lived through this moment – or something like it – before? Was that why the dark gods laughed so? He paused, considering. The black clockwork of his mind calculating.

The Mortal Realms were something new, built on the bones of the old. They were merely the latest iteration of the universal cycle and would one day shatter and reform, as had countless realities before them. As sure as the scythe reaped the grain, all things ended. Nagash knew this and understood, for he was death, and death was the only constant. But what if there had been a time that he had not been as he was?

And what if that time might come again?

What if this was the first step towards that unthinkable moment? And what if he had walked this path before, always with the same beginning and same ending?

Driven by this thought, Nagash let his essence fill the corridor like a graveyard mist, though his body remained in the core, wracked by amethyst lightning. He felt a bite of pain as the rite continued, and he rose up over the ratkin, crackling with wrath. He crushed the closest, snaring it in a foggy talon.

At its demise, he pushed all doubt aside. If this moment had happened before, so be it. The outcome would change. Must change. He would hold fast to his course, whatever the consequences. He would not – could not – be denied. Time itself would buckle before him.

Skaven squealed and scuttled away, fleeing the damp coils of fog. The slowest perished first, bits of shadeglass clattering to the floor as they convulsed and died. The mist filled their contorted forms, dragging them upright and sending them in pursuit of their fellows. The dead ratkin clawed at those they caught, ripping gobbets of fur and meat from their cringing forms. The skaven descended into an orgy of violence, hacking and stabbing at one another in their panic, unable to tell friend from foe.

If this was the first step, he had taken it, and there was nothing to be done. If not, then he still had a chance to see his design through. As the last of the intruders perished, in fear and madness, Nagash dismissed them from his thoughts. Their remains would join the rest of his chattel. There were more important matters to attend to now.

The presence of the intruders had thrown off the delicate balance of the pyramid's function. He could feel it, in the curdled marrow of his bones. They had polluted it somehow, tainted his Great Work. That had been their purpose all along. He could see it now – an antithetical formula, let loose among the Corpse Geometries, to gnaw at the roots of his perfect order. An artificial miscalculation, meant to break him.

Always, they sought to despoil the order he brought. Always, they made sport of his determination. They sent their servants to cast down his temples, and inflicted a hundred indignities upon his person. Again and again, they drove him to the earth, chaining him in one grave after another. They set stones upon him and sought to bury him where he might be forgotten forevermore. The laughter of the Ruinous Powers shook the pyramid, and shadeglass fissured all about him.

They thought him beaten. They thought that once more he would be cast down into a cairn of their making, to be safely ignored until the next turn of the wheel. Anger pulsed through him, and amethyst light flared from the cracks in his bones.

He was not beaten. And he would never be buried again.

'Stand not between the Undying King and his chosen course, little gods,' Nagash said. 'Nagash is death, and death cannot be defeated.' As he spoke, his thoughts raced through the structure, seeking a way to compensate for the damage. He was too close to fail now. There must be a way. There *was* a way. He merely had to divine it.

Skeletons were caught up in a grave-wind, disassembled and reconstructed as Nagash took shape at the points of greatest stress – many Undying Kings rose up, a hundred eyes and a hundred hands, driven by one will. These aspects of him set their shoulders against collapsing archways, or braced sagging walls. 'I will not be undone. Not again.' The words echoed from the mouths of each of his selves, as they fought against the pyramid's dissolution. A chorus of denials.

Shadeglass cracked and splintered as the oscillation sped up. Blocks of vitrified sand shifted and split, sliding from position to crash down around him. But still, the Black Pyramid revolved. Nagash reached out with mind and form, seeking to hold the edifice together through sheer determination. Despite his efforts, sections peeled away and crumbled to dust. Passages collapsed, pulverising thousands of servitors.

The core twisted as if in pain. Cracks raced along its length, leaking tarry magic. The mechanisms of rotation ruptured and burst, hurled aside by the core's convulsions. Skeletons were dashed against the walls, or sent tumbling into the depths of the pyramid. Nagash ignored all of this, focused on containing the magics that now surged all but unchecked and unfiltered through the structure. The power burned through him, threatening to consume him. But he held tight to it. His Great Work would not be undone. Not like this.

'I will not be defeated by vermin. I will not be humbled by lesser gods. I am Nagash. I am supreme.' His denial boomed out, echoing through the pyramid. Through the eyes of innumerable servants, he saw Shyish fold and bend like a burial shroud caught in a cold wind. Wild magic raced outwards, across the amethyst sands.

Across the realms, a rain of black light wept down from the convulsing sky. A million forgotten graves burst open. In vaulted tombs, the honoured dead awoke. Spirits stirred in shadowed bowers and hidden places. Nagash roared wordlessly and drew the power to him, refusing to let it escape. It was his. And he would not let it go. Let the realms crack asunder, let the stars burn out, let silence reign. Nagash would endure.

He could feel the realm buckling around him, changing shape, even as the dark gods laughed mockingly. Reality itself shook, like a tree caught in a hurricane wind.

Until, all at once, their laughter ceased.

And in the long silence that followed… Death smiled.

CHAPTER TWO

GLYMMSFORGE

FREE CITY OF GLYMMSFORGE

The sun set over the city of Glymmsforge.

The sky darkened, turning a deeper purple than Elya had ever seen before. Something about it chilled her, and she looked back to the heaps of refuse she'd been sorting through. She had to be quick, else the nightsoil men would catch and beat her. It had taken her days to recover last time.

Elya was small, thin and dark. Ten winters, or maybe eleven, but looked eight. Her clothes were loose and oft-mended. She went through the refuse with an experienced eye, picking through what had been dumped by vegetable sellers and butchers. She found a lump of fish meat and tossed it to one of the cats that hunted alongside her.

There were a dozen cats in the alleyway, eating scraps or hunting the vermin attracted by it. Most were the small, black cats native to Shyish, but some were strays from other realms – large, spotted hunters from Ghur, and sleek, almost hairless mousers from the sandy wastes of Aqshy, the Realm of Fire.

Wherever humans went, so did cats. They were as deadly an escort as ever padding through the dim streets. They loved Elya and had since the cradle. She knew this as well as she knew the sun would rise and the dead would walk. As she knew that the sky should not be purple. She glanced up again, chewing on something that was only a bit mushy. It wouldn't be enough, but it was something. A cat meowed, and she stroked it. The big, brindle tom flashed a scarred lip as it rubbed against her.

The cats were worried. She could feel it. It was as if they sensed something on the wind. 'Is it a storm?' she asked, softly. Sometimes sandstorms whipped through the streets. If she was caught away from home by one, she'd have to seek shelter wherever she could find it. 'I could go down to the catacombs. Pharus would understand.'

The tomcat meowed again, as if in agreement, then abruptly stiffened and hissed. Elya heard the clatter of a nightsoil cart approaching and darted from the alleyway, followed by the cats. She heard a shout behind her but didn't stop.

Elya ran through the concentric streets, trying not to think of the sky or how hungry she was. She followed the cats, trusting them to lead her along safe routes. She ran barefoot, her soles toughened by days at play on walls and rooftops of the Gloaming. The cobblestones were warm underfoot, for the moment. As night fell, however, they would become like ice.

Around her, the city woke up for the evening. Sprigs of icethorn and mistletoe were hung upon doorframes and silvered mirrors set in windows. Lamplighters, clad all in black and wearing protective posies of strong-smelling herbs, lit the lanterns that hung above every archway and lintel. Her father,

Duvak, would be among them, she hoped, earning money they desperately needed. If he hadn't crawled into a jug of wine and forgotten his duties.

She caught sight of Freeguild soldiers, in the mauve-and-black uniforms of the Glymmsmen, on their evensong patrol. Some carried long, sharpened stakes of Aqshian flamewood, just in case, while others carried mirrored shields or handguns loaded with salt-and-silver shot. The people of Glymmsforge knew well the dangers of the night and had long since made them routine and ritual both.

The cats led her through one of the twelve great market squares around which life in the city often seemed to revolve. She sprang over a nightsoil cart, eliciting a shout from the collector, and ducked through a vegetable stall, snatching a pallid carrot as she went. She was hungry, and stealing food wasn't really thievery.

Munching on the carrot, she leapt up onto the display board of a spice stall and danced through the bowls of spices without tipping over a single one. The cats ran alongside or ahead of her, streaking through the evening crowd.

While a few stones were tossed in her direction by angry market-goers, no one dared bother the cats. Not for no reason was a proud mouser a part of the city's amethyst-and-sable heraldry. Cats were among the most powerful of the city's defences. Besides keeping out vermin, they could detect the things that were not there. Many a haunting shade or alleyghast had been revealed by the warning hiss of a cat.

Elya followed the cats into a cul-de-sac, one of thousands in this district. Above her, windows clattered shut for the evening, and the smells of holy herbs and braziers of gloomweed filled the air. Somewhere, she could hear the clangour of iron funerary bells, and she knew that the Black Walkers were about and on patrol.

She scrambled behind an abandoned cask as the noise grew louder. A line of shuffling figures came into sight, passing the mouth of the cul-de-sac. The Black Walkers wore dark sack-cloth and heavy hoods of the same, hiding their features. Strange sigils had been chalked onto their robes and hoods, and the heavy chains they wore clattered and clanked as they brushed across the cobbles. The funerary bells they rang made the air tremble, as they sang a slow dirge in some language she didn't recognise. She didn't emerge from hiding until the last of them had vanished, heading west towards the mausoleum gate.

Her father called them priests, but she didn't know what god they served. Azyrites seemed to detest them. Elya, born in Shyish, was wary of them. In better days, her father had often told her stories of how the ghosts of dead gods haunted their ruined temples, and how some men still worshipped them, in secret places. Elya shivered. The ghosts of men were dangerous enough. She looked down at the brindle tomcat crouched beside her. 'We need to go down,' she said, as the sound of bells faded.

The cul-de-sac sloped downwards. The buildings to either side grew higher, as if trying to escape the shadows of the streets around them. They almost blocked out the sky, which had turned the colour of a bruise. The cats led her to the back wall, where dark thorn brambles and gloomweed grew wild, creeping across the cracked stones. She followed them through the brambles and into a crack in a wall, squeezing slightly, scraping her shins and banging her head. Behind the crack was a tunnel of sorts, a place where the stones leaned against one another in haphazard fashion.

Water collected here, running in chill rivulets between the stones. The dark swallowed her. It was cool and damp. The sounds of the marketplace and the clangour of the bells were muted. All she could hear was the constant drip of the water and the purring of her four-legged companions.

They led her around and down, through dark passages and cramped stairwells, into the deep catacombs. Elya scampered through the maze of forgotten rooms, through flooded cellars and beggar-warrens. She had made the journey a thousand times before, and felt none of the fear one might expect as she descended into the dark.

Elya liked the catacombs. They were far away from the bustle of the city. She liked the long, silent avenues that stretched for miles on end. She could wander for hours among the great mausoleums that had been carved into the sides of the curving tunnels and among the hills of crypts, one set atop the next, stretched up, up and up. Or down, down and down, depending on your perspective. She passed freely through the mirrored passages and the webs of silver chain that kept the unquiet dead at bay.

But most of the dead were at peace here, in the dark. Even so, mortals weren't allowed down here. Pharus said so. He lived down here, in the dark. He had only come up to the light once, that she could remember.

But she didn't like to think about that day. Her mind shied away from it, away from a red memory, full of sound and fury.

The cats stopped. So did she. She dropped to her haunches, watching the dark ahead. The walls moved, down here. Things were never the same way twice. Sometimes, she'd scared herself by walking into her own reflection, or found herself trapped in a tunnel that was no tunnel at all, but instead a construct of canvas and clever angles. The guardians of the catacombs liked to play tricks. But the cats always knew where they were and warned her.

The big, brindle mouser with the scarred lip hissed softly.

Elya flattened herself and scuttled off the path. A moment later, the tromp of heavy feet sounded in the dark. Armour rang against the stone, as clear as the bells of the Black Walkers. But these warriors served a living god, rather than a dead one.

From her hiding spot, she watched the giant warriors, clad in black war-plate and bearing weapons such as a mortal man might struggle to lift, stride down the path. Stormcast Eternals were a common enough sight in Glymmsforge. They guarded the city from danger – both above and below. These wore heavier armour than the ones she usually saw, decorated with morbid totems that made her skin crawl, and they carried heavy, two-handed hammers.

She felt a thrill of fear. The Stormcasts were frightening, though not in the same way as the Black Walkers. They were like statues come to life, too big and too strong not to evoke nervousness. But they meant no harm, she knew. Not to her, at least.

The two warriors stopped, just opposite her hiding place. They spoke to one another in low tones that set her bones to vibrating. Then, one turned and stared at her hiding spot. She held her breath.

'I see you, child,' he said, in a voice like crashing rock. He sounded disapproving.

'I wasn't hiding,' she called out.

'That is good to hear, given how poor a job you made of it.' He sank to his haunches, reaching one enormous hand out to a cat that rubbed itself against his greave. The animal accepted the touch with dignified grace and then ambled away, tail flicking. 'There are more of them today.'

Elya stepped into the open, holding the brindle tom in her arms. The cat glared at the Stormcasts as if they were rivals, rather than giants. 'They're keeping me company,' she said, with a hint of pride. 'They're my carters.'

'Your...?' the crouching Stormcast said, in confusion.

'She means courtiers, Briaeus,' the other interjected. 'She thinks she is their queen.'

The brindle tom snarled. Briaeus ignored the animal. 'Pharus told us you were not allowed down here, girl. Come, I will escort you to the entrance.' Briaeus reached for her. Elya flinched back, clutching her cat to her chest. The tom snarled again, and other nearby cats wailed in warning. The Stormcast paused.

'Perhaps you should let her go, Briaeus,' his companion murmured.

Briaeus glanced back. 'Our orders...'

Elya seized her chance. She dropped the cat and darted past Briaeus' outstretched hand, as swift as her limbs could carry her. He rose to his feet and made as if to lurch after her, but his companion stopped him. His words rumbled after her as she ran.

'Let her go. Pharus will deal with her.'

'This is a waste of time,' Gomes said, raising his lantern. The light washed across the path ahead, and long shadows stretched away into the sandy wastes outside the city.

The walls of Glymmsforge rose high above the small troop of Glymmsmen, soaring up into the black. From outside, Lieutenant Holman Vale could make out the irregular craters that scarred their surface – signs of the many sieges the city had endured.

More evidence of past wars littered the waste ground that sloped away from the walls. The mouldering wreckage of ancient siege engines loomed like lonely trees, and broken stones dotted the sands. Vale barely remembered the last war – he'd been a child. Gomes did, though he rarely spoke of it, and only when he was in his cups.

'There's no one out here. No one alive, anyway. And if they are, what of it?' Gomes continued. He was squat and broad, and his black-and-mauve uniform was untidy. But the blade he held in his other hand was well cared for.

'If they are, we must do our duty, sergeant, and see that they make it into the city safely,' Vale said, glancing at the men who followed him. He'd brought five, including Gomes. It didn't feel like enough, now that they were away from the gates.

It was too quiet out here. There were sprawling shanty towns clinging to the city walls to the south and the west, but none nearby. Too much blood had been spilled here. He cleared his throat. 'After all, can't have people camping in the spoil grounds all night, sergeant. That's dangerous.'

'And it also means they don't pay our private toll, eh, lieutenant?' Gomes said. Several men chuckled. Vale nodded.

'Exactly, sergeant. Everyone pays the toll, if they want to come through our gate.' Vale glanced back at the sloped walls of Glymmsforge's northern mausoleum gate. The mausoleum gates were strongholds unto themselves – dodecagonal bastion-forts, jutting from the compass edges of the city. Each was composed of twelve overlapping, triangular bastions, laid out in a semi-radial pattern from the curve of the wall. And each was manned by a company of Glymmsmen. In the case of the northern gate, it was Vale's company.

Vale was young, with a newly bought commission weighing him down. His family were traders – beer, mostly, though some silks and spices – with more money than influence. That was set to change, though, if Vale's father had anything to say about it. Vale had taken a posting with the Glymmsmen, while his sister had entered Sigmar's service. If all went well, in a few years the Vale name would rival that of the city's other leading families.

If all went well. If a deadwalker didn't feast on his guts, or a gheist didn't stop his heart. There would be promotions aplenty in his future, even if Captain Fosko didn't look as if he was going anywhere, anytime soon. He frowned at the thought. Fosko was old and hard and fixed in his place, like one of the gargoyles that adorned the city's walls. Worse, he was happy where he was.

'I know that look,' Gomes muttered, glancing back at him. 'Thinking about old Fosko, sitting in his warm quarters, sipping tea, while we're out here in the dark and cold?'

'Hoping he stays there,' Vale said, annoyed by his subordinate's perspicacity. 'Otherwise we won't be collecting any private tolls at all tonight. Where are these traders of yours? You said they came this way.' It wasn't unusual for people to duck out of line and seek an easier – or cheaper – way into the city. But only the foolish did so at night.

'I said someone said they might have,' Gomes corrected, testily. 'No one on duty saw them. One minute they were in line, the next they weren't. We're stretched thin on the gate – old Fosko wants men walking patrol, not searching people for contraband.'

'Maybe because he knows half of that contraband winds up in your private stores, sergeant,' a soldier said, eliciting a number of chuckles.

Gomes turned and gestured with his blade. 'Stow it, Herk. And the rest of you, keep quiet. Never know who or what might be listening out here.'

Herk and the others fell silent, as Vale studied his sergeant. Gomes was old for his rank. But he was a good line officer, when he wasn't inebriated. And he knew how to keep the books looking tidy, despite the fact they were drawing pay for around a third again more men than were actually in their section.

That, along with the private tolls they levied from those passing through the mausoleum gate during evensong, had allowed Vale to accrue a tidy sum. When he had enough, he intended to purchase a suitably comfortable commission. Probably somewhere in the inner city. There were precious few prospects in the outer. This line of thought was interrupted by the whicker of a horse.

Gomes stopped. Vale stepped up beside him. 'See something?'

'No, but I hear them.'

The unseen horse whinnied again, more loudly this time. It sounded afraid. The wind had picked up, and sand stung Vale's eyes. The lantern light flickered, and Gomes lowered it. Hooves thumped against the ground, as if the animal were turning in a hasty circle. Vale could hear metal clinking – the sound of tack and harness?

'What was that?' Herk said suddenly. Vale glanced at him.

'What was what?'

'I thought I told you to stow it, Herk,' Gomes growled.

'The stars… What's wrong with the stars?' Herk said, his voice edging towards shrill.

Vale looked up. The stars seemed to waver, as an amethyst radiance spread across the night sky in all directions. He heard the sands hiss, as if caught in a storm-wind. It almost sounded like voices whispering. He tried to ignore it.

Before his eyes, the stars vanished, swallowed up by the amethyst haze that occluded the sky. Vale tore his gaze from it and looked at Gomes. 'What happened to the stars?'

Gomes' reply was interrupted by a squeal of fear and the sound of galloping hooves. Vale shoved Gomes aside as a horse without a rider raced past, scattering the small group of soldiers. Vale heard a scream, somewhere out in the dark, as he picked himself up. It was joined by another, and another.

'Jackals,' he said.

'No. Not jackals,' Gomes said, swinging the lantern out. But there was nothing to be seen, save will o' the wisps dancing, drifting across the detritus of war. Corpse-lights bobbed along the tops of the far dunes, and Vale turned abruptly. He'd heard something close by, like the sudden, repeated intake of breath.

One of the men started, cursed, spun. 'Something touched me,' he said.

'There's nothing,' Herk said.

'It touched me, I tell you!'

Vale made to chastise them but closed his mouth without speaking. The air tasted sour. He felt ill. There was something wrong. Looking around, he could see that the others felt the same. He glanced up and then quickly away. Where had the stars gone?

'Lieutenant, we have to get back inside the walls,' Gomes said hoarsely, his face pale in the lantern's glow. He looked frightened. Vale had never seen Gomes frightened, and it sent a pulse of fear through him. He nodded, his hand on the hilt of his sword.

'I am fully in agreement, sergeant. At the trot, lads.'

No one argued. As they hurried back the way they'd come, all thoughts of tolls forgotten, the wind dropped.

To Vale, it seemed as if all of Shyish were holding its breath.

Lord-Castellant Pharus Thaum stood at ease on the edge of an abyss. The circular chasm lay hidden at the heart of the catacombs that sprawled far beneath Glymmsforge. Ancient pillars, carved from the rock of the walls and covered in indecipherable script rose about the cavern, holding up its ceiling.

Between the pillars rested hundreds of shallow alcoves, each containing a mummified corpse, wrapped in linen and cobwebs. Blessed chains of iron and silver had been strung across each alcove, as if to keep the cadavers within quiescent. More alcoves, similarly shrouded, ran along the curve of the abyss and down into lightless depths. Chains stretched like the strands of a great web between the alcoves, and from each link had been hung devotional ribbons and purity scrolls.

Mortal priests, their faces daubed with ash and sacred unguents, sat in leather slings and hauled themselves along the chains, murmuring constant prayers. Other priests, too old and wizened to traverse the chains safely, limped along the edges of the abyss. They rang silver bells and cast droplets of water gathered from the pure rivers of Azyr onto the alcoves along the walls. They went from nook to nook and back again, following a pattern set down years ago, in the first, black days of Pharus' time as seneschal of the Ten Thousand Tombs.

Pharus was an officer of the Gravewalkers Chamber, of the Anvils of the Heldenhammer Stormhost, second in command to Lord-Celestant Lynos Gravewalker. Clad in blessed sigmarite and bearing a halberd and warding lantern, it was Pharus' task to stand sentinel – an immoveable bulwark on which the stratagems of his lord-celestant could turn. For the past decade that had meant warding the Ten Thousand Tombs and their contents.

He took a bite of the apple he held, enjoying the bitter tang of its juices. A bag of them hung from his belt – one of the few pleasures he allowed himself. The apples were a reminder of better times and the garden he glimpsed, sometimes, in the memories that hung just out of his reach. At his feet, his gryph-hound, Grip, lay contentedly gnawing on the remains of a rat.

Any other Stormcast might have chafed at such a duty as this, monotonous as it was. But for Pharus, it was an opportunity to indulge his creativity. He was a lord-castellant, and where he stood, fortresses inevitably rose. Such was the case with the catacombs. He had turned the ancient necropolis into a confusing labyrinth of false streets, mirrored cul-de-sacs and avenues to nowhere, all in the name of keeping his charges safe. Pharus fancied that not even the Huntsmen of Azyr could find their way through his maze without aid.

'The sky has gone purple.'

Pharus sighed. 'Elya.' He looked down at the pale face at his elbow. 'I thought I told you not to come down here, child.' He wondered how she'd managed to avoid his patrols.

'Yes.' Elya flopped down beside Grip and sprawled over the gryph-hound. The beast grumbled and nudged the girl with her beak. Elya looked up at Pharus. 'Did you hear me? I said the sky has gone a funny colour.'

'I heard you. Have you eaten today?' The child looked undernourished. Her father spent most of what they had on drink, Pharus knew. The man was a broken soul, like so many in the city. Like Elya herself might one day be. If she survived. The streets were not safe for a child, even in one of Sigmar's cities. Her words registered, as he reached for an apple. 'Purple?' he asked. That was unusual. He glanced at one of the nearby tombs, reassuring himself that it was sealed shut.

'Purple,' she said. 'Like just before a sandstorm, only darker.'

He tossed the apple to the girl, still pondering this news. 'Eat it slowly. I don't want you to get a stomach ache like last time.' He watched her take a bite. 'How do you keep finding your way down here?'

'The cats help me.'

Pharus glanced down, as a black cat rubbed itself against his greave. 'Of course they do.' He looked at Elya. She was filthy and scrawny. Not much different than the first time he'd seen her, screaming. Crying as her mother – the thing that had been her mother – sought to draw the life from her. He pushed the thought aside.

'By rights, I should have you escorted to the surface,' he said. He'd done it before, with other intruders. He'd done worse to some, in fact. Sigmar had decreed that no living soul, save those who had been chosen for their faith and purity, were allowed anywhere near the Ten Thousand Tombs. 'And beaten, perhaps, for good measure,' he added lamely. She didn't reply, too busy with her apple.

Though he'd never admit it, he'd come to almost welcome her inevitable appearance. Sometimes, looking at her, he saw another face overlaying hers – another child, from another life. Like the apples, she was a reminder of who he had been before Pharus Thaum had existed. Before he'd lost and gained everything in a single blast of lightning.

It was a sign of weakness. A breach in his defences. But no matter how hard he tried to repair it, it always opened anew. And part of him was glad of it. Grip looked up, growling, the feathers on her neck stiffening. Pharus took another bite of his apple. 'You're late,' he said, chewing.

'My apologies, my lord. This place is… difficult to navigate.' A woman's voice, as resonant as his own, if not so deep.

'Thank you. I have laboured many years to make it so.' Pharus turned to examine the new arrival. Calys Eltain was a warrior and officer of the Gravewalkers Chamber, as Pharus was. The Liberator-Prime had her sigmarite shield slung across her back, and a hand resting on the pommel of the warblade sheathed on her hip. She had her helmet tucked under her free arm, exposing olive, freckled features, and close-cropped black hair.

Familiar, those features – enough to prompt a faint twinge of guilt. He'd seen it, the moment Eltain had arrived from

Azyr a few months earlier. Pharus glanced at Elya, but the child was ignoring the newcomer, concentrating on her apple. Relief warred with sadness, and he turned his attentions back to Eltain.

The Liberator-Prime had fought in a hundred battles or more, since her recent rebirth on the Anvil of Apotheosis, evincing a stubbornness that put even Pharus to shame, at times. She was a born defender, and her tactical acumen had marked her for high rank, eventually. 'Your cohort is the latest to be rotated down here,' he said, without preamble. 'Do you know why?'

Calys hesitated. 'I believe so, yes.'

Pharus nodded. 'Good. Saves me having to explain things. It will not be for long. A few months. Then you will be sent above. But every cohort must endure a term in the dark, if they wish to be allowed to war in the light. I trust that will not be an inconvenience for you?'

'My warriors and I are at your service, my lord. But I was unaware that there was anything in these catacombs that required a guard.' She looked around. Her gaze was keen. Calculating. She was observant. That was good. Too many Stormcasts ignored anything beyond the reach of their warblade.

'This is a realm for secrets, sister. You get used to it.'

Calys nodded absently. 'I know.' She glanced at Elya. The child peered at her now in open curiosity. Perhaps she'd never seen a Stormcast who wasn't a man. 'Also cats and children, apparently.'

'There are plenty of both in Glymmsforge. Another thing you get used to.' He looked down at the girl. 'I must speak to my sister. Go. Back to the city. And don't play among the tombs. You wouldn't want the nicksouls or the men o' bones to catch you, eh?'

Elya scampered away. Pharus waited until she had vanished back up the path and then turned to the new arrival. 'You will need to learn the safe routes through the labyrinth. They change daily, but there is a pattern.'

'Another thing to get used to?'

Pharus inclined his head. 'Even so. The dead find such things confusing. They are creatures of habit, haunting familiar places and stalking the streets they walked in life.' He paused, studying her. 'The weaker spirits can be trapped in mirrors or befuddled by moving walls.'

'Do the dead attack down here often?'

'More often than you might think.' Pharus peered down into the abyss. 'They don't always hurl themselves against the walls above. Sometimes they come by more circuitous routes. The catacombs that surround us are full of unquiet spirits. Some escape, from time to time, and must be hunted down.'

Calys nodded. 'The dead cannot be trusted.'

'Not here, at least.' Pharus smiled. An old saying, in Shyish. He wondered if she recalled where she'd picked it up. Part of him hoped not. 'But they have been quiet since Vaslbad the Unrelenting tried to crack the city several years ago. Besides the usual nighthaunts, shackleghasts and scarefingers, I mean.' He saw that the Liberator-Prime wasn't looking at him. Instead, she was staring off in the direction Elya had disappeared. He frowned. 'Speak freely.'

'The child,' Calys said. 'Is she a beggar? I thought I recognised her for a moment.'

'No. Her father is a lamplighter, when he's not the worse for drink.' He hesitated, choosing his next words with care. 'Her mother is... dead. Twice over.'

Calys looked at him. Pharus tossed the core of his apple to Grip. The gryph-hound snapped it out of the air and crunched it. 'Her mother – the thing that had been her mother – came for her one night, several years ago. Before you were made one of us, I believe. Smelling of tomb-salts and grave-earth. I banished the creature.' He smiled sadly. 'Since then, the child has become my shadow.'

'You let her come down here?'

'I cannot stop her. She's worse than the cats. Always finding new paths through the dark.' He scratched his chin. 'It's a challenge, to be sure.'

'She could be harmed.' There was a hint of disapproval there, and something else… Outrage? Or concern. He smiled without mirth.

'Yes. She knows that. I do not think she cares.' Pharus tapped the side of his head. 'Children often have an exaggerated sense of their own durability. I remember that much, from my time as a mortal.'

Calys hesitated. 'Did you have…' She trailed off, realising her lack of tact. Pharus waited. It was considered impolite, among the Anvils of the Heldenhammer, to ask about such things. The past was the past. It meant less than dust. And yet, like dust, it clung to you. Even when you thought yourself free of it, it was still there.

'Yes,' he said, and felt the old familiar pain, again. As always, he welcomed it. The pain reminded him of why he fought. As it would remind Calys, in time. If she ever remembered who she had been, and what she had lost. 'Perhaps I may find their shades one day, in one of the underworlds, once our war is won.' He shook his head. 'I like to think so, at least. However unlikely it is.'

'You think the war will end, then?'

'I think we must have hope. If not for ourselves, then for children like Elya. Else what is the struggle for?' He clapped her on the shoulder. 'You are new to Glymmsforge. You will learn in time that hope is the most potent weapon we possess in these dark lands. More, it may well protect you from the enemy.'

'And what enemy do we face here? Rogue spirits?' Calys tapped the pommel of her warblade. 'They cannot be worse than the servants of the Ruinous Powers.'

Pharus laughed. The sound echoed through the cavern, disturbing the bats in their high roosts. 'The dead do not rest easy here, however pleasant it may seem,' he said. 'A great voice calls to them out of the dark heart of this realm and stokes their rage. It drives them to madness.' He leaned on his halberd and stared down into the great well. 'Having heard it myself, I can understand.'

'You heard it – him, I mean. The voice of Nagash?'

'So have you. You were reforged recently, were you not?'

'Yes, but… I heard nothing.'

'You did. You simply may not recall. If you don't, you are a lucky soul indeed.' Pharus looked at her. 'Nagash is God of Death and when we perish, he seeks his due. He claws at us, even as we ascend to Azyr. Tearing away bits of us – of who we are – in his great greed.'

'How do you know this?'

'I listen. I learn.' Pharus smiled, his scars pulling tight. 'You would be wise to do so as well, if you wish to survive, sister. We are strong, but we must be wise, too. The realms are not forgiving of the foolish.' His smile widened. 'Still, there are pleasures to be had.' He reached down into the satchel hanging from his belt. He retrieved two more apples and extended one to her.

'Would you like an apple? I get them by the bushel from the market, on the rare occasions I seek the sun, such as it is. Nothing better than a good apple, I always say.' He held it out to her. 'A vice, I admit, but only a little one.'

Calys took the apple and stared at it, as if she had never seen one. He smiled and gestured. 'You eat it,' he said.

'I know what an apple is.'

'Just checking. Some experiences are not universal, I have discovered. For instance, I had never seen a megalofin, until after my reforging. And then I was eaten by one.'

Calys choked and stared at him. 'What?'

'I survived, obviously. Take more than that to kill me. Still, not an experience I am eager to repeat.' He bounced an apple on his palm. 'It's why I choose to take pleasure in the small things.'

'And why you choose to let a mortal child play down here?'

Pharus took a bite of his apple and looked at her. She hesitated then looked away. 'Forgive me, my lord. I spoke out of turn.'

Pharus took another bite. He knew better than to say anything. How to explain, how to say those words?

'I am not one to punish you for speaking truth,' he said, after a moment. 'Down here, we must trust each other. We must know without a doubt that the warriors to either side will stand. To perish in Shyish is a terrible thing, sister, and all the more so for we who do not die as men do. This you will learn.' *But I will do my best to see that you never do, for two deaths are enough for any soul.*

Before she could reply, a tremor ran through the chamber. Grip stood suddenly, every hair and feather stiff and trembling. Cats hissed and scampered away, seeking safety. The gryph-hound shrilled, and Pharus tossed aside his half-eaten apple. 'It sounds as if your first lesson is about to begin, sister. Something is amiss, and that usually means we're in for it.'

'What is–' Calys began, as the first shock wave hit.

Pharus was nearly thrown from his feet as the chamber

shuddered. Pillars cracked and twisted on their bases, before slamming into the chamber floor. Great clouds of dust rose from ruptures in the ground.

'What is this, what's going on?' Calys asked. She had retained her footing, but only just. 'Is this normal?' The chamber was shaking, as if it had been caught in the grip of ague. Pillars cracked and crumbled, and the web of chains clattered below.

Pharus snarled in frustration. 'No. It's an adventure every day down here.' He thrust the ferrule of his halberd against the floor, bracing himself. He saw priests scrambling for safety, and heard the cries of those still caught among the chains in the abyss. He thought of Elya and felt a moment of fear for the child. Briefly, he considered sending someone to search for her, but pushed the thought aside. He had a duty to protect the catacombs, and what lay within. Elya would have to look after herself. At least for the moment.

From somewhere within the labyrinth, funerary bells began to ring, sounding the alarm. He held up a hand. 'Listen – the bells.' Each of the twelve major thoroughfares in the catacombs had its own set of bells, with their own particular tone, high up in a reinforced tower. When a thoroughfare came under threat, the bells would be rung by the priests stationed there, summoning aid from the rest of the catacombs.

Some were silvery temple bells, while others were great, brass monsters, looted from ruined citadels. All of them were ringing now, thanks to the shock waves tearing through the catacombs, but only one set was doing so with purpose – a ponderous sound, like the thunder of inevitability. 'The Black Bells of Aarnz.'

'The what?'

'This way. Along the Avenue of Souls.' He started in the direction of the bells, Grip at his heels. As he strode out of the chamber, navigating against the convulsions, he gestured to nearby priests. 'All of you – get to safety. Let the chains look after themselves. Go!' The mortals streamed away, the able-bodied helping the wounded. Calys hurried in his wake.

'My cohort,' she began. They passed fallen stones, and Pharus saw broken, ash-smudged limbs sticking out from under piles of debris. Groups of priests worked frantically to free those who might be trapped, and Pharus was forced to send them on their way with gestures and curses. Anyone caught under those rocks was dead, or soon would be. He heard screams, echoing up from distant tunnels, and the crash of stones.

'Your cohort will already be heading in that direction, if they have any sense.' He glanced at her. 'Can you taste it? The air has gone sour.' Chunks of loose stone pattered against his war-plate. It felt as if the catacombs were collapsing in on themselves. For a brief instant, he had an image of them being buried under tonnes of mouldering stone, like the mortal priests. He shook it aside.

The Avenue of Souls ran along the northern rim of the abyss, beneath an uneven archway of hundreds of stone buttresses, illuminated by innumerable flickering candles. The buttresses had been fashioned at Pharus' request by the craftsmen of the Riven Clans – duardin, long dispossessed of their ancient homelands, who had come to Shyish seeking new ones. In Glymmsforge, they had found such a place.

The ramparts held back an unmoving mass of tombs and mausoleums, piled atop one another in untidy fashion. Once, they had lined the slope in neat rows, with great steps and porticos to connect one row to the next. But time and disaster had rendered them into a morass of stone, held from complete collapse only by the duardin-crafted ramparts.

A mausoleum broke loose from its perch and tumbled down

the slope, smashing aside smaller vaults in its plunge, before finally crashing into a buttress and collapsing it. An avalanche of broken stone swept dangerously close and spilled across the pathway, momentarily obscuring everything in a grey haze of dust. Coughing, Pharus waved a hand, trying to clear the air. His eyes narrowed as he noticed motes of purple light dancing through the cloud. 'Oh, no.'

'What?' Calys coughed.

'The air – feel it? It's...'

Grip snarled a warning. Pharus, acting on instinct, swept his halberd out. A decaying corpse slumped back, minus its head. More bodies stumbled out of the dust, reaching for the two Stormcasts with crumbling fingers. They were wrapped in burial shrouds, their mouths sewn shut and their eyes hidden behind folds of cloth. None of this seemed to hamper them, however. They pressed close, in eerie silence. Purple sparks danced across their juddering limbs and through the rents in their decaying flesh.

Grip darted forwards, beak snapping shut on a desiccated leg. The gryph-hound jerked the deadwalker off its feet and began to drag it away. Calys swung her shield into position as a corpse lunged towards her. Her warblade snipped out, removing the groping hands at the wrists. Pharus watched her fight, analysing her technique even as he swept his halberd out in a wide arc. The way a warrior fought was as good a look into their soul as any.

Calys fought like a miser. No movement wasted, every twist of her blade a thing of precision. She created a cage of steel about herself, and then expanded or contracted that cage depending on the needs of the moment. It spoke to a certain efficiency.

A corpse floundered against him, broken fingers scrabbling

at his chest-plate. He swept it aside and smashed it from its feet. More of them staggered out of the dust, twitching as the magics that animated them flared and pulsed, out of control. The ground shuddered beneath his feet. There was a sound like thunder, tolling up from below. He could hear screaming as well, and shouts.

More bells had begun to ring throughout the catacombs, as his warriors reacted to the threat. Pharus had devised a number of stratagems and drilled his warriors in them. The order in which the bells rang would tell them what to do, where to go. But never before had so many bells rung – and never all at once.

The dust grew thick on the air, coating his war-plate. He lost sight of Calys for a moment, as the cloud roiled. He felt the ground shake as another pillar fell. The ground shuddered so wildly he barely kept his feet. Stone ruptured and chains burst. Spectral faces congealed in the dust, only to dissipate moments later. He saw Grip drag another walking corpse to the ground as he spun his halberd in a tight circle, momentarily casting the deadwalkers back. There seemed to be hundreds of them, pressing in from all sides.

Calys fell back towards him. 'We're cut off. Nowhere to go.'

'Then we hold what we have,' Pharus said. He considered unhooking his warding lantern, but dismissed the thought. Its holy light would have little effect on the dead. Better to deal with them the old-fashioned way – brute force. He thrust his halberd forwards, crunching it into a deadwalker's chest. He heaved the twitching carcass up and hurled it into its fellows, knocking several of them to the ground. But more pressed in.

The air parted suddenly, as something fast and bright pierced the gloom. A sizzling arrow punched through a corpse's skull, spinning it around and casting it to the ground. More arrows followed the first, plucking the dead from their feet. The dust tore like cloth as Stormcasts charged through, falling upon the deadwalkers like wolves.

A trio of Retributors forced their way through the press, their lightning hammers casting broken corpses from their path. Liberators and Judicators advanced slowly in their wake, finishing off any deadwalker that managed to avoid the crackling arcs of the Retributors' hammers. Pharus recognised the warrior in the lead – Briaeus, Retributor-Prime.

He was clad in the heavy bastion armour of his conclave, decorated with tokens of death and good fortune. He swung and spun his hammer with graceful ease, wielding it like an artist might wield a brush.

He called out to Pharus as he smashed a quartet of corpses to the ground. 'Ho, lord-castellant, are you in need of aid?' One of the deadwalkers hauled itself erect, and he caught it up by the neck, as if it weighed nothing.

'If I were, you would be the first I'd call for, Briaeus. Now, tell me,' Pharus said, clasping the Retributor-Prime's forearm. 'I heard the bells.'

'The sleepers have awoken,' the big warrior rumbled. 'The lesser dead, all throughout the catacombs. It's as if someone reached into every mausoleum and tomb, and shouted them awake, all at once.' He glanced up and quickly stepped to the side as a chunk of masonry crashed down and shattered. 'And the catacombs are coming apart at the seams.'

'They'll survive,' Pharus said confidently.

'That's not what I am worried about,' Briaeus growled. 'These quakes are tearing open even the most tightly sealed of the tombs – there are things abroad in these tunnels that should not walk.' He hefted the struggling deadwalker and shook it, as if for emphasis. Its spine snapped, and the Retributor slung it away from him with a growl of disgust.

'What could be worse than walking corpses?' Calys asked.

Somewhere, out among the tombs, something screamed. A long, low wail of desolation, echoing down through the broken hummocks of stone. Pharus looked at Calys. 'I expected you to know better than to ask such a thing, and here, of all places.'

Calys shook her head. 'My apologies.'

Above them, specks of witch-light danced through the tombs. Behind them, a great clamour rose from the abyss, as of many muffled voices, shouting in their confinement. Pharus glanced uneasily past the pillared supports of the ramparts, at the edge of the pit. Briaeus was right. It was as if something had woken all of the dead beneath Glymmsforge.

'Is this some… spell, perhaps?' Briaeus asked.

Pharus shook his head. 'If so, it's unlike any we've seen before.'

Another scream sounded. More voices were added to that hellish choir. They echoed throughout the chamber and were joined by others from elsewhere. It sounded as if the entirety of the catacombs were howling.

'Lord-castellant – look.' Calys pointed.

Something like a mist had begun to drift down the slope, gathering speed. It flooded between the tombs and swept through the shattered gateways, pouring down over the broken porticos. Motes of violet light swirled within it, growing brighter as it drew closer to the Stormcasts. Pharus slammed the ferrule of his halberd down on the ground. 'Form up, form up. Shields to the fore!'

Liberators hurried to form a shield wall. Pharus was pleased to see Calys take her place, without waiting for his order. Sigmarite war-shields were locked together to form an unbreakable bulwark. Judicators raised their bows and sent a volley of crackling arrows arcing over the heads of the Liberators. The arrows sped down, and muffled explosions of lightning flared briefly beneath the mist. Undaunted, it rolled on, picking up speed, as the screaming intensified.

Pharus grunted. That wasn't good. 'Brace and hold,' he snarled. Briaeus and his Retributors stepped forwards, lightning hammers at the ready.

'I prefer deadwalkers,' the Retributor-Prime said.

'So do I,' Pharus said. He lifted his halberd. At his side, Grip crouched, feathers stiff, tail lashing. The gryph-hound whined shrilly as the mist billowed down the crest of the slope and spilled over the buttresses. There were distorted faces in its convolutions. Wide, howling mouths and bulging eyes that swelled, split and disgorged more of the same. A constant, churning mass of spectral agony.

Nighthaunts. Hideous spirits that had no corporeal body to speak of. Some were the restless souls of the wrongfully dead, while others had been wrenched from their living bodies by dark magics and cast adrift into eternity. Regardless of their origins, the result was always the same – a hateful creature of undeath.

The fog bank of howling souls struck the shield wall a moment later, and rolled over it. Sigmarite warblades, crackling with the lightning of Azyr, passed through the whirling storm of lost souls with no resistance. The weaker spirits came apart like smoke and fluttered away. But the stronger ones thrust aethereal claws through the joins in the Stormcasts' war-plate. The dead could not easily be killed, but they had little difficulty harming the living.

Wispy talons slid through holes in masks, and Stormcasts staggered, choking. Broken blades and phantasmal weapons crashed down, sometimes with no effect – but other times, the blades bit abnormally deep into armour. Only the Stormcasts' preternatural skill saved them from agonising death, as the host of spirits enveloped them. Warblades flashed, dissipating some spirits and causing others to retreat. But not enough.

'Hold them,' Pharus roared. 'Briaeus – drive them back!'

The blows of Briaeus and his fellow paladins were more effective than those of their brethren. The lightning hammers snapped out, trailing sizzling bands of energy, and spirits convulsed and came apart as they were struck. But there were only three of them, and they could not be everywhere.

'Judicators – loose,' Pharus shouted, whirling his halberd out to tear through the misty neck of a nighthaunt. At his command, the Judicators loosed arrows into the morass of tormented souls, further scattering them, though not permanently.

Pharus heard Calys cry out and saw her stagger back, a writhing spectre clinging to her. One unnaturally long hand was thrust into her chest. 'No!' He swept his halberd out. The blade chopped into the murky substance of the wraith's form, and it spasmed in apparent pain. His blow tore it from her and sent it whirling away. As she fell backwards, the shield wall began to crumple. Pharus sank down beside her.

'Do you yet live, sister?'

'I… believe so,' she gasped, clutching at her chest. 'That… I have… I think I have felt that cold pain before…' She looked at him, her eyes wide behind the mask of her helm. 'I can see…' She shook her head, as if confused. He knew what she was feeling, the sudden flood of half-forgotten sensations. 'What was that?'

'Death,' Pharus said flatly. Nearby, another Liberator gave a strangled scream as a ghost reached through his armour and stopped his heart with its chill claws. The warrior's body came apart in motes of crackling, azure lightning as he slumped. With a shuddering snarl of lightning, his soul was cast upwards, back to Azyr and the Anvil of Apotheosis, there to be reforged.

Pharus flinched away from that light. He had not yet endured a second death, and he had no intention of doing so, if it could be helped. He reached down and caught hold of the back of Calys' war-plate. 'We are giants, raised up and cast down, to rid the land of evil and keep safe all that is good,' he roared, as he dragged her to her feet. 'Hold fast and swing true.' He looked at her. 'Stand, sister.'

'I am fine. It… it… I felt it, in my heart. Squeezing my heart.' She clutched at her chest. 'My armour did nothing.'

'It kept you alive,' Pharus growled. He unhooked his lantern and hung it from the top of his halberd. Where its light touched, the spirits recoiled. They were not of Chaos, but they were corrupt nonetheless. 'Now ready yourself. They come again. If you must die, let it be on your feet.' He raised his halberd high, so that the light of the lantern washed across the shield wall. 'Stand, brothers and sisters. Not one step back.' He slammed the halberd down, and the light of his warding lantern blazed forth.

'Whatever comes – we hold!'

CHAPTER THREE

SIGMARABULUM

AQSHY, THE REALM OF FIRE

In the scented pavilions of Thurn, daemons were screaming. Mortal slaves and warriors, swaddled in silks and silver chains, fled the inhuman wailing, their hands pressed to newly burst ears and their bloody eyes clamped shut. Vainly they sought respite in the far pavilions, sprawled across the rocky convolutions of the Felstone Plains, or in the wilds, staggering into the smouldering darkness of the Aqshian night. But nowhere was free of the daemonic shrieks.

In the Pavilion of Roses, Havocwild, Headsman of Thurn and Lord of the Six Pavilions, winced as the screams grew in volume and poured himself another goblet of wine. He was a tall man, bronzed by the sun and clad in black silks and golden war-plate, engraved with the sixty-six verses of Slaanesh. He had been handsome once, but more than a century of warfare could wear the lustre off almost anything.

He stood on a basalt dais, festooned with thick cushions and closed off by curtains of tattered silk. Various weapons and pieces of armour were scattered around the dais and on its slabbed steps. Empty jugs of wine, and trays covered in rotting meats and fruits, lay among them, discarded where his slaves had dropped them before they'd fled.

Behind him, the screams of the daemons rose in pitch, and the jug in his hand vibrated, cracked and burst, spattering his armour with the dregs of the wine. He sighed and sniffed the contents of his goblet. It was an exquisite vintage, made from grapes grown in the volcanic soil of the Tephra Crater. He tasted it and frowned. The screaming of the daemons had turned it sour. He tossed the goblet aside and turned.

On the great rugs of magmadroth hide that covered the ground, dozens of daemonettes twisted and writhed. But not with their usual sense of elation. Normally, the Handmaidens of Slaanesh were poetry in motion, graceful and hypnotic. At the moment, however, they lacked all grace, twisting and twitching as if afflicted with ague. Their screams became even shriller, and his eardrums ached in a most unique fashion.

But like all new sensations, it quickly became tiresome. 'Enough,' he snarled, groping for the haft of his headsman's blade. The massive, two-handed sword had earned him his sobriquet as well as mastery of the Six Pavilions. 'Either cease screaming, or cease being – but do so swiftly.' He snatched the sword from its sheath of tanned human flesh and swung it up over his head as he advanced on the closest of the daemons. 'Whatever game this is, it has become tedious. Stop. *Stop!*'

The daemonette continued to howl, tearing at its own androgynous features with crustacean-like claws. It had gouged out its own eyes, as if it had seen something beyond its ability to bear.

One moment, the creatures had been cavorting for his amusement as usual. The next, they had succumbed to these strange convulsions. He had never seen the like before, but rather than exciting him with its novelty, the sight made him uneasy.

He held his blow, uncertain. Then, the ground shook. He was nearly knocked from his feet by the force of the tremor. The ground cracked and split, spewing volcanic gases. The shaking increased, as did the screams of the daemons. They began to tear at each other and the ground in a growing frenzy. It was as if they had been driven mad – or madder.

A daemonette lurched to its hooves and stumbled towards him, squalling. It slashed blindly at him, gibbering something that might have been a name over and over again. Disgusted, Havocwild beheaded the creature with a looping blow. He staggered towards the entrance as the ground buckled.

As he stepped into the open, he heard the creak of bone and looked up. The skulls of all those he'd killed, gilded and decorated with flowers and fine gems, covered the sides of the immense tent. An eerie green radiance flitted from skull to skull as he watched. Then, as one, they began to twitch and clatter on their barbs. He heard a sound as of a thousand voices, murmuring all at once and close by. Some of them screamed, in memory of pain they could no longer feel, or for a vengeance they would never claim.

He laughed, delighted, and his eyes were drawn to the sky above. It seemed to convulse, in time with the tremors that wracked the ground. Striations of amethyst light passed slowly through the dark, and the tremors grew fiercer. He watched in growing awe as the stars began to wink out, one by one.

'How *exquisite*,' he whispered.

* * *

SIGMARON, PALACE-CITY OF SIGMAR

Balthas Arum sat back with a sigh, his black-and-gold war-plate creaking. The lord-arcanum rubbed his eyes, more out of habit than because they ached. He closed the tome he'd been studying, set it atop the pile to his left and reached for the next. The wide table, made from a single slab of dark stone, was covered in small hills of paper – stacks of volumes and papyrus jostled for space with duardin bead-books and strange, golden plaques. Candles rose like wax towers and cast a pallid glow over the confusion.

Balthas, like all Stormcast Eternals, was larger than a mortal man. He bore the black-and-gold livery of the Anvils of the Heldenhammer proudly, and was clad in the war-plate and robes of his office. An ornate staff of sigmarite and gold lay against the table, the stylised lightning bolts that adorned its head flickering softly.

He bore a blade when he rode to war, but rarely used it, for such was not his purpose. He was no lord-celestant, to hurl himself into the thick of war, but instead a lord-arcanum – an aether-mage and master of a Sacrosanct Chamber. The fury of the cosmic tempest was his to command. Of what use was a sword or hammer, however well-crafted, to one who could wield lightning? With a word, he could crack stone or ride the aetheric winds, as swift as a thunderbolt.

Balthas ran his hands through his dark hair. He stared at the book before him, sizing it up the way a warrior might study a new opponent. The cover was made from the crimson scales of an Aqshian magmadroth, with brass clasps and bindings. Runes – but not duardin ones – were stamped on it. He tapped it with a finger, considering his avenues of attack. He had laid siege to this tome before and always come away defeated. It required careful thought. It was composed of unknown runic characters, etched by an unknown hand, on an unknown subject. An enigma.

He glanced at his helmet, sitting nearby. It was plated in gold, with runic sigils carved into the brow and cheek-guards. He tapped it fondly. 'I can draw down the lightning as easily as I draw breath. I am a master of the aetheric storm. I can peer into the heart of any living creature, and I have matched my will against those of the dark gods. But I cannot crack this cipher.' He frowned. 'Not yet, at any rate.'

Balthas opened the book, careful not to damage it. 'Perhaps today will be the day.' He scouted the first pages, studying the familiar, unintelligible lines of script, the strange illustrations – some species of herb, he thought. But what species, found where? He reached for a goblet, sitting near his hand. He lifted the cup without looking at it and found it empty, save for a few sour dregs. He peered into it, momentarily confused.

'I could have sworn I had a full goblet a few moments ago,' he said, out loud. He sighed and reached for a nearby jug. It too was empty. He set it aside, searching for any sign of the novice priests who attended to such menial tasks. He recalled, belatedly, that he'd asked to be left alone. Evidently, they had taken him at his word. He looked around.

The Grand Library of Sigmaron was silent. Shafts of light fell through the high, oblong windows to streak the dusty air. High, heavy shelves of smooth stone and fossilised wood lined the walls or else stood freely, stretching past even the limits of his preternatural sight. The concentric arrangement of these semi-circular shelves mirrored the circular shape of the library itself – a world within a world.

Azure-robed priests and priestesses strode silently through the shadowed pathways between shelves, retrieving books for patrons, or replacing those borrowed earlier. The priests wore heavy record books marked with the Sigendil, the High Star of Azyr, chained to their bodies. With these, they kept track of what books were read, when and by whom. Most were armed, too, however lightly. Libraries were dangerous places, even in Azyr.

The Grand Library was one of the oldest structures in the great palace-city, and one of the few that continued to grow and expand with every passing century. The agents of the God-King scoured the Mortal Realms for esoteric knowledge, bringing all that they found back to Sigmaron. Somewhere below him, in the Halls of Illumination, twelve-thousand monks – not all of them human or even alive – worked tirelessly to record and transcribe this knowledge.

The wisdom of nations long vanished, of generations past, of sages and seers without number, all gathered here, beneath a dome of glass and stone. All of it at the fingertips of any who wished to avail themselves of it. The thought made Balthas' heart skip a beat. Once, in a life he could but dimly recall, he might have wasted his days stumbling from one shelf to the next, seeking what revelations might come. Seeking knowledge for its own sake was a vice he had often indulged in.

But now, he had a greater purpose than his own aggrandisement. He had been remade, given form and function beyond that of mortal man. Made an engine of necessity, guided by the wisdom of a god. Balthas stared down at the book, willing it to surrender those secrets it so stubbornly held. He had defeated a thousand others just like it, and would defeat this one as well. There could be no other outcome.

'Lord-arcanum.' The voice was soft and thin with age. Balthas turned, irritated by the interruption. His annoyance evaporated when he saw who had addressed him. The priest was old, especially by the standards of mortals, and all but swallowed up in his blue robes and chains of office. His dark skin bore faded, celestial tattoos in the fashion of the Sword-Clans of the Caelum Desert, and his hands and cheeks still bore the scars of an earlier time.

'Chief Librarian Aderphi,' Balthas said, in polite greeting. He had known the old man since he had been anything but. Aderphi had come to the Grand Library as a novice, hands still stained with blood and his heart full of fire. Now, that fire had dimmed, and the blood had long since dried, but Balthas could still see the ghost of that young warrior in the bent figure before him.

'I trust I am not disturbing you,' the old man said. He took a seat opposite Balthas without waiting for a reply. He looked at the book. 'Ah. The Guelphic Cipher. A stubborn opponent, I'm told.'

'Fifty years,' Balthas said, with some bitterness. 'That's how long I've been trying.'

'I know. You were studying it the day I took up my post here, as a mere novice.' Aderphi smiled. 'Still not cracked it, then, my lord?'

Balthas raised an eyebrow. 'Is that a jest?'

'A small one, I assure you.' Aderphi picked up the empty jug and shook it. 'You are out of wine.'

'I may have been sitting here for some time.'

'Two days since you last asked for food and drink, according to the brothers. A long time to stare at dusty tomes and texts.'

Balthas frowned. That explained the slight ache in his back and shoulders. 'I have done so for longer, in the past,' he said stiffly. 'I beg your pardon, if my presence has disturbed you.'

Aderphi smiled. 'Only you could make an apology sound like an insult.'

Balthas' frown deepened. The old man made a habit of familiarity. As if his age exempted him from showing proper deference to his betters. 'If I am not proving disruptive, why have you chosen to interrupt me, Chief Librarian?'

Aderphi pointed. 'You have a visitor.'

Balthas blinked and turned. Another lord-arcanum, clad in the silver and azure of the Hallowed Knights Stormhost, strode towards his table. Tyros Firemane raised his staff in greeting. 'Fear not, Balthas, I come to rescue you from your self-imposed exile.' His voice boomed out, startling the tiny starwyrms that nested in the high places of the library. The little, winged reptiles hissed and swooped over the shelves, scattering clouds of dust. Tyros paid them no heed, even when one flitted past his ear. The ferrule of his staff clanged against the stone floor, and Aderphi winced slightly with each reverberation.

'Tyros,' Balthas said simply, as he turned back to his studies.

The Chief Librarian rose. 'I will leave you to it, my lords.' Balthas watched, somewhat bemused, as the old man hobbled off.

A moment later, Tyros leaned over the table, balancing on his knuckles, the silver sigmarite digging into the wood. The heavy-set, red-bearded lord-arcanum grinned. He had a wide face and hawk-like nose, lending him a fierce air. 'Still hunting, eh, Balthas? Caught anything yet?'

'Nothing of import, I fear.'

'Bit of a waste, then, wasn't it?'

Balthas sighed. 'How I spend my free time is my business, brother.'

'I merely question whether you've seen the sun, lately.'

'I have light enough.'

Tyros frowned and straightened. 'Yes, well, I come to tear you away from your dusty friends. Your duties await. We are required at the Anvil of Apotheosis.'

'Already?' Balthas sighed. Among the many duties of a Sacrosanct Chamber was to oversee the reforging process, as those Stormcast Eternals slain in battle were wrought anew and made whole. The process was not without its dangers, and required warriors of a certain mettle to meet to them. Ones more attuned to the aetheric, with the ability to wield the raw power of the Heavens in Sigmar's name.

'It's been a week, Balthas. Twelve chambers have stood their watch. Now twelve more must take their place – and that includes their lords-arcanum.'

'A week?' Balthas leaned back and stretched. 'That would explain the gnawing sensation in my belly, I suppose.' He had not bothered to eat before coming to the library. Knowledge sustained him – or if it didn't, it should.

Tyros snorted. 'That'll have to wait, I'm afraid.'

'Just as well. I'm in no mood to eat.' Balthas carefully stacked the tomes and stood. He pinched the flames of the candles out and retrieved his helmet and his staff. Tyros waited impatiently, thick arms folded over his chest.

'How many times have I had to come and dig you out of this mausoleum?' he growled. 'A dozen? Two dozen? Why do you spend so much time here?'

'As you said, I'm hunting. That is our duty, remember?' Balthas gestured to the tomes. 'I seek our prey in the forests of antiquity, following the ancient trails wherever they might lead.' He spoke with more passion than he'd intended, but he could not help it. The answer he sought was somewhere in these records. He was certain of it.

Somewhere within the Grand Library, within these tomes and scrolls, was the key to allaying the flaw that cursed all Stormcast Eternals. Death was not the end of a Stormcast's service, and those who fell in battle could be reforged and returned to the fray. But not without cost. The reforged, with few exceptions, became both more and less than they had been. Sometimes what stepped off the Anvil of Apotheosis was more akin to a tempest cloaked in human flesh than a mortal warrior.

These side effects of the reforging process were becoming steadily more pronounced as the war against the Ruinous Powers raged on. If victory – true victory – were to be achieved, a solution had to be found. Among the many duties of the Sacrosanct Chamber, the hunt for that solution was the most important.

Tyros shook his head. 'I doubt what we seek can be found in such records as these. The world-that-was is gone, brother, and all its secrets with it. We must look to the realms as they are, not as they once were.' Tyros was an explorer by temperament. He preferred to spend his days hunting through broken ruins and shadowed barrows, rather than studying ancient texts and scrolls.

Balthas frowned. 'That's ignorant, even for you, Tyros.'

Tyros glanced at him, his gaze equanimous. 'I know you forget how to talk to people when you spend all your time buried in books, so I'll forgive your lack of tact this once, Balthas.' He held up a fist. 'But call me ignorant again, and I'll bust that pretty nose of yours.'

Balthas blinked. Then, he nodded with a rueful smile. 'Forgive me, brother.'

Tyros grunted. 'I am technically your superior, you know.'

'Technically. What is a few months' difference in reforging?'

'I'll tell Knossus you said that. He'll be relieved.'

Balthas grunted sourly but didn't reply. Tyros chuckled.

Side by side, the two Stormcasts left the library. Sigmaron rose about them, a palace-city of ivory towers and golden aetherdomes, clustered on the cloud-wreathed upper slopes of Mount Celestian. It had grown over the course of millennia. Its ramparts and walkways now spilled across the thunder-shaken crags, connecting distant peaks – now given over almost entirely to forges and workshops – in an unbroken ring of sigmarite and celestine.

Far above, the High Star, Sigendil, shone down, casting its eternal radiance across the city and mountain both. Sigendil never moved from its appointed place, a source of unwavering certainty for even the sternest soul. Bathed in its light, Sigmaron was like an island in the starlit emptiness of the celestial sea, a starburst of gold amid the black. And at its peak, Balthas knew, lay the silent ruins of Highheim, the parliament of the gods. That vast acropolis had been deserted for aeons, since the dissolution of Sigmar's pantheon. It was forbidden to all but the most trusted of Sigmar's councillors, and even then, visits were only permitted in the company of the God-King himself.

Great storms vented their fury upon the highest of the aetherdomes; their strength was funnelled into the citadel's forges, and the rains were siphoned into the many gardens and groves scattered throughout the palace-city. The celestine vaults of the citadel rang with the clamour of unceasing industry, and great masses of humanity strode to and fro along the colossal walkways and ramparts. The whole of Sigmaron seemed to resonate with activity.

Balthas and Tyros made their way easily through the crowds. They were composed of servants, mostly, and so made way hurriedly for the Stormcast Eternals. Sigmaron was home to thousands of mortal attendants. Many worked in the vaults and gardens, while others were scribes or messengers, carrying armfuls of parchment. An honoured few were allowed to serve in the inner chambers of the palace, where Sigmar himself held court.

Besides the servants, there were representatives from Azyrheim and the other great cities of Azyr, including Starhold and Skydock, and their retinues. Among them were captain-generals of the Freeguild, dressed in their ostentatious uniforms, and the merchant-princes of the far-flung realmports, come to seek Sigmar's blessings for their financial ventures in the wider realms.

These last travelled with much pomp and circumstance, accompanied by retainers and exotic bodyguards, including gold-bedecked fyreslayers, brutal ogors and, in one case, a hulking gargant, who plodded along sedately in his mistress' wake.

'The palace-city has become crowded, of late,' Tyros remarked, as the great brute stomped past them. He turned, watching the gargant. 'Once, these walkways would have been empty of all save the chosen of Sigmar.'

'Once, we feared the realms lost to us, and Azyr adrift and alone.' Balthas strode along, heedless of the mortals scattering like quail before him. 'That Sigmaron boasts such life is a sign that we follow the correct course.'

'Spoken with the confidence of an academic.'

Balthas glanced at the other lord-arcanum. 'I have fought my share of battles, brother. But I can see the wider tapestry before me. If you would but open your eyes, you might as well.'

Tyros laughed. 'Sometimes, brother, I fear you are so concerned with your tapestry that you miss the finer details.' He lifted his hand in a gesture of surrender before Balthas could reply. 'But who am I to gainsay you? We are both masters of the storm, by Sigmar's grace.'

'Yes, a fact I will never cease to question.'

Tyros laughed uproariously, startling several nearby mortals. A moment later, Balthas joined him, if less boisterously. While the Hallowed Knights were, by and large, joyful souls, the Anvils of the Heldenhammer were more restrained. But for all their differences of opinion, there were few souls Balthas trusted more than Tyros. He was a rock of faith and dogged in pursuit of his duties. Qualities Balthas could respect. Tyros caught him by the shoulder. 'Come on, brother. Our chariot awaits. And the Sigmarabulum as well.'

Balthas glanced up. Far above Sigmaron, to the south of Sigendil, the Sigmarabulum encircled the broken remains of Mallus, the world-that-was. A fabricated ring of soul-mills, forges and laboratories, it was also home to the Chamber of the Broken World, and the Anvil of Apotheosis. There were only a few routes between the world-ring and the palace-city. Most were glacially slow – even the swiftest aether-craft would take days to reach the Sigmarabulum. But the Thunder-Gates could take one from Sigmaron to the Sigmarabulum almost instantaneously.

Designed by Sigmar and crafted by Grungni, the Thunder-Gates stood at the heart of the great orrery-bastions that revolved eternally on the outer ring of the palace-city. Each of the bastions was shrouded in a constant cascade of lightning from above. The lightning was caught in the massive, oscillating rings, to be stretched and subsumed, where it did not drip down to crawl in crackling patterns across the stones of the platform.

Only those clad in blessed sigmarite could pierce the veil of lightning safely and enter the bastions. Thus, these routes were barred to all but the Stormcast Eternals.

As they crossed the stone walkway that led to one of these orrery-bastions, Balthas cast his gaze over the wheeling stars of the firmament. The skies in Azyr were alive, in some sense. They roiled and crashed like the waves of the sea, albeit silently. Stars flared and dimmed, worlds spun in an eternal dance.

Sometimes, if one stared too long into the dark, great, inhuman faces seemed to take shape and look back.

These days, Balthas knew better than to stare. Whatever watched from behind the veil of stars was far beyond him, and he saw no reason to attract its attention. That was a matter for the gods.

They stepped through the curtain of lightning, and Balthas felt invigorated by its touch. He raised his hand, drawing it to him and letting it play across the contours of his gauntlet. He released it, as they entered the carefully carved stone archway that led into the orrery-bastion.

Within was a circular chamber, where the majority of the lightning was drawn down and reflected and refracted among innumerable celestine mirrors. As it shot back and forth, its fury was diffused and used to power the great clockwork mechanisms that clicked and groaned beneath a gigantic dais, composed of a number of concentric rings, which occupied the heart of the chamber. The air was thick with the smell of ozone.

As they entered the chamber, a heavy figure greeted them. The lord-castellant turned from the array of lightning-powered mechanisms, his face unreadable behind his war-mask. He wore the golden heraldry of the Hammers of Sigmar, and his armour bore the marks of heavy fighting. Only the truly worthy were given the honour of maintaining the orrery-bastions, having proven their valour against incredible odds. Lord-Castellant Gorgus had done that and more, by all accounts.

'Call down the lightning, Gorgus,' Tyros said, without preamble. 'We have business above and I would be about it.'

The lord-castellant set his halberd and studied them. 'I expected you before now,' he rumbled in a chiding tone. Nearby, a gryph-hound looked up from where it lay on its side, glared at them blearily and then flopped back down with a querulous screech.

'I had to go and dig him out of his books,' Tyros said.

Balthas ignored him and greeted the lord-castellant respectfully. 'My apologies, Gorgus. Time escaped me.'

Gorgus nodded, as if this was to be expected. He swept his halberd out, indicating the flat dais. 'Stand at the heart of the dais, lords-arcanum. The Sigmarabulum awaits.'

They did as he bade. Almost immediately, the dais began to turn. Somewhere below them, gears began to move with a grinding snarl. The rings that made up the outer edge of the dais rose of their own accord, until the whole apparatus resembled an orrery. The rings spun, faster and faster, stretching the lightning between them as they oscillated. In moments, all Balthas could see was a blur of cobalt light, blinding in its intensity.

'I hate this part,' Tyros growled.

Balthas said nothing, merely leaning on his staff. Thin strands of lightning played across the raised edges of his war-plate, or coalesced about the tip of his staff. The air tasted of iron and copper, and for a moment, his head felt as if it were stuffed with cotton wool. Then, there was a crash of thunder that shook him to his very bones, and the blue light began to fade. As it did so, the oscillation of the rings slowed and, one by one, they dropped flat, back into place around the dais. When the last glimmer of light had faded, they had arrived on the Sigmarabulum.

They stood on a wide dais – the mirror of the Thunder-Gate – but it was open to the stars, rather than being contained in a chamber. Flickering azure lanterns lined the path leading away from the dais. There were no guards – at least none that Balthas could see. But he felt them, watching him. The pathways of the storm were never unguarded, and the sentinels of the Sigmarabulum never slept.

Instinctively, he looked up, his gaze drawn to Mallus, rising above the highest towers of the Sigmarabulum. The red orb hung like a wound in the firmament, shining with a dull radiance. Unlike Sigendil's light, that radiance brought no certainty or comfort – only sorrow. Mallus was a reminder that the Mortal Realms were but the latest iteration of the universal cycle – and what awaited them, if Sigmar and his chosen warriors failed.

Balthas stared at the husk of a world and felt as if something were waiting for him there. Part of him longed to walk through the hollow caverns of its core, where Grungni's lightning-powered automatons excavated raw sigmarite ore. To see and touch the world that had come before all that he knew. All that he thought he knew.

But he knew better than to hope. Mallus was denied to all, save Sigmar. The most Balthas could hope for was to one day translate and read what few ancient histories of that world yet remained. They were kept locked away, deep in the heart of the Grand Library. Though they were available to any scholar, few could read them. Whatever tongue they had spoken in that distant age, it was all but unintelligible now.

'Beautiful, isn't it?' Tyros said, as they descended the steps of the dais. 'Like a haunting melody you cannot quite recall.' He peered up at the red world. 'I hear whispers, sometimes, when I look at it. The prickle of memories from a forgotten life. I think sometimes I might have walked there, in another age.' He sighed. 'That cursed light gets in your bones.'

'Maybe it was always there,' Balthas murmured. He'd often felt as Tyros had – as if Mallus were calling to him. As if he were a part of it, somehow. There were many among the Anvils of the Heldenhammer who felt the same. Something in them resonated with the world-that-was, but he could not say why. Balthas pushed the thought aside. He would find no answer to that question today, or possibly ever. 'Come, brother. We are late.'

CHAPTER FOUR

CHAMBER OF THE BROKEN WORLD

CHAMON, THE REALM OF METAL

When everything began to shake, Tonst fumbled at the control valves of his aether-endrin and let it carry him back out of the shipwreck, towards his tiny, one-duardin aether-hauler. His elbows scraped against the edges of the hole in the hull of the wreck as he floated free.

The remains of the Arkanaut Frigate hung awkwardly in the air, its endrin still functioning despite the massive amount of damage the vessel had endured. There was no way to tell what had happened, nor did he particularly care. That it was here, and still might hold something of value, was enough.

He'd tracked the derelict south, just past the Chimera Isles, following the air currents to where it had at last become snared in the tangle-clouds. What was left of the crew was still scattered about, in messy fashion, and whatever cargo they'd been hauling was relatively intact. Or so he hoped.

Tonst was a salvager by trade, and he had the certificates to prove it. That they were forgeries mattered not at all, so long as they had the golden stamp of Barak-Urbaz. He'd paid a hefty price for that stamp, but not so much as he would have paid for the real thing. Paper was paper. And salvage was salvage.

But he forgot all about what treasures the wreck might contain as he emerged and saw that the sky was crawling. 'Grombrindal's bones,' he muttered, watching as the sky's lustre was hidden beneath an amethyst shroud. The pressure gauges and valves that dotted his suit began to spin crazily, and his beard bristled in unease.

He'd thought it was just the ship settling, but instead it seemed as if the skies themselves were convulsing. He gritted his teeth and tried to compensate for the rising wind. If he weren't careful, he might be blown into the side of the wreck, or worse, carried out over the mountains, away from his own vessel. The aether-endrin on his back had seen better decades, and would only keep him aloft for a few hours at a time.

As he watched, the purple haze filled the sky, staining the clouds and erasing the stars above. The wind rose to a brittle shriek, and he felt a chill in his thick limbs despite his suit's insulation. It sounded as if the stars were screaming, somewhere out of sight. 'Get a hold of yourself,' he muttered, trying to ignore the sense of trepidation that filled him. 'Are you a beardling, to be frightened of the sky?'

Resolutely, he turned away, angling himself to float back into the hull. He extricated his anchor from his harness and hooked the edge of the gap. Carefully, he began to reel out the chain. The sky continued to quake, but the wreck seemed sturdy enough. At worst, its endrin would finally fail. If that happened, he would simply release his anchor and float free through one of the great rents in the deck above.

A fine layer of frost crystals covered everything in the hull, crates and corpses alike. He set down gently, bracing himself for the deck to fall away. When it didn't, he took a step. Frost crunched beneath his boots as he made his way deeper into the hold. The sun-stones mounted on his harness flickered to life, casting a soft radiance over the contents of the hold. Dozens of broken crates and shattered casks were revealed.

The wind keened through the wreck, causing scraps of paper and wood to tumble about. Things clattered in the dark, and the deck swayed beneath his feet. He started as the deck dipped and a body slid into view. The crewman had been gutted, his suit ripped open and his torso hollowed out. Frozen blood covered the carcass, and Tonst couldn't tell what had made the wounds. He swallowed, uneasy.

It wasn't likely that whatever had done this was still around. There were cloud-barnacles on the broken planks and no sign of tracks in the frost. Even so, he paused, listening. He'd heard stories about grot raiders, creeping down from the great spore clouds that blossomed in the dark above the highest peaks to set ambushes in floating wrecks.

But all he heard now was the creaking of the rigging. Through the gaps in the deck above, he caught flashes of amethyst light, cascading upwards. He squinted. Was there something up there, hidden by that glow? And where was it coming from? It looked like no atmospheric distortion he'd ever seen. The information might be of value to–

Thump.

Tonst tensed. 'Just a crate,' he muttered.

Thump. Thump.

He cursed softly and let his lights play across the opposite side of the hold. In the gloom, something moved. A soft sound – a groan? – echoed. 'A survivor?' he said, his voice loud in the quiet. He approached the place the sound had come from, moving quickly. A survivor could be bad for business – or exceptionally good, if they were from a sufficiently wealthy family.

'Anyone alive down here?' he called, hesitantly. 'If so, I claim salvage rights as per artycle eight, point three...'

Another groan. Followed by a fumbling sound. He closed in on it, wondering if it was just the wind making a fool of him. His lights fell across another corpse. He stopped. The dead duardin's boots had twitched. Tonst sighed. A survivor, and a poor one, to judge by his gear's lack of ornamentation. 'Just my luck. Well, come on then. Let's see you, you *wanaz...*'

Tonst reached down, and the crewman caught at his wrist. The wounded duardin lurched up, helm crumpled, revealing frost-blackened features. Eyes like misted glass glared sightlessly at him, as teeth champed mindlessly. He jerked back, yelling, as the duardin – not wounded but dead, he realised, *dead and moving!* – thrashed in pursuit.

The corpse of the crewman flopped towards him, making gabbling noises that sounded more like a beast than a duardin. Tonst backed away, reaching for his cutter. Something hissed from behind him, and he turned awkwardly, hampered by his endrin. Another crewman crouched atop one of the few intact crates in un-duardin-like fashion. Broken limbs quivered as the corpse crept closer. It lunged, groaning.

'No,' Tonst snarled, snatching his cutter from its sheath and sweeping it out. His blade sank into the corpse's chest with a wet crunch, and snagged there. He twisted a control valve and slid away from the stumbling corpse, as others nearby began to twitch and moan. Hands flailed at his boots as he hurtled back the way he'd come, anchor chain clanking in his wake. He caught it up as he half ran, half hopped towards the gap in the hull. The wreck was shaking worse than before, as if it might tear itself to pieces at any moment. Dead crewmen rose around him, lurching into view as he fled.

He had to get out. *Out, out, out!*

He exploded out of the wreck, trying to reel in the anchor. Cold hands groped, catching hold of it. The chain stretched taut. Tonst was jerked to an unsteady halt. He snarled curses as he twisted in place, endrin straining. He flailed at the release catch for the chain, but the sudden halt had jammed it. The chain trembled. He tried to angle himself to see what was happening. When he did, his flailing became more desperate.

He was still trying to release the chain when they dragged him back.

THE CHAMBER OF THE BROKEN WORLD, THE SIGMARABULUM

The Chamber of the Broken World occupied the aleph of the Sigmarabulum – the point from which the entirety of the ring, and Mallus itself, could be seen. It sat atop a great tower on the edge of the ring's inner curve, facing the world-that-was. The Tower of Apogee was said to have been the first part of the Sigmarabulum to be constructed, the seed from which the rest of the ring had grown.

Smaller towers, connected by hundreds of walkways, spread out around it. Lightning played about the great pylons that crowned each of them, and ran like water down their sides. These were the soul-mills: the storehouses of the slain. Often, fallen Stormcasts could not be immediately reforged – whether due to the sheer number of deaths or some more esoteric reason – and so their souls were instead drawn into the soul-mills, where they waited, unformed, but not necessarily unaware.

He could hear the towers shaking with the agonised fury of innumerable souls as he and Tyros climbed the steps of the Tower of Apogee. 'The soul-mills are active, more than I have ever seen,' he said.

'Count yourself lucky in that regard.' Tyros steadfastly ignored both the shuddering towers and the muted cries that came from them. Despite being reduced to raw soul-stuff, the dead could still scream, and their wails were audible throughout the Sigmarabulum.

'Something is going on – a new push into enemy territory?'

Tyros grunted. 'There is always a new push. Something is always going on. We are at war, brother. We fight on multiple fronts, in multiple realms, and every victory is bought at the price of our brothers' souls.' He sighed. 'But such is the way of it – much is demanded of those to whom much is given.'

Balthas could think of no fitting reply. He turned away from the soul-mills, leaving them to shake and scream as they would. Instead, he took in the tower before him. As ever, its scale staggered him. The wide, slabbed steps, numbering in the hundreds of thousands, spilled down the sides and back of the tower.

This cascade was broken at regular intervals by great porticos and enormous doorways. These were overlooked by high, semi-enclosed archways, where heavy artillery pieces known as celestar ballistae sat, ready to repel anyone foolish enough to attack the tower. Devised by the war-engineers of the Conclave of the Thunderbolt, the lightning-infused bolts they launched could punch through even the strongest shield, or the scaly hides of the star-born monstrosities that occasionally slunk down from the outer dark.

When they reached the uppermost portico, where the entrance to the chamber lay, two great clockwork gargants, made from gold and brass, stood to either side of an immense pair of double doors, covered in celestial carvings far beyond the skill of any mortal hand.

The two false gargants had been fashioned after the appearance of two of the ancient lords of that race, humbled aeons before by Sigmar. The Twin Kings, Mog and Gamog, had served for centuries as Sigmar's shield-bearers in penance for their defiance. Both had been slain in those final days before the Gates of Azyr had been sealed, leading their tribes into the safety of Azyr's mountains. Now, their death-masks adorned two great automatons, crafted by the Six Smiths in honour of the fallen brutes.

As one, the pair moved to admit the lords-arcanum into the halls beyond. The air shivered with the screech of the massive hinges, and the thunderous whirring of the gargant's gear-driven limbs as they hauled the doors open. Censers hung from the archway rotated in the sudden breeze, casting lazy comets of sweet-smelling smoke across the air.

The entry hall beyond the doors was enormous. It stretched beneath a curved roof, decorated with a faded mural depicting celestial phenomena. Great pillars of marble upheld the roof, and at the opposite end of the hall, two huge statues stood to either side of a set of massive double doors. The statues resembled Stormcast Eternals, if highly idealised, and were crouched and bent beneath the weight of the roof above.

An immense, contiguous bas-relief occupied the walls to either side of them. Among the many thousands of intricately carved figures, Balthas saw not just warriors, but delvers and masons, farmers, harpers and smiths. Not all of them human, but duardin, aelf and others. He spotted a looming gargant and the shuffling lines of the dead, as well. It was as if some unknown craftsman had attempted to capture the soul of the realms – the very stuff of life – in stone. A memory of a golden age, now long past, but preserved for all time.

Mosaics, crafted from innumerable small, polished stones, covered the floor. These depicted discrete stories rather than the vast sweep of history. Stylised moments of heroism and wonder, like Templesen's stand at Archiba, or the last charge of the Skyblood clans. Balthas, as ever, found himself distracted by the mosaics. More than once, he fell out of step with Tyros and lagged behind to better study one of the images.

After the fifth such momentary delay, Tyros turned. 'Much as we all might wish, death does not stop so you can look at pictures, brother.'

'I am well aware of that, Tyros,' Balthas said, hurrying to catch up with his fellow lord-arcanum. 'But one must make the time, on occasion, else we lose sight of where we've come from. The finer details, as you said, yourself.'

Tyros snorted. 'A fancy way of saying you're easily distracted today.'

Balthas glared at him. Tyros had little patience for anything that didn't produce immediate results. He relied on faith and instinct to guide him, where Balthas preferred a more considered approach. 'Sometimes I wonder why we are friends, Tyros.'

Tyros looked at him askance. 'We're friends?'

Before Balthas could reply, they reached the massive double doors that led to the Chamber of the Broken World and the Anvil of Apotheosis. A cohort of Retributors, comprised of warriors from several different Stormhosts, stood sentinel before the doors, beneath the great statues.

The honour of guarding the Chamber of the Broken World was much vied for among the champions of Sigmar. Only the greatest warriors of the paladin conclaves, as determined by the Trials of Culmination, were allowed to stand sentry here, for twelve days and nights, before they surrendered their places to the next cohort.

One of the Retributors, clad in the maroon-and-ivory warplate of the Celestial Warbringers, stepped forwards, one hand extended, his lightning hammer over his shoulder. 'Hold. Who approaches the Chamber of the Broken World?' As he spoke, the others spread out behind him, their hammers held at the ready. 'Speak and be judged.'

Balthas struck the ground with the ferrule of his staff. 'I, Balthas Arum of the Grave Brethren, seek entrance so that I might take up my duly appointed post.' Lightning crackled about the head of the staff. 'Will you bar my path?'

From far above, he heard a dim rumble. Without looking up, he knew that the eyes of the two statues were glowing with a sapphire radiance. The Retributors were only the most obvious of the Anvil's defences. There were protective runes and mystic wards woven into every surface, invisible to the naked eye. If he were not who he claimed to be, the consequences would be severe.

Balthas felt a moment of subtle pressure, and then the rumble faded as the two great doors swung slowly open. 'Enter, lord-arcanum,' the Retributor rumbled, and stepped aside. He glanced at Tyros and nodded. 'Tyros.'

'Kandaras,' Tyros said, as he followed Balthas, who shook his head.

'We have the rites of announcement for a reason, Tyros.'

'Waste of time. We wouldn't be here, if we weren't us.' Tyros gestured to the statues. 'Besides, they would know, rites or no rites.'

Balthas grunted. 'Still…'

Tyros clapped him on the shoulder-plate. 'Relax, brother. No reason to borrow trouble. The hard part is still to come.'

Balthas' second in command, Miska, was waiting for them when they arrived. She stood, frowning, in the doorway, her rod of office braced as if to bar their way. The Knight-Incantor was tall and slim, with pale, hard features and hair the colour of molten silver. Like Balthas, she was a gifted stormcaller, able to draw down the wrath of the heavens upon her foes. More, she knew the celestial melodies that could calm the spirits of storm and sky, and could sing a wrathful soul to peaceful slumber.

'You found him, then. Good.' Even now, after shedding her mortal life, the Knight-Incantor spoke with the faintest of accents. Some rough-hewn dialect that rasped against Balthas' attentions like a whetstone. She studied him with her usual expression of cool reproach. 'You are late, my lord.'

'I am well aware, Miska. There is no need to remind me.'

'It is my hope that by reminding you, you will cease to dawdle among forgotten stories and dusty tomes.' She spoke bluntly. 'You are needed here.'

'So I am told.' He said it sternly, striving to remind her solely by his tone of who was in charge. She smiled widely, seemingly pleased.

'Good, then. We will not need to tell you again.'

'Until we do,' Tyros murmured. Balthas glared at him, but Miska ignored the other lord-arcanum's comment. Balthas knew that as far as she was concerned, Tyros was incidental to proceedings. He was of a different host and thus someone else's responsibility. Tyros clapped a friendly hand on Balthas' shoulder and strode away, leaving him to his duties. The Hallowed Knight had his own chamber to see to.

Miska watched him go, and then said, 'The aether is in an uproar.'

Balthas nodded, though he'd felt nothing. While the aether held no secrets from him, Miska was attuned to it on an almost instinctive level. If she felt that something was wrong, it likely was. 'Today will be bad, I think,' she continued quietly. 'Be wary, brother.'

'I am always wary, sister.'

Together, they entered the great, pillared hall, where the Anvil of Apotheosis lay. The Chamber of the Broken World was immense, as befitted its purpose. The roof was a dome of dark glass, wrought from the sands of the Caelum Desert. It was divided into three Tiers of Trial – at the bottom of the chamber was the Forge Eternal, where the fires of creation were kept stoked by the celestial automata of the Six Smiths. Above that were the Cairns of Tempering, seven great stones plucked from the volcanic surface of Mallus by Grungni himself. And at the apex was the Anvil of Apotheosis.

The ensorcelled altar was a massive slab of pure sigmarite, wrenched from the core of Mallus by Sigmar's own hands. It still smouldered with the heat of the world's dying, and the air around it pulsed with the faint echoes of another time and place. It sat atop a dais fashioned in the shape of the High Star.

Each tier of the chamber was an assemblage of gargantuan clockwork platforms, perpetually moving in a slow, all but imperceptible fashion around the central core upon which the Anvil rested. They were the gears in some great mechanism of gold and glass, a machine crafted to refine souls and make them weapons.

The thought was not a pleasant one. Balthas thought of the soul-mills, and knew that the gods at their most callous often regarded mortal lives as little more than raw materials. Things to be changed, broken down and reassembled in a more pleasing or useful shape. Even Sigmar was not above crafting awful wonders in his drive to defeat the Ruinous Powers. He looked around. Knight-Incantors, clad in the heraldry of diverse Stormhosts, were taking up their assigned posts around the Anvil of Apotheosis. The Knight-Incantors surrounded the dais in a wide ring, each taking a position analogous to one of Sigendil's twelve points.

Behind them knelt a wider circle of Evocators – warrior-mages, second only to the Knight-Incantors. Duellists without equal, the Evocators wielded tempest blade and stormstave with deadly skill. They drew down the wrath of the storm not to strike their enemies, but to empower themselves. They knelt, blades and staves flat on the floor beside them, ready to aid the Knight-Incantors, should it become necessary.

One of the Evocators, in the black and gold of the Anvils of the Heldenhammer, rose to meet them. 'My lord Balthas, we were worried the Grand Library had claimed you for its own,' he called out, as he removed his helmet and tucked it under his arm. 'I knew you'd fight your way out eventually, though. I even composed a few verses, commemorating your victory. Do you wish to hear them?'

'Your confidence is heartening to hear, Helios,' Balthas said, somewhat sourly. Helios Starbane was lithe and graceful, even in his armour and robes. There were some who whispered that the swordsman had not been forged of mortal stock, but something rarer. Studying his lean, otherworldly features, Balthas could almost credit the rumours. 'But I must decline. There are more important matters to attend to.'

'Impossible,' Helios said. 'Poetry is writ in our very substance. What are we but motes of the divine, songs of heaven and loss, wrenched loose and encased in wrath and sigmarite?'

Miska shook her head. 'Enough. Now is not the time for poetry, Helios.'

'I disagree. When better than now? Where better than here?'

Miska looked at Helios, her face set in a disapproving expression. 'Remember your place, swordsman.'

Helios bowed his head, respectfully contrite. 'My place is at your side, as ever, Knight-Incantor. Where you go, I follow. What you command, I fulfil.'

Miska snorted and gestured. 'Go and take your place, then.' Helios laughed softly and straightened, pulling on his helmet as he did so. Miska looked at Balthas. 'The same goes for you, lord-arcanum. Your place is above. Your brothers await on the observation platform.' She hesitated. 'Remember what I said, Balthas.'

Balthas frowned. 'I will, sister. But see to yourself.'

She gave a terse nod and turned away to take up her place with the other Knight-Incantors. Balthas watched her for a moment, thinking about her warning. In truth, he'd felt ill at ease all day. As if something were coming, and he wasn't prepared. He looked at the Anvil and saw that it was growing white-hot.

As one, the Knight-Incantors raised their staves. With a single voice, they cried out a word in a language dead for uncounted aeons, that of the twelve lost tribes of Mallus. The word shivered on the air, and the temperature dropped precipitously. Then, the ferrule of every staff struck the floor with a sound like a meteor strike. As the echoes of that crash reverberated outwards, an answering thunder rumbled, somewhere far above.

Balthas stepped back as azure lightning, freed from the soul-mills, speared down from the glass dome overhead. It struck the Anvil and burst, spilling over the sides and trickling through the tiers. The glare of the impact cast long shadows, and Balthas was forced to look away, his vision filled with sparks.

The apotheosis had begun.

CHAPTER FIVE

NECROQUAKE

GHYRAN, THE REALM OF LIFE

In the Shadeglens of Hammerhal-Ghyra, dead shapes lurched through the gloom. They were packed so close together that they seemed almost a solid wave of shadow, rolling through the trees that marked the ancient burial gardens. A slash of silver parted the wave and cast back broken bodies. 'Push them back,' Aetius Shieldborn roared. 'Lock shields and advance.' The Liberator-Prime of the Steel Souls Chamber smashed a root-infested corpse from its feet and stamped on its skull, ending its struggles.

As one, the silver-clad Hallowed Knights to either side of him brought the rims of their shields together, forming an impenetrable bulwark against the frenzied corpses stumbling towards them. The dead were stymied, for the moment.

He glanced over his shoulder. Behind him, the remaining caretakers of the Shadeglens huddled, shocked and fearful.

The mortals were clad in robes of green, and where their flesh was visible, it bore the knotwork tattoos of those who had pledged their spirit to the Everqueen, Alarielle. He frowned and signalled a nearby Liberator with a twitch of his hammer. 'Serena, take Mehkius and three others – get the mortals out from underfoot. Reform a second wall, ten paces to our rear.'

'Aye, my lord.' Serena stepped back smoothly. The warriors to either side of her slammed their shields together, closing the gap instantly. She called out to Mehkius and the others, who repeated the manoeuvre with drilled precision.

As they escorted the mortals through the ivy-shrouded marble columns that denoted the northern entrance to the Shadeglens, Aetius turned back to the enemy. 'Who will hold until the last dawn breaks?' he cried.

'Only the faithful!' his warriors roared out in unison.

Aetius nodded in satisfaction. He could taste something sour on the wind – something that originated from further away than the deadwalkers scrabbling at the embossed face of his shield. Strange undulations of amethyst light made the night sky ripple in abominable ways. Hammerhal-Ghyra shook to its foundations, gripped by some unknown cataclysm. The echoes of collapsing stones and the screams of uprooted trees choked the air.

And the dead – the dead were everywhere. They clawed out of the blessed soil of the Shadeglens, or pounded on the walls of the crypts and mausoleums of the Azyrite necropoli of the southern districts. Shrieking ghosts crawled across the sky, and worse things stalked the deep shadows. It was as if the rule of life had been overturned and all the underworlds emptied. Aetius cursed as a deadwalker sought to tangle itself about his legs. He brought the edge of his shield down, separating its head from its neck.

'Advance,' he bellowed, as he kicked the head aside. The Liberators took a single step forwards, shields still locked. The line of deadwalkers staggered. Before they could recover, or those behind could press closer, Aetius struck the inside of his shield with his warhammer. The bell-like peal sang out over the line. 'Again,' he roared. His warriors took another step, and another, as steady as a millstone.

Deadwalkers fell, crushed beneath the Hallowed Knights' tread. But for every one that was pulped, three more surged forwards, silent and hungry. Aetius slammed his hammer against his shield again, and to his ears the ringing was unpleasantly akin to a funerary bell. He glanced upwards and felt a chill race through him as he saw the stars writhe and blink out, one by one.

As if Azyr itself were swallowed by the dark. He shook the thought aside. 'Hold the line, brothers and sisters – hold, until this cursed night ends and day comes again!'

THE CHAMBER OF THE BROKEN WORLD, THE SIGMARABULUM

In the Chamber of the Broken World, Balthas climbed to the semicircular observation platform, where his fellow lords-arcanum waited. Some, like Tyros, he had known for centuries. Others, like Knossus Heavensen, were newforged, with less than a century to their name. Heavensen, clad in the golden war-plate of the Hammers of Sigmar, greeted Balthas with a terse nod. Balthas returned the gesture and turned away to watch the proceedings below.

Tyros laughed, witnessing the exchange. 'Still sore, then, I see.'

'I have no idea as to what you're talking about.'

'I wondered why you've been burying yourself in the library more frequently. They say Heavensen is close to finding that which we all seek.'

'Good. The sooner it is found, the sooner a cure might be devised.'

'And all glory once more to our brothers in gold, the stars of our lord's eye. Vandus, Ionus, Blacktalon and soon Knossus – names of legend.' Tyros' tone was teasing.

'Much like Gardus or Tornus,' Balthas replied, more sharply than he'd intended. 'All of whom we have seen broken down and reassembled on that Anvil.' He pointed down, to where the Anvil steamed after the most recent lightning strike. 'I welcome my brothers' victories, for they are the stepping stones of my own glory.' He paused. 'Though, in your case, I might make an exception.'

Tyros laughed. Envy was an unknown to him, but he recognised Balthas' ambition well enough to gently mock it. They all had it, to some degree – the need to prove themselves, to grasp the subtlest arts, to show the God-King that they were worth the sacrifice he had made on their behalf. A shard of Sigmar's own divine essence was in each of them – in every Stormcast Eternal. Their lord diminished himself, so that his people might have a chance to win the final victory.

Knowledge of that sacrifice was one of the few things that made the reforging process bearable. It made Balthas wonder why any would resist it, even unconsciously. He watched a bolt of azure lighting scream down, to strike the Anvil. It spilled over the sides, dripping down into the lowest tier and the Forge Eternal. Light blazed up from below, where the Six Smiths laboured. The duardin demigods were only rarely seen away from their forges, and few Stormcasts were allowed there. Balthas had never even heard them referred to as individuals, only as a group.

The chamber shuddered slightly, as the hammers of the Six Smiths struck as one. The raw soul-stuff was hammered into shape, stripped free of the trappings of its demise and made ready for rebirth. The newly wrought souls were sifted upwards, into the Cairns of Tempering, where they endured seven times seven trials.

The nature of these trials was a mystery, even to the lords-arcanum of the Sacrosanct Chambers. Grungni had devised the trials, with the aid of Sigmar, to test the strength of a chosen soul. A part of Balthas yearned to know what his own trials had been like, but a greater, wiser part thought it better that he did not.

Once a soul had passed through the Cairns of Tempering, they were ready to be reforged and made flesh and blood once more. They rose upwards, through the shifting tiers of the tower, until they returned to the Anvil of Apotheosis, where the Knight-Incantors waited.

Down below, a soul erupted from the Anvil, rising above it in a crackling halo of lightning and starlight. Silence fell as the lords-arcanum watched. Balthas stepped to the edge of the platform, intrigued despite himself. Though he had witnessed the rites of reforging many times, they remained fascinating.

To his storm-sight, all souls were marked by a residue of the last realm they'd been in. This one was stained with a dark purple miasma, which clung to it despite the trials it had endured. The Realm of Death. He felt a flicker of unease. Something was wrong with the soul's aura – as if more than just its flesh had been injured.

The fires of creation roared upwards from the Anvil, engulfing the soul. It began to scream, and in the twisting flames, Balthas saw the memories of the warrior it had once been. Most were scenes from the warrior's final moments, but others were of a more personal nature – tattered recollections from a mortal life. The faces of kith and kin, the smell of walled gardens and the rustle of branches in a sea-wind, rising from the fire, like smoke. The pieces of who they had been, before they had been burdened with glorious purpose.

Miska and the other Knight-Incantors began to sing. Their voices split, overlapped and wound back, each singer a choir unto themselves. The chamber resonated with the song of the spheres, and the desperate thrashing of the soul calmed. There was a crash of twelve thunders, and something dark formed upon the altar. The soul contracted as motes grew within it, spreading outwards, like oil on water.

Balthas watched as a new body was formed from a seed of starlight and lightning. A web of newborn veins and nerve endings sprouted within the coruscating shell of energy, spreading outwards through the man-shape. Pieces of bone blossomed, spread and lengthened, as vestigial organs swelled to maturity.

Through it all, the Knight-Incantors sang the song of creation, their voices serving to shape the being before them. The soul began to writhe as it was clothed once more in flesh, and the pain of rebirth became more visceral – blood suddenly pumped through darkening arteries, as coils of intestine grew and slabs of muscle and fat sheathed bone.

As newly grown lungs inflated for the first time, a scream of rebirth burst from the mouth of the reforged warrior. For a moment, he stood upon the altar, wreathed in smoke. Then, as the echoes of his scream faded, he toppled. Evocators raced forwards, to drag the insensate warrior away. Even as they hauled him clear, the air above the altar was crackling anew. Another soul, another splash of half-formed images forming and burning away, as Balthas watched. Some of those memories would be lost forever.

To be reforged upon the Anvil was as traumatic an experience as it was transcendent. As the soul was broken down and rebuilt, it could lose part of itself in the process. Sometimes this loss was but a small thing – a memory, a name – other times, it was more drastic a sacrifice. Warriors came back... changed. Still loyal, still powerful, but lacking something.

But even that was not the worst that could happen. Balthas' grip on his staff tightened, and he closed his eyes, hearing again the screams of those souls that had succumbed to the elemental fury of the Anvil. Some souls inevitably resisted the process to the point that they, perhaps mercifully, simply ceased to exist. They rejoined the Great Tempest, where hopefully they might find some measure of peace. But others were too strong to die quietly. They were the reason the lords-arcanum stood on watch, high above the Anvil.

'I am the blade at my brother's neck,' Balthas said softly, as he watched memories turn to ash. Why would anyone resist rebirth, on behalf of such brief flickers of recollection? It seemed as strange to him now as it had the first time he had witnessed a reforging. He saw the brief flicker of the warrior's final moments. Something pale, without form or feature, reached out of the dark. Something dead. Another soul, bound in a shroud of purple, cast upwards from–

'Shyish.'

Balthas stiffened as, behind him, a familiar voice spoke. Slowly, he turned. As he did so, he saw that Tyros and the others were kneeling. He felt a pang of annoyance, as he realised he had been so engrossed that he had failed to notice the newcomer's arrival. An inexcusable lapse, in one trained to notice the smallest flaw in the aether.

'My lord Sigmar,' Balthas said, as he sank to one knee, head bowed. 'My apologies. I was lost in contemplation.'

'Do not apologise, Balthas. There are worse mazes to be lost in.' Sigmar's voice was like the crash of the morning tide against the shore. It echoed through the hollow spaces and made Balthas' very marrow grow warm.

The God-King stood before him, arrayed in golden war-plate. The air twisted about him, as if the realm were not quite able to bear his weight. He stood half a head higher than the tallest of his warriors, and there was an elemental strength to him – as if he were the raw fury of the storm, given solid form. But his presence was not merely physical. Sigmar's immensity stretched beyond the boundaries of the corporeal, into spheres beyond the sight of mortal men. He was the cold gaze of the moon and the warm laugh of the sun. He was the sound of clashing steel, of avalanches and howling winds.

To one possessing storm-sight, Sigmar appeared as a shard of the firmament itself. A being of pure starlight, impossible to look at for long. The God-King was Azyr, given mind and voice. In his merest gesture was the movement of worlds, and in his gaze, the flare of falling stars. Balthas blinked, trying to ignore what lay behind the mask of broad, too-human features. The face of a man aeons dead, out of whom a god had emerged.

'Rise, lords-arcanum. If you are not worthy of standing in my presence, then none who serve me are.' Sigmar gestured, and Balthas and the others stood, some more slowly than others. It seemed wrong somehow, not to kneel before the one who had made them. But the God-King had little patience for such niceties.

'We did not expect to see you here, my lord,' Knossus said. 'You honour us.'

'Do I? Some might disagree. What about you?' Sigmar looked down at Balthas, and he found himself at a loss for words. 'Do I honour you?'

Unable to speak, Balthas bowed his head. Sigmar laughed softly. 'If I do, I suspect it is not enough. You hunger for things other than my appreciation. As it should be.' He waved a hand. 'Return to your contemplations, please. I would speak with Balthas.'

'Me, my lord?'

'Your name is Balthas, correct?'

'Yes.'

'Then yes.' Sigmar smiled. He pointed. 'Tell me what you see, Balthas. Not just with your eyes, but everything.'

'I...' Balthas hesitated. 'I see death. The stain of Shyish is upon their souls.'

'Yes. The servants of Nagash wage war upon our territories – Glymmsforge, Gravewild, even the Oasis of Gazul. The dead hurl themselves at our ramparts, seeking to drive us from their ancient demesnes.'

'Madness,' Balthas said.

'Is it?' Sigmar looked down at him. 'One could argue that we are interlopers, with no more claim to those territories than any other invader.'

'Nagash ceded those lands to us himself.'

'Under duress. And now he wants them back. Such is the prerogative of a god.' Sigmar held out a hand, and the light contracted about it, turning cobalt. 'It is in our nature to be changeable. We are not omniscient. We are but manifestations of the realms, a part of them, given voice and thought. Some of us are stronger than others. Some more in tune with the raw stuff of creation that flows through the realms we claim for our own. Nagash has ever desired to be more than what he is. To be more than a manifestation of Death, to be Death itself. A universal force, mightier even than the entropy of the Ruinous Powers.'

'He is a monster.'

'Now? Yes. Once... perhaps. Perhaps even then, he was mad. But I do not think so. I cannot think so. For if there was never anything else in him, then my sin in freeing him was worse than any other I have committed.'

Balthas stared at him. It was unnerving to hear a god speak of such things. To admit failure, as if he were no more certain of events than those who served him. He cleared his throat. 'Forgive me, my lord, but the way you speak of him...'

Sigmar nodded. 'Once, we were friends. If we can be said to have friends. We fought side by side against ancient horrors undreamt of even in the nightmare realms of the Ruinous Powers. The King of Broken Constellations and the Devouring Light. The Abyssal Dukes and Symr, the First Fire. They and a thousand others came against us, in those first dim days before the Mortal Realms settled into firm shape. And we fought them all, Nagash and I.'

Sigmar smiled sadly, and for a moment, Balthas almost forgot that the being before him was a god. Instead, he seemed merely a man, tired and alone. Then the moment passed, and the God-King was himself again.

'Others came later. Alarielle and Tyrion. Gorkamorka and Malerion. The brothers, Grimnir and Grungni. Aye, and many smaller gods as well. Little gods and powers, like the Six Smiths, whose names have been forgotten by all save myself, seeking to join our pantheon. But always, there was Nagash. My brother.'

'He betrayed you,' Balthas said softly.

'You do not have to remind me, Balthas. I was there. As was he. And whatever the truth of that moment, only we can say, and yet neither of us knows.' Sigmar looked down at him, and Balthas felt the heat of his power. Not just the storm, but the stars and the sun. Sigmar's gaze encompassed things vast and inconceivable.

Balthas looked away, unable to bear it. Sigmar set a hand on his shoulder. 'They say you spend too much time studying what was.'

'Who says? Miska? Tyros? *Knossus?*' Even as the words left his mouth, he felt ashamed. 'Perhaps they are right. But I cannot shake this shadow that clings to me, my lord. I feel as if there is some piece of knowledge, just out of reach. If I could but grasp it, I might...' He trailed off. Sigmar's grip on his shoulder tightened.

'You might be made whole.'

Balthas looked up. 'Yes.'

Sigmar nodded, not looking at him. Instead, he watched the reforging, his expression unreadable. 'A good thought, Balthas,' the God-King said, after a moment. 'Hold fast to it, whatever others say.' He looked down at Balthas. 'I need you to hunt this prey for me, my lord-arcanum. Such is why I drew your soul – and the souls of your brothers and sisters – up from lightless depths and clad you in raiment of star-iron.'

Before Balthas could reply, shouts from below drew his attention. 'Something has gone wrong,' he said, gripped by a sudden unease.

Sigmar frowned. 'A soul is not listening to the song. He is–'

Down below, a soul erupted from the Anvil, lashing out with tendrils of crackling lightning and bellowing in agony. Its human form, unfinished, slipped away as something new took its place: a thing of all shapes and no shapes – a living bolt of lightning, driven mad by the agony of its own existence.

A Knight-Incantor was swept from his feet by a wild blow. The armoured warrior crashed down several yards away in a broken, smouldering heap. The lightning-gheist hauled itself off the dais, growing and shedding flaring limbs as it rampaged towards the other aether-mages. Helios and the other Evocators darted towards it, seeking to corral the rogue soul. It shrieked and lunged to meet them.

Balthas caught the edge of the platform's balcony and made to swing himself over, but Sigmar's voice stopped him. He glanced back at the God-King and saw Sigmar clutching at his head, as if it pained him. 'Lord Sigmar–?' Balthas began.

Sigmar screamed.

Thunder rumbled, shaking Balthas to his bones. He heard glass break and stone grind against itself. The chamber – no, the entire tower – was shaking. Cracks speared upwards along the walls. The Anvil blazed up, brighter than before, not with a holy light but something darker. An amethyst radiance that shone forth, drawing long shadows and causing those Stormcasts it touched to spasm and fall. The lightning-gheist swept aside those that dared to confront it, seeming to grow larger as the tower's shaking grew worse.

The observation platform shuddered, and lords-arcanum were knocked sprawling. He heard Tyros shouting curses as a pillar twisted on its base and toppled to the floor, shattering into hundreds of jagged chunks. The platform bent and swayed. Balthas, already off balance, had no choice but to move with it. He dropped from the shuddering platform and landed heavily, cracking the marble floor beneath his feet. He rose, staff in hand.

He glanced back and saw Sigmar standing atop the buckling platform, lightning cascading from him. The God-King was still gripping his head, and his voice echoed out, wordless and furious – a solid pall of frustration, perhaps even pain, that washed through the chamber and across every soul in it. Nearby Stormcasts staggered, holding their own heads or crying out in shock. Balthas could feel the God-King's pain as keenly as if it were his own, but he forced himself to turn away.

All was confusion. The ground bucked and ruptured as the marble floor split. Pillars collapsed, and jagged cracks ran along every wall. Through the dust and smoke, he could see several Knight-Incantors, including Miska, struggling against the amethyst energies blazing from the Anvil. They had it contained for the moment. He heard the crackle of lightning and the crash of steel, but could see nothing for the smoke. Voices shouted battle-prayers or called out for aid close to hand.

He stepped back, just as the body of a Evocator tumbled past him. Balthas knelt by the unconscious warrior. The swordsman's armour had been scorched free of all heraldry, and he was barely breathing. He murmured a healing incantation, soothing the warrior's hurts as best he could while he scanned the smoke. He could hear the crackle-scrape of something moving, just beyond the limits of his vision.

Abruptly, the lightning-gheist reared up over him, tearing through a shroud of smoke and dust. It shrilled, its cry that of a man stretched to the limits of audibility. Something that might have been a face wavered within it, distorted features twisted in an expression of unending pain. It had grown, and its agony swelled unchecked.

Balthas gritted his teeth and flung up a hand as a crackling tendril swept down towards him. The aether solidified at his gesture, forming a shield of celestial energy between himself, the unconscious Evocator and the lightning-gheist. It battered at the shield, every blow echoing like thunder. It snarled and gibbered, spitting out pieces of half-forgotten conversations as it attacked.

He pushed aside all thought of what was going on around him. He had his duty, and he was the only one standing between the rampaging entity and freedom. He took a step forwards, using the shield to push the creature back, away from the fallen Evocator. If he could contain it atop the anvil once more, they might stand a chance of salvaging the soul it had been – and if not, it would be easier to destroy it there. The creature resisted, fighting him every step of the way. It was growing stronger with every passing moment.

He forced it back, matching it lightning for lightning. But as he stepped into reach of the amethyst radiance, he felt his connection to the aether dim. Just for an instant, but it was enough. The lightning-gheist lunged, squalling. Crackling fists, larger than a mortal man, slammed down on him, and through him.

He bellowed in agony, every muscle contracting as the lightning inundated his armour. His staff fell from his hand, and he staggered. The creature's connection to the aether had enabled it to breach the mystic wards that adorned his war-plate. Almost blind, Balthas clawed at it, seeking the nexus of its consciousness.

When he found it, it was like plunging his hands into a freezing river. Images, memories, hopes, dreams buffeted his consciousness. All the pieces of the person the creature had been. He saw a sea of tombs, sealed with silver chains, and heard the purring of cats. He tasted the sweetness of an apple and saw the face of a child – a girl. The face rose to the surface of the maelstrom, and the lightning-gheist wailed desolately. A moment later, the image sprang apart, like a leaf caught in a fire. A torrent of raw emotion threatened to engulf him: shame, anger, fear, sadness.

Balthas weathered the storm, enduring the confusing sensations. They weren't what he sought – he wanted the thing's name. Names were the key to identity. With a name, he could draw the warrior from the monster, if there was anything left of them. Despite the pain, the crash of disordered memories, he groped for the silvery thread of the warrior's self. When he caught it at last, the lightning-gheist twisted, screaming.

'Thaum,' Balthas roared. 'I name thee Pharus Thaum, lord-castellant of the Gravewalkers. I name thee Anvil of the Heldenhammer and loyal son of Azyr. I name thee and I bid thee cease, in the name of he who forged us!'

At the sound of its name, the creature smashed him from his feet and sent him tumbling backwards. He rolled across the floor, trailing smoke. The lightning-gheist surged after him, wailing. Its moans were like a storm-wind, racing across an unsettled sea. It struck him again and again, preventing him from mustering any sort of defence.

He could hear the shouts of the others and feel the floor shuddering. Whatever cataclysm gripped the Sigmarabulum, it hadn't ended. A pillar cracked, and he only just managed to hurl himself aside. It fell, striking the lightning-gheist, momentarily splitting the creature in two. It reformed itself and shattered the fallen pillar, casting fragments in all directions. Several slammed into Balthas, knocking him sprawling even as he got to his feet. He rolled over, unable to catch his breath, head spinning. He looked up as the creature loomed over him, multifarious limbs crackling and snapping.

Suddenly, Tyros stepped between Balthas and the snarls of lightning, raising his staff to block it. The lightning crashed against Tyros, and clawed at his war-plate, leaving black scars on the silver. 'Up, Balthas! There's work to be done.'

'Where did you come from?' Balthas said, clambering to his feet. 'Where is Sigmar? Is the God-King injured?'

Before the other lord-arcanum could reply, the lighting-gheist attacked again. Tyros grunted as the force of its blow knocked him to one knee. As he sank down, Balthas stepped forwards.

'Leave him, Thaum – look here!' He spread his hands, drawing the aether into a coruscating orb between his palms. The lightning-gheist swatted Tyros aside, sending him skidding across the floor, as it reached for Balthas. Its human features surfaced again, mouth open in a scream, eyes wide, glaring at something only it could see.

Balthas thrust his palms forwards, unleashing the power he'd drawn from the aether. The explosion knocked him backwards, but it hurled the creature back as well. It crashed away into the smoke, still screaming. Balthas scrambled to Tyros' side. As he did so, he heard a resounding groan echo down from above.

He looked up and saw that the cracks had reached the roof. Great chunks of masonry were tearing loose, as the roof shifted and the walls bent. It felt as if the whole tower were coming loose from its foundations. The glass dome shattered and thousands of glittering shards rained down, joining the falling stones.

There was no time to run. Balthas raised his hands, trying to draw the aether to him, to shield them both. Strong as their war-plate was, the bodies within could still be pulped. But the celestial winds resisted his call, barely twisting into momentary knots above him before dispersing. It was as if the heavens were in an uproar. The spell fragmented, uncast, even as the first chunks of stone plummeted towards them.

'No.'

Sigmar's voice rumbled out like thunder, momentarily overcoming the tumult. 'No. This shall not be.' The God-King was suddenly there, swelling like a storm cloud, growing larger, his glowing form piercing the smoke. He caught a cracking pillar in either hand and forced them back into place with a roar of tortured stone. He thrust his shoulder against the slumping roof and held it steady. 'This will not be.'

As his words struck the air, lightning snarled and stretched in crackling lines across the crumbling walls. Damaged stone grew hot and reformed, and the ruptures in the floor sealed themselves. With the pillars in place, Sigmar raised his hands and slammed them against the roof. More lightning flashed, shrieking from the point of impact. Falling stones reversed course, tumbling upwards to reform most of the roof.

Balthas stared in wonder until a cough from Tyros shook him. He looked down at the other lord-arcanum. 'Brother – are you…?' Tyros' armour had been burnt and crumpled in places, and his azure robes were tattered and blackened.

'Still breathing,' Tyros panted. 'Just cracked my ribs. And broke several other bones. I'll be fine.' He caught hold of Balthas' robes. 'Go after it, brother. Don't let it escape. Do your duty.'

Balthas nodded and stood. He extended his hand and exerted his will. His staff hissed through the air like a crossbow bolt. He caught it and spun it in a slow, precise circle, calling the celestial winds to him. It was more difficult than it ought to have been, but slowly, the smoke was dispersed, revealing the far side of the chamber.

He saw the Anvil, still spewing purple light. The floor was still shaking as he strode past, hunting his prey. He could see the scorch marks where his blast had cast the lightning-gheist. And more, he could see the marks on the wall, where it had climbed, seeking escape. His eyes followed the black trail up and up, to the shattered dome overhead. He saw a flash of light, past the broken glass.

'There you are.' He had to get up there, and swiftly, before the lightning-gheist escaped. He raised his hands. The aetheric winds were still in upheaval, but he managed to find the edges of the power and draw it to him. Lightning leapt through the dome and arrowed down to strike his staff. He spun, dragging the lightning around him, as if it were a cloak. It resonated with the storm-magics that permeated his body, and he felt himself thin and stretch as he was reduced to a ghost of hissing aether.

Spells of translocation were dangerous. It was all too easy for even the most skilled mage to lose themselves in the celestial currents and become part of the aether. But Balthas saw no other option. He shot upwards, his form twisting and curling like smoke.

As Balthas rose, his perceptions expanded. He could feel Sigmar's presence, as heavy as Mallus itself and as blinding as the sun. He saw the soulfire parts of his fellow Stormcasts and felt the twisting currents of the aether. It was akin to trying to swim through storm-tossed waters, and it took all of his concentration to avoid being swept away by the cosmic riptide. Time and space stretched around him. He could hear the dolorous, bone-deep groaning of Mallus, and the wild screaming of the stars. More, he could hear something that might have been darksome laughter, booming up from some distant realm. The sound clawed at his soul, threatening to drag him back down, but he tore free. As he cleared the dome, he wrenched himself loose from the aether.

He fell to the roof and rolled to his feet, wreathed in steam and spots of light. His senses swam, readjusting to the physical world. He braced himself with his staff, as the tower shook. Shaking his head to clear it, he glanced up.

Balthas froze. Stared. The heavens were burning. Shimmering ribbons of amethyst fire rippled upwards and outwards, rising from the lightless gulfs below. Where the ribbons touched, reality shuddered, as if in revulsion – or fear. The Sigmarabulum shook as from a shock wave, and towers collapsed in clouds of dust. He could hear the screams of those caught in the wave of devastation as it passed over the ring. Far below, fires burned as the weapon-forges and ore-processors ruptured and spat molten sigmarite into the streets.

He spun, as a soul-mill cracked open with a roar of splintering stone, disgorging a storm of lightning into the tortured air. The freed souls swirled in a riotous tempest, their cries joining the general clamour. Some dissipated, their essences lost to the cosmic winds. Others fell towards the streets, their shapes twisted out of joint, becoming crackling nightmares.

A hiss of burning air reminded him that they were not the only lightning-gheists at large. He turned, slashing out with his staff. The creature jerked back, distended maw snapping. It had lost all semblance of human shape and rationality. Faces made from pure energy formed on its body, all screaming in the same voice. It slithered towards him, growing new limbs in its haste. Balthas faced it, staff held across his body.

It surged towards him, setting the air aflame as it moved. Balthas thrust his staff out, catching it between the jaws and focusing his will. A lightning-gheist was nothing more or less than a living storm – and how to control the storm was the first lesson an aether-mage learned. He spat incantations, matching his voice against the creature's screaming. It writhed, caught suddenly by bands of air and light. Tendrils of lightning flailed down, battering him. His war-plate grew warm, then hot, as the strikes washed over him. His robes and cloak smouldered, then burst into flame. Even enchanted cloth had its limits.

Balthas twisted his staff, drawing some of the lightning-gheist's substance into it. The creature shrieked and redoubled its struggles. 'Hear me, Pharus Thaum – hear me, Anvil of the Heldenhammer. Yield – do not let pain and fury lead you to destruction. There are wars yet to be fought, brother – do not force me to destroy you!'

The creature howled like a hurricane. Its struggles turned the stones beneath their feet black. It squirmed away from him, dragging against his magics, trying to pull free. But it was caught fast, and he braced himself, resisting its attempt to break away. He began to weave an incantation to cage it.

Another shock wave struck the Sigmarabulum. Purple light blazed up, blinding Balthas momentarily. He staggered, losing his hold on the lightning-gheist. As his vision cleared, he saw it tear away from him, and he leapt after it, staff raised.

He drove his staff down, like a spear, trying to ground the creature. But as his staff struck, the edge of the tower sheared away beneath them. Instinctively, Balthas flung out his hand and caught the broken periphery. He slammed back against the tower, hard enough to rattle his teeth. He saw the lightning-gheist spinning away, not towards the Sigmarabulum, but the starlit void. Balthas watched it fall, unable to prevent it. It shrieked as it receded, tumbling faster and faster, until it was merely one more shimmering speck in the firmament.

Breathing heavily, Balthas hauled himself to safety. He bowed his head and whispered a silent prayer for the soul of Pharus Thaum. 'I am sorry, brother,' he said softly. He used his staff to push himself to his feet. He looked out over the ring, trying to gauge the limits of the devastation. But all he could see was fire.

The Sigmarabulum was aflame.

And somewhere, a god was laughing.

CHAPTER SIX

NADIR

FREE CITY OF GLYMMSFORGE

The taste of victory was not so sweet as Calys Eltain recalled. The Liberator-Prime sat on a toppled pillar, staring at the gryph-hound that lay listlessly beside her. Calys reached down, and Grip pulled back, out of reach, growling softly. Calys retracted her hand. 'I am angry as well,' she said softly. There was no telling whether the beast understood her or not. 'He seemed to be a good leader. A good warrior. That he is not here now is a… mistake.'

Warriors died. That was their purpose. To die, so that another might not. That was why the Stormcasts were reforged – so that they might die as many times as was necessary, until the war was won. She took a grim satisfaction from the thought. Only Sigmar's chosen had the will to endure such torment.

But it had gone wrong.

She had been ready to die again. Pharus had saved her, at the cost of himself. A debt she would do her best to repay, when he returned. If he returned. Sometimes it took longer than it ought. Some souls could not be reforged in days, or even months. They took years. Some were lost on their way back to Azyr, drawn to the edges of the realms, where the raw stuff of magic gnawed at the borders of existence.

She feared that whatever disaster had gripped Glymmsforge was not limited to Shyish. She felt it, deep in her bones – a sense of something wrong. As if the fundamental alignment of the realms had been thrown off somehow.

'What was it?' she muttered.

'A cataclysm,' a deep voice intoned. 'One unlike any this realm, or any other, has ever weathered before.'

Calys looked up. Lord-Relictor Dathus stood nearby, watching her. He had his skull-faced helm under one arm, and his black mortis armour was covered in ash and other, less identifiable substances. 'You did well, Calys Eltain. Took command, when it was needed, and held the line. Such qualities are much sought after.'

'My thanks, my lord. But I did only what was necessary.'

The lord-relictor of the Gravewalkers nodded. 'Yes. But you recognised what that was, at the time. Few warriors do.' He came and sat beside her. 'He requested that you be sent down here, you know. He asked for your cohort, specifically.'

Calys blinked. She hadn't known. 'Why?'

Dathus looked away. 'Who can say? Pharus could be ridiculously cryptic when he put his mind to it. It was one of two reasons he was stationed here, in the dark.'

'And what was the other?'

'He was a brave warrior.'

Calys looked away. 'He liked apples.' She didn't know why she said it, but it seemed appropriate.

Dathus looked away. Somewhere, in the dark, bells were ringing. 'The aftershocks of the cataclysm have faded, but the dead are still in uproar, still stalking the lightless avenues. It will take many weeks to lay them all to rest.'

'Then it was necromancy?'

Dathus frowned. 'Some are calling it a necroquake. As good a term as any.' He looked at her, his face expressionless. 'Lord-Celestant Lynos has agreed that it is best that I take command down here for the duration of the current crisis. I have spoken to Briaeus and the others. Now I come to you.' He studied her. 'You have only recently come down here. If you wish your cohort to be rotated out, I feel it only fair to give you the opportunity.'

Calys glanced down at Grip. Then she shook her head. There was no need to consult with her cohort. Tamacus and the others would follow her lead. 'No. We will stay.'

'Good.' Dathus did not sound as if he had doubted that she would. He leaned on his staff and stared out into the dark ruins. 'The aether is in uproar. The winds of magic blow strong, even down here. The gate of every tomb rattles, and the shadows are full of faces. We will need to be wary, in the coming weeks and months.'

Calys looked around, though there was nothing to see. 'It sounds as if Nagash has declared war on Azyr.' Calys glanced at the lord-relictor.

Dathus laughed harshly. 'He did that long ago, sister. This is just a renewal of hostilities.' He lifted his staff. 'Azyr and Shyish. Apex and nadir. The Heavens are potential writ large. They stir the soul and feed the soil. They bring light to the darkness and cast long shadows. All things are possible, if one but looks to the stars.' He gestured to the roof of the cavern. 'But in Death, potential ends. It damps the fires of creation and brings silence to all places.'

He tapped the side of his head. 'I hear him, in the hollows of my soul. Like a great bell, tolling the end of all days. He wishes to recast us all in his image and make all souls one with his own. He will devour us, wholly and utterly, if we let him.'

Calys ran a hand through her hair. 'Is the city safe?'.

'For the moment, and so long as we keep watch over the Ten Thousand Tombs,' the lord-relictor said. 'Do you know what lies within them?'

Calys shook her head. 'Rumours, only.'

'An army. A legion of the dead, sealed away against the day of Nagash's return, many centuries ago.' He smiled coldly. 'But we found them first and ensured that they would never awaken. Not while the Anvils of the Heldenhammer stood watch here, in the dark. That was Pharus' task, and one he relished.'

'And now?'

'It will be mine, until a suitable replacement can be found.' He studied her for a moment. He looked as if he wished to say something, but the sudden clangour of bells interrupted him. He sighed and got to his feet. 'Another empty tomb has been found. Another black soul, loose in these catacombs.'

Calys made to follow him, but Dathus waved her back. 'No. Briaeus and I will deal with it. You will see to the evacuation of the wounded. We will speak more later.' He turned, eyes narrowed. 'I fear that the cataclysm was but a prelude to something worse. Keep your sword close, Calys Eltain.' His words echoed after him as he strode away. She watched him go and then looked down at Grip.

'What was it Pharus said? An adventure every day?'

The gryph-hound yawned. Calys snorted. She needed to rejoin her cohort and resume her duties. She looked up. The dark seemed to stretch out in all directions and swallow every sound. An eternal void. She lost herself in it for a few moments.

Or perhaps longer. Then, she heard Grip growl. She blinked and shook herself.

A cat was watching her. No, more than one. They prowled among the tombs, tails lashing. Thinking of Dathus' instructions, she suddenly recalled the child – Elya – and wondered whether she had managed to escape the catacombs. Ordinarily, the child would have slipped her mind entirely. What mattered one child, in such devastation?

Yet… the girl had been important to Pharus. And something about her puzzled Calys. There were hundreds of urchins like her roaming the streets above. So why did this one feel… *important?*

She shook her head, annoyed. Ever since the wraith had touched her, she had been plagued by wisps of memory. Nothing solid, just snatches of a song that might have been a lullaby, the feel of a small hand in hers; frustrating glimpses of a forgotten time. She looked down at the cats. 'Well? What do you want?'

The cats scampered away. She followed them. They led her along winding paths, through a field of fallen pillars and crushed tombs. She heard the voices of her fellow warriors, echoing through the ruin. A crowd of Stormcasts and several mortal priests were gathered around a small, angry shape. 'Where is he? Where did he go?' Elya screamed, pounding small fists against a hapless Stormcast's armour. The warrior held his arms a safe distance from the child, perhaps worried about accidentally injuring her. 'Bring him back!'

The cats scattered into the dark as one of the priests noticed her arrival and bowed low, making way. 'What's going on?' she demanded.

A Liberator looked at her. One of the ones who had arrived with Dathus. 'The child – she somehow got past the traps. Our orders–'

'Our orders are to ward against the dead. Not the living. Let her go.'

'But–'

Elya squirmed out of her captor's grip and darted towards Calys. 'Where is he?' she cried. 'Why isn't he here?'

Calys sank down to one knee, and the child rushed into her unprepared arms. Instinctively, the Liberator-Prime caught and held her. The child felt fragile in her grip, like a thing of spun glass, and small. So small. Murmuring soothingly, she smoothed the girl's tangled hair. The torn edges of her memory fluttered again across her mind's eye. It was as if she had lived this moment before, many times. Calys wondered if somewhere in Shyish there were children with her eyes. And if so, did they remember her at all? She pushed the thought aside. 'Why are you here, Elya? It is not safe.'

'Where is he?' Elya glared up at her, on the cusp of panic. She seemed to realise for the first time who she was speaking to. Tear tracks cut through the mask of filth that covered her thin features as she tried to free herself from Calys' grip. Uncertain, Calys released her. The child backed away, features sharp with fear and fatigue.

'You mean the lord-castellant?' None of the other Stormcasts would meet her gaze, as she looked around helplessly. 'He… I… Child, he is…'

Elya stiffened. 'He's gone, isn't he?' she said, in a voice old beyond her years. 'The nicksouls got him. He said they wouldn't, but they did. The way they got my mother.'

Calys nodded and pressed a hand to her chest. Her heart still hurt, where the wraith had touched it. 'Yes.'

The child's eyes were dry, as if she had cried all the tears in her. 'Father says you come back, when you die. Like Mother.'

Something in the way she said it caused Calys' heart to

spasm. 'No. We do not come back the way… the way your mother did. But sometimes we do come back.'

'Will he come back?'

'If Sigmar wills it.'

'Will I come back, when I die?'

'I…' Calys trailed off. How did one answer such a question? Instead, she opted to avoid it entirely. 'Your father will be worried. It is still dangerous on the streets. You must go home.' She rose to her feet. 'Someone will take you home.' Then, a moment later, 'I will take you home.'

The child frowned. 'You don't know where I live.' It almost sounded like a question.

'You will show me.'

'Liberator-Prime?' one of the other Stormcasts said. 'Shall we accompany you?'

For a moment, Calys imagined a cohort of Stormcasts, tromping through an embattled city to deliver a child back to her father. She shook her head, smiling slightly. 'No. Stay here. Hold position and continue repairing the defences. I will see her safely home.' She paused, searching for a rationalisation they would understand. That she understood. 'It is my duty to evacuate those who need it.' She looked down at Elya. 'Come, little sister. It is past time for all children to be asleep.' She would find Tamacus and the others, and see to beginning the evacuation.

Elya looked up at her. 'They say Elder Bones takes you when you die. Did he get Pharus?'

Calys felt a chill at the girl's words. Elder Bones was the name some in Glymmsforge used for Nagash. 'No,' she said hurriedly. 'No, he didn't.'

And she hoped and prayed that it was so.

* * *

NAGASHIZZAR, THE SILENT CITY

In the darkness of Shyish, Nagash looked upon his works and found them good. He stood, rising to his full height, shards of shadeglass falling from his shoulders. He heard the Ruinous Powers howling in fury as a cataclysm not of their making rippled out across the Mortal Realms. He drew some small satisfaction from their impotent rage, even as his own frustration boiled over.

'It was imperfectly done,' he intoned. He looked down. Arkhan the Black met his gaze. The Mortarch held an orruk skull in his hand. They stood in the ruins of Nagashizzar, among heaps and mounds of smouldering greenskin bones. Deathrattle work gangs numbering in the thousands laboured in silence to clear the avenues and rebuild what had been destroyed. Arkhan tossed the skull over his shoulder.

'I have always been of a mind that success should be judged only on its occurrence,' he said, his voice a hollow imitation of his master's. 'That it was done is enough, surely.'

'Perhaps.' Nagash looked up. His mind was measureless, a cosmic instrument of many parts. At any one time only small slivers of his true consciousness were active – facets of himself, moulded to conduct particular errands, while the bulk of his attentions were bent to more important matters.

Idly, his awareness passed across these lesser selves, following the amethyst threads that connected them all back to him. He listened as Bal-Nagash, the Black Child, soothed the final moments of a plague-touched mother and her infant, singing to them in a high, sweet voice. He watched as Nagash-Morr, the Reaper-King, manifested upon a battlefield in some forgotten corner of Shyish, wielding scythe-blade in defence of the living and the dead alike. There were darker aspects as well.

Things of broken fury and madness, who reaped a steady toll of souls for his eternal legions.

All were him. All were one, whatever their name. Like Arkhan, they spoke with Nagash's voice and acted on his design. And like Arkhan, they would grow stronger, thanks to the completion of his design. They – and he – would wax in might, until the realms bent beneath their weight. Until even the farthest stars dimmed and far worlds went silent.

He gazed at the sky and saw that it was filled with souls. A thousand – a million – more, innumerable, all spinning, falling, screaming. A flood of souls, descending together in an unceasing tide, drawn down by an irresistible force: him. No longer would they resist his call. No longer would other realms take what Shyish was owed.

To mortals, the changes he had enacted would be all but imperceptible. Their minds were not capable of processing such a dramatic metaphysical shift without help. Some would have an inkling of what had occurred. But they would not know for certain.

To Nagash, however, the change was obvious. Where once the realm had stretched like an endless field of wheat, awaiting the scythe, now it was a whirlpool. A maelstrom of lands and lives, stretching down, down to Nagashizzar and the Black Pyramid. An abyss deeper than time, where even death might die.

'Look, Arkhan… A void is gnawing at the sky. An absence – an unlight. The circle of time is broken all out of joint, and the sun has become as a black tunnel. The sky becomes an inverted mockery of itself – a shadeglass reflection.' Nagash reached upwards, as if to touch the sun. 'I have made it so. I have willed it. This realm is mine. It is me. Sigmar might be the stars, but I am the darkness that stretches between them. All things recede into me, as motes of light dwindle in the black.' He looked down at Arkhan. 'I have come into my inheritance at last.'

'You have cracked open the skies, master. Not just here. The other gods–'

'There are no other gods before me, my servant. Merely falsehoods, masquerading as divinity. Life, destruction, light, shadow… What are these things but preludes to the inevitable? I am become the totality of existence. And I will cast my light upon all these realms.' He lowered his hand. 'I have bent the world, my servant, and made it a shape more to my liking.'

'You have made it a nadir,' Arkhan said softly. The Mortarch looked around in what might have been wonder, or perhaps awe. 'We are truly the lowest point of the Mortal Realms now. The bottom of a well of bones.'

'Yes.'

Nagash thrust aside a shattered pillar with less effort than a man might have used to swat a fly. He felt swollen – bloated – with the energies he'd called up. They would fade, in time, but for the moment, he was supreme. It was just as well that the Howlers in the Wastes had fled back to their own realms. He might have been tempted to match his newfound strength against theirs in a battle that surely would have compounded the cataclysm.

'Was this destruction what you intended, my lord?'

'No. The transformation was to have been silent. The false gods would have been none the wiser, if my formulas had not been altered by the presence of intruders. Now, as you said, they will see and know what I have done.'

'Given what has been unleashed I should hope so. Otherwise they are blind.'

Nagash looked down at his Mortarch. 'Humour?'

Arkhan looked up. 'It seemed appropriate, given the situation.'

Nagash studied him for a moment. 'Very well.' He looked up. 'The outer wave of the cataclysm will have reached even the outermost edge of Azyr by now. Sigmar will know what I have done.'

'You sound pleased.'

'I am. Despite my earlier intentions, I find that I wish him to know. I want the betrayer to see that I am at last supreme, in my realm. He is a fleck of starlight, an echo of thunder, but I am Shyish itself. I am death, and death's shadow. All things come to me eventually. Even gods.' He turned, staring across the wastes. 'But for now, I will be content in retaking my realm at last. The squatters will be driven from the temples, and the last underworlds bound to my will.'

'They will try to stop you.'

'Let them. Let Sigmar himself come and meet me in battle once more.' Nagash snatched up a block of shadeglass and tore it in two. He cast the pieces aside. 'I will break him. I will snuff the stars themselves, if I wish. The God-King will not stand against me.'

'It is not Sigmar that concerns me, my lord.'

Nagash drew himself to his full height. 'Sigmar is the only concern. The Ruinous Powers are but vermin, clustered at the threshold of my realm. I will deal with them as and when they choose to pit their wiles against mine. But Sigmar…' Nagash touched his skull. He remembered things, sometimes. Events that had not happened, or rather, had happened to another him, in another turn of the universal wheel.

In his mind's eye, he saw a flash of gold and felt the impact – a hammer, wielded by one who was not yet a god, but would be. He felt his skull shiver to fragments and his spirit fly free, seeking escape from the reverberations of that terrible blow. He heard a voice then. The same voice he had heard at the dawn of the Age of Myth, when he had been freed from his mountain-cairn. A hand, blazing like the heart of a star, had plucked him from his cage of eternal night. The one who had freed him, fought beside him… betrayed him.

'Sigmar is the only concern,' Nagash said, again. 'I will cast down the stars and reduce the sun to a cinder. I will topple his golden towers and make of his people a feast for crows and jackals. This, I command.'

Arkhan hesitated. Then, he bowed his head. 'And as you command, it must be, my lord. Nagash is all, and all are one in him.'

'Yes. It is good that you remember this, my servant.'

Arkhan looked at him. 'Humour, my lord?'

'No. A statement of fact.' Nagash looked up, as something drew his attentions. The sky above was in constant flux, rippling and twisting as it became used to its new shape. Light pierced this fluttering shroud at a hundred points – souls, some of them, being drawn down into Shyish. But one of them was different. Stronger.

The fiery comet screamed as it fell through the sea of stars. Caught up in the glacial echoes of the cataclysm, it tumbled faster and faster, burning itself a path through the spaces between realms. It blazed with cold fire as it tore through the purple-black skies. It spun in all directions at once, its crackling form twisting and bending with the celestial wind.

As Nagash watched, the firmament seemed to fold around it, twisting and spinning, stars stretching across the curve, becoming scars of light. It tumbled down through the tunnel of worlds and stars, falling faster and faster, until its very shape seemed to stretch across vast distances, and its screams became a sonorous drone.

He could hear its voice now, and taste the echoes of its memories. He even knew its name. Intrigued, he rose up to meet the thing, as it fell screaming through the void. Nagash expanded as he rose, until he filled the sky. He lifted his hands, cupping them beneath the shimmering comet to catch it. As it tumbled into his grasp, he closed his hands about it and peered into its soul. 'Ah. What a curious thing you are. Fury, with no form to contain it.'

The lightning-gheist had no shape, no true awareness save that it was in pain, from which there was no respite. The broken shards of its memory would bite into its limited consciousness, briefly flashing into perspective before being torn away. These shards became explosions of colour and sensation, and brought a new type of agony. Its screams redoubled in ferocity as it boiled in his grip, lashing out with claws of lightning.

It reeked of Azyr, and of Shyish as well. He knew a reforged soul when he held one. But never had he beheld one in such a state of flux. 'You stink of the stars, little thing,' he intoned, reaching out as if to caress the crackling mass. 'You smell of clear waters and lightning. Are you a new thing under the moon, or something familiar in a new shape?'

Lightning crashed against his talons as the soul tried to squirm free. It was mad and blind, unable to perceive the nature of the being that held it. Slowly, idly, Nagash sank his claws into it and pulled it apart, strand by crackling strand. He unwound it like a knot of thread, studying each strand for some sign of its identity – its original identity, before Sigmar had twisted it into a shape of his choosing.

'Ah,' he said finally. 'Look, Arkhan – a prodigal soul has returned. One born of Shyish and stolen by Azyr. How strong it is. What a warrior it might have made for my armies, in times past.' Nagash pulled his hands apart, stretching the soul between them. Its screams rose in pitch as its essence was drawn taut.

'Perhaps it might still make one, my lord.'

'And why would I waste my strength on such a deed, Arkhan?' Nagash asked. Some part of him was genuinely curious. It was not often that Arkhan made such suggestions.

'Fate, my lord. You are its epitome – the ultimate and untimely. Is this, then, not your will? Such a gift, here, now?' Arkhan stretched up a hand, as if to touch the crackling, shrieking thing. 'A portent of things to come. You are superior. What better way to show it than to undo what Sigmar has done?'

Nagash cocked his head. He studied Arkhan for long moments, considering. If such a suggestion had come from one of his other servants – Neferata, for instance, or Mannfred – he would have questioned the motives behind it. But this was Arkhan. Arkhan lacked even the *illusion* of free will – he was but the echo of his master and thought nothing, save that some part of Nagash had thought it first.

And his suggestion was one Nagash had contemplated at length, since the first moment he had realised what Sigmar had done. Sigmar the Usurper, who had taken the souls of the rightfully dead and made them over into something impossible.

Sigmar, whose work Nagash would now undo.

'You are correct, my servant. Let us begin as we mean to go on.' Nagash looked down at the struggling thing in his grip. 'First, we must strip away all falsehood.' Nagash spread his talons, stretching the struggling soul even more taut between them. He could see the true soul within, the seed of substance from which this shape had grown.

The Stormcasts were not possessed of mortal souls – instead, something of the divine was grafted to them. A bit of the eternal tempest, nestled within them and growing ever stronger, over time. As Nagash did, so too did Sigmar – hollowing out his worshippers, so that something of him might flourish within them. Whether he admitted it or not.

Nagash could not pluck that mote of celestial power loose, no matter how much he might wish to. It was inextricably intertwined with the essence of the soul. To rip it loose would be to destroy the soul and render it useless. In a way, the Stormcasts were as much a part of Sigmar as the Mortarchs were a part of Nagash. Thus did the God-King seek to protect what he claimed, whether it was rightfully his or not.

He could almost admire such tenacity. Whatever else, Sigmar was strong, and Nagash had always respected strength, even though he sought to humble it. But strength alone was not enough. Not now. Nagash was beyond strength. Beyond tenacity. He was the inevitable, and the inevitable could not be denied, even by gods.

Jaws wide, he shrieked at the stars, and in the sound was the creak of uncounted crypts and the rustle of leather wings. Then, with a roar, he tore the crackling shape in two. Husks of tattered lightning wrapped themselves about his forearms as something pallid and lacking substance sluiced to the ground from within them. The lightning coiled and spat like a thing alive, even as it faded away into nothing.

Arkhan knelt beside the hazy shape. He thrust a hand into its centre and rose, dragging it with him, as if it weighed no more than smoke. It was the barest intimation of a human shape, and its misty substance pulsed and roiled. 'Even shorn of the lightning, it still persists, my lord.'

'Not all of it. A spark yet remains within it – a spark I will fan into a fire of my shaping.' Nagash took hold of the shape and gestured, casting strands of its substance into the air. In moments, the shape was reduced to scattered skeins of soul-stuff, which curled and twisted slowly on the air. Nagash studied them for a moment. 'Now, we begin.'

And slowly, artfully, he began to weave it together once more.

Pharus Thaum stood alone. The air sparked with lightning, and a flat, grey haze hung over everything, hiding the sky as well as the ground. Something shifted beneath his feet, as he took an uncertain step. He wore unfamiliar armour, and the broken sword he held in his aching hand was of an archaic design. He looked down at his breastplate, with its crowned skull and comet markings. 'What is this?' he croaked. 'Where am I?' Somewhere far above him, something that might have been a carrion bird mocked his question. He looked up and saw only grey clouds, rolling across a colourless horizon. For a moment, those clouds seemed to twist into a shape he half recalled, before they drifted apart.

He looked around. The echo of old pain lanced through him. Not just physical, though there was that as well. His joints ached, as if he had been fighting for days. His skin felt raw, and his throat was dry. Through the haze, he saw what might have been great walls of wood or stone, as if there were a city somewhere in the distance.

Pharus knew he should recognise it. A name danced on the tip of his tongue. He felt as if he knew this place… as if he had lived this moment before. What was its name?

He took a step towards the distant walls, and heard a clatter. The ground shifted beneath his feet. The mist dispersed, for just a moment. He froze. The ground was covered in bones. He hesitated. No. Not covered. He was standing on a hill composed of skulls and femurs, of snapped ribs and broken spines. Everywhere he looked, great white dunes rose in silent undulation: a desert of the dead.

His stomach lurched, and the sword slipped from his hand. As it struck the bones, the air throbbed with the reverberation of an unseen bell. A great wailing rose from all around him, like the din of startled birds. But no birds had ever made a sound such as this. It pierced his ears and raced through him, driving out all thought. The world began to spin, and his stomach with it, as the din rose to painful volume. Pharus clapped his hands over his ears and sank down. Everything shook. He heard the bones rattling, as if something huge were moving beneath them, circling him with slow, lethal interest. The mist thinned, and he saw what might have been the trunks of immense trees, rising from amid the bones.

From above, he heard screams – not the cries of birds, but human voices, stretched in unknowable agonies. They echoed thinly, trickling down from impossible heights. He climbed awkwardly to his feet and took a step towards them, not wanting to see, but needing to. The mist swirled about the heights, momentarily revealing the great spiked branches that jutted from the trunks at impossible angles. And on those branches…

Pharus looked away. But he could not block out the screams. A long shadow, as of great wings, swept over him, and the air boomed with the thunder of their passing. He did not look up, even as bones were cast about to slam into him. Even as a red rain began to fall, staining white bones pink.

'Do you hear them, Pharus Thaum?'

The voice seemed to come from everywhere and nowhere. A deep, basso rumble that shook him to his marrow. A sepulchral voice, harsh and grating. Pharus shook his head. 'Who are you? Where am I?'

'You are where all men eventually must go,' the voice continued. *'You are in the nadir, where all things settle.'* There were shapes in the mist now, horrid, moving things that he could not

identify. Stick-legged and jackal-eared, they prowled among the bones, and he turned, trying to keep them in sight. They never came close enough to see clearly, for which he was grateful, but he could hear their hungry, eager panting. Bones cracked between long teeth, and blunted nails pried open runnels of marrow.

'You are where jackals prowl and beetles scurry. Where bats roost and rats nest. This is the cremation ground, the black hour, the final moment. A place both merciless and of infinite mercy.'

Overhead, things that were not birds swooped and spun in a macabre dance, riding a grave-wind. They dived down through the red rain, as if luxuriating in it. Sometimes, they swooped close, and he thought he glimpsed pale faces set atop leathery bat-like forms. They cackled, circling him, and trilled hungrily as he tried to find some route of escape.

'Here, the flesh of reason is eaten and the marrow sucked from its bones. Here, only the night wind stirs, and all that there is to see is the abyss between stars. Rejoice, little soul, for you have at last reached that point where all fear dies and true understanding begins. Rejoice, and be welcome.'

Pharus felt something catch hold of him. Fingers like meat hooks fastened upon him and spun him about. A lean figure coalesced out of the mist before him. A tall man, taller than any Pharus had ever seen. Built spare, and dark, with lean features. He was clad in ornate robes of an unfamiliar style, and his head was shaved to the quick. The man released Pharus and spread his arms. Pharus backed away, his shoulder at once frozen to numbness and burning with pain. 'Who are you?' he demanded, his voice a shrill rasp.

'I am he to whom all men must eventually kneel. I am the end of all things.' The newcomer smiled, but there was no warmth in it. No light. His voice resonated through Pharus, shaking him to his core. The man looked up. Red rain stained his face and robes, but he seemed heedless of it. 'Do you hear them? I think they scream your name.'

'That is not my name,' Pharus said. His heart spasmed in his chest. What was his name? Not Pharus. Why did he think his name was Pharus? He'd had a different name once, hadn't he? He shook his head again, trying to clear it. As if amused by his confusion, the swooping shapes cackled again, and he heard the throaty, growling chuckles of the unseen carrion-eaters. The tall man's smile widened, becoming almost a rictus.

'It is the name of the man you were. A forgotten name for a forgotten life. And those who scream it were known to him. The detritus of a wasted moment. You were taken, and they paid the price. Look.' The man gestured, extending a brown hand to the mist. It roiled and cleared, and the rain slackened, revealing what had heretofore been hidden. Unwilling, but unable to stop himself, Pharus looked.

He could see their faces, or the echoes of such. Faint, and growing fainter with every moment that passed. Like a tapestry tossed into a fire, the edges of his memories blackened and shrank. He remembered a battle and a sound like a vast gate, swinging shut. He remembered the smell of burning flesh and the yelping howls of cannibal tribesmen. But mostly, he remembered the soft sound of a woman weeping, and a child, crying in fear. He wanted to speak to them, to beg their forgiveness, though he did not know why.

'Look upon the faces of those you abandoned. Seek their forgiveness.'

'No. That's not true. I did not abandon them.' But as he said it, he knew it to be a lie. Perhaps he had not meant to. Perhaps he'd had no choice. But he'd left them, and his last memory of them was of screaming. Oh, how they had screamed, and he had screamed as well, but his cries and theirs had been drowned out by thunder. By that treacherous thunder. His groping fingers found the sigil on his breastplate and traced the fiery silhouette of the comet, with its twin tails. 'Sigmar…' He had prayed for deliverance, and the god had heard him and answered. But not in the way he had wished.

'Yes. Sigmar did this to you. Do you see it now?'

Pharus flung out a hand as if to push the words away. 'No.' He saw the hilt of his broken sword, rising above the bones. He tore it free and turned, anger giving him strength. The tall man spoke lies. They had to be lies, else the truth would tear the heart from him. 'No. Who are you? Name yourself!'

'You know my name. All men know it. It is the first name you learn and the last you speak. I am your fellow traveller, accompanying each of you, from cradle to grave.' The lean face split in a rictus smile – a slash of bone-white through the brown. 'Say my name, man. Call out to me, as you called out to him, and I will give them back to you. That is in my power. That is your due. I am a just god. But speak my name, and you shall see them again.'

The man drew close, ignoring the blade. As he walked, he swelled in size, until his shadow swallowed Pharus whole. Flesh drew taut beneath robes gone suddenly ragged, and tore, exposing bone. 'Speak it, Pharus Thaum. Recognise me, and rejoice.' Long fingers plucked papery skin away, exposing the skull beneath the mask. Eyes like beacons fixed on Pharus, and the sword grew impossibly heavy in his hand. 'My name, in the tongue of the first men, means nothing. Absence. Null. I am nothing, and I am everything. Do you know me now, man? Will you call out to me, as all men must?'

Pharus sank to his knees. 'Nagash,' he croaked.

'Yes. I am Nagash. I am the end of all flesh.' Each word was a hammer blow. The bones that made up the ground rattled with his laughter. 'And I am your lord and master, little spirit. Whatever your name, you belong to me. Sigmar has given up all claim to you. Bow, and be born anew.'

'No.' Pharus turned away, the word like ash on his lips. The mist swirled about him, hemming him in. He could no longer see the faces, but he could hear their cries. He wanted to weep, but tears did not come. Nagash's face seemed to leer at him from every direction.

'Yes. Sigmar has cast you aside. And now, in my benevolence, I take you up. Bow, little spirit. Bow, and rejoin those you love.'

'No,' Pharus said, but the denial sounded weak. He heard the sound of wings again and felt the world quake. Something circled the spiked trees, and the screams grew louder. Or perhaps there were more of them now. Were those whom he'd left behind among them? He staggered, trying to reach the trees, but they receded further from him with every step, and the red rain fell thick and stinking upon him. He could barely see for the blood.

'Do you deny the truth of your own eyes, then? Look. See. Memories are wounds in the psyche, little spirit. They leave deep scars and tell stories, if one but has the wit to see and listen. Look. *Look.*'

A massive hand, as cold as the grave, encircled his head, forcing him to look. Sigmar's face, as vast as the open sky, was staring down at him, from some impossible distance. Those great eyes, as cold as the arctic wind, met his own, and Pharus felt himself shrivel beneath them. Sigmar had judged him and found him wanting. That was why he had been cast down. Wasn't it?

'Sigmar is not just,' Nagash intoned. 'Sigmar is a deceiver. Treacherous and cruel. He takes what he wishes and leaves nothing but ash in his wake. Do you see?'

Pharus remembered it all, now. He could still feel the fire of the Anvil, burning his soul clean. It had eaten away at all that he had been, from his last moment to his first, and he'd thought it might consume him entirely. He'd burned and become something else. Burning and becoming, over and over again. The pain had been too great, and when the world had begun to shake, he'd ripped himself from the flames, unable to bear them any longer.

'Because they were changing you into something you were not. They were burning away all that you had been, and changing it into something… simpler. Easier to grasp. A tool. A lie.' Nagash's grip tightened, and Pharus squirmed, instinctively trying to free himself.

'No,' he said, his voice sounding high and frightened to his ears. 'No. That's not right. That's not what happened.'

'But it is. Look. Look close. See the betrayal.'

The mist swirled, and for a moment, he was elsewhere – a great chamber, which echoed with the screams of the newly born and the heat of creation's fire. The pillars of heaven shook as abominable thunder sounded in the dark. Figures, clad in gleaming war-plate – they had tried to stop him, to thrust him back into the fire.

Pain…

Thunder coursing through him…

The feeling of armour crumpling beneath his fists, the sound of their screams…

He'd crushed them and cast them down. He felt no pleasure at this, only shame. Why could they not see that he did not wish to go? Why did they not understand his agony? Why could he not make them understand?

I name thee Pharus Thaum, the warrior cried, as he cast his lightning…

More pain, so much pain...

He felt again the panic – the nauseating fear – the pain – as he lurched for freedom. Away from the storm, the pain.

'The stars, the tempest, they called out to you, though you did not know how or why, only that you must reach them and find an end to pain,' Nagash said. 'But it was not the stars you heard. It was me. It was my voice, tolling you down to where you were always meant to be. You were born in this realm, as all living things are born only to die. And you recognised that truth, in your torment.'

'No,' Pharus said, his voice barely a whisper. Nagash's grip tightened.

'Yes,' Nagash said. 'You sought to find peace in the dark of creation's light. Was that not your right? Did you not deserve it – you served and fought and died, and now only desired peace. Silence. Oblivion. Not to burn and become someone new, someone else.

'But they would not stop. Again and again, they tried to drag you back. They took those you loved from you, and then, when that was not enough, they sought to take all memory of them. To leave you empty, save for the storm.'

Pharus twisted, feeling again the agony that grew with every passing moment. He could not think – could not see, could not feel anything save pain – and then... and then... 'Sigmar,' he said, half pleading. He reached out, stretching a hand that burned and smoked. Reaching towards Sigmar. Rising above him, a mountain walked. A titan made from starlight, in whose voice echoed the litany of war.

Sigmar, looking down at him, his eyes... sad?

'No,' Nagash whispered. 'Disappointed. A craftsman, briefly examining a broken tool, before casting it aside.'

'No,' Pharus said. 'No, he didn't.'

'But he did. Sigmar saw you, saw your pain and looked away.' Nagash laughed, and the sound tore strips from Pharus' soul. 'Why did he look away? Had you not served him?'

'I... I...' Pharus tried to find the words but could not. The question filled him.

'You were no longer of use, and so you were cast aside,' Nagash said. 'The fate of all useless things, in his realm. But you have use yet, Pharus Thaum. I will remake you. I will cast you into fires of unlight and forge a weapon from your tattered shroud. If you but bow to me, I will give you back what you have lost.'

Nagash released him, and Pharus fell onto his hands and knees among the bones. Broken skulls stared up at him, witch-light dancing in their sockets. Again, he heard screams and smelled smoke. His limbs trembled, as he felt the hammer-stroke of his final blow, as the city – his city – burned. What was its name? Why couldn't he remember? Why couldn't he remember anything about the time before the fire and the Anvil?

'Why can't I see their faces?' he croaked.

The skulls spoke with Nagash's voice. 'The memory was stolen. Sigmar stripped it from you, as he snatched you away from the predestined end of your story. He took of you what he needed and cast the rest aside.' The bones began to shift and roll beneath him. He staggered upright, trying to find stable footing. His legs sank into the clattering, churning mass, and something sharp dug into his calves. He screamed – or thought he did – and clawed at the bones, trying to haul himself free.

Pharus looked up and stretched a bloody hand to the starlit expanse now visible above. 'Sigmar, help me,' he begged. Sigmar gazed down at him. His eyes were not cold now, but hot. They had swelled to encompass suns, and their glare beat down on him, burning him as the Anvil had done. Sigmar spoke, but Pharus could not understand the words – it came as the roaring of a tempest, driving him flat, deeper into the churning maelstrom of bones. Fleshless hands tore at him, clinging to his limbs, dragging him down.

'He denies you, Pharus Thaum. You are a useless thing.'

'That's not my name!' Pharus tore himself free and lashed out at his captors, until his knuckles were bloody and exhaustion gripped him. He clambered free and started to wade away from the voices, the thunder and the churning. He had to escape. To get away. To… to… what? A carrion bird flapped alongside him, easily keeping pace. It cocked one black eye at him.

'It is the only name you have now,' the bird croaked. 'The name he gave you. The name on your tomb. Embrace it, and I will give it meaning. Bow, little spirit, and you will have justice. That is my oath to you. Bow, and I will give back all that he has taken.'

Crude stones erupted from beneath the bones, and Pharus staggered back. They rose all around him, like the bars of a cage. He spun, and the black echo of him, trapped in the flat panes of the stones, spun with him. The reflection changed as it moved through the stones, shedding its mortality to become a hulking engine of divine wrath. 'No,' he begged. 'No, do not make me, please.'

'It is inevitable,' the carrion bird cawed, from its perch atop one of the stones. 'Rejoice, for you have found true purpose. All are one in Nagash, and Nagash is all. Bow, Pharus Thaum, and find new meaning.'

Pharus backed away as a massive gauntlet, the colour of midnight, emerged from the stone. The rest of the armoured figure followed, lurching across the bones that cracked and crumbled beneath its tread. As it reached for him, it seemed to lose all cohesion, becoming a tarry mass. Pharus twisted away from it, but the bubbling substances splattered across him. It burned, and he screamed. He tore at his own flesh, trying to scrape away the steaming tar. But his desperate movements only spread the substance.

'Bow, and become greater than that which was lost. Bow, and see again the faces of the forgotten. Bow, and justice will be yours.'

Pharus sank to his knees, still screaming. He tipped forwards, abasing himself, as the pain ate away at him. He screamed their names, though he thought he had forgotten them, and heard them crying out in welcome. Or perhaps mourning. Nagash's voice filled him like cold fire, burning him inside as he was burned out.

'Yes. We shall have justice for the wrongs done to us, you and I. This is my will, and so shall it be. Now sleep, and be made whole.'

Pharus felt the ground beneath him begin to rise. The stones – no, not stones, he saw now, but the tips of great black talons – drew close, folding over him, entombing him. He was caught fast, burning and screaming, as he had been on the Anvil.

Burning, and becoming.

CHAPTER SEVEN

FIRES OF WAR

THE CHAMBER OF THE BROKEN WORLD,
THE SIGMARABULUM

Sigmar Heldenhammer, God-King of Azyr and Lord of the Storm Eternal, looked out over the burning ruin of the Sigmarabulum and bowed his head. For a moment, he'd thought he'd heard something. A voice, crying out in the wilderness, seeking his aid.

But that was nothing new. A thousand voices cried in his ear with every moment. Too many to hear them all clearly. Some prayed. Others wept. There were few he could aid in any tangible way. But this one had been different. Louder, somehow. Before being suddenly silenced, as if by a great wind.

He stood at one of the huge cracks that gaped in the walls of the Chamber of the Broken World. Through it, he could see the full extent of the devastation that afflicted the great citadel-ring. Smoke rose towards the stars in spindle-legged shapes, and fire boiled up from cracked foundries. Strange shimmers of heat folded across entire districts, hiding them from view. Lightning flashed as the dead were put to rest.

He could taste the after-echoes of the great cataclysm, still resonating outwards. For all he knew, into universes undreamed. Everything stank of death. Every stone and star was soiled by the energies that had surged up from Shyish. The realms still shuddered, their very substance threatened by the sudden realignment of ages-old patterns. And still, aftershocks radiated upwards, as he suspected they would for some time.

Even Mallus had been affected. The dead world was gripped by tectonic disturbances such as it had not suffered in centuries. The fires in its core blazed, threatening to consume even more of the remaining surface, and the storms of broken souls that swept eternally between the poles had grown in ferocity. Sigmar half expected it to rip itself from its place in the heavens and cast itself down. But some things were beyond even Nagash.

There was no question that the God of Death was the author of this upheaval. It had originated in Shyish and shaken the Tree of Worlds from root to bough. 'Nagash,' he said softly. Then, more loudly. 'Nagash. Always Nagash.'

Nagash. The Undying King. Brother and betrayer. Sigmar saw again the great cairn where Nagash had been imprisoned, its stones piled by unknown hands, and heard a voice, whispering in the dark. Unafraid, he had torn at the stones until his hands had wept starlight. When Nagash had reached out, Sigmar had held out his hand. And for a time, that had been enough.

But that time was long past, and almost forgotten.

Unaware of what he was doing, he raised his fists and slammed them out against the edges of the crack. Stones hewed from comets cracked, as lightning snarled about his clenched fingers. The fists came up and drove out a second time, with piston-like force, further shattering the walls and cracking the floor beneath.

Sigmar stepped back, as the ancient stones crumbled away and fell from sight. Rage undimmed, he fought to control himself. It was like trying to wrestle a storm into a box, but he'd had aeons of practice. Long past were the days when his fury might shake the heavens, or flood the lands below. He was a different god now, to the one he had been. Arrogance had been burned out of him by the fires of shame.

'But some things never change, eh?' he said, half to himself. 'And some gods are as foolish as they were millennia ago.' He turned to the golden-armoured figure standing behind him. 'Let this be a lesson to you, Knossus Heavensen – some things never change, no matter our desires.' He noticed the paleness of Knossus' tattooed features and the stiffness of his posture, and realised belatedly that the lord-arcanum was disturbed by his display of anger. 'Do not fear, lord-arcanum. My anger is not directed at you.'

'I did not think it was, my lord.' Knossus spoke with all due reverence, and bowed. He had his helmet clutched under one arm and his staff in the other hand. His war-plate was marked by signs of battle and stained with ash. Knossus and his warriors had fought for hours alongside other Sacrosanct Chambers to recapture those souls that had escaped from the soul-mills and rampaged across the Sigmarabulum.

Sigmar grimaced. 'Do not bow, Knossus. I require no worship from you.' He looked past the lord-arcanum. The Chamber of the Broken World was being repaired, but slowly. He had prevented its collapse, but the cataclysm had damaged more than just the walls and pillars. At the heart of the chamber, the Anvil had at last returned to normal, shedding the purple miasma that had clung to it.

Knossus straightened. 'I know, my lord. But I give it freely.'

Sigmar looked down at him. 'Perhaps I should have clad you in silver, instead of gold.' He smiled as he said it, but Knossus took the statement at face value.

'If such be your will, my lord.'

Sigmar sighed. 'It was a jest, Knossus.'

A brief smile played across the lord-arcanum's features. 'I am aware, my lord.'

Sigmar laughed, and somewhere far away, thunder rumbled. He clapped Knossus on the shoulder, nearly knocking the Stormcast from his feet. 'Good. Now tell me what there is to be told.' He turned back to the crack in the wall.

'The soul-mills are repaired. The aftershocks are fading. The dead...' Knossus hesitated. Sigmar glanced at him.

'The dead do not rest easy,' he said.

Knossus nodded. 'Even in Sigmaron, they rise and attack. The Vaults of the Firmament cracked wide in the cataclysm. Thousands of suddenly ambulatory corpses have spilled out into the streets, attacking any they come across. Some are no more than feral husks. Others are possessed of more malign awareness. It is as if a call to war has gone out, and now even the honoured fallen turn on us.'

'A call to war,' Sigmar repeated. 'Perhaps that is what it was.' He was already aware of everything Knossus had told him. He could feel the dead, clawing at the insides of their tombs, and hear the wailing of souls driven to madness.

He looked out, past the edges of the Sigmarabulum and down into Azyr itself, where high, snow-capped mountains rose over great plains and seas. The dead walked in Sigmaron, as Knossus said, and in Azyrheim, below it. In every great city of Azyr, the dead stirred. And not just there. Wherever one of his cities rose, he could see. Deadwalkers stumbled through the streets of Excelsis and Greywater Fastness. Cackling spirits threatened the Phoenix Temple in Phoenicium, and long-forgotten armies of fleshless deathrattle warriors stirred themselves from the boiling mud-flats and marched on the walls of Hammerhal Aqsha.

The embers of his rage flickered, threatening to blaze forth once more. He watched all that he had built in these scant decades since the opening of the Gates of Azyr come under attack, and his hands itched for the weight of his warhammer, Ghal Maraz. He longed to take it up once more and hurl himself down into Shyish. To at last answer the questions that lay between himself and the Undying King. But he had learned his lesson.

He turned from the wall and strode past Knossus. 'I suspected this day would come the moment Nagash chose to reject my offer of alliance. He was always stubborn. But I hoped he'd see sense.'

Knossus followed him, shaking his head. 'Perhaps there is method to his madness. We have pushed back the dark gods on almost every front. They are not defeated, but they are on uncertain ground. The other gods rally against them, and even Archaon cannot be everywhere at once.' He hurried to catch up to Sigmar's longer stride. 'This may well be Nagash's only chance – we are stretched thin, and our eyes are on other foes.'

Sigmar slowed and glanced down at him. 'There is more to this than simple strategy. I think this was the culmination of something set in motion long ago. Nagash has always taken a longer view than most gods. Even myself. I think in terms of centuries. Nagash thinks in terms of epochs.' He stopped. 'He has already foreseen the moment that the last star flickers out, and prepared accordingly.'

'Surely that will never happen.' Knossus sounded aghast.

Sigmar looked around before answering. The detritus of the battle against the lightning-gheist lay scattered everywhere. Scorched weapons and torn armour lay mixed among the rubble. Half a dozen Evocators and a Knight-Incantor had perished, attempting to bring the rogue soul to bay. That the lord-arcanum known as Balthas had managed to survive, and defeat it, was a testament to his strength.

Balthas. There was a soul to be watched. An old soul. Sigmar glanced up, at Mallus, and then away. Balthas had requested that his Chamber be sent in pursuit of the escaped soul. Sigmar was still considering that request.

He glanced at Knossus. 'It is not in my power to say what will happen, or won't. All things move towards their end, whatever the will of men or gods.' He picked up a crumpled helmet. The warrior who'd worn it was now in one of the soul-mills. He could feel the last moments of their life and the echo of their death. He could hear their soul screaming, begging for release. Sigmar closed his eyes. The helmet fell to the ground. Someone would clean it up later. It would be reforged and made ready for war again. All things could be reforged. Even gods.

'But that end is not here yet, my lord,' Knossus said.

Sigmar opened his eyes and looked up at the dark curve of the sky. He could see every star, and beyond. In the quiet between battles, when the affairs of the realms did not distract him, they sang to him, sometimes, calling down to him, bidding him join them in the eternal dance. He felt their pull now and knew that one day, he might no longer be able to resist their call. But not today. Not until the war was won.

'No. It is not. You will go to Shyish.'

Knossus bowed his head. 'As you will it, my lord.'

'As it must be, Knossus.' Sigmar approached the Anvil. The Knight-Incantors who had been working to cleanse it retreated, bowing low. Sigmar gestured, catching up some of the skeins of magic that emanated from it. He could feel the heat of the world from which the substance of the Anvil had been drawn.

Mallus. It'd had another name, once. In another age, in another life. Once, it had been as vibrant as the realms and dearer to him than anything. Now, it was simply raw materials for a war beyond comprehension. A world and all those who might have once lived on it, made over into weapons.

'As it must be,' Sigmar said, again. 'Until the war is won.'

SIGMARON, PALACE-CITY OF SIGMAR

Balthas whipped his staff up and about, striking the dead thing as it lunged for him. A skull, brown with age, cracked, expelling a violet light. The corpse, a scarecrow of leathery skin stretched over thin bones, wrapped in mouldering robes of azure and rusted armour, collapsed in a heap. It was not alone. A dozen more stumbled along the parapet towards the lord-arcanum, clad in the finery of ages. They wore the tattered vestments of healers and philosophers, generals and diplomats. In life, they had been heroes. In death, they were little more than beasts.

Some stumbled on limbs that did not function correctly. Others scampered across the crenellations of the World-Wall – the highest rampart of Sigmaron, and the closest one to Mallus – with simian ease. Balthas braced himself as the quickest of these leapt for him, fleshless jaws champing. He swept his staff up, catching it in the chest and pitching it over the side. For a moment, Sigmaron seemed to fall away from him, in descending tiers of pale stone. A vertiginous slope of towers and buttresses. Now, clouds of smoke obscured some of those structures. He turned back and reversed his staff, thrusting it out to catch a second corpse. A brittle sternum crumpled, and he drove the dead-walker back with two quick steps.

As the corpse reeled, Balthas slammed his staff down, a corona of corposant playing atop it. A bolt of lightning thundered down, striking the cadaver and immolating it. Smaller chains of lightning leapt out to strike the rest, one after another. The celestial energy cascaded through the dead, reducing them to ashes and blackened bones. He watched them burn with no small amount of satisfaction.

'Neatly done, my lord. Even if you have once again declined the use of your blade.'

He turned as Miska joined him on the parapet of the World-Wall. She eyed the smouldering lightning scars with approval. 'Then, you have ever possessed a talent for the aetheric.' As ever, her voice rasped across his hearing, like a whetstone across a blade.

'It was but the work of a moment and of no import,' he said modestly. 'Any aether-mage could have done the same.'

'That is true.'

He ignored her dismissal. 'The others?'

'Scattered along the World-Wall, as you ordered. We have cleansed all but the lowest tiers of these hungry corpses.'

Balthas nodded in satisfaction. He had claimed the honour of cleansing the World-Wall for his chamber the moment Sigmar had ordered their chamber despatched to Sigmaron. 'Good. We will regroup and descend to the lower tiers.'

'Azyrheim is still shaking, they say.'

'Who says?' Balthas grunted, as he glanced upwards. Above them, the Sigmarabulum was still burning. It hung in the sky like a caged comet, thick scars of smoke stretching out towards the uncaring stars. Mallus, too, burned. The red world shuddered, as if it were a great beast disturbed by some distant sound. He looked away, unsettled by the sight.

Miska shrugged. 'Many people.' She looked down at the palace-city. Something flashed, over the western slopes of the mountain. 'Reinforcements, departing through the Shimmergate,' she said, shading her eyes. 'The city of Glymmsforge is under threat. The armies of death ride full upon it.'

Balthas snorted. 'When do they not?' He'd already known that. Shyish, more than any other realm, had suffered from the cataclysm. Sigmar's territories in the Realm of Death – those underworlds and ruins ceded to him by treaty or omission – were under threat from the resurgent forces of the walking dead.

Miska gave him a disapproving look. 'They are under siege.'

'They are always under siege. Azyr itself is under siege. Besieged is our default state.' He gestured impatiently. 'Forgive me if I am not shocked that a cataclysm of such resonance is soon followed by opportunistic savagery.' Balthas shook his head. 'Whatever this *necroquake* was, it had its origins in Shyish. That much I am certain of. Of course the legions of the Undying King see this as the time to attack – Nagash probably caused this!'

He realised belatedly that he was shouting. He calmed himself and ignored Miska's raised eyebrow. She looked away. 'Knossus will be in command, they say. He goes to reinforce Glymmsforge.'

Irritated, Balthas frowned. He'd known that as well, though he'd given it little consideration. It was of no import to him where Knossus Heavensen went. '*They* are very well informed, whoever they are.' He glared at her, though without any true rancour. Miska was immune to his glare, in any event. She peered at him.

'It is the talk of the palace. You should unstop your ears and listen – you might learn something.' Her tone skirted the edge of insubordination. 'Sigmar throws open the vaults of our temple, and sets us loose at last. The veil of secrecy is cast aside. We will march openly with our brethren, now, for the first time.'

'We? Is our chamber to march upon Shyish as well, then?'

'A figure of speech.'

Balthas grunted. Miska was right – he hadn't been listening. He had buried himself in the hunt for the dead, as penance for his failure on the Sigmarabulum. He had never before allowed a soul to escape, and it weighed on him. Removed from the moment, he knew that it was not his fault. Not truly. But there was a difference between knowing and believing.

He was conscious of Miska's eyes on him, and straightened. 'It is of no import. Until I am informed otherwise, our chamber has a mission. There are still maddened souls racing loose through the citadel-crags of Sigmaron. Someone needs to chain them.'

'As you say, lord-arcanum.' She knelt and ran her hand through a pile of dust and bone fragments. Something that shone with an azure radiance clung to her gauntlet. It crackled softly as she brushed it into one of the vials that hung from her belt.

She held the vial up to her lips and whispered softly to it. Or perhaps sang. Balthas was never quite sure. Regardless, the spirit would be contained in the vial until such time as she chose to release it – usually with explosive results. She stood.

'Do you think they resent you, those spirits you hold captive?' he asked. Some of the vials hanging from her waist held the souls of fellow Stormcasts, reduced to frenzied storm-spirits by a failed reforging process. He couldn't imagine they were happy with the current state of affairs.

'I doubt they think at all. To be reduced to such a state is to lose all comprehension of one's self and one's surroundings.' She smiled sadly. 'They are nothing more than echoes of pain and fear. In my vials, they slumber until such time as Sigmar calls them home.'

'You hope they slumber.'

Miska sighed. 'You are more snappish than usual. Is it because Knossus is going to Shyish, and not you?'

He paused. Then, annoyance overwhelmed his reserve. 'Glymmsforge was founded by our Stormhost. But we are not sent – why?' He slammed the ferrule of his staff against the stones. 'I will tell you why,' he added quickly, before she could speak. 'Because of my failure. This is punishment.'

'Do you truly believe that?'

Balthas didn't answer immediately. He didn't know. He simply felt. 'I have asked Sigmar to allow us to go to Shyish,' he said. He was not asking for her approval, or so he told himself. He was lord-arcanum, and his commands were to be obeyed. Even so, he felt a faint flicker of relief when she nodded.

'Good. It has been too long since we have gone to war.'

'War? No. The rogue soul. It escaped – I can feel it. Pharus Thaum yet persists, somewhere in the realms. I suspect Shyish, if only because of what has happened – a simplistic theory, I admit, but we must start somewhere.' He clenched a fist. 'I will drag him back to the Anvil, and purge his soul of madness.'

'He is beyond reforging now, even if we find him.'

'Then he will be destroyed. But I will drag him back regardless.' He slammed his staff down again, and lightning crawled across the stones of the parapet. 'He was chosen, and he must submit. If he cannot bear the weight of such responsibility, then he will add his strength to the cosmic storm.' He shook his head. 'This must be done. That is our purpose.'

Miska nodded agreeably. 'So it is.' She looked out over the palace-city. Though she said nothing more, he could almost hear the thoughts running through her head. He became suddenly possessed of the urge to explain his determination.

'Why would a soul fight so hard?' Balthas looked out over the city. 'Only pain results from such struggle.'

Miska was silent for a moment. Then, she said, 'Perhaps some part of him feared losing those things that made him who he was. Memories are the landmarks by which we find our way.'

'They – we – do not need to find our way, sister.' He gestured up at Sigendil. 'There is our way. There is our guiding light. As bright now as it has always been.'

'And do you not dream, brother? In those rare, few moments of sleep you allow yourself, do you not see what life was, before the thunder claimed you?'

Balthas hesitated. 'Do you?'

Miska smiled thinly. 'I know my name, brother. I know the feel of ice, weighing down my furs, and the sound of sled-runners biting the ice.' Her accent thickened slightly as she spoke. 'I know the taste of a deer's heart, steaming and still bloody, on a cold morning. I know the songs of my brothers and the way my father taught a bear to dance, to the delight of our village.' She looked up at the High Star, her expression almost wistful. 'I know all these things and hold them close in me. Were I to fall in battle, I do not know that any could take them from me, easily. I, too, might lash out on instinct, if it seemed I might lose myself in the pain of reforging.'

Balthas shook his head. 'I remember things as well, but nothing I would risk eternity for.' Idly, he glanced up at Mallus, and then away. 'Nothing at all.'

'And that, then, is why you are lord-arcanum. You have the

proper perspective for the task at hand.' She didn't sound as if she believed him. 'Let us hope it stays that way.'

Miska was not prone to cryptic pronouncements. If she did not elaborate, that meant she didn't know. 'Earlier, before the cataclysm… you sensed something. What was it? The cataclysm itself, or something more?'

She leaned on her staff, her face pensive. 'Sometimes the Anvil shows us things. There is a pattern to everything, if you can but see it.' She held out a hand. 'The air feels wrong, somehow. As if the very realms have been wrenched out of shape.' She looked at him. 'I think that this is merely the beginning, brother.'

Balthas looked out over the palace-city and felt a moment's apprehension. After a moment, he said, 'I think that you are right, sister. Something has awakened in the depths of Shyish, and I think we must be ready for whatever is to come next.'

NAGASHIZZAR, THE SILENT CITY

Arkhan the Black strode through the ruins of Nagashizzar, alone save for his thoughts. He needed no bodyguards, for what could threaten one who was second only to a god? Besides, he wanted no spies present for this, save the one always present in his head. That he thought that way at all was, he suspected, merely the habit of a life he might once have lived.

It was hard to recall, after all these centuries, what mortal life had been like. Sometimes he wondered if he had ever been mortal at all, or had sprung fully formed from the dust of Shyish. Half-formed memories clung to the underside of his mind like bats to a cavern wall, occasionally fluttering up to disturb his equanimity. Were they truly his, or were they merely fabrications? Was he himself, or was he merely another facet of

Nagash, given shape and voice so that the Undying King might have someone to talk to? Could a god, even one like Nagash, become lonely?

Arkhan pushed the thought aside with a familiar weariness. An aeon of experience had taught him that such questions were an ouroboros, circular and without end. Perhaps that had been Nagash's intention all along – to trap his vizier in a cage of introspection and thus force him to second-guess his every decision. Maybe it was simply a game to Nagash. A dark joke, played on his most loyal servant.

Arkhan laughed hollowly to himself. That he could do so was proof enough that Nagash was otherwise distracted, as he'd hoped. He could still sense the tang of lightning on the air and hear the echoes of the spirit's screaming. What it had been was as good as forgotten. What it would become, under Nagash's careful ministrations, was impossible to guess.

The Undying King shaped his servants to suit his needs. Would he create a thing of bones and dry marrow, or a howling spectre? Maybe he would weave bits of flesh and muscle together, in a monstrous conglomeration. Whatever the result, it would be Arkhan's duty to teach it its place in the hierarchy of death. Soon enough, it would join the others.

The call had gone out, and the servants of the Great Necromancer answered. Great flocks of bats – or things that resembled bats – covered the face of the moon. The dunes were trampled flat by the unceasing tread of fleshless feet. The air was thick with the stink of rotting meat and grave-miasma. The masters of the restless dead – the Deathlords of Shyish – were returning to Nagashizzar, to heed the word of their lord and master.

Arkhan stopped, sensing something. The faint brush of a familiar mind. Some deathlords, it seemed, were swifter than others.

'Well, old liche, this is a pretty mess you've allowed.'

The voice – cultured, disdainful – echoed over the empty avenue. Arkhan looked up. A lone pillar stood, commemorating a fallen temple. Atop it, a lean shape, clad in baroque, ridged armour, crouched.

'I allow nothing. I merely do his will. As we all must, Mannfred.'

Mannfred von Carstein stood and stretched. Arkhan wondered how long the Mortarch of Night had been crouched there, waiting to make his presence known. Probably some time. Mannfred had always possessed a flair for the theatrical. The Soulblight prince was tall and muscular, beneath his archaic war-plate. Bare arms, marked by scars, some ritual, some not, folded over his chest as he looked down his nose at Arkhan. 'Speak for yourself, liche. I serve my own ambition, always.'

'And here I thought it was pragmatism.'

Mannfred's supercilious expression melted into a snarl, as a woman's voice pierced the shadows of the avenue and echoed up. Both Mortarchs turned, as the third member of their triumvirate revealed herself. Neferata, Mortarch of Blood, stepped into the light of the moon and stood for a moment, as if awaiting applause. When none appeared forthcoming, she moved to join Arkhan.

'Do come down, Mannfred,' she called out. 'We have much to discuss.' The Soulblight queen was formidable, for all her slight build. She moved with a predator's grace, and her armour had been crafted by the finest smiths – living or dead – in Shyish. Her bearing was regal, and something in her gaze pulled at Arkhan, stirring the embers of the man he might once have been.

'Neferata,' he said. She smiled. He knew that she saw into

the hole where his heart might once have been. Whether she was amused or disappointed by what she found there, he neither knew nor cared.

'Arkhan. You seem surprised to see me.'

'Perhaps he's simply astonished that you deigned to appear in person, O Queen of Mysteries,' Mannfred said. A moment later, he leapt from his perch and landed lightly before them, his tattered cloak swirling about him. One hand on the hilt of his sword, the bald-headed vampire strutted towards them. 'I know I am. Then, perhaps he expected neither of us to attend this gathering.' He wagged a finger at Arkhan. 'A miscalculation, liche.'

'Lower your finger, or I will rip it off.' It was no surprise to Arkhan that they were here. Only that they had arrived so soon. Both had their spies in Nagashizzar. Perhaps they had already been racing towards the city. But to aid Nagash – or hinder him? He looked at Neferata. 'You felt it?'

'Impossible not to,' Neferata said. She looked around, taking in the shattered pillars and piles of rubble waiting to be cleared. 'He's done it at last. I don't know whether to feel elated or terrified.'

'I'd settle for understanding how he did it,' Mannfred growled. 'All this time – this is what he's been planning? What's the point?'

'Efficiency,' Arkhan said. He looked up. The stars still shone in the heavens, but they seemed further away, somehow. 'He has upended the natural order. Whether it will remain so is a question I cannot answer.'

'Which means the Undying King, in all his wisdom, doesn't know,' Mannfred said, smiling nastily. He cocked his head, as if scenting the wind. 'Can you smell that? It smells like… opportunity. How delightful. Is that why you called us here?

Are we to finally topple him?' It was said in jest. Mannfred was too cunning to think such a thing was possible, especially now. Nonetheless, Arkhan felt a flicker of anger at the vampire's temerity.

'Quiet. This is no time for foolish ambition.' Neferata gestured dismissively. 'Nagash has endangered us all with this ploy. The Ruinous Powers will not stand to be challenged so. They will seek to claim Shyish now.'

'You mean they haven't been doing that already?' Mannfred spat. He threw up his hands. 'Oh, that's right. I forgot. You've been hiding in one concealed city or another for the past few centuries, while the rest of us were fighting a war.'

Neferata whirled, a snarl rippling across her face. 'I have not been hiding, fool. I have been doing as anyone with a brain would do – gathering resources and preparing for the greater conflict to come. My spies are spread across the Mortal Realms and beyond – even in the Varanspire itself. The very stronghold of our enemy!'

'And what have they told you that's of use, eh? Did they warn you that this was coming?' Mannfred leaned towards her, fangs bared. The two vampires snarled at one another, each only moments away from lunging at the other's throat.

Arkhan struck his staff against the ground. 'Cease. Your bickering serves no purpose here, save as a distraction to the Great Work.'

They turned to look at him. Neither was particularly cowed. They did not fear him – they had known each other too long for that – but they respected him, as much as they hated each other. Or perhaps they simply hated him less.

'Nagash has called out into the dark, and the lesser deathlords answer,' he intoned, before either could speak. 'They seek his favour, and he burdens them with purpose. The cities of

Azyr will fall, and he will reclaim lordship of those underworlds lost to us.'

'We know this. We heard his voice echoing out of the night as they all have.' Mannfred flung out a hand. 'That is why we came.'

'And that is why he is telling us to go,' Neferata said, smiling slightly. She understood, even if Mannfred didn't. She looked at Mannfred. 'Nagash seeks new Mortarchs from among those who answer his call quickest. The wars to come will be tests, as well as battles to reclaim territory.' She laughed softly. 'How... efficient.'

Mannfred frowned. 'He intends to replace us,' he said.

'No. Merely to add to our ranks. To find those worthy of being his heralds in a new age of gods and monsters.' Arkhan turned and studied the ruins around them. 'Nagash has played the miser since the Three-Eyed King shattered his skull and cast us all into disarray. He has hoarded his power and played the long game.'

Mannfred smiled slowly. 'And now we approach the end game, is that it?' He laughed. 'I see it now – I didn't before, I admit. But you're still the same old Arkhan, whatever has happened. You fear we will interfere with things. Undermine the others for our own benefit.' He glanced at Neferata. 'I wonder, who do you think is speaking to us now, really? Arkhan, or our master?' He leered at Arkhan. 'Who delivers this warning, eh?'

'Does it matter?' Arkhan said.

'Always.' Neferata looked at him. 'Context is as important as the message itself. If you speak with his voice, then we know this is his will. If it is you – well, one might be inclined to wonder why you are so eager for us to stay away at this time?' She tapped her lip with a finger. 'Then, of course, there is the probability that this is some esoteric trap – a test, perhaps, of our loyalty. Why call us here, only to tell us to leave?'

'You would have come anyway,' Arkhan said. 'Indeed, both of you were already on the way here, were you not?'

Mannfred chuckled. 'He has us there.' He bowed mockingly. 'I sensed a disturbance in the aether and came only to see if I might aid our great lord.' He glanced sidelong at Neferata. 'What about you, O Queen of Mysteries?'

She ignored him. 'It matters not why I came. Now that I am here, I am loathe to depart without some assurances.' She leaned close. 'What game is being played here, Arkhan? And what is our part in it?'

'The only game that matters. And your part is the same as it has always been.' He pointed at her. 'To serve Nagash's will, in all things. And it is his will that you depart.'

She frowned but did not protest. She knew the truth of his words. She could feel them, in whatever passed for her blood. She glanced at Mannfred. He grinned at her and she turned away. 'As you say, Arkhan. But be warned, if this is a ploy of some sort, I will learn of it, and I will punish you for it.'

'Promises, promises,' Mannfred murmured. Neferata did not deign to reply. Instead, she lifted a hand in a regal gesture. Overhead, something shrieked, and the dark shape of Nagadron, Neferata's dread abyssal, dropped to the street. Paving stones splintered beneath its weight, and a cloud of dust swept over Mannfred and Arkhan as they retreated. Nagadron glared at the Mortarchs, despite its lack of eyes. Its tail lashed in barely restrained fury, and its snarl echoed over the avenue.

Neferata trailed pale fingers along the beast's crimson-armoured skull as she climbed gracefully into the saddle. 'Remember what I said, Arkhan. Do not test my favour, for you will soon find yourself out of it entirely.' As she straightened in her saddle, Nagadron loosed an ear-splitting screech and sprang into the air. In moments, the dread abyssal was gone, loping towards the southern horizon.

Mannfred turned to Arkhan. 'She won't forget this insult, old liche.'

'And what about you?'

'Forgotten and forgiven. Neferata's problem is that she wishes to be the spider at the centre of every web. If there is a scheme in the offing, she wishes to be a part of it. But I am wise enough to recognise when something holds no value to me.' He looked around. 'Nagash has made this realm the battleground of existence now. He has drawn a line in the sand and dared the other gods to cross it. We must be ready when they do.'

So saying, Mannfred bowed low and turned away, drawing his cape about him as he did so. He stalked off – not in the same direction as Neferata, Arkhan noticed. The Mortarchs had not truly been united in centuries. Once, in better days, they had been Nagash's hands and will – united in purpose, if not outlook. Now, they were an alliance of rivals, each seeking their own benefit at the expense of the others.

Even he was not immune. Nagash had indeed called for them; had desired that his Mortarchs lead the assaults upon the Azyrite enclaves. Now, he would have to make do with lesser champions, when neither Neferata nor Mannfred deigned to appear. Champions like the one he would make from the Azyrite spirit he had acquired.

If Arkhan had still had a face, he might have smiled. A new age had begun. The old spheres of influence crumbled, and new ones rose to replace them.

For too long, he had played nursemaid to deceitful children. He had aided and abetted his fellow Mortarchs in their intrigues, allowing them to think him a neutral party. A puppet-thing, empty of all ambition.

But ambition took many forms. There were many types of power, even in the Realm of Death. Mannfred was right. Opportunity was rife.

And Arkhan the Black intended to seize it.

CHAPTER EIGHT

THE WINDS OF AZYR

FREE CITY OF GLYMMSFORGE

The air tasted sweet, for all that it still stank of smoke. Calys Eltain drew another discreet breath of fresh air through the mouth-slit of her war-mask. She'd never thought that she could miss such a little thing, but after many days down in the dark of the catacombs, a taste of relatively clean air was worth its weight in sigmarite. Grip seemed to agree. The gryph-hound fairly pranced in Calys' wake, chirping softly.

Calys was careful not to let the sweet air distract her from her duties. Her gaze swept the barred storefronts and shuttered windows to either side of the cobbled street. Buildings slumped in ruin, having collapsed during the cataclysm. The street before her was cracked and broken in places. Dark stains marred the cobbles and walls, and she could taste the tang of faded lightning.

She and her brotherhood moved in loose formation around

Lord-Relictor Dathus, warding him from all possible harm. Not that she expected any. The city was quiet after the necroquake. Even the occasional aftershock did little to break the fearful serenity that had descended over Glymmsforge. The citizens were hardier than they looked, inured against the horrors of the dead, to some degree.

'Things are quieter than I recall,' Dathus said. His voice echoed against the stones of the street. 'Where are the hawkers of wares and the urchins running underfoot?' He turned, his skeletal war-mask catching the dim light of the lanterns that burned above the nearby doorframes. Calys could feel mortal eyes on them, watching from the dubious safety of crippled buildings.

'They watch us,' Tamacus, one of her Liberators, murmured. 'They are frightened.'

'They are wary,' Calys corrected, without looking at him. 'They have weathered cataclysms, if not so far-reaching, before. The underworlds are less stable than most places.' She caught sight of a pale face, watching through the gaps in a boarded-up window. The face vanished a moment later.

'The lamplighters have been out, at least,' Dathus said.

'It is almost morning,' Calys said, without looking at him. It was hard to tell, these days. Since the necroquake, the sky rarely brightened beyond the colour of a new bruise. Dark clouds hung thick above the Zircona Desert, and not even the highest spires of Glymmsforge pierced them. She'd begun to wonder if the sun was even still there.

As if reading her thoughts, Dathus gave a harsh laugh. 'I've long since given up trying to tell. Day and night are one and the same, now. And I fear it will be that way for some time.' The lord-relictor sounded tired, but moved with brisk energy.

Since the cataclysm, he and Calys and the others had worked

to reseal every open tomb and shattered alcove in the catacombs. Luckily, the Ten Thousand Tombs themselves had remained inviolate. Whatever magic sealed them still retained its potency. But the mortal priests tasked with securing the chains and saying the prayers of binding had reported sounds from within some. As if whatever terrors were contained within them were slowly beginning to stir.

Dathus had grown increasingly taciturn, as if mentally preparing himself for the worst. But at the moment, he seemed positively ebullient. Calys had allowed herself to hope that the worst might be behind them. Especially since word had come from Lord-Celestant Lynos that reinforcements were on their way.

Glymmsforge had been under siege since the quake. The dead had risen in the city's burying grounds, despite the precautions taken to prevent that very thing. Deadwalkers roamed the slums, preying on the poor. Flay-braggarts and roof-walkers prowled the tomb yards of the aristocracy. Black hounds had been seen loping through the walls of Mere Gate, their ghostly howls causing the waters to turn to ice.

Worse were the tales brought to the city by the ever-increasing numbers of refugees, seeking safety behind high walls. The dead had never rested easy in this realm, but the sheer number of ravenous spirits and shambling corpses now flooding the underworld was unheard of in the annals of Lyria.

Shyish was the Realm of Death, and there was not a stone in it that did not have its own ghost. And now, it seemed as if all of those ghosts were awake and thirsty for the blood of the living. Reports from Fort Alenstahdt said that the packs of deadwalkers that roamed the desert were growing in number, and that the great wagon-fortresses of the Zirc nomads were beginning to circle, as if in preparation for a storm.

'The child was back again, yesterday,' Dathus said suddenly.

Calys didn't react. 'What child?' She felt the gazes of Tamacus and the other Liberators in her cohort flick towards her and then quickly away.

'I caught her creeping among the highest tombs, watching me.'

'How many cats were with her this time?' Tamacus said, before Calys could silence him. She glared at him, and he bowed his head in silent apology.

'More than I felt comfortable confronting on my own,' Dathus said. It was hard to tell if that was a jest. He drew close to Calys. 'I got the impression she was looking for you. Why?'

Despite herself, Calys glanced at the lord-relictor. Elya had become a nuisance, of late. She'd thought – hoped – the child would avoid the catacombs for a time. At least until Pharus' return. If he returned. Instead, it seemed as if she lived in the tunnels now. Then, having seen the hovel she and her father inhabited, perhaps the tunnels were preferable. They lived in the Gloaming – the slums that clung to the outer edge of the city.

It was an unpleasant place. Hovels made from scavenged material pressed up against cheap rooming houses and taverns that were little more than benches and some tents. Most were refugees from elsewhere in Shyish, seeking a better life under the aegis of Azyr. Others were the poor of Azyrheim and a hundred other great cities, seeking new opportunities in a younger metropolis.

Elya's remaining parent was a wastrel lamplighter named Duvak. He'd already been well on his way to drinking himself into a stupor the first time she'd escorted the child home. He'd panicked at the sight of Calys and begun screaming. She wasn't sure why. Elya had managed to quiet him, with an ease that spoke to long experience. Calys had left swiftly, after eliciting a promise from the child that she wouldn't be caught in the catacombs again. A promise the child had since skirted around the edges of.

'Is that what she said?' she asked carefully. 'That she was looking for me?'

'She said nothing. I intuited. Briaeus and the others have seen her often. She is always quick to scamper out of reach, save when you are around. I'm told you've escorted her home twice since the necroquake. Unless I am mistaken, that is not one of your duties, Liberator-Prime.'

'The child should not be down in the dark.'

'Pharus allowed her to come and go as she pleased. Or so Briaeus swears.'

'Pharus is not here.' She looked away. He was right to chastise her. It was a dereliction of duty, whatever her rationalisations, whatever she had promised. 'I shall ignore her in the future, lord-relictor. My apologies.'

'I said nothing about ignoring her. I merely asked why she might be looking for you.' He looked away. 'Mortals are a gift fraught with heartache. We who fight in their name exist outside time, while they are slaves to it.' He paused, as if considering his next words carefully. When he continued, his voice had lost some of its harsh edge. 'There was a boy – a son of one of the Freeguild officers who ward this city. His name was – is – Fosko. When he was a child, I used to bring him trinkets to occupy him, whenever we had need to confer with his father on military matters. He reminded me of someone, I think. A son, a brother – I cannot say.' He fell silent. Calys looked at him.

'What happened to him?'

'He got old, Calys. In the blink of an eye, he went from a

child to a man, weathered by time and war. He joined his father's regiment. He is a captain in their ranks, now. Soon, he will die. Either from natural causes or battle. When I look at him, I still see the boy he was, rather than the man he has become. And it pains me, Calys. For I can preserve the souls of my brothers and sisters, but not him.' He gestured about him. 'Not any of them. We can but protect them for a short time, and then it is in the hands of Sigmar.'

'Is that your way of telling me not to get attached?'

'If you like.'

Calys shook her head. 'It's not my idea, I assure you. She seems fixated on those catacombs. She says the cats lead her where they will.'

Dathus nodded. 'That may well be the case. The cats of Glymmsforge are strange beasts, even in a realm full of such. Perhaps I should speak to her.' He paused. 'If I can catch her, that is.' Another pause. 'I suspect my mortis armour frightens her.'

Calys almost laughed, but managed to restrain herself. The thought of Dathus trying to catch the child as she sneaked about the catacombs was a deeply amusing one. Thunder rumbled through the city, shaking the rooftops and setting birds to flight. Lightning flashed, somewhere above them. Dathus gestured with his staff. 'The Shimmergate opens, sister. We had best proceed swiftly, else Lynos will wonder at our absence.'

They moved quickly through the streets. Calys felt the eyes of the citizenry on them the entire way. Despite her earlier words, not all of the gazes were wary. Some were indeed fearful. But that fear was not directed at the dead. There had been purges in the past. Revolts against Azyr's rule were not common, but neither were they unknown.

In every instance, it had been the Anvils of the Heldenhammer who had put the rebellion down. Calys had participated in one such purge only a few months ago, dealing with a coven of Soulblight vampires hiding among the city's gentry. The leeches had turned entire Azyrite families of impeccable lineage into blood-hungry fiends, and then sought to manipulate the city's growth for their own ends. Calys had sought out and beheaded the coven-leader, casting the creature's still-shrieking head into a bonfire herself.

She wondered if it had been that action which had brought her to the attention of Lord-Castellant Pharus. She'd had no time to ask him – and no intention of asking Dathus. There was a time and a place for such things, and now wasn't it.

'Behold, the Shimmergate – the path of starlight,' Dathus said. She looked ahead. The streets had widened, spreading into a vast plaza. It was lined with massive statues of jasper and gold, only a few of which had been broken during the cataclysm. The statues, she knew, depicted the city's founders, the Glymm. Curious, she studied those carven faces as they passed through the shadows of the statues.

'They were from Azyr, originally,' Dathus said, noting her attentions. 'Warrior-mages from the Nordrath Mountains, they came seeking new opportunities in the years after the Gates of Azyr had been cast wide. New lands to conquer, new fortunes to be made. Minor aristocrats like the Glymm became veritable kings in the underworld of Lyria.'

'Glymmsforge doesn't have a king,' Calys said. The last royal son of the Glymm line had died defending the city against Vaslbad's legions, leaving no known heir. Now, the city that bore his family's name was overseen by a conclave of aristocrats, merchants and philosophers.

'No. Perhaps it is for the best.' Dathus sounded bleakly amused.

The representatives of the conclave stood at the other end of the plaza, waiting for their honoured guests to arrive. Most were clad in the finery of their office, though the representative of the Freeguilds wore his mauve-and-black uniform. His only concession to formality was an engraved, silver-plated breastplate and a high-crested helm of the same. Unlike the others, he was armed, though the blade was ceremonial.

Towering above the mortals were a trio of Stormcast Eternals. Two of them wore the black of the Anvils of the Heldenhammer, but the third wore the gold of the Hammers of Sigmar. The security of the city was shared between the two Stormhosts, though the latter had no permanent garrison in Glymmsforge. Instead, they rotated chambers, on a seasonal basis. At the moment, it was the task of the Adamantine – a Warrior Chamber that had earned its battle-honours mostly in Aqshy, from what little Calys knew of them. The lord-celestant of the golden-armoured warriors stood beside the commander of Calys' chamber, Lynos Gravewalker, and the Lord-Veritant, Achillus Leechbane.

At the other end of the plaza was the foot of the Shimmergate. The realmgate that connected Lyria to Azyr sat at the top of twelve, spiralling stairways of purest amethyst. The stairways intertwined as they rose to meet the shimmering blur of light that hung in the skies over the city, like a tear in the firmament.

At the moment, a cloud of cobalt mist billowed from the light and rolled down the steps. It brought with it the smells of clean water and cold heights. The air thrummed with aetheric tension. Calys shifted uncomfortably as the tang of lightning played across her senses. Beside her, Grip fluffed out her feathers and scented the air with a contented chirrup. 'The winds of Azyr,' Dathus murmured. 'So clean as to pain the senses.'

The plaza, normally full of merchants and citizens going about their business, had been cleared for the evening. Bands of Glymmsmen stood watchfully at the entry streets, leaning on halberds or carrying crossbows. The Freeguild soldiers seemed on edge. Then, perhaps it was understandable. For most of them, the Shimmergate was as close to Azyr – and Sigmar – as they would ever get.

Calys led her cohort towards the gathering of notables. Dathus walked beside her, his previous good humour seemingly evaporated. As they drew close, she studied the golden-armoured lord-celestant. She'd heard stories of the Hero of Klaxus. Most Stormcasts had. Orius Adamantine had been among the first of their kind to march to war, and the list of his battle-honours took up an entire tome in of itself.

He stood at ease beside Lynos. The two lords-celestant were of a similar size, though where Lynos was pale, Orius was dark. He held his tempestos hammer in the crook of his arm, and his black hair was bound in long, serpentine locks and tied back. His golden war-plate showed the signs of hard use, and his heraldry was chipped and marred. Orius, it was said, had little interest in appearances – only in effectiveness.

He nodded in greeting. 'Dathus. I thought you hidden away forever, down in the dark. Tell me, do the dead still sleep uneasily?'

'When they sleep at all, lord-celestant.' Dathus bowed slightly to the two lords-celestant. 'I trust I was not called away from my responsibilities simply to see old friends?'

'Hardly,' Lynos growled. 'The Shimmergate opens. Reinforcements from Azyr. Command of the city is to be turned over to them.' He said it flatly and with no small amount of bitterness. Calys understood. Lynos had led the defence of the city for three decades, and in that time had turned back enemies both living and dead. Now, apparently, he was expected to turn his responsibilities over to another – and an unknown, at that.

'So I heard,' Dathus said mildly. 'Who?'

'We do not know. Sigmar has not seen fit to tell us.' Orius smiled mirthlessly. 'Perhaps he was busy keeping the stars from falling out of the sky.'

Lynos glared at him, in a not altogether unfriendly fashion. 'We will know soon enough, I suppose,' he said, somewhat grudgingly. He turned to the representatives from the city's rulers and moved to speak to them.

Calys relaxed slightly, having safely delivered Dathus. She peered up at the statues that rose like siege-towers around them. 'They were a mighty people in their day,' a deep, harsh voice said, from behind her.

She turned to see Lord-Veritant Achillus watching her. His war-plate was covered in marks of purity and warding, as was the cloak of rich crimson he wore. The Lantern of Abjuration mounted at the top of his staff flashed softly as he joined her. Unlike most Stormcasts, who were warriors first and foremost, the duty of a lord-veritant was to root out corruption and evil in those territories claimed by Azyr.

'It has been some time, Calys,' Achillus said, nodding to her. 'The last I saw you, you were covered in gore and carrying the head of a Soulblight vampire.'

'It was an honour to assist you in that matter, lord-veritant.' Calys bowed her head.

'You did well. One of the reasons I recommended your cohort to Lord-Castellant Pharus. You have the stomach for war against the dead. A trait we are in need of.'

'Is it to be war, then? The cataclysm…'

'Was a precursor to something greater, yes.' Achillus looked down at Grip. He sank to one knee, and the gryph-hound sidled towards his outstretched hand. 'This is Pharus' gryph-hound,' he rumbled, stroking Grip's neck. He looked up at Calys. 'Are you caring for her now?'

'She cares for herself, mostly.'

Achillus stood. 'They do that. Pharus would be pleased to see it, nonetheless.'

'Is there…' She hesitated. It was not her place to ask such things.

Achillus shook his head. 'No.' He looked towards the realmgate. 'Perhaps our reinforcements bring word.' Calys turned.

The mist pouring from the Shimmergate had thickened noticeably. There was a sound, like crystal breaking, and lightning flashed within the tear. Then, shapes appeared in the mist, moving with disciplined swiftness. Stormcasts, from their bulk, but unlike any she had ever seen before. They wore the heraldry of the Hammers of Sigmar, but crackled with a strange radiance. 'Who are they?'

Achillus grunted. 'Someone I had not thought to see here. Things must be dire, indeed.' He and Lynos shared a look. Calys could tell the lord-celestant was as puzzled as she was.

Lynos looked at Orius. 'Brother, they wear your heraldry.'

Orius frowned and shook his head. 'Even so, I do not recognise them.'

At the head of the column came a warrior all in gold, save for his azure robes and cloak. He bore a staff in one hand and rode atop a storm-grey gryph-charger. The great beast squalled in challenge as it loped down the wide steps with a familiar feline grace. Like its smaller cousin, the gryph-hound, the great beast was a blend of cat and bird, save that it was large enough to bear an armoured Stormcast on its back with ease. Its bifurcated tail lashed as it descended, and its rear hooves thudded as they struck the steps.

Behind the beast and its rider came phalanx upon phalanx of similarly clad warriors. Some bore blade and staff, others wielded heavy shields and maces that crackled with aetheric energies. Behind them came warriors in pale robes, bearing baroque crossbows.

As the gryph-charger touched the bottom step, the beast leapt forwards, as if enjoying its sudden freedom. It bounded towards the city's delegation, screeching in challenge. Calys saw the mortals pale, and the Freeguild representative instinctively grasped for the hilt of his sword. She didn't fault him – a hungry gryph-charger was a match for most things that walked or crawled in the realms. A normal man had little chance against one.

The rider hauled on the reins, and the beast slid to a halt, its back hooves drawing sparks from the plaza stones. The Stormcast slid easily from the gryph-charger's back, and strode towards the waiting delegation, staff in hand. 'I am Lord-Arcanum Knossus Heavensen. I come bearing the word and wrath of the God-King of Azyr, Sigmar Heldenhammer. Glymmsforge stands imperilled. But it shall not fall. Not while I stand with it.' His voice boomed out across the plaza.

'Sacrosanct Chamber,' Achillus murmured, glancing at Dathus, who nodded tersely.

'Then the worst is yet to come,' the lord-relictor said.

Lynos and Orius met the newcomer. After a moment's hesitation, the three warriors exchanged handclasps. Knossus pulled his helmet off, and Calys noticed an immediate resemblance between his tattooed features and the great statues. She wondered if the mortals who bowed so respectfully saw it as well. She thought that perhaps a few of them did, given their hasty glances between the newcomer and the nearest likeness.

The last Glymm had returned to his city, in its hour of need.

* * *

NAGASHIZZAR, THE SILENT CITY

Pharus awoke in darkness.

It was not a true awakening. Not a slow climb from sleep. Instead, it was akin to a candle being lit. One moment, nothing. Then, light. Awareness. Weight. Pain.

He tried to collect his scattered thoughts. They slipped through his grasp like frightened fish. He remembered some things but not others. He knew his name, but not who he was. What he was. It was there, dancing around the edge of his consciousness, but he couldn't bring it to mind. He looked around.

Faint motes of purple light danced along the air, casting an amethyst haze across a sea of shattered pillars and broken stones. Something about his surroundings was familiar, but he could not say why. Instinctively, he looked up. He didn't recognise the stars.

He was shrouded in heavy chains, pitted with age and hairy with mould. He tried to shrug them off but found that he could barely move them, no matter how much he thrashed. The air was thick with dust and smoke, but he had no difficulty breathing. A moment later, he realised that it was because he wasn't breathing at all. He looked down at himself. Something was wrong. He couldn't focus on his limbs, on his body. As if he were no more substantial than a mirage. But he hurt all over. It felt as if he had swallowed an ember, and it was slowly burning its way through him.

'Where… where am I?' he croaked. His voice sounded odd. Broken. Like a distorted echo. And something out in the dark replied. A murmuring whisper, as of many voices speaking swiftly and quietly. Then came the hiss-scrape of bones on stone. Lights appeared in the dark. Not motes, but flickering, indigo flames.

The creatures were dead, their crumbling forms wreathed in purple fire. As they drew close, the dark retreated. Pharus saw that he was chained atop a shattered dais that might once have belonged in a temple. Glimmering dust heaped against the sides in untidy dunes and scraped against his chains as the breeze kicked up.

Despite the macabre appearance of the newcomers, Pharus felt no fear. Even as they gathered about him, and the heat of their flames washed over him. He knew that he should, but instead felt only a sense of resignation. As if this were somehow expected. Unavoidable.

'Inevitable.'

The word hung like the peal of a bell. Pharus jerked in his chains as a tall form stepped out of the dark and followed the burning creatures up onto the dais. The skeletal being, clad in robes and armour, and clutching a staff, drew close, and fiery corpses drew back, to make way. 'That is the word you are looking for, I believe.'

'Who…?'

'Who am I, or who are you?' A fleshless hand extended, and Pharus flinched back. 'The answer is the same, save for details. I am Arkhan the Black, Mortarch of Sacrament. I am the Hand of Nagash. When I speak, it is with his voice. When I act, it is with his will.'

Something coalesced within Pharus' mind. 'Shyish. I am in Shyish.'

'Yes. And you are Pharus Thaum. Once of Azyr. Now of Shyish.'

Pharus shook his head. 'I… no. No, I am not – I…' The chains seemed heavier all of a sudden. The world seemed to grow thin at the edges. He felt stretched out of shape. He shook his head, trying to focus. 'Why am I here?'

'You are dead.'

The word sliced through him. 'No.' The denial was instinctive. Again, he tried to throw off the chains, as he felt certain he should have been able to do. He had been strong once, stronger than this. Or had that merely been a dream? Everything was muddled – foggy. It was as if he were watching things from a distance.

'It was not a dream,' Arkhan said, as if reading his thoughts. 'But as you have shed the mortal coil, so too have you shed the strength that came with it. The spark of the divine that once ran through you, now consumes you. Can you feel it?'

Pharus could. It wasn't an ember now, but a full fire, crawling up through his insides, spreading through the hollows of his non-existent bones. If he had no body, why did he hurt so? 'What have you done to me?' he snarled, still struggling futilely. Rage flared in him, a hungry, howling wrath that made his chains clatter and his not-limbs ache.

'Nothing, yet.' Arkhan extended his staff and used the tip to lift Pharus' chin, somehow, despite the insubstantial nature of his form. 'You are shapeless, still. Held to a familiar form only by the chains that bind you. Soon, they will not be necessary.' He stepped back, and Pharus slumped, pulled down by the weight of the chains.

'Who am I?' he muttered, trying to force his scattered thoughts to coalesce. It was hard. The anger made it hard to focus. He saw broken images – a necropolis. Warriors in black armour. A child. 'Elya?' he whispered. Was that her name? Who was she? More images now, growing firmer in his mind. A woman and child. Blood on pale stone. A cat's eye, gleaming in the dark. A great chamber. Lightning slamming into him, filling him, remaking him. 'Sigmar,' he groaned, and the name burned as it passed his lips. 'I was… I… Why am I not reforged?'

Memories circled his awareness like a flock of crows. As they dived and spun, he recalled his life in disordered bits and pieces. The smell of a garden in the cool of evening. The weight of a practice blade, and his father's voice, cautioning him. And… a woman's hand, in his. Her lips, close to his ear. He shook his head, trying to clear it, trying to force the pieces into place. He smelled smoke and heard the crash of gates being battered open. The scream of a woman – the same woman as before – and… children? No, a child. 'Elya,' he said again. Why was that name important? Who was she? A child's face swam before his eyes, but was soon supplanted by another. Two children, but only one name.

Then, the lightning. Again, the lighting. Dragging him away from the garden, from the woman and her child – his child – away from it all. Away even from his memories. They slipped out of reach, like smoke on the wind. 'They are dead.'

'All things die,' Arkhan said.

Anger burned in him, and amethyst lightning crawled across the chains that bound him. 'I might have saved them.'

Arkhan nodded. 'Perhaps.'

'Why did he take me, then?'

Pharus felt the liche study him. Arkhan made a sound that might have been laughter. 'He needed weapons. And you were to hand. You are chattel, little spirit. Best get used to it.'

'No. No. I…' Pharus shook his head, trying to clear it. The lightning snarled and snapped like an enraged beast, and the chains began to smoke. 'Am I a prisoner?'

'No more so than myself. You will bear a blade of black iron and shadeglass, shaped by the heat of dying stars, in Nagash's name. Does this please you, little spirit?'

Pharus glared at the liche, trying to muster his strength. There was a heat, building in him. A dull pain, made worse by the lightning that flickered across his form. 'I feel no pleasure. Only pain.'

'It will pass. It is not true pain, only its echo. Soon, you will forget.'

'I will believe that when the fire beneath my skin goes out.' Pharus clawed at himself, to no avail. His form wavered and billowed in its chains, like a plume of smoke. It felt as if there were a storm crackling inside him, seeking freedom. 'I have no flesh, and yet it burns.'

'Is that so surprising? Your soul fell through the firmament. It burst through the walls between realms and burned itself a path back here – to your place of creation.' Arkhan chuckled. 'You should be proud. Few souls could have survived such a fall.'

'I did not survive.' The words dredged up a new geyser of pain, and Pharus screamed and thrashed, rattling his chains.

Arkhan ignored his display. 'You still speak.'

'So do you,' Pharus hissed. 'And you are not alive.' The chains creaked as he fought to stand. The spirits that had accompanied Arkhan drew back as the iron nails holding the chains pinned to the dais began to pull loose.

'And yet, I exist. Survival is persistence.' Arkhan circled him, like a trader studying a bit of livestock. 'The power of Azyr strengthened you. Fortified your soul. And now Nagash will make use of what Azyr has cast aside.'

'Be quiet,' Pharus snarled. 'I was not… I wasn't cast aside. I… I…' His thoughts were a confusing tangle. He remembered the God-King's eyes and the disappointment in them. It had pierced him, made him hesitate. Made him fall. He threw back his head and howled. Lightning licked out, scorching the nearby stones.

'Yes,' Arkhan said. 'You remember.'

'Quiet,' Pharus roared, jerking towards the liche. His form

blurred and crackled, threatening to come apart. He felt the lightning course through him, and he groaned. It ached like a wound gone septic. The chains held him back, despite his frenzy, trapping the storm within him.

'You remember. That is good. It hurts. That is also good. Let the memory of that pain sustain you, warrior. For all too soon, you will forget it.' Arkhan raised his staff and slammed it down. An amethyst light spilled from it, driving back the shadows, revealing what lurked among the ruins.

Corpses stood, watching the dais in awful silence. So many, Pharus could not count them all. Among the tottering carrion flitted phantasmal shapes, wrapped in chains or bearing implements of execution. The burning spirits that surrounded Pharus on the dais gripped the links of his chains, hampering his struggles. He fought against them, but to no avail. They had the strength of the dead.

'They come to honour you, for you are unique among the dead,' Arkhan said. 'And not just them. Look.' The Mortarch extended his hand as something passed silently among the ranks of the dead. 'They come bearing gifts.'

Robed and hooded, with tall antlers the colour of obsidian crowning their heads, a line of women – or things shaped like women – wound its way towards where Pharus stood, chained. He stared in wonder and horror as they drew near. What was left of his spirit shuddered, as he saw pale flowers sprout in their wake and wither before the passing of their shadows. From within their hoods, pale faces, blanched of all colour, looked out at the world with eyes as black as the nadir itself. They came barefoot and burdened with weapons and armour, wrapped in burial shrouds.

'The daughters of the underworld,' Arkhan intoned. 'They have come, bearing the tools with which you will break through the gates you once defended.' He lifted his staff. 'Kneel, spirit. Kneel and receive the gifts of the Undying King.'

Something sparked within Pharus. 'I do not kneel,' he said, raggedly. 'I did not bow…' Something in Arkhan's words stirred yet more memories. He remembered the necropolis again, but more, he remembered that he had defended it – or defended something else from it. 'I did not bow.'

At Arkhan's gesture, burning spirits retreated, hauling on the chains as they did so. Pharus was dragged to his knees a moment later. Arkhan looked down at him. 'It seems that you do. And it seems that you did. Else we would not be here now.'

Pharus snarled and tried to rise, but the chains were impossibly heavy. He had no form to bind, no body to bear the weight, and yet he did. He bowed his head, suddenly weary. He was so tired, more tired than he had ever been in life. This place bore down on him, crushing all thought of resistance. He looked again at the approaching women. 'Who – what – are they?'

'The wives, daughters, sisters and mothers of those who would not bend knee to Nagash. Ancient kings and prideful chieftains, highborn queens and savage warlords – they defied him, so he took what they loved most and made them love him. He bent their souls into shapes more pleasing to him and made them his chatelaines. They rule the lesser underworlds in his name, watching over the forests of souls, and they guard those relics he deems to have no immediate purpose, until he calls for them once more.' Arkhan looked at him. 'It is a high honour he does you to call them forth, in such a manner.'

Pharus said nothing as the spectral women drew closer. Spectres retreated before them, giving them a wide berth. Vicious as the spirits were, these creatures were worse. The air twisted about them, forming strange patterns. The flowers that bloomed and died in their wake whispered shrilly for the entirety of their short existences. Worst of all were their faces – impossibly young, with eyes like black pits. They were ancient things, wearing pretty masks, and Pharus could not meet their gazes.

They ascended the dais, moving silently. Arkhan met the one in the lead and bowed respectfully. 'Welcome, O brides of night, O enemies of the day. Welcome, ye maidens, mothers and crones, those who go to and fro amongst the places of tombs, and by paths of sullen moonlight. Welcome, thou who does rejoice in the howling of jackals and the spilling of warm blood.' Arkhan struck the stones with his staff. 'I bid thee welcome three times, and three times that span shall your binding be lifted for this night's labours.'

A sigh went through the newcomers, and, as one, they spoke. 'Greetings, O Prince of Forgotten Deserts, O Lover of Night's Queen. We have been called, and we have come.' They knelt among a spill of flowers, creeping across the stones, and lifted their burdens high. 'We have brought the tokens of our love, and offer them up.'

Arkhan nodded and stepped aside. 'Gird him, ye daughters of benighted spheres.'

The women rose, their black eyes fixed on Pharus. He forced himself to his feet as they encircled him. 'Get away from me, hags,' he spat, giving vent to the anger. They ignored him and began to unwrap the objects they had brought. He looked at Arkhan. 'I will not let them touch me. I will break them… *burn them*.'

'Choice is an illusion.' Arkhan stepped close. 'Once, this war-plate was meant for another. A soul like yours, humming with lightning, twisted and broken by years upon the wheel… but not fully. Not to the satisfaction of our lord and master. And so he discarded it, as he does all things that prove to be of no use.' Arkhan's gaze flickered. 'Something to remember, perhaps.'

He caught hold of the chains. 'Nagash is all, and all are one in Nagash. But do not confuse certainty of purpose with infallibility. The dead can be destroyed as surely as the living, if one knows how. I am the Hand of Death, and I will crush you, if he deems you to be of no further use.'

Enraged, Pharus twisted in his chains, writhing against the hooks that bit into his aethereal form. 'Free me, and let us see who crushes whom.' He thrashed, trying to get at the Mortarch. 'Perhaps it is you who will prove to be of no use, liche.'

Arkhan laughed hollowly and let the chains fall slack. He stepped back and gestured with his staff. The black links burst, and Pharus lunged forwards, free, the storm unfettered. He groped for the Mortarch with crackling talons, wanting nothing more than to rip him limb from limb. Arkhan reached out and caught him – somehow – by the throat. Fleshless fingers tightened, and Pharus' essence contracted painfully.

'You are a little thing, and young besides. I have been dead longer than these realms have been alive. Sometimes I think that, perhaps, I was born dead. You are nothing, next to me, as I am nothing, next to him.' He lifted Pharus easily. Pharus writhed, clawing at Arkhan's arm. The liche's sleeve began to smoulder, but he paid it no mind. His grip tightened even more, and Pharus screamed. His lightning, his substance, coiled in on itself, and he felt his soul burn. His screams quavered through the air, and the gathered dead groaned in amusement, or perhaps sympathy.

Arkhan released him. 'But you have your uses yet, and so I will spare you the chastisement you deserve. I am patient, and perhaps… perhaps you will learn.' Pharus sank down, his form wavering like a candle-flame caught in a draught. Weakened, he barely struggled as the women went to work, cladding him in his new armour. Wracked by pain, he looked up, seeking the stars, but saw nothing save the vast, hungry black of the sky. An abyss, rising upwards forever.

He looked up at Arkhan. 'Learn what?' he asked, more quietly than before. As each piece of war-plate was set in place, the pain began to diminish and so too did his rage. Even so, his soul squirmed at its touch. Somehow, he knew that it was a cage, more than a protection. But he desired an end to the pain more than freedom.

'Your place.' Arkhan watched the proceedings with a flickering gaze. 'Nagash yearns for order. Only when the cosmos is united under a singular consciousness, with every spirit and body bent towards the directives of that consciousness, will he be satisfied. Only when all things know their proper place, will he be content.'

'All are one in Nagash,' the women intoned, as they worked. 'Nagash is all.'

Pharus stared at them. 'But I still think… I still have a will. A mind.'

'Whose mind? Whose will? Nagash is vast and contains multitudes.' Arkhan turned. 'We are all a part of him, and he acts through us.'

'Then we are slaves.'

Arkhan looked at him. 'Something you should be used to. And there is freedom in this sort of slavery. At least it is honest, if nothing else.'

Pharus fell silent. His broken thoughts jangled in his skull like shards of broken glass. The harder he sought to grasp them, the more pain it caused him. He cradled his head. It had no weight. Nothing about him had weight or solidity, save when he concentrated. It was as if he and the world were held separate by unseen walls.

'I cannot think. I cannot remember. It is as if the past is a foreign country.'

'You get used to it, in time,' Arkhan said. 'As one century bleeds into the next, you will forget that you were ever anything other than what you are now. Once time ceases to have meaning, so too does the past fade and the future become intangible. You will exist in an eternal present, unburdened by worry or regret.'

'I do not want that.' He looked away. 'I was promised something. Nagash promised me something… but I cannot remember what it was.'

Arkhan laughed hollowly. 'It is not about what you desire. It is about efficiency. Clear your mind of such thoughts. Does a sword think of its time as raw ore, or the day it will be rusty and useless?'

'Do you feel regret?' Pharus asked. 'Do you feel anything that is not his will?'

Arkhan's eyes blazed suddenly. Then, like a fire burning itself out too quickly, they dimmed. 'If I do, it is only because he allows it. Nagash is a just god, little spirit.

'And justice is often cruel.'

CHAPTER NINE

THE LIVING AND THE DEAD

SIGMARON, PALACE-CITY OF SIGMAR

'It is not seemly for our lord to hide himself away, so,' Helios said. The Evocator turned, moving swiftly, sword rising. Miska stepped back, out of reach, and thrust her staff towards his abdomen. Helios twisted aside, light on his feet, despite his war-plate.

'We all seek answers in different ways, brother.'

Around them, the Garden of the Moon stirred with a breeze. The great, silver trees that made up the garden had been caught in the fires that raged across Sigmaron, and many had warped and blackened, as had the pale grasses that grew in their shadow. But they would recover, in time. Aelf treesingers roamed the groves, encouraging new growth, and their lilting song provided accompaniment to the clashing of blades.

Helios' cohort of Evocators sat or stood nearby, watching

the duel. The swordsmen looked less battered than might be expected, given their efforts over the last few days. Then, that was simply the general mark of their competence. Not all of them had eyes for the bout between their Evocator-Prime and the Knight-Incantor. Some duelled amongst themselves, while others saw to the care of their weapons.

'And what is the question?' Helios thrust his blade like a spear, but without speed or force. Miska tapped the point aside with her knuckles. 'What gnaws at him so, that he ignores us for days on end and vanishes into a tomb of paper?'

'The only question that matters,' she said, whirling her staff towards his ankles. He leapt straight up, avoiding the blow. The watching Evocators applauded cheerfully. 'The question we were forged to answer. Balthas is diligent. That is no sin, whatever your feelings on the matter.'

'I do not judge him harshly, sister. I merely think it unwise to allow him to wall himself off from the world and all its wonders.' He slid towards her, blade whirling. She backed away warily. Helios was as swift as the solar wind for which he'd been named.

Helios continued, pressing with words as well as his blade. 'He has ever been brittle in his manner, but of late, he has become harsh as well. It is as if he has judged us, and found us wanting, in some manner.'

Miska laughed. 'You say that as if it's an impossibility.'

'Isn't it?' Helios stepped back, arms spread, inviting attack. 'Am I not incomparable in my prowess? Are my brothers and sisters not exceptional?'

Miska lunged. The head of her staff crackled with energy as it darted towards him. He twisted, batting it aside at the last moment. He stumbled slightly, but she recognised the ploy for what it was and held back. He straightened a moment later, grinning ruefully. She raised an eyebrow, and he shrugged. 'You are more observant than most, sister.'

She sighed and stepped back, signalling the end of the bout. 'Yes. And I have noticed what you speak of as well, brother. Balthas finds fault in his own actions, and his anger at himself has spilled over. He means no offence.'

'Nor have I taken any. None of us have. He is our lord-arcanum, however prickly he might be. I do not doubt his courage or his skill, having witnessed both. But someone must speak with him, and soon. An absent leader is no leader at all.'

Miska frowned. At any other time, such words would have earned Helios a rebuke. Then, at any other time, he would not have felt free to say them. Balthas had always been remote, from his peers as well as his subordinates. But his isolation of late was beyond the norm, even for him. She shook her head. 'Do the others feel the same?' she asked quietly.

Helios hesitated. Miska gestured impatiently. 'It is a simple question, brother. Answer me honestly, please.'

'I have spoken to the others, yes. Mara and Quintus both agree. Porthas keeps his own council, as always,' he said, naming the most senior officers of the chamber. 'The others are of mixed opinion on the matter.'

'You have been diligent,' she said, not without some disapproval.

Helios accepted her chastisement without comment. He merely nodded and planted his sword point-first in the ground before him, his hands resting on the crosspiece. Miska ran a hand through her hair and tugged on her braid idly, considering the problem before her.

For as long as she had served under him, Balthas had delegated much of his responsibility. She was the intercessor between him and those he commanded. Many lords-arcanum encouraged a more informal relationship with those they led into battle – Knossus Heavensen participated in training bouts with his own Sequitors, while others, like Tyros Firemane, led their warriors in the rites of preparation and purification.

But Balthas did none of those things. Saw no reason to do those things, in fact. He was lord-arcanum and took the title at face value. Not for him was the easy camaraderie of the battlefield. He was above it all, and removed from it, save in gravest necessity.

Miska felt a twinge of guilt. In some small way, she had encouraged this behaviour. It was often simpler to work around Balthas, rather than include him. In battle, he had few equals. Off the field, however, he bristled at what he perceived as tedium, and often became obstinate when things did not align perfectly to his assumptions.

'His failure to contain the lightning-gheist gnaws at him,' she said slowly. 'He cannot conceive of failing at a task he has accomplished a hundred times before. He will not be satisfied until he is given the chance to make amends.'

Helios nodded. 'Then perhaps we must add our voices to his, and ask Sigmar to let us slip our chains. The others go to war – why not us?' He looked around, and the other Evocators nodded in agreement.

Miska gestured for silence. 'Quiet. We have a guest.'

Helios turned, startled. So too did the other Evocators. An aelf, impossibly pale and inhumanly thin, stood among them, clad in robes of soft indigo and radiant white. The aelf's narrow features were tattooed with celestial designs, and her dark hair was bound back with a clasp of silver. She had come among them, her tread as silent as moonlight, and none of the burnished giants who surrounded her had noticed.

Miska bowed, and the aelf returned the gesture. 'My apologies if we have disturbed your efforts, my lady,' the Knight-Incantor said.

'It would take more than you to do that,' the aelf said, with a swift smile. She reached out and touched the trunk of a silvery tree. 'Indeed, the trees enjoy your presence. You are vibrant with starlight, and they drink it in. The grasses too grow thick beneath your feet. Stay as long as you wish.'

'Our thanks, my lady,' Helios said, taking the aelf's hand and bowing low, as if to kiss it. 'Such words are welcome to my ears.' It was a courtly gesture, from another age, and one Miska had not expected of Helios. The aelf inclined her head solemnly, as if in acknowledgement, and pointed to the sky.

'I did not come merely to compliment you. There is a message from the God-King.'

Miska looked up. Above, a star-eagle circled the garden. It cried out with serene savagery and swooped towards Miska, trailing sparks of light in its wake. The birds normally dwelled in the aetheric clouds high above Mallus, hunting the strange things that drifted there. But some came occasionally to Sigmaron, impelled by some instinct to serve as the eyes and ears of the God-King.

Miska lifted her hand, and the eagle landed on her forearm. It had almost no weight, though she knew it was strong enough to tear through anything save sigmarite. It screeched, flapping its great wings, and she heard a word – just one – echo in her head, like the distant thunder of a summer storm.

Then, with another flap of its wings, the bird launched itself upwards once more. Miska watched it go and felt a pang of longing that she could not explain.

'Well? What message did it impart?' Helios asked.

She smiled and tapped his shoulder with her staff. 'Our prayers have been heard.'

* * *

In the Grand Library, Balthas sat silent, not seeing the pages open before him. His stack of books had been right where he'd left them, as if Aderphi had known he was coming back. Then, maybe the librarians simply hadn't got around to putting them back before the necroquake had shaken Sigmaron to its core. But he paid no attention to them.

Instead, he was listening to the thunder of realmgates opening and closing throughout Azyr – not only with his ears, but with his soul, attuned as it was to the movements of the aether. The air twisted in seeming confusion, as the dimensional apertures yawned wide, allowing in strange winds. He felt the raw, hot pulse of Aqshy and heard the rasp-scrabble of Ghyran, as ancient pathways were opened. He felt the grinding, tomb-creak of Shyish and twitched as a cold grave-wind whipped through Sigmaron.

It had been decades since there had been such an exodus – not since the battle for the All-Gates. But never before had that exodus included the warriors of the Sacrosanct Chambers. They'd waged wars in secret, fighting only where there was some great need. Few of their fellow Stormcasts even knew of their existence, and those that did had been sworn to secrecy by Sigmar himself. The Sacrosanct Chambers had a sacred duty, and they could not afford distractions.

But it seemed that time had come to an end at last. Balthas had always suspected that it would, though he'd hoped for another century or two. Wars were maelstroms, drawing all things to their centre. That boded ill for his studies.

Even so, he could not deny a sense of anticipation. With no need for secrecy, there would be nothing keeping him from the great libraries of the Mortal Realms, and nothing preventing him from consulting with sages and philosophers without need for go-betweens. He might begin his hunt in earnest.

'If I am ever allowed to do so,' he murmured. He heard the rattle of sigmarite on stone and sighed. It seemed his ruminations were once more at an end. Some new difficulty had reared its head, somewhere in the palace-city.

'Here you are again. Back in your lair, among the cobwebs and forgotten stories.'

Balthas blinked. 'Miska,' he said aloud. 'Something to report?'

'Why else would I intrude on your solitude?' The sound of the Knight-Incantor's voice startled the lizards on their high perches. 'Though, one would think you'd be half sick of shadows at this point.' The Knight-Incantor peered down the rows as she strode towards his seat. 'Then, maybe you were just here dealing with the ghosts of librarians past, eh?'

Balthas didn't turn. 'You would be surprised.' He had come back to the library, seeking a moment's respite from his duties. But even here, the dead had risen. Long-dead librarians, entombed beneath the structure, had awoken. They had clambered from their nooks, eye sockets full of cobwebs and lungs full of dust. Balthas had made short work of them, with the aid of Aderphi and the others.

Miska studied the table. 'More books.'

'This is a library.' Balthas sighed inwardly. He knew she would come to the point of his interruption eventually. He shook his head and bent forwards. He pulled a book close and scanned it quickly. He'd had an idle hope of finding some mention of a similar cataclysm to the necroquake in the history of the Mortal Realms. But so far nothing had revealed itself. Whatever had happened, it was a new thing under the sun. That annoyed him to no end.

Miska leaned over him, as if to read the titles of the books he'd gathered. 'I don't see how you can bury yourself back in here, after all that has happened.'

'I am merely taking a moment to gather my strength.'

'By sitting in the dark, surrounded by dusty tomes?'

'You kneel in prayer. I sit in study.' Balthas set aside the grimoire he'd been perusing and reached for another. 'We commune with the aether in our own ways.'

'You're looking for answers. You won't find them in here.'

Balthas let a hint of the annoyance he felt creep into his words. 'Well, I won't know until I try, will I?' He glanced at her. 'If you are bored, you may leave.'

She was silent for a moment. 'Why?' she asked simply. 'Why here, Balthas? Why not with your brothers and sisters? Why seek answers in the dark?'

Balthas sighed, openly this time. 'Sometimes, I think what we seek is like air and cannot be grasped. Nonetheless, I strain to do so and become a shadow of myself. A shadow among shadows.' Balthas looked at his second in command. 'I am close, I think. The answer is here, somewhere, in this library. In these books.' He picked up the Guelphic Cipher and gestured with it. 'The accumulated knowledge of centuries. As I've said before, what better hunting grounds for such as we?'

'I can think of several.'

Balthas set the book back down. 'I'm sure you can. Why are you here, Miska?'

'I came to tell you that your petition has been heard.'

Balthas blinked. 'What?'

'Be of good cheer, Balthas. We are loosed to hunt at last. You got your wish.'

Balthas shook his head. 'My wish was not to have failed in the first place. That a rogue soul escaped was my doing. I must make amends. That is all.' Despite his words, a sense of elation filled him. He had not expected Sigmar to allow him to go. Perhaps he was not being judged so harshly as he feared. He stood. 'When?'

'As soon as possible.'

Balthas hesitated. An unwelcome thought had occurred to him. 'I suddenly realise that I do not know where to start looking,' he said, chagrined that he hadn't thought of it earlier. Miska snorted.

'Late to worry about that now, brother.'

'Quiet. Let me think.' He turned, scanning the shelves, seeking an answer. He recalled those last moments so clearly – the lightning-gheist had fallen away, into the maw of the cataclysm. For all he knew, it had been destroyed. But he did not think so. And obviously Sigmar didn't either. If it – if *he* – had survived the Anvil, he could survive almost anything. But that didn't bring him any closer to finding it.

It might well have become trapped in any one of the realms. He needed to pick up its trail, somehow. He heard Miska say something, but was already elsewhere in his head, seeking the answer to the problem before him. He looked down at his armour and the marks it still bore – great, scorched scratches. He could sense the touch of the aetheric on them. The lightning-gheist had left some of itself behind. 'Ah. That will do.'

Balthas touched the marks, lightly, teasing out the aetheric energies that still clung to them. He could feel the residue of the lightning-gheist's anger and pain. A disordered mind, distilled to the basest impulses. That was the danger of the Anvil. To remake a soul, it first must be broken down into a more malleable shape. That was where things inevitably went wrong. Broken into its base elements, reduced in such a manner, a soul was protean. It lost pieces of itself, or made new ones out of whole cloth. Old memories gave way to new ones, conjured up from dream or nightmare.

One person became another. Almost like the one who had perished, but yet not, changed in some often imperceptible fashion. In that way, a lightning-gheist was akin to an infant – if a singularly dangerous one.

Slowly, he drew out the residual energies. They sparked and hissed about his fingers as he extracted them, and caught them between his hands. He rotated his wrists, shaping the wriggling corposant into a more compact form. 'Look, Miska. Memories made into talons. That is what a gheist is, after all – a tangle of memories and fears, gone feral. Is it any wonder that they must be put down?'

'And what memory is that, brother?' Miska asked. After a moment, she added, 'Should you be doing that here? Perhaps we should take it elsewhere – somewhere safer.'

Balthas didn't reply. He had the scent now, and no concern for irrelevant minutiae. He was a lord-arcanum, and there was no place safer than where he currently stood. He raised the flickering essence, studying it from all angles. With the proper rites, he might make it a tether, to lead him to his prey. It would have left vestiges of itself, as it fell away. It would be like stalking a blood trail. Only the creature at the other end would not have weakened appreciably from its loss.

In the squirming facets, he saw rags and tatters of images – a woman's face, streaked with blood. A blossom of deepest purple. Fire, and the flash of swords. A memory of death, then? The first death or the second? Perhaps it didn't matter.

He probed deeper, trying to find the strongest thread. The one that would lead him to what he sought. More images now – tombs, rising like crags. Cats, padding through dark passages. Apples, ripe and red. Impatient, he pushed these aside. He needed something more tangible. Something more – ah. 'There,' he murmured.

Stormcasts, in the black war-plate of the Anvils of the Heldenhammer, fought against a swarm of nighthaunts. The cackling spectres swept over the battle-line like a fog bank. Warriors staggered and fell. Balthas saw – felt – his hand fasten on one and haul her to her feet. She looked at him and spoke, but there was no sound save for a wild roaring, as of water crashing against rock.

And then, one of the nighthaunts was there, a frenzied mist, laden with howling, grimacing faces. Distorted claws plucked at him, seeking a weak point. Blind, he staggered. Felt pain, as something slid between the plates of his armour. He tasted blood. And then… the black swallowed him. A hook of lightning speared through him and drew him up through a twisting tunnel of stars, faster and faster until the innumerable lights bled into a singular radiance that was blinding in its intensity.

Balthas' heartbeat thundered in his ears. He felt heat, such as he had never known. It ate away at him, burning him from the inside out. He tried to pull back from it, to remind himself of who he was, where he was, but the heat and the pain held him. It tore at him, and he thought he screamed – and then, in a flash, he was elsewhere, falling away from the light, the heat, into a yawning chasm of cold that reached up from below to claim him.

Stars spun, bleeding away into scars of light. Coloured hazes, the stuff of the realms, surrounded and suffused him, before being ripped away as he fell. Then, there was no light, no radiance save a pale amethyst glow that leeched his strength from him.

Balthas twisted and turned, trying to free himself, but it was like tar. It weighed him down – no, he reminded himself, not him. He tried to focus. This was no longer a memory. He had followed the thread back, and down, to its source. He could taste the iron bitterness of fear on his tongue, and his limbs ached. His lungs strained, as if filled with smoke. Something in him was burning. He was burning.

And through the smoke, through the flames, death looked down at him and smiled.

'Balthas!'

Miska's shout brought him back to himself. He staggered back, lightning crawling up his arms and playing across his chest and shoulders. It was not the clean azure radiance it ought to have been. Instead, it was a deep, angry violet. The colour of death. The lightning swelled, expanding, sprouting bestial jaws and something that might have been a face. Crackling teeth snapped shut, barely missing him. He fell backwards, trying to control what he had inadvertently unleashed.

'Balthas, hold still. I will–' Miska began, moving to aid him.

'No. Stay back!' Balthas dug his fingers into the crackling brambles of energy, seeking the nucleus. 'I have it under control.' He twisted his fingers into it, piercing its essence. Savage as it was, it was nothing more than a remnant – the echo of a dying scream, given life by some fell power and left as a trap.

He clambered to his feet, still holding the struggling essence. It twisted in his grip like a serpent, hissing and striking weakly at him. A lesser aether-mage, or one not so well-versed in the art of spirit-control, might have been overwhelmed. 'I require a spirit-bottle, Miska,' he said, through gritted teeth. 'Do you have one about your person?'

'Yes, here.' She unstopped one of the crystalline vials and extended its mouth towards the struggling energies. There was a sound like a strong wind, blowing through the crags, and the energies were drawn swiftly into the bottle, with a despairing shriek. Miska quickly sealed it. 'I've never seen a spirit like that. What was it?'

'A warning,' Balthas said, after a moment. 'But what it means for us, I do not know.'

CHAPTER TEN

THE UNDYING KING

NAGASHIZZAR, THE SILENT CITY

Pharus Thaum passed beneath a broken archway of black stone, encrusted with skull-like barnacles. Will o' the wisps danced across the barnacles, casting a pallid glow over the path ahead. As he walked, Nagashizzar twisted and bent around him, like a shroud caught in a fierce wind. Every street and boulevard was a ripple, an undulation, rising or sinking to reveal new mustering grounds, new tombs, new citadels of necessity.

'Nagashizzar is vast,' Arkhan said, as if reading his thoughts. The liche strode easily alongside him. Despite everything, Pharus was beginning to find Arkhan strangely companionable. 'It swells like the night ocean, receding as the dawn breaks. Our gates spill forth upon every land, our towers spy every border. The desert around us is every desert in the realm. We are a single moment, a last breath, held and stretched into infinity.'

'Sigmaron is much the same.'

'Do you remember Sigmaron then?' Arkhan looked at him.

Pharus scraped the flat planes of his memory. 'I remember golden towers and the light – so much light. Starlight, moonlight, sunlight.' He shook his head. 'It is as if those memories belong to another man.'

'What else do you recall?'

Pharus was silent for a moment. 'The taste of apples.'

Arkhan turned away with a rattling sigh. 'Ah. A good memory. I have not tasted food or drink in time out of mind. I have lost even the memory of such memories. Hold fast to it, Pharus Thaum. And remember who deprived you of such simple, impossible pleasures.'

Pharus did not reply. Around them, ancient vaults creaked open, disgorging deathrattle legions to march in silent lockstep to mustering fields scattered across the city. Primeval cisterns were uncapped, unleashing wailing tempests of nighthaunt spirits, long bound in darkness, but free now to take their vengeance on the living. These spirits swirled up into the air over the city, joining the storm of souls that was ever-growing there.

As the dead spilled into the sky, the winds picked up, casting sand and shards of shadeglass everywhere. A living mortal would have been blinded in moments, and flayed to the bone a few seconds later. For Pharus, clad in his new war-plate, it was no more disconcerting than a summer rain. He looked down at himself. Rather than the hammer-and-lightning sigils of Azyr that he kept half expecting, the war-plate bore the morbid heraldry of some long-vanished city-state of Shyish.

A stylised hourglass occupied the centre of his chest-plate. Crossed scythes marked the backs of his gauntlets, and heavy chains draped his shoulders and torso like a sash. His helm was a skull, topped by great, curving antlers of bone, and the cheek-guards swept back into bat-wing shapes. Thick robes, stained with grave matter, draped his limbs and lower body. Though when his concentration lapsed, both seemed no more substantial than smoke. 'This armour… It does something to me.'

'It suits you,' Arkhan said. 'Then, it was made for one of your kind. A cage and crown both.' He paused. 'Your head is clearer now, I trust. You have control over yourself. That is good. Otherwise you would be little more use than these broken things.'

He gestured to a flood of spirits swirling upwards nearby, howling their fury. The chainrasps were spiteful things, broken by Nagash's will, their forms dictated by the circumstances of their death – and they surrounded him and Arkhan in a dolorous tempest, whispering and wailing.

They struck the walls like water, spreading and spilling to the ground. They crawled towards him in jerky fashion, begging for absolution or demanding vengeance. A part of him felt revulsion at the sight of them. But another part felt a strange sort of kinship with the tormented souls. 'So many,' he said.

'There are more dead in Shyish than the living can comprehend,' Arkhan said, as they paused to allow a ghostly black coach to thunder past. The fleshless steeds that drew it snorted amethyst fire, and the driver was a shapeless thing, clad in rags and laughing wildly. 'Even the stones here have their ghosts. Even the trees.' He gestured, and Pharus saw what he at first took to be a grove of skeletal trees, rising from among the crumbled temples. When one of them turned to look at him, he realised his mistake.

'Sylvaneth,' he said, drawing the word from memory.

'Of sorts. The Everqueen has first claim on what passes for their souls, but some sought a different lord, in the days when she turned her face from the realms. As her song faded, they heard a different, more pleasing melody.'

The ghostly tree-spirits lurched silently past them, lumbering through the ruins, their bare branches shaking in the wind. Their features were jagged masks of ravaged bark, and their eyes burned with a terrible light. As they drew close, Pharus thought he heard a shrill keening on the wind. The sound was at once joyful and despairing.

That sound – or something like it – echoed throughout Nagashizzar. Every laugh was tinged with sorrow, every sigh with melancholy. Great funerary bells rang in the depths, and the dead shuffled from their centuried slumber and once more took up the devices of war. Chariots, coaches and hooves rattled along the avenues, as the kings and queens of forgotten bloodlines arrived to make their obeisance before Nagash. Flocks of carrion birds swirled through the storm of souls, or else perched on the high towers, croaking out Nagash's name. Jackals prowled the alleys, their eyes glowing amethyst.

Pharus felt a great sense of anticipation building in him. He was at once cold and hot, hungry for something he could not put into words. His gauntlets creaked, as he clenched and loosened his hands in strange expectation. 'What is that sound? Can you hear it?'

'All dead things hear it. Nagash calls to you, on the wind and in your bones.'

Pharus twitched, feeling a sudden need, an urge, to turn and walk until he was commanded to stop. He could not resist it and did not wish to. 'I am… hungry,' he said, his voice no more than a whisper. 'Thirsty. It hurts.' Not as bad as it had, though. The war-plate he wore might be a cage, but it kept the pain at bay. Even so, he could still feel the storm, surging within him, seeking escape. He traced the hourglass shape on his chest-plate.

'It will grow worse. Pain is the price we pay, to serve the Great Work. Even Nagash feels it – and your pain is but a shadow of his own. Remember that, Pharus Thaum. Remember that you are but a shadow of the Undying King, a part of him now and forevermore. When he reaches out, it is with a thousand hands, and you are one of them.'

'Yes.' The word felt wrong, somehow. Pharus' hand fell to the sword now belted at his waist, in a sheath of rotting leather. It was a wide blade, meant for brute strength rather than finesse. Its hilt had been carved from a femur, and its crosspiece was made from the fangs of some large beast. Both the blade and the hourglass pommel had been made from some sort of dark, impossibly hard crystal – shadeglass, Arkhan had called it. It seemed to flex in eagerness as he gripped the hilt, and the sands in the hourglass hissed weirdly.

He hesitated, feeling the malignant hunger roiling within the deceptively crude weapon – the weapon longed to part flesh and gorge itself on the final moments of the dying. And part of him longed to allow it to do so. He realised Arkhan was watching him. 'You understand now, I think,' the liche said.

'I understand nothing. I know nothing. But I…' Pharus hesitated. 'It does not seem so important to know, as it did earlier.' He flexed his gauntlets, watching the haze of his substance flicker through the gaps in the iron plates. For a moment, he wondered if he was no more than a memory of who he had been. He felt a spark of anger flicker within him.

Before it could ignite, Arkhan said, 'You have been remade, and all useless parts of you have been cast aside. If you have questions, it means he wishes you to ask them.'

'Will he send me against Azyr?'

'Do you wish him to do so?'

'What I wish is not important.'

'Good. You are learning.' Arkhan sounded pleased.

'Yes. I remember more of who I was. What I was.' Pharus looked at him. 'I also remember that you are the reason that Nagash spared me. He wished to destroy me. But you did not. Why?'

Arkhan glanced at him. 'Tell me – what do you know of Nagash?'

Pharus hesitated. 'He is... all.' What else was there to know? Nagash was the sum totality of all things. All things were one, in him. Or so the voice beating in his brain insisted with monotonous rhythm.

Arkhan extended his staff. 'Look to the east. What do you see?'

Pharus looked and saw an unlight – a black sun, squirming against the dark curtain of the sky. It boiled and burned amid the ruins, eating away at the world around it. It swelled and receded with the voice in his head, and he found himself unable to look away. Vastation built in him, purging his lingering uncertainties.

'Nagash is the black sun – the true sun's shadow and twin,' Arkhan said. 'As Sigmar holds the sky suspended, so too does Nagash draw down the earth. They move in eternal opposition, pushing against one another.'

'I do not understand.'

Arkhan's teeth clicked in what might have been an expression of amusement. 'In some ancient texts, the black sun illuminates the truth of the soul. Nagash is the totality of truth – an absence of all lies, even the most comforting. He is the black sun, burning in an inverted sky. He is the truth, and Sigmar, the lie. Sigmar is a husk, filled with falsehood. He demands much and gives little in return. Nagash, at least, offers justice.'

'Justice,' Pharus echoed. He looked down at himself. 'Is this justice?'

Arkhan laughed. 'This is Nagashizzar. The place of final justice.' He stopped and thumped the ground with his staff. 'We are here.'

They had come to a long avenue that stretched eastwards, towards the black sun. It had been cleared of much of the rubble, but work-gangs of skeletons still toiled along the edges. Clusters of bodiless spirits – chainrasps and flickerhaunts, gallarchs and lane-hags, scregs and flay-braggarts, masses of drifting, moaning spectres – bunched and floated through the ruins to either side, responding to the same call that drew Pharus.

'What is this place?' Pharus asked.

'We approach the base of the Black Pyramid. Here, the Undying King has set his throne, so that he might receive the oaths of fealty owed him, by his most loyal servants.' Arkhan turned west, towards the closest end of the avenue. 'There, see? Three of the most prominent come now, to kneel at the Undying King's feet – at their head comes Vorgen Malendrek, the Knight of Shrouds.'

A silent host of deathly riders paraded down the avenue, past Pharus and Arkhan. At their head was a towering figure – darkly magnificent, balefire bleeding from his eyes, wrapped in spectral shrouds. He wore a black iron helm, topped by great, curving bat wings, and bore a fine sword belted to his hip, an hourglass set into the hilt.

'Like you, Malendrek once served the God-King,' Arkhan said. 'And like you, he has seen the truth of Sigmar's perfidy.' He sounded almost amused. He pointed. 'And there, Crelis Arul, the Lady of All Flesh.' Behind Malendrek's nighthaunt riders came a shuffling tide of rotting flesh. The deadwalkers moved with no grace or precision, stumbling along like confused livestock. The greatest mass of them bore upon their backs and shoulders a palanquin made from bone and raw, bloody flesh.

The woman seated atop the hideous palanquin was draped in rotting and stained finery as of ancient days, her features hidden behind a crudely stitched leather mask. Two great dire wolves, their ribcages showing through tattered fur and their skulls bare to the moonlight, crouched to either side of her. Occasionally she stroked one or the other of them, as if they were living things.

She raised a crumbling hand as if in greeting, and Arkhan returned the gesture. Then, he turned and lifted his staff. 'And last but not least – save perhaps in his own mind – Grand Prince Yaros, Lord Rattlebone.'

The deathrattle warriors who brought up the rear of the column marched as one, in perfect synchronisation. They bore heavy kite shields and long spears, to which had been affixed rotted pennants. Archaic armour sheathed the brown bones, and the rhythmic clamour of their passing was all but deafening.

At their head rode a princely figure, wearing a battered crown of iron and a cloak of dusty fur. The Deathrattle King rode a skeletal steed and had a single-bladed axe balanced across his saddle. He lifted the axe in salute as he passed.

'Three lords of death, come to serve he who forged them.'

'Where are they going?'

Arkhan silently extended his staff east. Pharus turned. Dust clouds rolled across the far end of the avenue, momentarily blotting the black sun from sight. When they cleared, Pharus saw, at the far end of the avenue, an immense structure of black shadeglass. It resembled a dais, but was leagues across and surmounted by a towering throne, taller than any gargant, and circled by flocks of carrion birds. A great figure reclined atop the throne, and Pharus recognised the being who had remade him.

Nagash. Unspoken, the name echoed through him regardless, down into the hollows of his spirit. The confusion he felt, the doubt and anger, it vanished all in an instant. The storm in him subsided, like a startled beast. Hoar frost crept suddenly across the panes of his armour, and he felt a chill digging into the marrow of his non-existent bones. Cries echoed up around him, so many as to occasionally merge into a single, great howl. He stepped back as something that might have been fear stirred in him.

The Undying King sat on his throne, amid a slow typhoon of souls, swirling about him in desperate celebration. Broken skeletons, crawling along the avenue, reached out to the distant figure as if in supplication. Pharus felt the pull himself. Impossible to ignore or defy. It was as if there were a great weight pressing down on him and pulling him all at once. Somehow, all things bent towards Nagash, even the winds and the light of the distant stars. It was as if he were a hole in the realm, and all that existed fell into him, to be lost forevermore.

He groaned, and looked away, unable to bear such awful majesty for long. 'He is all, and all are one in him,' Arkhan said. 'Do not resist. Let the silence of him fill you and smother all doubt in its cradle.'

'I hear something.' Pharus cradled his head. 'Like a swarm of insects, rattling in my skull.' He twitched, trying to escape the sound. 'Is that him?'

Arkhan gave a rattling laugh. 'Come. He calls to you, and you must answer.' He stepped onto the avenue, and Pharus followed. The spirits that huddled along either side set up a great wailing, which Pharus thought must be akin to applause.

A hundred thousand souls clustered among the ruins. Some were nothing more than bobbing motes of witch-light, while others seemed almost alive, save for their pallor.

More souls drifted down like ash from above, falling towards Nagashizzar from the dark skies. Some of these joined the throng that lined the avenue, while others were caught by the wind and whisked away, trailing despairing moans in their wake.

'Where are they all coming from?' Pharus asked.

'Everywhere and nowhere. Wherever a mortal's story begins, it ends here, and here is where all men must eventually come. Some will stay in Nagashizzar, caught fast by their crimes. Others will pass through the Sepulchral Gate and into whatever underworld calls them home. As it is inscribed there – by the manner of their death shall ye know them.'

The avenue quickly became crowded by swaying deadwalkers and eerily still deathrattle warriors. They made way for Arkhan, their ranks shuffling aside as if shoved back by invisible hands. Arkhan led Pharus through them, towards the great dais at the end of the avenue, where Malendrek and the other deathlords stood waiting for the word of Nagash.

Pharus felt their gazes on him as he approached, and he wondered what they made of him. Yaros seemed as stoic as any skeleton, the hollow sockets of his eyes burning dimly. Arul, the Lady of All Flesh, greeted them softly, her voice a liquid slur.

'Lord Arkhan – it has been too long since you have visited my charnel gardens. They wax vibrant these days.' She held out a mouldering hand, and Arkhan took it with courtly aplomb. His fleshless jaws brushed across her bruised knuckles.

'I am sure their fragrance is as potent as ever, my lady.'

Her flat, milky eyes fixed on Pharus. 'And who is this handsome spirit? He wears the raiment of a deathlord, and yet I do not know him.' She held out her hand to Pharus. He hesitated, but only for a moment. He took it and bent. Had he been alive, he thought the stench of her would have choked him. She was a dead thing and stank of rot.

'He is called Pharus Thaum, and he is newly made,' Arkhan said.

'Ah, a new soul. How charming.' She reached up and traced crumbling fingers across the side of Pharus' helm. 'He smells of… lightning.'

Malendrek stirred. The burning slits of his eyes, visible within his helm, narrowed. 'What game are you playing, Mortarch?' he rasped. 'The glory to come will be mine and no other's. Certainly not any pet of yours.'

Arkhan turned. 'Remember to whom you speak, Knight of Shrouds. You are not so high in our lord's esteem that I cannot rend you asunder and reweave your soul into a more fitting shape.' Malendrek drew himself up, one hand falling to the hilt of his blade.

'Careful, Black One,' he said. 'You serve as his hand for the moment, but there are worthier souls in creation.'

Arkhan laughed. 'Your ambition is admirable, though wasted, Knight of Shrouds. If you wish to supersede me, you must get in line. Be warned though, I am told it is quite lengthy.'

Malendrek hissed. 'Speak, then. Who is this? Some broken liche of your circle?' He looked at Pharus. 'Arul is right. He stinks of lightning.' He laughed suddenly. 'Wait. I know him, now. Pharus Thaum – guardian of the dark places. One of Sigmar's revenants. Another who received the blessings meant for me. And now you are here. The wheel of fate surely turns in strange directions.'

Pharus gazed at him in incomprehension. 'Do we– did we know each other?' Something in the creature's words stoked the storm in him. Amethyst lightning sparked and crawled across the gaps in his armour.

Malendrek's eyes blazed bright as his pale hand fell to the hilt of his blade. 'We fought side by side, against the soulblight warlord, Vaslbad. In Glymmsforge.'

'What was your name?'

'You know my name. I was the commander of the southernmost gate. The slayer of the Slender Knight. *I was a hero*.' Bitterness swelled in the dead man's voice. There was naked longing there, a desire now impossible to fulfil.

'I do not recall you,' Pharus said. Then, more maliciously, 'Perhaps you were not as important as you claim.' He was surprised by his own venom and the pleasure he took in saying the words.

Malendrek shrieked and made to draw his blade. Arkhan stepped between them, his eyes glowing with a witch-light greater than Malendrek's own. 'Will you strike a servant of your master without cause?' He slammed his staff down, and amethyst fires sprang up. 'Are you a living man, to let hot anger stir your turgid blood?'

Malendrek snarled curses. Pharus reached for his own blade, but a glance from Arkhan stopped him. 'Cease,' the Mortarch of Sacrament intoned. Malendrek drifted back and glared at them.

Before he could speak, Yaros gave a dusty chuckle. The wight king stood nearby, watching the confrontation. 'One more pawn, or one less, the game is set already. And the true winner sits there, watching us play at influence.' He raised his axe. 'Hail, Nagash. Hail, O Undying King.'

Pharus turned. Nagash was indeed watching them, slumped on his throne, his talons pressed together in a steeple before his bowed head. The Undying King sat as if engaged in some inconceivable calculation. Spirits writhed about him, whispering and singing hymns to his might and mercy. Massive, skeletal morghasts crouched to either side of his throne, their cruel glaives held ready to defend their master.

Nagash flicked a finger, and what Pharus had at first taken to be a pile of bones and rags heaped on the wide, rough-hewn steps of the dais, rose awkwardly to its feet. Arul clapped her hands gently. 'Oh, how delightful – he has resurrected dear old Blood-a-bones to amuse us. It has been so long.'

Blood-a-bones proved to be a tatterdemalion of colour and injury. A court jester, clad in rotting costume and dented bells. He twitched up and bowed low. 'Greetings, gentles all,' he shrilled in a childish voice. 'Our king welcomes you to his hall – see there, the stars shine through the holes in the roof, and the dead sweep away the dust on the floor.' He flung up a broken hand and spun in a madcap circle, jaw sagging. 'He strives, oh he strove, to make it pretty for you.'

'Dance, jester,' Nagash intoned.

At his words, the jester capered in awkward circles, as the carrion birds that circled Nagash's throne pecked at him. His ragged costume was sewn to his mouldering flesh, and bare bone poked through his peeling features. Despite the state of him, he seemed in good humour. He bounced and spun, moving more swiftly than any dead thing ought, and the tarnished bells attached to his costume jangled piercingly. As he whirled, he sang without melody.

'Our king is kind, so kind, and he will take what grows in every creature's womb and make it his own,' the jester screeched. 'He will make every house a tomb, and as his great hand sweeps across the sea, all the fish will rise with their bellies up. The jackals bow to him, and the birds as well.' He batted at the birds as they dived for what remained of his eyes. Jackals darted through the ranks of the dead and snapped at his flailing limbs.

'He leaves a trail of fire across the desert, so that all who seek him might find their way. Rejoice! Rejoice! The Undying King is come again, in all his glory!'

Pharus felt no horror, no disgust at the display, though he knew he ought to. Only curiosity. Was there some message in the jester's song, or was it merely gibberish? The question vanished from his mind as Nagash gestured once more, and the jester began to twirl faster and faster. He careened from one side to the other, losing bits of himself as he danced. 'Rejoice! Rejoice! He is all, and we are him, and all are one! Rejoice!'

With a final despairing ululation, the jester collapsed into a heap. Light still burned in the sockets of his skull, but his song was finished. Jackals worried at his carcass, snarling and fighting with one another. Nagash gazed down at the remains in silence.

'Behold,' he intoned, in a voice like the grinding of stone. 'I am risen.' He looked up, and his burning gaze swept across the ranks arrayed before him. As one, the dead sank to their knees. Pharus found himself drawn down with the others, unable to resist the unspoken command. Like the jester, they moved as the Undying King willed.

Nagash stood. 'I cast forth my hand and the trees raise up their roots.' He threw out a talon, and great roots, colourless and sickly looking, erupted from beneath the avenue with a rumble and a roar. They rose high, coiling about nearby pillars, stretching towards the dark sky. Twisted faces blossomed on the pallid bark like fungus. They wailed. Some cursed Nagash's name, while others begged for mercy. Pharus looked away.

'Where I set my foot, the earth buckles,' Nagash continued. He stepped down onto the steps of the dais, and the stone cracked loudly. Dust geysered as he descended, and the ground shook. 'My gaze boils the sea and my voice calls down the stars.

I am risen, and all is silence.' The words echoed from the pillars. Nagash gestured. 'Arkhan. Come forth and attend me, my most faithful servant.'

'I am at your command, my lord, as ever,' Arkhan called out, as he strode towards the steps leading up to the dais. 'But speak, and I shall move the realms themselves.' He climbed to stand beside Nagash. The liche looked tiny, next to his towering master.

'There is no need, my servant, for I have already done so. I have realigned the heavens themselves.' Nagash looked down, his flickering gaze fixing on Pharus for a moment, before sliding back to Arkhan. 'Is this all, then? Am I abandoned by my servants?'

'Never, my lord. A thousand wars are waged even now, in your name. A hundred deathlords march across the amethyst sands, travelling from the north, the east and the south. Spirit, bone and meat answer your call.'

'And my Mortarchs?'

Arkhan set his staff and rolled his shoulders in an elegant shrug. 'They go where they will and kill where they wish. As you made them to do, my lord. Rest assured, they have tendered their apologies for their absence and assure you that they strive ever in your mighty name. They build empires to your glory, O Undying King.'

Nagash gave a rumbling laugh. 'I am sure that is what they say.' He gestured dismissively. 'No matter. The vagaries of the soulblighted do not interest me this day. I seek to raise up new champions and conquer old lands.' He looked out over the gathered dead. 'The time has come. Shyish must be cleansed. All who do not kneel before me must be made to do so. As it once was, so shall it be again, forevermore. Stand forth, my Knight of Shrouds.'

Malendrek drifted forwards silently. Nagash stretched out his hand. 'You sought my favour, Vorgen Malendrek, and thus I have bestowed it. I have made you more than you were and raised you up, so that you might take vengeance for yourself upon those who used you so cruelly. Will you do this for me, my servant?'

'Speak the name, my lord, and I shall cast them into ruin,' Malendrek said, in a voice like the cawing of many birds. Pharus thought he detected a note of eagerness in the ghostly warrior's tone. As if he already knew what Nagash intended to ask of him.

'Glymmsforge,' Nagash said. Malendrek gave a lingering sigh. Nagash gestured. 'The way is already open. A gap in the defences. Use it. Crack the city wide and reclaim it, and the underworld of Lyria, for me.' Nagash looked at the others. 'Crelis Arul and Yaros of Dmezny – you shall serve my champion in this. Aid him. Break the city. Glory awaits.'

For a moment, Pharus thought one or the other might protest being subordinated to the ghostly warrior. But neither did. The hierarchy of the dead was set, it seemed – spirit, bone and then meat.

'And what of your newest servant, my lord?' Arkhan asked. He gestured to Pharus. 'One once of Azyr's heights, now of Shyish's depths. What task shall he be bent to?'

Nagash turned his lamp-like gaze upon Pharus once more. For long moments, he stared, as if puzzled by the presence of the being before him. Finally, he looked at Arkhan. 'By your whim was I encouraged to show mercy. Thus, to your whim I yoke him. Let him prove himself worthy of my mercy, howsoever you see fit, my loyal Mortarch. And if he should fail, you shall bear the brunt of my ire.'

Arkhan bowed low. 'As you command, so must it be, my lord.'

Nagash returned to his throne, and the audience came to an end. The other deathlords turned away to depart, though not without a few backward looks and a glare from Malendrek. Pharus wondered if he'd made an enemy there, and what it meant. He waited, uncertain, as Arkhan descended the steps of the dais. If a skeleton could look pleased, Arkhan did so.

Nagash, for his part, looked neither pleased nor pensive. The fleshless rictus of the Undying King's features did not change, as he sank back onto his throne in a clamouring of armour and bone. Carrion birds circled him, and swooped down to perch on his shoulders and knees. They set up a raucous chorus, screeching and cawing, as if advising the god of some mischief elsewhere. The jackals began to howl, casting their eerie song to the wind.

Pharus stared up at Nagash and knew, somehow, that the god did not notice him. It was as if, having delivered his commands, his mind had withdrawn to other spheres. Arkhan confirmed this, a moment later.

'Shyish stirs, and so the reaper must ready his scythe,' the liche said, as he joined Pharus. 'You and the others will be its edge, and Glymmsforge, the harvest.'

'I cannot feel him anymore – my head feels... empty.' Pharus touched his helm. 'I feel empty. He is silent.' He wanted to hear that awful voice again, to feel it resonate within him. It drove out all fear and worry, and crushed doubt and uncertainty.

'Fear not, Pharus. He is with you always. He is hidden within even the deepest of your thoughts, and in the hollows of your soul. What you see, he sees. What you feel, he feels. You are his hands and eyes and mouth. Even when you think yourself alone, he is there.' Arkhan caught him by the shoulder. 'This god will not abandon you, Pharus. That I swear to you.'

Pharus looked at Arkhan's hand and felt the crackle of the

lightning raging inside him. As if sensing this, Arkhan stepped back. 'You were a jailer, once. Do you recall this?'

'I… yes.' Pharus dredged the slow currents of his memory. 'The Ten Thousand Tombs. Beneath Glymmsforge. I… guarded them.' The words came with difficulty and only brought more questions. Like sand, the memories sifted through his fingers no matter how tightly he grasped at them.

'Yes. And now you will crack open the prison you built, and free those within.' Arkhan studied him, his gaze revealing nothing. 'Ten thousand souls, entombed by my hand, in the waning days of the Age of Myth. I had done so many times before, and since, to aid my lord and master. I would see these awakened. They will prove the undoing of the false city and shall march through the Shimmergate, with you at their head. You will be a sword, thrust into the heart of Azyr.' He clenched a fist. 'Thus Nagash has commanded, and thus it will be done.'

CHAPTER ELEVEN

SHIMMERGATE

'Easy, Quicksilver. Easy.' Balthas stroked the gryph-charger's feathered neck. The great beast felt his impatience and pawed at the ground in unsettled fashion. 'We will be away soon. Won't we, sister?' He glanced at Miska. 'They are late.'

'They will be here.' She stood beside him, staff in hand. Helios and his Evocators stood just behind them, acting as honour-guard. The swordsmen were the most skilled of his warriors, and Balthas valued their capabilities. Behind them, the remainder of the Grave Wardens Sacrosanct Chamber made ready to depart through the Shimmergate.

He studied the realmgate, his fingers tapping against the massive, scabbarded broadsword hanging from his saddle. He could not remember the last time he'd drawn it. Though he was as capable a swordsman as any, the blade lacked the elegance of aether. And he felt more comfortable with a staff in his hand than a blade.

The realmgate was a blur of light, encompassed by a circle of stone. It had been carved in ages past by unknown hands, though legends as to the mason's identity abounded. Some thought her a sorcerer, seeking her lost love in the underworld of Lyria. Others said it had been shaped by a duardin craftsman, seeking a path to a hidden treasure. Whoever they had been, the Shimmergate was all that remained to mark their memory.

'Nervous?' Miska asked, not looking at him.

'And why would you think that?' he snapped. Suddenly ashamed, he made a show of studying the two cohorts of Sequitors that stood in disciplined ranks behind the Evocators. Mara and Porthas, their commanders, spoke quietly to one another, with a casual friendliness that Balthas sometimes envied. Mara was stocky, wielding a heavy, angular stormsmite maul and soulshield, much like her warriors. Porthas was built like an ox, and he had his two-handed greatmace balanced across his shoulders.

The Sequitors resembled Liberators, but their similarity to the rank and file of the Warrior Chambers was merely cosmetic. Unlike their brethren, the Sequitors were able to channel the limited magics that coursed through them into the armaments they bore. Thus empowered, their weapons were capable of slaying things resistant even to the touch of holy sigmarite. As they had done often, at Balthas' command.

Miska looked up at him, eyebrow raised. He sighed and sat back. 'Fine, yes. Somewhat. I have grown used to the veil of secrecy woven about us. To discard it now feels wrong…'

'It is necessary.'

'Unfortunately.' He sighed again. 'Perhaps I am simply annoyed. My researches were at a delicate phase.' They hadn't been, and they both knew it, but he refused to give her the satisfaction of admitting it.

'They will keep.'

Balthas looked at her. 'You're excited, aren't you?'

A half-smile quirked at the corner of her mouth. 'Aren't you?'

'Not particularly.'

'But this is what you wanted.' She sounded as if she were asking a question, rather than simply stating fact.

'Yes,' he said, after a moment. He let his gaze drift past her, to where the final elements of his chamber were assembling. Quintus and his cohort of Castigators were diligently checking over the functions of their thunderhead greatbows. Resembling large crossbows, the bolts they loosed were heavy things, resembling a smaller version of a stormsmite mace. The heads of the projectiles were filled with the condensed breath of a stardrake. On impact, they unleashed a tempest of aetheric energy that would tear through foes, mortal or otherwise.

Miska gave a bark of laughter. 'You've never been one for the battlefield.' She shook her head. 'Remember that city in Chamon – Agnostai? Rather than lay siege to the city, you turned their gold stores to granite.'

'It worked, didn't it?' Balthas smiled. He had always possessed an affinity for the transmutive magics of Chamon. The alchemical winds responded to his will with an ease that surprised him at times. It was as if they recognised him, somehow. 'Their army surrendered en masse, without a single arrow loosed or sword drawn. Mercenaries are loathe to fight without the promise of pay.'

'Was that really the reason? Or were you more interested in getting into the Silver Sepulchre than wasting time taking the city?'

Balthas frowned. 'The Sepulchre contained certain remains necessary to my research.'

'So you assured me at the time.'

Balthas heard the unspoken criticism. 'Finding a way that does not work is not failure. Only through meticulous trial and error will we discover that which we seek, sister.'

'Spoken like a true alchemist.'

Balthas sniffed. 'I trust you recall that I am your lord-arcanum and not a mere Sequitor, to be spoken to in such a disrespectful manner.'

Miska peered at him. After a moment, she inclined her head. 'You are correct. Forgive me, my lord. Discipline is the foundation of victory.'

'You are forgiven.' He turned as a sardonic cheer went up from his warriors. Two figures, heavily encumbered, climbed the rocky slope. One of them waved slowly, in sombre acknowledgement of the cheers. 'Finally.'

He urged Quicksilver towards the two warriors as they carried their burden up the slope. 'Gellius, Faunus – you're late,' he said. The armour of the two Sacristan Engineers was hung with the tools and oddments of their duty, and they rattled as they climbed.

Gellius, the larger of the two, shifted the weight of the celestar ballista he carried on his back. 'Better late than never, my lord,' he said solemnly.

Balthas frowned. 'I would reprimand you, if there were time.' He looked at the other engineer. 'I trust you will apologise on behalf of your brother-engineer, Faunus?'

'If you require it.' Faunus hefted an ornate astrolabe and peered through its scope. 'A few final calculations and we'll be ready.'

'I've heard that before,' Balthas said, annoyed.

'Have we ever failed you, my lord?' Gellius asked, patting the ballista he carried. 'She's a temperamental one, but faithful. As are we.'

Balthas made to reply when Quicksilver shrieked suddenly. He felt the aether tense and shiver. He turned, following the pull of it. Nearby, the arctic winds spun, casting up snow and sunlight alike. There was a snap of air, followed by the crunch of snow beneath a heavy tread. Sigmar appeared, striding across the snow, his golden war-plate gleaming and the heavy fur cloak he wore swirling about his shoulders.

Warriors sank to their knees, heads bowed, as the God-King passed among them. Balthas slid from his saddle as Sigmar drew close. Gellius and Faunus both dropped to one knee, and Balthas made to do so as well, but Sigmar stopped him. 'Up.' The God-King gestured sharply. He studied the Shimmergate for a moment. The light seemed to brighten beneath his attentions. He turned.

'Come with me, Balthas.' Sigmar turned and crunched through the snow. Balthas hesitated and glanced back at Miska, who motioned for him to go. As he followed Sigmar, he tried not to stare at the ground – the God-King left no tracks. The snow shifted beneath his weight, but there was nothing to mark his passing.

Sigmar glanced back at him, a half-smile on his face. Balthas realised, with some embarrassment, that the God-King somehow knew what he was thinking. 'I forget, sometimes, about leaving tracks,' he said. 'I remember the sound. The wet crunch of snow beneath my feet, the feel of the icy wind, cutting through my furs. The weight of Ghal Maraz in my hands. But I forget other things – the way your weight displaces the snow. The ache that comes with hard travel, the way your lungs strain. Sweat.' He stopped before an outcropping. 'It's easy, to forget.'

They stood in silence, gazing out over the horizon. Somewhere, a mountain eagle shrieked, as it took wing over its kingdom. Sigmar watched the bird, for long moments. Then, he turned. 'You wish to go to find the rogue soul.'

Balthas nodded, uncertain as to where this was going. Had Sigmar not already given his permission? 'Aye, my lord. It – he – escaped me. But he shall not do so a second time. I have the scent of his soul.' He hesitated. 'And there is only one place he could go, now.' He glanced back towards the Shimmergate. 'The boughs of the World-Tree bend low.'

'Nagash has broken the order of things. The dead stir in every realm, shaken from their long sleep. I see the soil shift on forgotten graves, and bones gleam in the moonlight. Ghosts wander through the streets of the cities of men.' Sigmar frowned. 'Even here. Even here, the effects of his imprudence are felt.' His hand clenched, and the sky shuddered with thunder. Lightning flashed in his gaze.

'He has unleashed a cataclysm from which the realms will be slow to recover,' Balthas said. He could still feel the echoes of that hellish reverberation in his bones. Wild magic boiled on the air, invisible to all save those with the wit to see.

'We have entered a new, more deadly age,' Sigmar said, watching the horizon. 'Only time will tell whether it proves to be the last, or merely the latest.' He smiled, but there was little humour in it. 'Many crimes can be laid at the feet of the Undying King, but being boring was never one of them.' Sigmar threw back his head and laughed.

The sound boomed out, shaking rocks and snow from the high peaks, and nearly pitched Balthas from his feet. 'The wars we waged, Nagash and I. The schemes we concocted. We stole fire from the belly of Symr, Balthas. We cast up mountains and filled seas with the blood we shed against our enemies.' His laughter trailed off, and his smile grew thin and strained. 'And now we are at war once more. Heaven and Death, and all the realms caught between them.' He looked at Balthas. 'I can see your guilt burning in you.'

Balthas froze, but only for an instant. Sigmar sighed. 'You blame yourself for your brother escaping. You think of it as a failure, rather than simply a thing that happened.'

'It was my weakness that allowed it – him – to fall…'

'It was not. Others had the opportunity to stop him. They did not succeed.'

'Others are not me.' Balthas cursed himself the moment the words left his mouth. But Sigmar merely nodded, as if he had expected nothing less.

'I have heard similar sentiments before.' He sank to his haunches and scooped up a handful of snow. Even crouched, he was massive, and Balthas felt as a child must, when a parent seeks to impart a lesson.

Sigmar held his hand out, and the snow swirled and shifted, taking shape. For a moment, it resembled a tree, and then something that put Balthas in mind of the interior of an anthill. 'You hold yourself to a higher standard than your brothers.'

Balthas did not reply.

Sigmar did not look up from the snow as it twisted and changed shape. 'You see yourself at odds with them, even if you do not admit it.'

'Not at odds, my lord,' Balthas said softly. 'Never that.'

Sigmar nodded, not looking at him. 'No? Perhaps not. Perhaps you are wiser than the gods, Balthas. I hope so.'

Balthas did not flinch. 'If I am wise, it is because you made me so, my lord.'

Sigmar rose to his feet. 'You flatter me.' He held out his hand,

and gestured to the swirling snow. It had expanded, taking the shape of a walled city. 'Do you recognise the city?'

'Glymmsforge,' Balthas said, after a moment.

'Yes. In the underworld of Lyria. That is where you are going. That is where you will find what you seek.' Sigmar gestured again, and the snow melted and reformed – a man's face, this time. Balthas recognised Pharus Thaum. 'I felt his soul shatter as the cataclysm caught it. The energies of the Anvil ran wild, and a true son of Azyr became something less. A moment repeated too often for my liking.'

'And mine, my lord.'

'I told you before, Balthas, that you must hunt this prey for me. But for now, set your eyes upon a new quarry. Look.' Again, the snow changed. It rose and spread, became a sphere, and then a column. Something was familiar about it. Balthas thought he had seen it before. Sigmar nodded, as if he had spoken. 'You saw this in his mind as you confronted him, did you not? Do you recognise it?'

'He was… guarding it?'

'Yes. The duty he gave his life for. The Ten Thousand Tombs.' Sigmar turned his hand, causing the image to rotate and spread. 'A warren of catacombs, old when Lyria was young. A poisonous crop, planted by the hand of a dead man, against the day it might be needed. The souls of fallen heroes and bloodthirsty conquerors, imprisoned and awaiting the day of their freedom. Black souls that might rend the city asunder, if they were to be freed.'

Balthas grunted. 'Does Knossus– do they know?'

Sigmar nodded. 'It was discovered soon after the Shimmergate was claimed. The city was built atop it, in part to protect the tombs from those who might try to open them. One of the many unspoken responsibilities your Stormhost bears.'

'Pharus has fallen. Who guards it now?'

Sigmar looked down at him, and Balthas nodded in understanding. 'That is why you are letting me go – I am to take up where Pharus left off.' He looked away. 'It is fitting. I failed him in life. In death, I must make amends.'

Sigmar nodded. 'If that is the way you wish to view it.'

'And what of Pharus Thaum, my lord?' Balthas asked. 'Am I to just… abandon his soul to its fate?' He shook his head. 'Let someone else play the sentry, my lord, please. Let me find Thaum and bring him to Azyr's light once more. Let me wash clean the stain of failure. Please.'

Sigmar's expression was sad. 'Would that I could, my son. But I cannot.'

'But why?' Balthas asked, knowing he shouldn't, but unable to stop himself. 'How can we abandon him?'

Sigmar sighed. 'Nagash has his soul now, Balthas. I can feel it. I felt it too late to stop it – did not recognise what was happening in time. It is as if a piece of me is trapped, somewhere in the dark.' The God-King opened his hands and let the snow drift to the ground, to rejoin the carpet of white.

He looked down at Balthas. 'He is lost to us – to me – whatever his fate. But as you saw into his mind, so too will Nagash. And he will know the secret of reaching what we have hidden from him, all these years. His servants will seek out the Ten Thousand Tombs and attempt to open them. This cannot be allowed. Even if Glymmsforge itself falls, the Ten Thousand Tombs must remain sealed.' Sigmar set a heavy hand on Balthas' shoulder. 'Do you understand?'

'I do, my lord.'

'That means that you will be under Knossus' command.' For a moment, Balthas thought he saw the God-King smile. 'Do you understand that?'

'I do.' Balthas fought to keep his voice even. The elation he'd felt earlier was gone. He bowed his head and said, more firmly, 'I do, my lord.'

Sigmar gave a satisfied nod. 'I know that you do, Balthas. And it pleases me. Now go. Glymmsforge awaits.'

'I will not fail you, my lord.'

'None of you ever have, Balthas. I do not expect you will start now.'

Balthas turned and hurried down the trail. 'Balthas,' Sigmar called out. Balthas stopped halfway, and turned.

'I told you that there was a time when I wandered the snows. In those days, I too was a hunter. I hunted meat rather than knowledge, but the two things are not so different. One fills the belly, one fills the mind. But sometimes… sometimes the prey escaped.' Sigmar stared up at the stars, his expression unreadable. 'This was not failure. The time simply was not right. So I learned to wait. To hold my shot. To seek a better spot from which to observe my prey. To seek the proper moment.'

'And how did you know when that moment was?'

Sigmar chuckled, and the sound throbbed through Balthas. 'You'll know, Balthas. When the moment is right, you will let your arrow fly. And I will be there to guide your aim.'

Balthas bowed his head. When he rasied it again, Sigmar was gone, with only a flurry of loose snow to mark his passing.

'I will not fail you,' Balthas said again.

His words were carried away by the wind.

'Hold the lantern higher, Verga,' Calys barked. 'Even my eyes can't pierce this murk.' At her words, the Liberator behind her raised the storm-lantern she held, allowing the flickering blue radiance to wash across the interior of the mausoleum. 'The last of them came in here. I'm certain of it.'

The storm-lanterns held a shred of lightning culled from the eternal storm. No shadow could resist their light. In theory, at least. But the gloom that lurked among the catacombs beneath the city was thicker than any shadow. It seemed to seep from the stones and collect in every tomb and mausoleum. And it hid monsters.

A plague of spirits haunted the catacombs. They'd already destroyed or imprisoned many, but there were always more. Lurking just out of the corner of the eye.

Calys glanced at the warriors who followed her. 'Stay alert. This one is shrewder than the others.' Some gheists were like rabid beasts, lacking even the basest cunning. But others were possessed of a dreadful wisdom. She had only brought two others – Verga and Faelius – with her into the maze of tombs, leaving Tamacus and the rest of her cohort to watch the entrance to the avenue. Their prey was a monstrous thing – shroud-like, with long, spindly limbs and clacking jaws. It seemed impossible that it could hide in such a confined space, but it had left a clear trail.

The air had turned cold in its wake, and a glimmer of hoar frost hung over the walls, marking where it passed through the crypt. A stone bier rose up before her, the carved lid cast aside and laying broken on the floor. All that remained within it was a clutter of burial wrappings and dust. The nooks that lined the walls were much the same, save that they were filled with cobwebs as well.

'Something is here,' Faelius murmured behind her. He lifted his grandhammer and tilted his head, listening to the wind that whipped through the tombs. 'I can feel it watching us.' He turned. 'Waiting.'

'Waiting for us to lower our guard, you mean,' Verga said. She jabbed the tip of her blade into the rubble on the floor, disturbing a flood of tomb-spiders. The pallid insects scuttled across the floor, seeking the safety of the shadows.

Scrape-thump.

The sound was soft. Barely audible. But Calys heard it. She froze, and the others followed suit, listening.

Scrape-thump. Scrape-thump.

'Like a shroud being dragged over rocks,' Faelius said. 'And the air… Smell it? Like milk gone sour.' He turned. 'Or a corpse.'

'Those two things don't smell anything alike,' Verga said.

'Quiet,' Calys said, sharply. She could hear a quiet rustling. Her breath puffed out through the mouth-slit of her war-mask. Hoar frost crept across the panes of her armour, cracking and scattering as she moved.

Scrape-thump. Clack.

Instinct compelled her to look up. The thing was splayed across the roof of the crypt, like some great bat. Long, thin limbs bent with a sound like ice cracking as it flopped down towards her, equine skull rattling. Calys yelled and slashed at it with her war-blade. The sword passed through the folds with ease, tearing the voluminous shroud but striking nothing solid. She found herself swallowed in its flabby embrace, tangled in the ragged cloak. Claws skittered across her war-plate, too-long fingers seeking a way in.

Then, the crypt echoed with a boom of thunder as Faelius' grandhammer slammed down. The nighthaunt wailed and swept away from Calys, sending her staggering back against the bier. It spiralled towards Faelius, fleshless jaws wide. The Liberator whipped his hammer up, trying to smash its skull. The spectre plunged through him as if he weren't there. A bullseye of ice crept across the warrior's chest-plate, and he stumbled, the hammer slipping from his hands. The night-haunt tore through his back and turned, lunging for Verga as Faelius toppled forwards, limbs twitching.

'Fall back, Verga – get into the open,' Calys shouted. She tossed aside her sword and lunged for the grandhammer. The creature seemed to fear it. Faelius groaned and tried to sit up as she stepped over him and snatched up his weapon. 'Stay down, Faelius,' she said, as she hurried after Verga and the nighthaunt. The other Liberator had done as she commanded and retreated into the open.

The avenue beyond was lined with mausoleums, one piled atop the next in tottering walls that stretched up to the roof of the passageway. Drifts of dust and bone fragments pressed thick against the stoops of the lowest crypts. Walkways of timber or bridges of stone stretched between the highest crypts, forming a second ceiling, thick with grave-mould and cobwebs. Gallows-cages hung from the bridges, and the chained skeletons within them thrashed in silent fury as they caught sight of her.

Calys saw Verga immediately. The Liberator backed away from the spectre as it darted from side to side, trying to avoid the glare of the storm-lantern. It moved like oil on water – there, but not. It slid through the air, stretching itself impossible distances, before contracting suddenly. She could see its pale shape through the swirl of the shroud – emaciated to the point of inhumanity. Ribs stretched pearlescent flesh taut, and its limbs were all sharp, broken angles.

Clack. Clack. Clack.

Its equine jaws snapped as it circled Verga, drawing closer with every circuit. She swept her blade out, trying to hew through it, but it avoided her blow. Long talons scratched across her arm, leaving trails of ice. She stumbled, and the spectre reared up over her, claws groping for her throat.

'Verga – move!' Calys roared, swinging the hammer up. The spectre turned with a hiss, and the grandhammer met its skull.

Bone cracked and burst as the hammer passed through it and slammed down. The ground ruptured, and lightning speared up, burning the spectre from the inside out. Wreathed in flames, it hurtled upwards, broken skull gaping in a silent scream. It clawed at itself, until it at last came apart in a shower of burning rags.

Calys took a slow breath as the spectre was consumed. She looked at Verga and gestured with the hammer. 'Go and help Faelius.'

A voice echoed down from above. 'A well-struck blow, sister.'

Calys looked up and saw Lord-Relictor Dathus watching her. He stood atop a set of stairs that led nowhere above, set in an open space between crypts. The steps curved up and then around and back down in a stony loop, winding through the crypts. As he descended, the upper steps swung away, and a false archway, resembling a crypt opening, crashed down in its place. Dust sifted down across her armour, and a sudden breeze from somewhere washed over her. She grimaced. There were always mysterious draughts and smells down here, and Calys had yet to become inured to them. Sometimes, she wondered if Pharus had ever grown used to the stench and the damp before… She pushed the thought aside.

'I have struck better,' she said as Dathus reached the bottom. The lord-relictor had been gone for several days, conferring with the new commander, Lord-Arcanum Knossus, as well as Lord-Celestant Lynos and the others in charge of the city's defences. 'Any news?' she asked, resting Faelius' hammer across her shoulders. 'About Lord-Castellant Pharus, I mean.'

'None,' Dathus said. 'I am sorry, Calys. Knossus had nothing to share in regard to his fate.' He looked out over the sea of tombs and grunted. 'He had nothing at all to share, in fact. Other than that the necroquake reached Azyr itself, and shook the pillars of the heavens.'

Calys felt the cold weight of dread in her belly. 'Azyr…'

'It endures, as ever. Be at peace, sister. The God-King would not let the realm fall now, not after all this time.' Dathus shook his head. 'Though, to hear Knossus tell it, it was a close thing. Even the Anvil of Apotheosis was affected, if only for a short time.' He looked at her. 'We live in dangerous times, sister. Come. Walk with me a spell.'

Calys fell into step with the lord-relictor, after retrieving her blade and checking on Faelius. The Liberator had already recovered somewhat, and she returned his grandhammer. As they walked, she signalled to Tamacus and the others, alerting them to the nighthaunt's destruction. They would continue to sweep this section, hunting for any other lingering spectres that might be lurking in the tombs.

The path inclined upwards as she and Dathus walked along the avenue, and the mausoleums to either side grew sparse. Statues loomed out of the dark, staring down at them with unseeing eyes. Soon, they were walking along a stretch of path that took them towards the Ten Thousand Tombs.

The ground shuddered beneath her feet as unseen sections peeled away with a scrape of stone and clouds of dust, swinging out and up or down. New twists and turns were added to the path ahead, and from behind came the rumble of a new wall sliding into place. The outer catacombs were always in motion these days. Those dead things still loose in them wandered the confusing tangle of passages, unable to escape.

She heard a shout from overhead and saw the arch of a bridge drift towards its new position. A cohort of Stormcasts stood atop it, braced against the shuddering of the stone. As the bridge locked into place, they strode across it, shields raised against whatever awaited them in the dark beyond. 'It never ends, does it?' she said.

'Duty never does.'

She looked at Dathus. 'What news from above?'

'The same, but worse,' Dathus said. 'The city is in upheaval. It is all we can do to keep it in hand. The dead rise in greater numbers, and every day, refugees bring word of fresh horrors rising from oases and slipping down out of the high crags. Every restless soul in Shyish has been stirred to wakefulness, and all of them thirst for the blood of the living.'

'None have slipped past us,' Calys said, firmly.

Before Dathus could reply, there was the sound of scrabbling at the entrance to a nearby tomb. It was a sound that had become all too familiar to Calys of late. The stones cracked and crumbled, as if something were trying to dislodge them. Calys made to draw her blade, but Dathus waved her back. He set his hand on the face of the tomb, and a blue radiance played across the cracks. 'Sleep, child of death,' the lord-relictor growled. 'Your time is not yet arrived.'

The scrabbling faded, as if the occupant of the tomb had resumed its fitful slumber. Dathus stepped back, allowing a nearby group of mortal priests to go about their duty. They would re-bless the tomb, and that which lay within, anointing it with sacred unguents and marking it with sigils of warding, as they and their predecessors had done for almost a century. Calys doubted it would hold for long, despite their efforts.

'That happens too often for my liking,' she said.

Dathus turned away from the tomb. 'The constant fluctuation of the catacombs causes stress fractures in the stonework – a hazard of Pharus' cleverness.'

Calys nodded. Any spirits that escaped would be confused by the eternally shifting underworld, and easily trapped. But that same shifting allowed some to escape in the first place.

Luckily, those that most often did so were the easiest to recapture. She suspected that too had been part of Pharus' design.

A shadow passed over them, as an archway bridge swung out over the slope of tombs and graves. Dust rained down in a constant patter, dulling her war-plate. She strode to the edge of the slope, walking across the roof of a crypt that jutted out over the abyss below.

From this highest point, the catacombs somewhat resembled a massive orrery of interlocking stone rings. Mausoleums and crypts clung like barnacles to each ring, as well as the tumbledown slopes that filled the gaps between. The great mechanisms that controlled the movement of the catacombs hung suspended in great orbs of stone, which hung directly over the Ten Thousand Tombs.

Dathus joined her, his eyes following hers. 'I've set a guard on them, just in case. They have orders to activate the final sequence, should it appear that the tombs are in danger of being opened.'

Calys frowned. The sequence would collapse the catacombs, burying them forever. But destroying the catacombs would almost certainly destroy Glymmsforge as well. Not immediately, perhaps. But the reverberations of such an act would ripple outwards, weakening streets and foundations. Not even duardin craftsmanship would survive such devastation. 'It won't come to that,' she said firmly.

'The dead are remorseless,' Dathus said. 'And we must stand ready to deny them this place, whatever the cost.'

'Why do they hate us?' The question slipped from her lips before she could stop it.

'They do not,' he said, after a moment. 'Not truly. Nor, I think, does Nagash. To hate, one must care. And the God of the Dead cares for little save himself.' He looked out, over the edge of the crypt. 'Sigmar delights in us, as he delighted in our fathers and their fathers. Our creations, our courage, even our hubris – it delights him.'

'A funny word, that, to use in relation to a god.'

'But fitting.' Dathus looked at her. 'It is said by some, among my brotherhood, that the realms spin in eternal opposition – one pulling against the other. Azyr pulls against Shyish, Ghyran against Ghur, Hysh against Ulgu, and Aqshy against Chamon. Each the mirror image of the other, some in subtle ways, others more obvious. And as Azyr and Shyish stand in opposition, so too do the gods. Sigmar is the beginning and Nagash, the ending.' He gestured, and a spark of lightning danced across his knuckles and palm as he turned his hand, this way and that. 'But Nagash is a greedy god and seeks to be both beginning and end. So he raises the dead from their sleep of ages and sends them to attack the living.'

'Like Elya's mother,' Calys said absently. The child was never far from her thoughts these days.

Dathus studied her and she looked away, suddenly uneasy. The music of the catacombs had become louder. She heard the creak of stone, and the slow drip of water, from somewhere. Bats stirred in the high roosts, chittering in fear.

And down below, the dead, in their ten thousand tombs, began to moan.

'Something is coming,' Dathus said. Calys nodded silently. She could feel it, on the damp air. Like the quaver of silent thunder. 'Glymmsforge is slowly sealing itself off from the rest of the underworld,' the lord-relictor continued. 'Even so, huge numbers of refugees still clamour at the outer gates, seeking entry. Every hamlet and trading outpost within a hundred leagues has been denuded of inhabitants, as the dead rise and stalk the living with a greater frequency than ever before.

Mortals come to the city in their hundreds, in search of sanctuary.'

'A dangerous journey,' Calys said. 'There are deadwalkers in the desert.'

'Indeed, and they are congregating in ever-greater numbers – immense herds of corpses stumble in the wake of the refugee caravans, pulling down stragglers and adding them to legions of the dead,' Dathus growled. 'In the corpse-yards of the southern districts, and the walled gardens of the aristocracy in the north, spectral shapes prey on rich and poor alike. We are under siege, within and without.'

'What of this new lord – Knossus – what has he done?'

'He strikes down the dead where he finds them,' Dathus said. 'And with a power beyond any that even I possess.' He stopped as the archway ahead cracked in half and fell away with mechanical smoothness, revealing a sharply angled wall, marked with mystic sigils. Mirrored walls closed in about them as the floor descended, carrying them downwards in response to their weight. 'This place truly is a marvel.'

'The duardin are a clever folk,' Calys said.

'Pharus was clever,' Dathus corrected. 'Duardin traps are stolid things. Efficient, but not so creative as this. Only a mind like Pharus' could have calculated all of this. Finding weak points and turning them into a strength was his gift. I once thought he would guard this place until the end of time itself.' He fell silent.

'He will return,' Calys said.

'But in what form?' Dathus murmured. Calys was about to ask him what he meant, when he stopped and turned. 'The city is closing in on itself. Every avenue and gate, save the main thoroughfare, is slamming shut. Knossus has commanded that Glymmsforge isolate itself from Lyria, to better weather the coming storm.'

Calys nodded. That made sense. The city – and by extension, the Shimmergate – would be easier to protect if it were sealed off. But that meant cutting off support to the outlying communities, as well as outposts like Fort Alenstahdt. Necessary sacrifices – but even so, she was glad she wasn't the one giving the order.

Dathus continued. 'To that end, we must seal off the Ten Thousand Tombs, so that no servant of Death might reach them. Do you understand?' He gazed out over the sea of tombs that stretched in all directions around them. 'Even I am not sure how it works. Briaeus and the others who served with Pharus the longest assure me that they can do so. But it is not something that might be undone at a whim.'

Calys understood at once. 'Once sealed, it cannot easily be unsealed.'

The lord-relictor nodded. 'Someone must stay above, to ensure that it is the case. And to defend the gateway, should it come to that. That responsibility is yours, if you wish it.' Dathus looked at her, the light of the lanterns playing across his skull-helm.

Calys hesitated. Then she nodded. 'I will bar the path, brother.'

Dathus returned her nod with one of his own. 'I expected no less.' He set a fist atop her shoulder-plate. 'I will be staying down here, with Briaeus and the others. We will hold this place from within, as you hold it from without. Gather your cohort and go, sister. Lord-Arcanum Knossus has commanded that we seal off this place immediately, and I would not wish you caught in those tunnels when the process begins.' He extended his hand. 'May Sigmar bless and keep you, Calys Eltain.'

She caught his hand. 'May he do the same for you, Dathus.'

Dathus laughed softly. 'I have no doubt he will, after his own fashion.'

CHAPTER TWELVE

RAZOR'S EDGE

Elya ran through the crowd thronging the street.

The tide of humanity was larger than any she'd experienced, even during high market days. Thousands of new faces, voices and smells, packed into the long, central avenue that linked each of the city's rings, moving towards the heart of Glymmsforge.

She saw two women, one old, one young, dressed like traders from the distant city of Gravewild, in yellow linen and golden ornaments, and a fat man, dressed like a nobleman, in rich brocade and an embossed breastplate. There were duardin as well, clad in dusty travel robes, and she saw men and women dressed in the rough leathers of miners. Many carried weapons, and most looked as if they had been forced to put them to use recently. Everyone, whoever they were, had that pinched, hungry look she knew well. Everyone in the Gloaming looked like that, especially of late.

Glymmsmen threaded among the crowd in knots of black, inspecting the people, seeking signs of soulblight infection or cult markings. You could never be too careful, that's what her father said. The Freeguild seemed to agree – they were out in force. And more besides. On one of the high, stone plinths that overlooked the avenue, a massive figure stood watching the crowd. With a shiver, she recognised the figure as the lord-veritant of the Anvils of the Heldenhammer. There were stories about the Leechbane – all of them bad.

Folk in the Gloaming said he'd led the purges of the northern slums, when they'd been overrun by grave-eaters, many years before she'd been born. And that he'd done the same more recently in the districts of the wealthy, when several families had come under the sway of a soul-leech. Not all Stormcasts were like Pharus or Calys. Some were much, much worse. She shivered again and moved quickly away from him, startling a flock of pigeons that were searching the street for food.

The purple-hued birds sprang into the air and rose high and away. Some folk claimed they collected the souls of the dead for Elder Bones, but the cats claimed that wasn't so. It was the big, black carrion birds that served the King of the Dead, and the spindle-legged jackals that wandered the desert. The pigeons served a smaller god, and a quieter one by far. Or so the cats said.

The sky overhead was the colour of a bruise, and the wind rolling in off the desert was cold. She dodged around a burly road-agent, who cursed at her as she ran by. She spotted a pickpocket she knew from the Gloaming and gave him a wide berth. A moment later, she heard shouting and knew he'd been spotted. The crowd heaved suddenly as the thief ran past, and she was nearly trampled. Dodging bodies, she thought about climbing to a higher vantage point and seeking somewhere quieter to watch things, but decided against it.

She'd taken to the streets when she'd felt the ground begin to shake, earlier. Dust had geysered from the cracks in the street, and the buildings had shuddered. Something was happening down below, and people were worried. She would have asked Pharus about it, but he was… gone. She rubbed her face.

Calys had said he would come back, but Elya wasn't sure she trusted the Stormcast. Pharus had been her friend, she thought. Calys wasn't. She wasn't sure what Calys was.

Calys scared her father. All Stormcasts scared her father, but he'd never yelled as he had when he'd seen Calys for the first time. He'd looked at her face and just screamed and screamed, as if he'd seen a nicksoul. The way he had the night her mother had died. Elya shied away from the thought. She hugged herself, suddenly cold.

She didn't like to think about that night or any of it. She'd been too little to remember much of it – much of her. She recalled her mother's face, twisted up and wrong somehow, and the sound of her father weeping. And then Pharus, with his lantern. The light had been so warm and her mother had gone away, but her father had kept crying. He still cried, some nights, when he didn't get enough to drink. Or had too much to drink.

Her mother was dead. Had been dead. She'd become sick and died. Then she'd returned, and Pharus had killed her again. And now Pharus was dead too. Part of her hoped he wouldn't come back, because if he did, she might begin to wonder why he had and not her mother. She stopped and for a moment became a little island in the sea of people. She scraped the heel of one palm across her eyes and frowned. She heard shouting.

There was a commotion going on up ahead. Voices rose up and the crowd convulsed like a thing in pain. Metal flashed, and a cry went up. Elya's eyes widened, all thoughts of Pharus and her mother forgotten. The fat man she'd seen earlier had shoved one of the trader women – the older one – to the ground. The man drew a knife from within his robes. 'Grave-eater,' he screamed, kicking at his victim.

At his words, the crowd surged back from him, Elya included. Men and women had shouted those words from street corners since she'd been a baby. Sometimes, when people died, they came back. Not as nicksouls or wailgheists, but as grave-eaters – hungry corpses that had no mind, only appetite. Overcoming the sudden spurt of fear, she winnowed closer, trying to see. The fat man gestured at the old woman on the ground as her companion tried to intervene.

'She is sick,' the younger woman shouted, crouching beside her companion. 'She is hurt – please. We have done nothing...'

'She's infected,' the fat man spat. 'Look at her! She's turning already.'

More shouts as a Glymmsman forced his way through the crowd. 'What's going on here?' The soldier reached out to grab the fat man, startling him. The fat man's blade flashed, and the Glymmsman spun away, clutching a red arm and cursing. His cries drew the attention of his fellows, and those soldiers closest moved to confront the fat man, who stared at the Glymmsman he'd injured in shock.

'I didn't mean...' he began.

On the ground, the old woman had begun to thrash and twitch, her heels and head striking the cobbles. The young woman was scrambling backwards, her face twisted up in a horrified expression. 'No, Takha, no – oh, blessed Sigmar, no!'

When the old woman sat up, the young woman began to wail. The soldiers hadn't noticed yet. The fat man had their attention. Two Glymmsmen had tackled him to the ground. The three of them rolled in the dust, the man's cries muffled.

Fists thudded into flesh, and the knife clattered away. More Freeguild hurried towards the brawl, fighting through the crowd.

When the old woman attacked, she went for the fat man first. She caught him by a flailing arm and sank her teeth into the meat of his forearm. He screamed a high, thin wail, and Elya shrank back. Her sudden movement attracted the attentions of the grave-eater, and the old woman scuttled towards her on all fours, bloody mouth working. People screamed and fought to get out of the way, as Elya turned to run. The corpse bounded through them, snapping its jaws wildly.

She ducked the dead woman's flailing hand and scrambled under an abandoned cart. The grave-eater groped blindly for her, teeth gnashing like those of a maddened cur. Elya pulled all her limbs close, huddling away from the dead woman. 'There she is – seize her!' a man shouted, from close by.

The old woman whirled, snarling, as a Glymmsman grabbed for her. She leapt on the soldier and bore him backwards, biting at his throat. Elya crawled out from under the cart, hoping to put some distance between herself and the old woman. She tried to ignore the screams. Glymmsmen raced past her, cursing and shouting.

She caught sight of the fat man, trying to crawl away. He wouldn't get far. Sometimes, when the grave-eaters bit you, you became like them. It might take days, or just a few seconds – but it would happen. That was probably what had happened to the old woman. She'd been bitten, somewhere out in the desert, and had turned after entering the city.

The Freeguilder was screaming, as the old woman gnawed at him. He would turn too, just like the fat man. Worse, he probably knew what would happen to him, if he had the bad luck to survive his mauling. Elya heard the crash of metal on stone and saw the crowd part with a frightened murmur for the Leechbane. The lord-veritant strode towards the confrontation, the lantern atop his staff glowing as brightly as the one Pharus had carried. But he wasn't Pharus. Pharus wouldn't have done what the lord-veritant did next.

'Move back,' he said, his voice cutting through the confusion like a blade. Glymmsmen drew back, and the Leechbane drew his sword.

He took off the old woman's head with the first sweep of his long blade. He killed the wounded Freeguilder next, as easily as a cat might kill a mouse, before any of the soldier's comrades could speak up. And then he stalked towards the fat man, who tried to get to his feet, his face pale. Elya closed her eyes as the fat man began to scream and then stopped, suddenly, as the sword flicked out a third time.

Silence fell across the street. Elya huddled beside the cart, trying to make herself as small as possible. If the Leechbane thought she'd been bitten, he wouldn't hesitate to take her head as well. The only way to put down a grave-eater plague was to stop it before it got started, or kill everyone who might turn.

But if he'd noticed her, he gave no sign. Instead, he'd turned, as high up above the city, the Shimmergate was shining again, blazing like a small sun. Every eye in the avenue turned towards it, drawn with lodestone certainty, wondering what it portended.

Elya took the opportunity to slip away, moving as quietly as a cat.

Balthas watched the sun rise over the walls of Glymmsforge, and wondered why anyone would come to such a place as this. Everything in the underworld had a faded, colourless quality, to one used to the vibrancy of Azyr. Did this place really have so much more to offer than Azyrheim, or any of the Cities of the Dawn? Why would mortals flock to places like this?

Then, he'd long ago come to the conclusion that many mortals were simply contrary. They simply did not know what was good for them. Like those attempting to flood the city, seeking the protection of its walls. Congregating in one place, however well-defended, was tantamount to inviting attack. They did not see that their numbers only added to the burden borne by the defenders.

His Sacrosanct Chamber had arrived to little fanfare, just before dawn. The city was readying itself for war and had no time to spare greeting late arrivals. He felt no insult, and had set about determining the location of the Ten Thousand Tombs, only to find the catacombs barred to him – barred to everyone – by order of Knossus Heavensen.

Messengers had come. Knossus requested his presence, here on the walls that surrounded the steps to the Shimmergate. The final redoubt, from which the city might make a last stand, and the oldest, strongest walls in Glymmsforge. There were soldiers on the parapets here, Freeguild in the mauve and black of the city's largest regiment. They gave Balthas a wide berth, which suited him.

He watched as a woman hurried up a set of nearby steps, carrying a basket of bread. Soldiers crowded around her as she handed the loaves out. One kissed her, and they spoke quietly. Intently. Balthas watched their soul-fires intertwine, briefly, before they broke apart and went their separate ways. He could taste their shared memories on the air, as well as the love they felt for one another. Annoyed by the intrusive sensation, he turned away.

He could sense Miska and Helios, waiting below on the avenue that ran between the two innermost city walls, as he stood impatiently here, awaiting his fellow lord-arcanum, even though he was far senior to the younger warrior. He found his thoughts drawn to Agnostai and the Gilded Reach. Places his careful studies had taken him, and places impulsive Knossus had already been.

It was not a rivalry, for rivalry implied competition. Knossus went where he would and did as he willed, driven by the same desires that drove Balthas. And like Balthas, he did not deign to notice those who lagged in his wake.

It was Knossus who had solved the audient puzzles that sealed the Chiming Vault, and unravelled the riddle of the shadeglass mechanisms within. It was Knossus who had at last translated the alchemical texts taken from the Silver Sepulchre. And it was Knossus who had been honoured by Sigmar, for his victories.

Perhaps Tyros was right, and some part of him resented the other lord-arcanum's success. Glories that should rightfully have been his had they not fallen into the lap of another. It was irksome. Frustrating, even. He did not like to think of himself as prey to such weaknesses. And yet, here he was, gnawing at himself as he considered the situation.

'What are you doing, brother?'

'Calculating, Knossus. How much grain is in the city's stores?' Balthas turned as Knossus Heavensen joined him on the top of the wall. He pretended not to notice as the Freeguild sank to their knees, heads bowed. 'How much water in the wells? How many more men can be mustered to the walls at notice?'

'I have done those calculations, brother. I have waged this war a hundred thousand times, in life and beyond.' Knossus took off his helmet and hooked it to his belt. His tattooed features turned towards Balthas. 'This was my city, once.'

'Yes. Perhaps it will be so again, in the event of this war's successful prosecution.' Balthas did not take off his own helm. He'd always felt more comfortable with something covering his face, when he had to walk abroad. In Sigmaron, it wasn't so noticeable, but here, something in him wanted a wall between him and this realm.

He caught sight of a small, slinking shape padding across the parapet. And another, crouched on the parapets curving above them. 'We are being watched. Cats. And a child.' Balthas looked at the other lord-arcanum. 'Why are there so many cats here, Knossus?'

'And children?' Knossus was smiling.

Balthas grunted. 'I am well aware of how that particular infestation comes to be.'

Knossus laughed softly. 'She is an urchin, I expect. There are thousands of them in the city. There always have been.' He frowned. 'Despite the best efforts of some.'

Balthas looked away. 'Mortals are fragile,' he said. Soldiers glanced at him, and then hurriedly looked away. Balthas paid them little mind.

'More than you know and less than you think,' Knossus said. He took a breath, as if preparing for something painful. 'Sigmar sent your chamber to aid mine.'

'And so we will. By descending into the Ten Thousand Tombs and guarding them.'

'They are already under guard, by Lord-Relictor Dathus, of the Gravewalkers Chamber. I have ordered them sealed off. There is no way down. Not without destroying the very defences that have been erected to protect them. I have been assured of it, by the duardin engineers who created them.'

Anger speared through Balthas. 'Are you mad? How am I to defend something I can't even get to?'

'By helping me defend the city,' Knossus said. 'I have had

reports of what is coming. Three of the desert outposts set along the Great Lyrian Road have been attacked, all contact with them lost. I fear my chamber will not be enough to stem the tide. I need you.'

'I have my mission, brother. Given to me by the God-King himself.'

'As do I. They are one and the same.' Knossus pointed, out over the desert. 'An army of mad souls, charnel leavings and bird-picked bones is on the horizon, whether we can see it or not. Every dead thing for a thousand leagues is coming here, to Glymmsforge. You know that. You can feel it on the air, as well as I.'

'Which is why I must defend the Ten Thousand Tombs. The city is secondary to that, brother. Even you must admit that – or perhaps you are letting your nostalgia override your wisdom.' Balthas regretted the words, even as he spoke them. But it was too late to take them back. He straightened as Knossus stared at him.

'What are you saying?'

'I know who you were, Knossus. And I know that is why Sigmar sent you here.' It came out as an accusation. 'This city was yours, you said. An attachment of your mortal self – something you ought to have left behind. Tell me, did you ask him to let you garrison this place? Is this your reward for glories accumulated?'

'How can you think that?' Knossus asked, his face tight with anger. 'He sent me here to defend his holdings. And that is what I will do. This city will weather the deathstorm that threatens it, and its people will survive.'

'This city is no concern of mine. Only what it rests atop.' Balthas gestured dismissively. 'You are the greatest of us, a scion of the mightiest Stormhost.' He indicated the nearby soldiers.

'You have an army, and the blessings of Sigmar. You have command of a city. What need is there for me?'

'Are you still so angry with me, then?' Knossus said softly, after a moment. 'After all this time, have you still not forgiven me for Agnostai? Will you make me wage a war on two fronts, Gravewarden?'

Balthas looked at him. 'Wage however many wars you like, brother. You'll hear not a word from me. It is what you do best, after all.'

Knossus sighed and looked away. 'Always so stubborn.'

'If I am stubborn, it is because my mission was given to me by the God-King himself.' Balthas drew himself up. 'The Ten Thousand Tombs are my only concern, brother. Not whatever grudge you imagine I bear you.' He tried to keep his voice mild, but an edge crept in regardless.

Knossus' tattooed features quirked in something that might have been a smile. 'That I bear you,' he said slowly, repeating Balthas' words. 'Is that how you think of it, Balthas?'

'I do not think of it at all.'

'You were always a bad liar.'

Balthas grunted. 'Perhaps. Then, perhaps I have never seen the need.' He made to step past Knossus, but the other caught his arm.

'What have I done? What offence have I given you?' Knossus demanded. 'From the moment we met, you have snapped and snarled at me, beneath your breath.'

Balthas shook him off. 'I do not know,' he said, after a moment. He looked out towards the desert. 'I do not know,' he repeated, more quietly. 'Maybe I am envious. Maybe I see in you what I should be, and am not. Or maybe, I simply find you off-putting.'

Knossus snorted. He too looked towards the desert. 'You

would not be the first.' He glanced at Balthas. 'You frustrate me, brother. All of us, really. You were among the first of our number, but you wall yourself off from all save Tyros, and even he must make effort to speak to you.' He leaned against the parapet, his palms braced on the crenellations. 'Look, brother. Look around you. See what you dismiss so casually. For once, look past yourself.'

Balthas sighed but did as Knossus asked, looking with his storm-sight as well as his eyes. He saw the fear on the faces of every mortal stationed on the wall. More, he saw the hope in their eyes and heard the prayers on their lips. They were frightened, but not broken. Not beaten. They would stand, as surely as the Stormcasts themselves. They would fight and perish, and perhaps, some few among them might return, clad in sigmarite, to fight again. He flinched away from the thought.

It was an honour to be called to Sigmar's service. But that honour weighed heavy on even the strongest soul. He looked at Knossus. 'What is it that you want me to see, brother? That they are afraid? That they are brave, for all their fragility? I know this.' Then, after a moment, 'I never doubted it.'

'If you know it, then you know nothing is more important than what we do here. Glymmsforge must stand. Whatever else, it must stand. Else these people – our people – will perish, and their souls will be added to the tally of the dead.'

Balthas glanced back at the Shimmergate, rising above them. He groped for an answer – a logical solution to the problem at hand. 'Why not evacuate them?'

'Would you abandon Sigmaron? Or would you fight to the last, to defend it?'

'This is not Sigmaron.'

'But it is their home.' Knossus stepped back. 'I need you, Balthas. The deathstorm approaches, and we must stand against it. All of us – mortal and immortal alike. The Ten Thousand Tombs are defended. I need you here, in the open air.'

He sighed and looked out over the desert. Balthas waited, growing more uncomfortable by the moment. Finally, Knossus shook his head. 'If Sigmar sent you, that means he suspects that there is an ulterior motive for what is to come. Perhaps I should let you do as you wish. Even if it means weakening the defence of the city.' Knossus looked away. 'For the first time, in a long time, I do not know the best course ahead, and it troubles me.'

Balthas hesitated. Part of him rejoiced, for here was victory. Knossus at a loss, for once. But instead of enjoying it, he remembered Sigmar's words.

You see yourself at odds with them, even if you do not admit it.

Not at odds, my lord. Never that.

Perhaps you are wiser than the gods, Balthas.

'If I am wise, it is because you made me so, my lord,' he murmured, feeling small within his shell of sigmarite. Knossus looked at him in confusion. Balthas sighed. 'Perhaps we should find common ground upon which to make our stand, Knossus.'

He reached up, as if to clasp Knossus' shoulder, but could not bring himself to go that far. He let his hand drop. 'Sigmar placed me under your command, brother. So command me, and I will do all that I can to see it – and my own duty – fulfilled.'

Knossus smiled. 'Sometimes, Balthas, I am proud to be your brother.'

'As you should be,' Balthas said.

-

From the avenue below, Miska watched the two lords-arcanum converse, and sighed. Helios shook his head. 'He wastes so much energy on resentment.' He stood nearby, balancing his stormstaff on the end of his blade, much to the enjoyment of the urchins lurking nearby. He had his helmet off, as did she. It eased some of the discomfort mortals felt in their presence, if they could see the faces of the Stormcasts who walked among them.

'It is not resentment.'

'What would you call it?' Helios flipped his staff with his blade, caught it with his free hand and sent it spinning up into the air. The children laughed and clapped.

Miska watched them, unsmiling. 'Balthas is akin to a mechanism. He has his lines, and he runs on them. The messiness of the world causes him much consternation.' And this was a messy situation, to be sure.

The city wore a mask of order, but beneath that was only confusion. Glymmsforge had been rocked by the necroquake, its foundations cracked and the certainties of its citizens cast to the wind. Now, as people from outside sought safety in its walls and the dead rose, the city was balanced on the razor's edge. One misstep, and it would be lost.

Helios laughed softly and caught his staff. 'He will have to get used to it.' He bowed slightly to the urchins, who cheered. 'The masque is finished, the veil cast aside. We stand revealed, for good or ill.'

Miska grunted and leaned against her staff. Helios spoke the truth – few mortals gave them more than a second glance, now. One Stormcast was very much like another, to them, barring differences in heraldry. 'Very poetic.'

'Well, I am a poet.' He looked around the courtyard, his stormstaff bouncing against his shoulder. Miska followed his gaze. Soldiers, scribes and citizens hurried about their business around them. A man selling hot potatoes from a rickety cart called out his wares as he navigated the press of bodies. Fishermen, coming from the Glass Mere with baskets of fish on their backs, threaded through the crowd, pursued by opportunistic cats. Life continued.

Miska did not often lose herself in the few memories of her mortal life she possessed. But here, for a moment, she was tempted. Instead, she shook the thought off and signalled to Porthas, who loitered nearby. The Sequitor-Prime ambled towards her, bouncing a steaming potato on one palm. He took a bite and chewed noisily. 'Do we have our orders?' he asked, around a mouthful.

'Not yet, but I have no doubt we will, soon enough. I want you ready to move, when it happens. Where are the others?'

Porthas swallowed a chunk of potato. 'Waiting in the plaza beneath the Shimmergate.' He looked around. 'The city is on edge. I can feel it.' He took another bite. 'Good potato, though.'

Helios laughed. 'It's the simple things, eh, Porthas?'

'A potato is a potato, whatever the weather,' the big Stormcast said. He looked at Miska. 'You can feel it, can't you, mage-sacristan? The fear. The confusion.' He popped the last of his potato into his mouth and chewed thoughtfully.

Miska watched the faces of the mortals around them. There was fear there, to be sure. Uncertainty. They could smell death on the wind as easily as she. But also determination. That was good. They would need that resolve.

She heard a sharp sound – the clangour of small bells – echoing from somewhere close by. Curious, she turned in the direction of the noise. 'Stay here,' she said to the others. 'I would see what that is.'

'Not unaccompanied, you won't,' Helios said mildly. He glanced at Porthas.

'She won't be,' Porthas said. 'You wait here, for the lord-arcanum.' He fell into step beside Miska. She shook her head.

'I do not require a bodyguard.'

'It is not about what you require,' Porthas said. His blunt, scarred features twisted up in a smile. 'You are our mage-sacristan, my lady, and due a certain respect.'

'Only when it suits you, I notice.'

Porthas shrugged. 'And it suits us now.' He patted the haft of his greatmace. 'Besides, we are strangers here, and this city is on edge. No telling what might happen. Helios and I are expendable, my lady. You and the lord-arcanum are not.'

'We are all expendable, Porthas,' Miska said. 'That is why the Anvil of Apotheosis was made.'

'Now you sound like the lord-arcanum.'

She glanced at him. 'He has his moments, brother.'

Porthas grunted, but didn't reply. Miska frowned. Porthas rarely let anything resembling an opinion slip. Taciturnity was his art, and he was a master of it. That was why Balthas favoured his cohort over others. The lord-arcanum preferred his followers to act without speaking, when possible. Sometimes, she thought Balthas would prefer an army of automatons over living warriors.

The sound of the bells continued, leading them through the press of the avenue and out into the western market square. It was a wide, twelve-sided plaza, banded by market stalls and storefronts. Wooden buildings rose at awkward angles, tottering arthritically over the open space of the plaza. Broadsheet sellers wearing heavy wooden placards wandered among the crowd, shouting out the latest news or getting in brawls with one another. There were at least four active printing presses in the city, locked in an unending battle for dominance. Elsewhere, spice merchants hawked their wares to passing trade, and fishmongers chopped away at the bounty of the Glass Mere.

Miska paused for a moment, enjoying the anarchic vitality of the city. There was nothing like it in Sigmaron. Even Azyrheim was more orderly than this. Porthas nudged her. 'There – look.' He pointed.

She followed his gesture and saw a thirty-foot statue of silver rising from a plinth of black stone. A crowd of the devoted, clad in sackcloth and ashes, and wearing chains hung with a profusion of tiny silver bells, prostrated themselves before the statue. The sound originated with their movements, and the market crowd gave them a wide berth.

Miska approached the statue, Porthas trailing after her. Mortals moved quickly from their path, but Miska paid them little mind. The statue was that of a woman – proud, clad in the robes and armour of the Collegiate Arcane. 'She looks familiar,' Porthas murmured.

'She should,' a woman's voice said. 'She once beat you at arm wrestling.'

Miska turned. A Knight-Incantor, clad in gold and azure, strode towards them. 'Zeraphina,' Miska said, in greeting. 'I wondered where you were.'

'I came looking as soon as Knossus mentioned that you'd arrived,' Zeraphina said. They knocked their staves together in greeting. Zeraphina glanced at Porthas. 'Come for a rematch, then, you great ox?'

Porthas laughed. 'Once was enough, my lady. I learned my lesson.'

Miska smiled and nodded to the statue. 'Did you pose for that?'

Zeraphina looked at it and frowned. 'No. Nor would I have, had they bothered to ask.' She shook her head. 'Ugly great thing. There's one for Knossus, as well.' She pitched her voice low. 'Waste of silver, in my opinion.'

'Do not judge them harshly, sister,' Miska said. 'They merely sought to honour your sacrifice.' She looked at the statue. 'I expect that it has brought great comfort to them, in times of need.'

'Perhaps,' Zeraphina said doubtfully. 'I'm told pilgrims come from across Lyria to pray before it.' She smiled sadly. 'I only wish that I could answer their prayers.'

'We can answer one at least, sister.' Miska looked at her. 'Come. Balthas and Knossus should be finished yelling at one another by now. They'll need our counsel, I expect. There is much that needs doing.'

Zeraphina laughed. 'Need? Yes. Will they listen? I'll not give odds on that.'

The three Stormcasts departed. Behind them, the devoted continued to pray, unaware that the object of their veneration had stood before them, only moments earlier.

CHAPTER THIRTEEN

INEVITABLE

SHYISH, THE REALM OF DEATH

Ayala turned, peering east. The wind brought with it a grave-chill, and the hint of a sour meat stink that was unpleasantly familiar. The old woman pulled her tatterdemalion robes tight about her, suddenly cold. Her hand fell to the curved knife sheathed on her hip. It was a good knife, blessed and edged with silver, but it made her feel no safer.

This was not a night for safety. No night was safe, not in Shyish. But this night especially – something felt wrong. Something had changed, though she didn't know what. A few days ago, the sky had twisted in on itself, and the ground had shuddered. Tremors weren't unknown in the desert, but never were they so forceful.

There was something coming. She felt it in her water, the way a sand-rat felt the shadow of a bird's wings. From close by, music rose towards the stars as her kith and kin held back the shadows with the old songs. They would be dancing too, around the fire, whirling so that their robes caught the light and made the air swim with reflected colour. Noise and colour – these were the strongest proofs against the dark.

'The wind in your bones, grandmother?' her granddaughter, Uskya, called out as she drew near. Ayala turned. Uskya was the image of her mother, Ayala's daughter, dead these past two turns of the season. The young woman was dark of eye and hair, with the slim build that characterised the Zirc. Her robes were of many colours, the same as Ayala's, the same as those worn by every nomad in the nine hundred tribes. 'Come back to the fire, we'll soon drive it out. Feytos has made dinner.'

'I know, child. Why do you think I'm out here?' Feytos, her other grandchild, was chieftain now, like his father before him. Among the Zirc, it was tradition that a chieftain prepare the evening meal. Unfortunately for all of them, Feytos was a terrible cook.

Ayala glanced back towards the quintet of towering wagon-fortresses that bore her tribe across the desert sands. The enormous conveyances resembled wheeled citadels, their frames studded with balconies, garrets and towers. Higher than all of these were great pipes of bronze. Thin streams of steam wafted from the pipes, signalling the cooling of the massive boilers that turned the wheels.

The wagon-fortresses were arranged in a rough circle about the gigantic bonfire that the nomads had started. Feeding the fire had taken more of their precious supply of wood than Ayala approved of. But if there was ever a night for it, this was it.

Uskya laughed and interlaced her arm with Ayala's. 'He is not that bad a cook, grandmother. And the meat is good – the best the Azyrites had.'

Ayala sniffed. 'The best they were willing to trade, you mean. They keep the best for themselves, always.' The traders at Fort Alenstahdt were shrewder than she liked. They made her brothers, sneak-thieves all, look like naïve children when it came to bargaining. All of the Azyrites were like that, though.

She looked up at the stars. They seemed so cold and remote, this night. The Zirc worshipped Sigmar, who wore the firmament as a nomad wore robes. The Azyrites claimed to worship him as well, though their golden man-god seemed nothing like the Wind-Walker she and her tribesfolk venerated.

The wind shifted, bringing with it the sound of moaning. Out in the dark, jackals began to yelp. Uskya shuddered. 'Deadwalkers,' she said.

Ayala nodded, eyes narrowed. 'And close.' The hungry dead roamed the desert in grave herds, usually only a few dozen, but sometimes numbering in the hundreds. She listened and heard the slow shuffle of feet across the sand.

'Getting closer,' Uskya added. She tugged on Ayala's arm. 'Come. Let us go back.'

Ayala resisted. She'd seen something – starlight, glinting off steel. 'There's something else out there. Do you hear it?' Like the rattle of war-plate, and the slow rasp of bone on bone. Her hand fell to the hilt of her knife.

The wind was howling now. Sand scraped her cheeks. Something – a man, perhaps – staggered over the top of the nearest dune, stumbled and fell. It rolled across the sand, leaving a wide trail. Uskya took a step towards it. 'Is he…?'

Ayala caught her wrist. 'No.'

The body flopped over and lurched upright with a crackle of strained ligaments. It gave a ghastly moan and sprang forwards, faster than Ayala expected. Usually, the dead were slow. But this one moved almost as quickly as a normal man. She jerked her granddaughter out of its path and reached for her knife. The corpse floundered into her, teeth gnashing.

As they fell, she saw more deadwalkers begin to stagger down the dunes. She fumbled at the dead man's face, trying to keep his teeth from her throat. Uskya appeared over the deadwalker's shoulder, her own knife in her hand. She drove her blade into the corpse's neck, trying to sever its brainstem. The corpse jerked, knocking her sprawling. It lurched half-up, eyes fixed on new prey.

Ayala slashed out, recapturing its attentions. Her blade ripped the dried flesh from its cheek, exposing bone. It turned with a groan and snapped at her. She felt a jolt of pain and jerked back. The corpse followed, and she slammed her knife into the rotting hole where its nose had been. Angling the blade, she sliced into what was left of its brain. Black ichor gushed over her hand, and the corpse toppled off her. She jerked her blade free and Uskya rushed to her, helping her to her feet. 'Hurry, grandmother, hurry! They are coming!'

Corpses shambled towards them, slower than the first, but not by much. And marching in their wake, skeletal forms, clad in rotting leather and tarnished armour.

Behind them, cries of alarm rose from the bonfire. Someone had finally noticed the dead. Something shrieked past, riding the night wind. Ayala looked up, as Uskya caught her uninjured arm. The old woman's eyes widened as she saw ghostly shapes, swooping down through the black, skimming past the stumbling corpses. They seemed to fill the sky, from end to end, like carrion birds drawn to the feast.

Her folk had many names for them. So too did the Azyrites. She shoved Uskya towards the wagons. 'The light, we must get into the light.' Uskya didn't argue. She had known what those shrieks heralded since childhood. All Zirc did.

The sands boiled behind them as they ran for the gap between wagon-fortresses, and the firelight beyond. Things cackled, just out of sight. Unseen hands tore at Uskya's robes, and Ayala turned, slashing the silver blade out. The cackling things retreated, but only for a moment. And the walking dead drew ever closer.

'Cold… so cold…' Uskya said, clutching at herself where the dead had gripped her. Ayala nodded.

'So are they,' she said. 'Hurry.' The glow of the bonfire washed over them. The camp was in an uproar. Men and woman huddled together, fearful of the things that spun like great moths or bats, just out of the glare of the light, while others ran for the wagons or slashed uselessly at the spirits. Shadow-shapes stretched across the sands, clutching at the inattentive. Nomads shouted and thrust spears or blades into the gauzy things, trying to pin them to the ground. The dead slipped away, only to return like nightmares.

'What is this, grandmother?' Uskya asked. 'Why is this happening?'

Ayala said nothing. Her kin raced about, gathering up what belongings they could, before hurrying to reach the safety of the wagon-fortresses. Steam belched from the copper pipes, as desperate crews stoked the boilers. Horns blew, and lanterns were lit, washing the sands with light. She saw her grandson, Feytos, bellowing orders to his kinsmen.

He wore his armour beneath his robes, as was habit with most of the men. He gestured with a silver sword, bought at great expense from some Azyrite merchant. 'Get to the wagons,' he roared. 'Full steam west. Make for Fort Alenstahdt!' He caught sight of them. 'There you are – quickly, get aboard.'

His eyes widened slightly as he noticed Ayala's wound, but before he could speak, something crashed down on him from above. It screamed like a water-panther as it landed, and Feytos died with its blade in his back.

The thing rose, jerking the blade free. It was like no dead man Ayala had ever seen: a thin, stretched shape, wrapped in black iron and grave shroud. Eyes like amethyst light blazed from within a shadowed helm, and the face that held them twisted and changed from that of a man to a fleshless rictus as she watched.

It took a step towards them, moving with an awkward, stuttering gait. It twitched and was suddenly closer. Every spasm brought it nearer. The world around her seemed to slow, and the night became as tar. She heard Uskya shouting, as if from a vast distance. But she could not look away. His eyes blazed brighter and brighter, drawing her in. The world closed about her and fell away.

And then the dead man was staring down at her.

Pharus stared down at the old woman, studying her. She gazed up at him, as if frozen. Everything seemed frozen, as around them, the dead went about their bloody work. The air was filled with screaming. Of the spirits that surrounded him, the chainrasps were the most numerous. Spiteful things, broken by Nagash's will, their forms dictated by the circumstances of their death, they filled the clearing amid the wagons in a dolorous tempest, whispering and wailing.

But there were others as well. Black-eyed dreadwardens, scythe-wielding reapers and glaive-bearing stalkers swooped and drifted among the panicking nomads, killing any who tried to resist or were too slow to reach the dubious safety of the wagons. Some of the nighthaunts served him, while others were bound to Malendrek.

The Knight of Shrouds was howling out his contempt nearby.

Malendrek had ridden his skeletal steed into the heart of one of the wagons, leading his ghostly horsemen in an orgy of bloodshed. Somewhere out in the desert, Grand Prince Yaros and Crelis Arul would be making their own way towards the slaughter, leading their forces.

A mass sigh ran through a knot of nearby chainrasps, and they scattered, revealing a hunched, broken shape, wrapped in a rusty shroud of keys and locks. The spirit's face was hidden beneath a helmet that might once have been in the shape of a dog's muzzle, or a bird's beak, and it wore a crude, rusting hauberk of scalloped plates. In its colourless hands, it gripped handfuls of chain, which flickered with nauseating energies.

Those chains, Pharus knew, could draw in a soul, and trap it. Fellgrip was a jailer of the dead. It was trailed by a coterie of lesser phantasms – its wardens. These spirits clustered about the hunched thing, whispering to it and lashing out at the other, lesser chainrasps with clubs and rusty axes, driving them away from their master.

'Fellgrip,' Pharus said. Fellgrip twitched its chains at the sound of his voice, and their rattling sent a shiver through Pharus' soul. The temptation to strike the Spirit Torment down was almost overwhelming – something about it unsettled him, and instilled in him a sense of terrible foreboding. It stared down at the old woman with malign intensity, and he extended his sword between them. 'Go. Collect the tithe. This one is mine.'

Fellgrip gave a disgruntled warble and drifted away, followed by its lackeys. Arkhan had bound the creature to him, somehow, as he had bound several other powerful spirits. Pharus turned back to his prey.

The old woman still stood as if frozen. Steam billowed, mingling with the smoke of the bonfire, enveloping them both. Several of the wagons were starting to move, their great wheels shaking the earth. Pharus reached out, almost gently, and caught the old woman by the throat. She barely struggled. There was a wound on her arm, and he could see the black strands of deadwalker poison spreading through the flickering light of her soul. A quick death would be a mercy for her.

He raised his blade. It yearned to taste her blood and flesh, and he yearned for it as well. To sup on the moment of her death, to take some of her warmth into himself. He was cold. So cold. So empty.

Something silver flashed out of the corner of his eye. He felt a blow and flung the old woman aside. The younger nomad stood before him, holding the silver sword of the man he'd killed. She darted past him, to the side of the old woman. 'I won't let you hurt her,' she shouted. Her voice echoed strangely, and he paused. Her face reminded him of another… younger, but with the same eyes, full of fear and determination…

…hurt her…

…won't let you hurt her…

He twitched the echo aside and raised his blade.

…the dead were everywhere in the streets, everywhere he turned…

…his halberd swept down, chopping through a door as dead hands caught at him…

'Elya,' he croaked. A name. Whose name?

…a small girl – Elya? – wailed as something from the grave clutched her to its bosom…

He stopped, sword raised. It was as if something held him fast.

…he had raised his lantern, and there was thunder…

He heard the hiss of a voice inside him.

Free them, Pharus. Life is a cage, and only the dead are truly free.

It was not the first time Pharus had heard that voice, since leaving Nagashizzar. It had been barely audible, at first. A soft murmuring. But it had grown louder, the farther they travelled from the Silent City. It spoke to him of what he must do, of the justice owed him. He could not ignore it, and so he listened.

Still, he hesitated. The words felt wrong, somehow.

Nagash freed you. Nagash will free them all. They will see, as you now see.

But the very notion seemed somehow antithetical to him. He shook his head, trying to clear it. A human gesture, more from instinct than need. The doubts fluttered like moths and receded. The sword felt heavy in his grip and slowly, he lowered it. The old woman, on her feet now, caught the younger by the hand and dragged her away from him. He did not move to stop them.

He caught sight of something that might have been the hint of a skull in the facets of his sword. Its gaze burned into him, and he shuddered as a sense of displeasure radiated through him. He tore his eyes away and turned, needing something… hungry for something…

'You hesitated.'

He spied a thin shape, stretched and too tall, wafting towards him, dragging a massive axe in its wake. Spirits hurried from its path, almost as quickly as they had made way for Fellgrip. The newcomer's face, half-hidden beneath a ragged hood, lacked definition, save where it was forced into shape by the mask of ashes and dried blood she wore. She smiled at Pharus, revealing blackened teeth.

'Why did you hesitate, my sweet lord? Even in life, I never hesitated.'

'It is not for you to question me, spirit,' Pharus snarled.

She bowed mockingly. 'Have you forgotten my name already, my lord? Shall I remind you? I am Rocha, my lord. Entyr Rocha, Lady of the Fourth Circle. In life, I was High Executioner of Helstone. In death, I am the axe in your hand. But speak, and I shall mete out justice to those who defy you.' She looked past him, in the direction the women had fled. 'Shall I hunt them down, lop off their heads and present them to you?' She lifted her axe, and Pharus saw that the blade had been stained black with blood.

'No,' he said. The air smelled of death. Bodies lay in heaps and piles. One of the wagons burned, and chainrasps cavorted in the flames, as nomads screamed. Deadwalkers and deathrattle warriors stalked through the haze of smoke, pursuing the living.

'The Mortarch of Sacrament bid me serve you,' Rocha hissed, drifting closer. 'He casts forth his hand, and a thousand gallows-ropes snap taut. A true lord, wise and mighty.' She peered at him. 'But you are not. Not yet. Light still flickers in you. I can taste it and – oh – it is a deceitful thing. It will lead you astray, that light.' She hesitated. 'I thought to grasp it, once. I was betrothed to a prince. A mighty prince.'

She trailed off, her gaze unfocused, lost in memories. The spirits that clung to her began to moan and wail, and her gaze sharpened once more. 'But he is gone, and I am here. I sent a thousand or more souls to face the Black Judge when I was alive, and many more since.' She ran a thumb along the pitted edge of her axe. 'It was my duty then, and my only pleasure now. As it should be yours.' Her voice was as harsh as a raven's caw. 'Rejoice, for you have found justice at last. The guilt of life is taken from you, and you are free.'

She shuddered slightly, and Pharus saw that the weak spirits were clutching at her arms and pulling at her hair. He could hear their voices clearly now – high, thin accusations and curses. She floated back to the slaughter, muttering to the gibbering spirits in resigned tones. He watched her go and felt a flicker of something – unease? Sympathy?

'Do not waste your sorrow upon her, my lord. Innocent blood stains her hands, and her crimes fill volumes in the Libraries of Mourning.'

Pharus turned. The spectre behind him was tall and clad in black burial robes. He wore a sword on his waist, its sheath tattered and the bare blade etched with dolorous sigils. His face was hidden behind an iron death-mask, such as those worn by the ancient folk of the Ghurdish Hills. The mask was a beast's head, complete with tusks and curling horns.

A suit of shattered armour hung from his starveling frame, and in one pale hand he clutched a staff, topped by an ancient lantern. Within the lantern, a shrivelled hand sat, each of its fingers topped by an eerie, green flame. The light of the creature's lantern was… warm. Comforting almost. Part of him longed to bask in it.

'Omphalo Dohl,' Pharus said. 'Come to chastise me as well?' Dohl was another servant, gifted to him by Arkhan.

'Not so, my lord. Never. I am but a humble shepherd of broken souls.' Dohl's voice was reminiscent of a funerary bell. Each word was like a portent of doom.

The nighthaunt drifted closer, and the light from his lantern washed across Pharus. The gnawing hunger and cold that had begun to build in him faded momentarily, and he sighed. 'That light – it reminds me of something else. I think… I think I used to carry such a light, once.'

He looked around. The battle – if it could be called that – was all but over. Deadwalkers crouched over unmoving forms, tearing mindlessly at the cooling flesh. Deathrattle stood silent and unmoving, awaiting commands. And the nighthaunts flocked like carrion birds to the high tiers of the fortress-wagons, hunting any who might still be hiding.

Dohl drifted closer. His eyes were black behind his mask. As pitiless as the void. But not malignant. Not evil. Merely… empty. 'It was taken from you, along with all that you were or could have been. You were denuded of your power and strength, and cast down by an uncaring god. Gaze into my light, if you would see the truth.'

Pharus looked away. 'I know the truth. Why would a god lie?'

'What is a lie but the shadow of a truth?' Dohl pulled his staff back, so that the light faded. Pharus grimaced. The hunger was back and worse than before. It clawed at his non-existent insides, and he felt ravenous. Not for meat or drink but for something else. He wanted to lash out. To tear open living flesh and draw out the screaming soul within.

'No,' he muttered. 'No. No, I do not want that.'

But he did. That need pulsed in him, loud and insistent. What right had the living to the pleasures now denied him? What right had they to the sun, to the breeze, to the touch of a loved one? Or even something so simple as the taste of an apple? Was it not just, then, to take such unearned and unappreciated privileges from them?

As if reading his thoughts, Dohl said, 'In death's shadow, all men are equal, in misery and reward. For the Undying King bestows blessings as well as curses. But only upon those who acknowledge his primacy.'

Pharus closed his eyes. But even then, he could see the light of Dohl's lantern. It was inescapable. 'He gave me my form,' he said softly. 'Remade me from nothing.'

He freed you from captivity. He will give you justice.

'Sigmar abandoned you,' Dohl said. 'Nagash saved you.'

As he will save all that is.

Pharus bowed his head. 'Yes.'

Dohl loomed close. 'I sense your doubt, my lord. It hangs heavy over you. Look into my lantern light, and your doubt will burn away. You will see the truth, and all doubt will be lifted from you.'

Pharus opened his eyes. He turned, ready to look, when a harsh laugh caught his attention. He whirled, and Dohl hissed in annoyance. 'Who dares–?'

'Only me, spirit. I come to confer with your master.'

Grand Prince Yaros stood looking down at the body of the man Pharus had killed, his axe cradled in the crook of one arm. His steed stood behind him, its rotting reins held by a skeletal servant. Yaros turned to look at Pharus. 'Your blade is barely wet, my friend.'

Pharus waved Dohl back and sheathed his sword. 'And yours is wet not at all.'

Yaros nodded. 'True. I have no interest in wanton slaughter. I am a warrior, not a butcher. As you are, I suspect.' He patted the blade of his axe fondly. 'I will contain my fury until we reach the walls of Glymmsforge. There, I shall drown the streets in blood.'

'Nagash will be pleased.'

'Perhaps,' Yaros said, in dry tones. 'For our lord and master, Glymmsforge is but an academic quandary. It is not a city to be humbled, but a symbol of Azyr. It is to be cracked asunder and no stone left atop another. He will send armies to do this, until it is done, and then his mind will turn elsewhere, to the next quandary. For him, the spheres.' He gestured about him. 'For us, the sand. And here we shall wage a war of liberation.' He pounded his chest-plate with a fleshless hand. 'Our soldiers merely wait for our call.'

'Soldiers?' Pharus asked, looking away from the wagons.

'There are armies undreamt, slumbering beneath these sands. It is my honour to awaken them, in the days to come. My task, as Malendrek has his, and you have yours.' Yaros gestured expansively with his axe. 'In my youth, there were a thousand oases in the Zircona Desert, and around each a kingdom sprouted.' He gave a rattling chuckle. 'They are gone now, alas, those grand fiefdoms. But the seeds they planted – the fallen heroes and soldiers of forgotten wars – yet remain, awaiting the call of one of royal blood.'

'You,' Pharus said.

Yaros gave a harsh laugh, like sand scraping stone. 'I am the son of kings, am I not? Did I not lead their descendants to glory at Akakis? Did I not pull down the citadels of the Wolf-Duke? Am I not the Hero of Orthad?'

Pharus, who could not recall ever hearing of those events, merely nodded. Yaros peered at him, witch-light flickering in the sockets of his skull. 'I am, my friend, as surely as you must be. We Deathlords are, all of us, heroes. Even Malendrek, for all that he is a spiteful shade.' He turned away. 'We are heroes,' he said again, and Pharus wondered if he too had a voice inside, whispering certainties.

The living fear you as the prisoner fears freedom.

'They fear us,' he said, echoing the voice.

'Of course they fear us, my friend. How could they not? We are lords of death.' Yaros glanced at him. 'You stand in august company, you know. Our names are legend, in the halls of twilight. Not Malendrek's perhaps, but mine certainly. And I am not alone.' He pointed his axe north. 'There, in the lands of ice and snow, the Rictus Queen rules a country of the dead. I pledged my troth to her, though she refused me.' Yaros loosed a doleful sigh. 'And Count Vathek, whose soul Nagash keeps locked away in an iron box. I rode beside him at the Battle of Lament. Him and a hundred others. Heroes, my friend. Heroes, all.'

Tools, the voice whispered in Pharus' ear. *Tools put to good use.*

'Why did you wish to speak to me?' Pharus said, growing tired of Yaros' rambling. The deathrattle prince seemed easily distracted.

Yaros laughed again. 'Why, to take the measure of you, little spirit. To see whether there is steel in you, or only spite.' He leaned close, almost conspiratorially. 'Malendrek says you stink of Azyr. And I can smell it on you.' He tapped Pharus' chestplate with his axe. 'There is an ember, smouldering inside you. But it grows smaller by the day. And soon it will be gone entirely, and you will be one of us.'

Pharus drifted back, and Yaros turned. His servant sank down, and Yaros used the skeleton as a step-stool to climb into the saddle. He hauled back on the reins, causing the fleshless horse to rear silently. 'Be of good cheer, my friend – death is the end of strife, and your course is set,' he called out, as he turned his steed about and galloped away to join his warriors. The skeletal servant trotted after him.

Pharus watched him ride away, and then turned to Dohl, who hovered nearby. 'How many wagons escaped?'

'Three, my lord. Should we pursue?'

'In time,' he said distantly. There was no escape. No matter how far they went, or where they hid, they would all come to Nagash, in time.

It is inevitable. You are inevitable.

He glanced down at his blade and saw again the hint of a skull, leering at him from within its depths.

The living are weak. They know fear and doubt. It is a burden on them.

'Life is a burden,' Pharus said.

Life is a cage. In death are all slaves freed. All are one in Nagash.

Pharus paused. His hand fell to the hilt of his blade. He could feel the sands shivering through the hourglass there. 'And Nagash is all,' he said finally.

CHAPTER FOURTEEN

INVIOLATE

FREE CITY OF GLYMMSFORGE

'Welcome to the Gloaming,' Lord-Veritant Achillus said.

Balthas looked around, unimpressed. His surroundings put him in mind of a honeycomb, perforated by courtyards and blind alleys. He saw wretched structures with broken windows patched over with rag-and-board, dirt-smeared walls and rotting foundations. A canopy of crude bridges and gantries stretched above the street, from one side to the other. The sounds of singing, fighting, squabbling and screaming echoed all about him. 'It's a slum,' he said.

'Yes. And a large one.' The lord-veritant stopped, as something crashed down on the street ahead. Balthas glanced up and saw a head vanish inside an open window. Shouts and curses echoed down from other windows, and rooftops. The city was in uproar. Not fully fledged panic, yet. But tensions were high. The Glymmsmen were stretched thin, handling the influx of new people to the city, all of whom brought with them tales of the dead.

In the wake of the cataclysm, it was too much. Flagellants roamed the streets, howling prayers. The citizens, inured to siege mentality, resignedly readied themselves for another assault. But this was different, and they knew it – for the enemy was already here.

More things – bricks – crashed down. People ran along the rooftops, shouting warnings. Balthas glanced back at the cohorts of Sequitors and Castigators following in his wake. They had orders to ignore such provocation, where possible.

'They seem unhappy with our presence,' Mara said. The Sequitor-Prime looked around, her gaze sharp behind her war-mask. She was not used to this, Balthas knew. The enemy was normally in front of them and clearly defined.

'It is rare that we bring glad tidings,' Achillus said. He raised his staff, and the lantern atop it flashed. 'Especially to the Gloaming.' As the light washed across the nearby storefronts and walkways, the catcallers above fell silent. 'But they know me, here. And they know not to cross me.'

'How many times have you had to do this?' Balthas asked.

Achillus shrugged. 'Enough to know that it is never simple.' He paused. 'Shyish is not simple. The dead are too close, here. Their whispers are shouts, and some among the living are too willing to listen.'

'This is not the same thing. Deadwalkers are more akin to a pox than anything else.'

'I know what deadwalkers are, lord-arcanum,' Achillus said bluntly. 'I have fought them since the first stones of Glymmsforge were set.' The light from his lantern drove back the shadows and revealed huddled beggars in alleyways and cats slinking through gutters. Pigeons burst into flight, startled by the radiance. And something else – a warmer glow, like a current of hot air, tinged with amethyst. 'This way.'

'You have the trail?' Balthas asked, following the lord-veritant down the street. They'd come into the Gloaming seeking several individuals who'd escaped a riot elsewhere in the city. A deadwalker had been involved – a trader from Gravewild, Balthas had been told. The creature had bitten several others, before it had been put down. Not all of the injured had been caught before they slipped away.

Achillus didn't reply. Balthas frowned in annoyance. He did not require companionability in an ally, but Achillus seemed disinclined to give him the respect his position warranted. He wondered if this were some jest of Knossus', to assign him so surly a liaison. His Sacrosanct Chamber, along with Knossus', was scattered across the city, investigating a thousand and one problematic incidents.

The dead no longer rested easy in Glymmsforge, and the fear in the streets grew stronger hour by hour. Deadwalkers haunted the slums, as ghostly shapes loped along isolated streets. A colony of great bats had descended upon a private park, in the inner ring of the city, and drained the life from the scions of a noble family. Undead street curs hunted cats in the back alleys, and phantom fires danced across the rooftops.

But so far, the city held. Balthas had to admit, if grudgingly, that this was mostly due to Knossus' efforts. The other lord-arcanum was everywhere, fighting to hold together the fragile calm. His warriors walked the streets alongside the city's defenders, and carried hope with them. It wouldn't last, but for the moment, Glymmsforge stood inviolate.

'There,' Achillus said, loudly.

Balthas looked up. The tenement was a tottering pile of wood and stone with a slanted roof and haphazardly arranged chimneys. Rickety steps climbed up the sides, and crude gantries of wood and rope connected the building to those on either side, as well as one directly across the street. Washing lines stretched beneath these paths, and sodden clothes hung dripping from the highest. The doors and windows were seemingly boarded over from the inside, as if the inhabitants were afraid of someone getting in.

There was a smell on the air – subtle and foul. To Balthas' storm-sight, the structure was bathed in a dark, amethyst radiance. Soulfire flickered somewhere inside. 'Yes,' he said. The magics he sensed were savage things – wilder than they should have been, and more potent. It was as if the winds of magic had grown stronger following the necroquake. But that was a problem for another time.

He turned to his Sequitors. 'Mara, your cohort will enter the building with us.' Mara nodded and turned, barking orders to her Sequitors. Balthas glanced at the Castigator-Prime. 'Quintus, take your warriors and block off the surrounding streets. Nothing gets out, unless I say otherwise.'

'As you will it, my lord,' Quintus said, and genuflected. The Castigator-Prime gestured and his cohort scattered, two warriors to each street and side-passage. Balthas nodded in satisfaction and looked at Achillus.

'You are certain of this, brother?'

'I am.' Achillus studied the doorway. 'Several of the injured fled the attack. They might turn, if they haven't already. If the curse spreads, this city will face a war on two fronts. The deadwalkers will scatter, and every new death will only feed their number.'

'And if they are not gripped by this curse?'

Achillus said nothing. Balthas looked at the building. 'A graceless structure,' he said.

'Function over form,' Achillus said. He started forwards. Balthas fell into step with him. Mara and her warriors followed them, the clank of their armour loud in the quiet. Achillus drew his blade and shattered the boards blocking the doorway. A thick stink washed out over them.

Crossbow bolts splintered on Achillus' chest-plate. He looked down, and then up. 'That was foolish,' he said solemnly. Then, he was through the doorway, blade singing out. Balthas followed him, staff held low. He saw Achillus cleave a mortal in two, and another standing at the top of a set of stairs, hastily reloading his crossbow. The man was a bravo, clad in rattletrap gear and bearing the scars of a life lived on the wrong side of Azyr's law. Balthas saw the story of him at a single glance and chose a fitting end.

He gestured, drawing the skeins of aether tight, and the second crossbowman screamed as his form stiffened and became stone. The newly made statue rocked slightly and then toppled from the top of the steps to crash into the floor below. Achillus glanced at him and nodded. 'Well done.'

'It lacked subtlety,' Balthas said. He looked around. Cheap lanterns hung from the walls. The bottom floor of the structure had been broken open, revealing the cellars below. Planks of wood crossed the hole like makeshift bridges. From below, he heard a dull moaning, muffled by the confines of the cellars.

Sequitors pounded past him, assuming defensive positions. He stepped to the edge of the hole and peered down. Deadwalkers shuffled aimlessly in the great pit below. Some scratched at the walls, while others gnawed on their own flesh. Many were old things, dried to sticks and covered in decades of filth. Others were fresh – their wounds only hours old, if that. 'What is this?' he said.

'A plague pit,' a voice said, from above. 'Or it was.'

A man clad in thin, patched robes, stepped onto the landing above, accompanied by several warriors who had the look of sellswords. They looked distinctly unhappy about the situation, unlike their employer. He had a thin, haunted look, and the ghost of a smile passed over his face. 'I spent months, digging through records and reports, until I found it. You burned it, once. I suspect it looks different now. But they were still here, buried in the dark. Truly, the dead are persistent.'

Achillus glanced at Balthas. 'I thought this place looked familiar.'

Balthas shook his head. 'Not all of those corpses are old.' The man was mad. Worse, his soul was a tattered sack, leaking a sickening amethyst light. Balthas had fought sorcerers steeped in death-magic before, and began to draw strands of aether tight, readying himself.

'Fresh ingredients, gathered by my… aides,' the necromancer said, gesturing to the sellswords. 'They were infected, you know. They would have turned, regardless. This way, they shall serve a greater purpose. They shall be tools of war, rather than mindless beasts.' He glanced at one of the bravos. 'Deal with them.'

The man, scarred and missing an ear, goggled. 'What?'

'I'm paying you to ensure that my studies are not interrupted, am I not?' The necromancer gestured. 'Kill them.'

'But they… they're…' the bravo began.

The necromancer sighed. 'Fine. I'll do it myself.' He raised a hand. Achillus lunged for the steps, as Balthas felt the aether quaver. Sickly green flame speared through the gathered sellswords, slaying them instantly. As they fell, the necromancer spun and flung out a hand. He spat a single, deplorable word that echoed like a cemetery bell.

From the cellar, the dead answered. Swiftly, more swiftly than seemed possible, the deadwalkers began to climb, one atop the next, scrambling over the lip of the pit with bestial agility. They rushed towards the Sequitors, slavering and snarling.

Balthas turned. 'Mara – look to the pit. Leave the necromancer to Achillus and me.' The Sequitors braced themselves, and Mara set herself between the deadwalkers and the doorway. Stormsmite mauls thudded down, pulping flesh and bone, as crumbling hands scraped against soulshields. Satisfied they would keep the dead corralled, Balthas turned back to the steps.

Achillus was already halfway up. The necromancer was chanting. The bodies of his sellswords twitched and rose, but not to attack the approaching lord-veritant. Instead, the dead slumped over the necromancer, intertwining their broken limbs.

Amethyst light danced across them, and flesh ran like wax, until one body bled into the next. The necromancer rose up, borne aloft on the hands and feet of the dead. Skulls cracked open and stretched over the necromancer's head, forming a hood of bone and hair. The bodies had become akin to a twitching, steaming suit of war-plate, crafted from meat rather than metal.

'Nagash calls and his faithful answer,' the mortal shrieked. 'When he reaches out, it is with a thousand hands. When he speaks, it is with a thousand voices. Hear the word of Nagash – hail Nagash! Hail the Undying King!'

The conglomeration took a plodding step forwards, towards the edge of the landing. Floorboards bent beneath its grotesque weight. The mortal swung out a hand, entombed within a number of others, creating a massive paw with hundreds of writhing fingers. The hand slammed into Achillus as he reached the top step, and there was a spark of azure light. The lord-veritant was sent tumbling down the steps, cursing the entire way.

The necromancer followed, shattering the steps as he descended, one great paw gouging apart the wall alongside him. A massive knot of fists barrelled down. Achillus rolled aside and scrambled to his feet. The necromancer heaved himself around in pursuit. 'I will crack open your shell and offer up your soul to Nagash,' he screamed.

'No. You will not.' Balthas stepped quickly between them, his staff raised. The conglomeration lurched forwards and grappled him. It was stronger than it looked. Faster. But Balthas held it at bay.

The necromancer snarled at him, baring rotten teeth. 'Stand not between the Undying King and his kingdom!' Balthas felt a preternatural chill slither through him at the words. He caught hold of the skull-and-scalp helmet, and felt the pulse of its wearer's twisted soul. It was like broken shards of black glass, biting into his palm. The necromancer had used what was left of his own soul to weave together his grisly war-plate – the binding spell was a thing of brute force and crude edges, lacking in any subtlety. It was easy enough to find the loose strands of magic and tug apart the knot holding it all together.

As Balthas unravelled the spell, he felt the mortal's soul twitch and flutter in his grasp. Panic rose in the necromancer's gaze, and he thrashed, trying to free himself. Balthas held fast, however, and the mortal could not pull away. 'N-no, no you cannot...' the necromancer whined. 'I was promised justice – justice against those who hounded me.'

'Is this justice, then?' Balthas said. The first flap of flesh-plate peeled away from the whole. More followed, with a hideous sucking sound. 'This abomination? If you think so, you are as broken as these husks.' Broken limbs and meat sloughed away all at once, leaving the necromancer dangling in Balthas' grip. He shook the pathetic creature. 'Answer me.'

The necromancer cursed and clawed at his forearm. Dark strands of aether tightened about his crooked fingers. Balthas saw the spell forming before the mortal spoke. He squeezed, cutting off the necromancer's air. The mortal gasped, and the spell turned to ash on the air. Disgusted, Balthas tossed him aside.

The necromancer clambered to his knees, wheezing. 'You… you are too late,' he coughed. 'The dead outnumber the living. And the lords of death march upon you. They are coming, and all who are imprisoned shall be freed by–' He was silenced by Achillus' blade, as it parted his head from his neck. Balthas looked down at the decapitated body as it twitched in its death throes.

'He was no threat,' he said, after a moment.

'Not to us,' Achillus said, glancing meaningfully at the bodies in the pit. He took down one of the lanterns hanging on the wall and cast it down, where the dead lay thickest. The cheap salamander oil spread quickly, carrying a trail of flame.

'Come, brother,' Achillus said, stepping over the flames. 'The shadows lengthen and other tasks await us.'

'Whatever else comes, we must hold the Shimmerway,' Lynos Gravewalker said. 'If our route to the Shimmergate is compromised, there will be no retreat.'

'I thought the Anvils of the Heldenhammer never retreated,' Orius Adamantine said, smiling slightly. The two lords-celestant stood atop the Mere-Wall, overlooking the Glass Mere and the hundreds of thriving fish farms that clung to the shore, and the villages that spread along and up the sides of the wall like barnacles.

Meeting here had become something of a tradition for the

two. It was quieter here than along the outer walls. Fewer soldiers, fewer people making their way from one section of the city to the next. Fewer distractions. And something about the smell of fish and the sound of water lapping against the shore put Lynos in a contemplative frame of mind. One more conducive to the discussion of strategy.

Birds cried out raucously as they circled the freshwater lake, and Lynos could hear the shouts of fishermen as they went about the business of the day. They seemed to have no idea of what was coming. No understanding of the tensions that gripped the city. Or perhaps, they simply didn't care. Even with war on the horizon and the city in upheaval, fishmongers needed fish and fishermen needed coin. Was that bravery, he wondered, or foolishness? He looked at his fellow lord-celestant. 'We prefer not to retreat, on the whole. But sometimes it is unavoidable. Besides which, who are you to talk of such things?'

Orius laughed. The Adamantines had a similar reputation for stubbornness in the face of long odds. 'True. But you are right, brother. We must ensure that the city's main artery remains in our hands.' He frowned. 'I do not like to think of the armies of the dead spilling into Azyr. Or of what slumbers beneath us waking up.'

Lynos bowed his head. 'Were Pharus with us, I would have no fear of that.' He shook his head and looked up at the dark sky. Clouds covered the sun, and what little light managed to get through was weak and muddy. 'But he is not, and we must press on, regardless.' Despite his words, it felt wrong, going into battle without his lord-castellant. Pharus was the rock upon which the Gravewalkers stood. Without him, everything felt off-kilter somehow. He took a deep breath and pushed the thought aside. 'Another debt added to Nagash's tally,' Lynos rumbled. 'Like Makvar, at Gothizzar. He fell, waiting for aid that never came.'

'And has born enmity for the dead ever since,' Orius finished. 'Yes, you've told me this tale before, Lynos. I've fought alongside Makvar – I know his anger as well as I know my own. Or yours, come to that.' He shook his head. 'This is different. Nagash played Makvar false, but did not openly move against him. The same when the Shadowed Soul invaded his demesnes thirty years ago on his ill-fated expedition – then, too, Nagash ceded the field rather than risk open war.'

'Something has changed,' Lynos said, nodding. 'The air tastes different. Feels different. As if the game has changed.'

'We have relied on the Undying King being, if not an ally, then the enemy of our enemy. If he moves against us, things become less certain. Nagash is a different sort of foe to the servants of the Ruinous Powers, or the orruks.' Orius looked down into the waters of the Glass Mere, as if seeking his reflection. From this high up, and in the weak light, Lynos knew that even his eyes would discern nothing save stretches of dark on dark. 'And we face a different sort of war. One I fear that we are not prepared for.'

'And there you would be wrong, brothers,' Knossus Heavensen called out as he approached, his helmet under one arm. 'Sigmar foresaw this moment the day Tarsus Bull-Heart failed to return from Stygxx, and his Warrior Chamber came back in pieces. We of the Sacrosanct Chamber have been raised up to face that which is coming. It is our sacred duty, and now Glymmsforge is protected by, not one, but two such chambers.'

'Which can only mean that Sigmar foresees this city enduring the brunt of whatever is coming,' Lynos said flatly. It had been almost a week since the second Sacrosanct Chamber – this one bearing the colours of his own Stormhost – had arrived.

As yet, the lord-arcanum – Balthas, Lynos thought he was called – had avoided him. He suspected he knew why. Pharus had not yet been reforged. In fact, none of those who'd died in the necroquake had.

One way or another, Lynos intended to bring the lord-arcanum to task and get some answers. Orius nudged him. 'Smoke,' the other lord-celestant said. He pointed. 'The northern district.'

'The Fane of Nagash-Morr,' Knossus said, without looking.

Lynos peered in the direction of the smoke. 'I thought it sealed not long after the cataclysm. Has some fool attempted to reopen it?'

'Not fools. Worshippers. Mortals who believe in the lie of Nagash's benevolence. They seek his protection from the dead.' Knossus sighed. 'Perhaps for them, there is safety there. But the Undying King is our enemy, and he can be allowed no foothold, however benign, in this city. I ordered Lord-Veritant Achillus and Lord-Arcanum Balthas to clear it, and bring the temple down, stone by stone.'

'I should have been there,' Lynos growled. He felt a pulse of frustration. This was his city, when all was said and done. The responsibility was his.

Knossus looked at him. 'You cannot be everywhere, brother. The deed is done, or soon will be.' He sighed and looked out over the Mere. 'I forgot… I forgot how beautiful it was.' He spoke so softly, Lynos almost didn't hear him. Then he sighed again and turned. 'Come. I came to collect you both. It is time to hold what might be our final council of war, before things reach the end.'

'Is it so close, then?' Orius asked, looking towards the desert. The horizon had grown steadily darker as the days passed, and the nights seemed longer.

'Closer than we know,' Knossus said, solemnly. 'Come, brothers. The others will be waiting. We must ready Glymmsforge for war.'

'I dislike burning temples, brother,' Balthas said, as he and Lord-Veritant Achillus climbed the stone steps to the council chambers of the stormkeep. The fortress of the Anvils of the Heldenhammer crouched at the city's heart, within sight of the Shimmergate. It was a squat, black edifice, built for chilly efficiency rather than grandeur. Balthas approved.

There had been more to do, after the necromancer's death. The tasks seemed endless. Mystic wards to be strengthened and places of ill-repute searched. Ghosts to lay and bodies to burn in cleansing fire.

'Even ones devoted to Nagash?' Achillus asked, not harshly. He had become less surly after the battle with the necromancer. Not friendly… but tolerable.

'They were doing no harm to any but themselves.' Balthas shook his head. 'Also, I mourn the loss of their libraries – those who spend their time in the company of the dead have long memories, and keep good records.'

'They will rebuild,' Achillus said. 'They always do.' He sighed. 'Peaceful as the adherents of Nagash-Morr are, they are still a warrior-cult, and dedicated to a god we are now at war with. Sooner or later, they would have made the wrong choice.'

'To serve their god, you mean?' He thought of the mortals, standing disconsolate as their place of worship was erased in mystic fire. They had not resisted – indeed, they seemed to have expected it. The priests, in their amethyst robes and with their faces painted in ash and dust, had calmed the crowd. They had spoken of inevitability and acceptance. Of how all things died, and death was not the end.

'To make war on ours,' Achillus said. He looked at Balthas. 'You are new here, lord-arcanum. You do not understand the ways of Shyish. The ebb and flow of this realm is unlike any other. This is the realm of a god who – at his *best* – is inimical to all that we represent. We cannot allow him a foothold here, in this enclave of Azyr. Not now. Perhaps not ever again.'

'You say that as if you think this war will end with the status quo restored,' Balthas said. 'Nagash has upended the status quo. Things will never be the same.'

'All the more reason to burn his fanes and scatter his worshippers, then.' Achillus stopped, one step above Balthas. 'This is the red edge of the frontier, Balthas. Here, the influence of our god wanes as another grows. We do what we can to shine Azyr's light here, but some shadows are too persistent, even for us.' He gestured to the lantern atop his staff, its soft blue radiance washing over the stones around them.

Balthas stared into that light for a moment. Then he looked away. 'You are correct, of course. The thought of all that knowledge – going up in smoke...'

Achillus snorted. 'If you think they allowed us to destroy anything of any real value, then you are not half the sage people claim.' He turned and began to ascend once more. 'I've burned that temple eight times in the past eighty years, brother. They keep rebuilding it. And they invite me to the first service they hold, each time.'

Balthas paused. 'Do you go?'

'Every time.' Achillus laughed. A moment later, Balthas joined him.

The council chambers rested at the heart of the stormkeep. A circular space, it was dominated by a map of the city. The map was the height of a man, and nearly as long as the wall to which it was affixed, showing every alleyway and beggar's gate in Glymmsforge.

It had been drawn with a care and precision beyond that of any human cartographer. Only duardin draftsmen were so precise, for all that they disliked the use of such ephemeral materials. Their mapmakers preferred metal and stone to ink and parchment. Similar maps stretched nearby. One was of the known regions of the underworld of Lyria, while the other was of the Zircona Desert and the outposts along the Great Lyrian Road.

There was no table, no chairs. A rough-hewn bench occupied one wall, and a number of stools were scattered about, for the use of mortals. A few ragged battle-banners covered what the maps didn't, and other trophies hung here and there – skulls taken from great beasts, mostly. By and large, the Anvils of the Heldenhammer put little stock in trophies.

Flickering storm-lanterns hung from the rafters, casting a cerulean light over the chamber. Balthas saw the two lords-celestant, Lynos Gravewalker of the Anvils of the Heldenhammer, and Orius Adamantine of the Hammers of Sigmar, studying the map closely and conferring in low tones with a mortal soldier, wearing the mauve and black of the Glymmsmen. The Freeguilder held a war-helm, wrought in the shape of a skull, beneath one arm, and his close-cropped hair was crimson.

'Varo Tyrmane, Lord-Captain of the Glymmsmen,' Achillus said, softly. He indicated a burly duardin sitting perched on a stool nearby. 'And that's Grom Juddsson, representative of the Riven Clans.' Juddsson was clad in rich robes and fine war-plate, and his beard was oiled and curled into tight ringlets, threaded with silver. He stared pensively at the map, gnawing on the stem of a pipe.

Tyrmane and Juddsson weren't the only mortals present. A representative of the Collegiate Arcane, clad in fine purple robes, stood off to the side, murmuring instructions to the bevy of scribes surrounding her. A group of Freeguild officers, wearing the uniforms of several regiments other than the Glymmsmen, spoke quietly in one corner.

Balthas recognised some of them – a captain of the Silver Company, out of Chamon, with his pristine white doublet and polished armour; a line-sergeant of the Ironsides, a gun-company normally contracted by the Ironweld Arsenal; and a *boyr* of the Sons of the Black Bear, a lance of knights from the northern baronies of Azyr. The knight was the biggest of the three, his bearskin cloak making him seem massive next to the others.

Achillus went to speak with Knossus, who stood conferring with the representative of the Collegiate Arcane and his Knight-Incantor, Zeraphina. Balthas stood, slightly ill at ease in this gathering of strangers. He wished he hadn't left Miska to oversee the deconstruction of the temple, but someone had needed to ensure that the fires didn't spread.

He felt, rather than saw, someone approach. 'You have been avoiding me, lord-arcanum.' The voice was stern and somewhat morose.

Balthas sighed and turned to face Lynos Gravewalker. The lord-celestant was a sombre titan, as befitted one who had spent much of the past century seeing that the dead rested easy in their tombs. From what Balthas knew of him, he knew better than most the dangers of Shyish, and had a keen mind for one whose whole purpose was war. 'I assure you that I have not, lord-celestant,' he said. A lie, but a kind one. 'Circumstances have prevented me from making a proper introduction, for which you have my apologies.'

'They tell me that Pharus has not been reforged.'

Balthas looked at him. 'Who says this?'

Lynos shrugged. 'The aether speaks. I listen.' He frowned. 'Is it true?'

Balthas studied the map. 'It is as Sigmar wills.'

'That is not an answer, lord-arcanum.'

'No. It is not.' Balthas sighed. 'There were... complications.'

'Tell me,' Lynos growled.

'His soul was... lost during the necroquake.'

'Lost?' Lynos ran his hand through his hair. 'Lost.' He looked away. 'Pharus was my shield. The rock upon which I built my strategies. And now he is gone. I feel as though I have lost my hand.'

Balthas hesitated. He reached out, some half-formed thought of comforting the lord-celestant on his mind. But he pulled his hand back at the last moment. Lynos would not thank him. For all the lord-celestant knew, Balthas had been forced to destroy Pharus. Instead, he stared at the map, analysing the city, noting its weaknesses and strengths.

Glymmsforge had grown from humble beginnings. A rough palisade, erected around the Shimmergate had been reinforced time and again over the course of five decades, expanding into a dozen concentric rings of stone. Man, duardin and aelf had worked as one, to erect a monument to civilisation amid the wilderness.

His eyes slid across the map. The bulk of the city, as well as a vast freshwater lake known as the Glass Mere, was confined within the innermost rings. The outer rings formed a defensive network that had been refined over decades. But the city's most powerful defences were not its high walls and batteries of cannons.

Every brick in every wall had been blessed, or else marked by holy sigils. The bones of common saints were interred in every market square and byway. The districts of the city spread outwards from the temples of the gods – not just Sigmar, though his were the most prominent. In the Dweomervale, in the city's southern district, a basalt shrine to Malerion crouched amid gloomy streets. In the Lyrian Souk, a vine-shrouded sanctuary to Alarielle, the Everqueen, spread living branches over the rooftops. There were others.

The largest was the Grand Tempestus – an imposing edifice of stone, built by the first devoted to set foot in Glymmsforge. It rested at the heart of the original city and had grown as Glymmsforge grew – from rough palisade chapel to a veritable fortress of faith.

These temples radiated an aura that made it difficult for the dead and the damned to gain a foothold in the city. It was cleverly done. Balthas traced the ley lines – the currents of celestial power – running through the city. 'Like a spirit trap, writ large,' he murmured. 'Who built it, I wonder?'

'My ancestor,' Knossus said, from behind him. 'Or, rather, the ancestor of the man I was. He built the city. Designed it. And the generations that followed built on his work.'

Balthas glanced at him. 'He knew of the Ten Thousand Tombs?'

Knossus nodded. 'Parts of the city were built with them in mind. The Grand Tempestus lies over the only stable entrance into the catacombs below. All of the others were found and sealed by the Anvils of the Heldenhammer, over the years.'

'Wise. And now you've sealed the final entrance.' Balthas tapped the map with his staff. 'Even so – is it guarded?'

'It is. A cohort of Liberators – specially chosen – ward the Grand Tempestus.'

'Is that enough?'

Knossus smiled sadly. 'I suspect not. But we will come to that in a moment.' He struck the floor with the ferrule of his staff. 'Friends, let us begin.' He looked around, as all eyes turned towards him. 'There is a storm on the horizon. We can all feel it. All who live in Glymmsforge can feel it. From the highest seat on the city's conclave, to the meanest beggar in the Lyrian Souk. Shyish is in upheaval. The hills rise wild, and the dead rise with them. They will come to Glymmsforge, if they are not already on the way here.'

'You are certain then?' the duardin, Juddsson, growled.

'We have the word of refugees flooding the city. The Zirc nomads are circling their fortress-wagons around their oases, and we have lost contact with more outposts than I care to consider – all along the Great Lyrian Road. As it stands, only Fort Alenstahdt is still sending regular reports.' Knossus indicated the desert map. 'And those reports are dire indeed – deadwalker herds massing in the dunes, and men going missing in the night.'

Balthas peered at the map. Fort Alenstahdt was only a few days' travel from Glymmsforge. If the enemy were on the move towards the city, following the road, Fort Alenstahdt would fall right in the likely path of attack.

'None of that is what I'd call hard evidence,' Juddsson said. 'The deadwalkers are always massing, and men always go missing.'

'The aether is alive with malign portents, Master Juddsson,' the representative from the Collegiate Arcane said. 'Even your own runelords must have some concerns.'

'Aye, but it's always best to confirm such things, Lady Aelhad,' the duardin said, gesturing at her with the stem of his pipe. 'Manlings have been known to panic over a change in the weather. No disrespect intended.'

'It's more than the weather, Grom, and you know it,' Tyrmane said, flatly. 'Don't think we don't know that the Riven Clans have been quietly sealing off their tunnels from the rest of the city. If there's panicking, your folk are the ones doing it.'

Juddsson peered at Tyrmane. 'There's a difference between being sensible, and losing your head over a few deadwalkers, Varo.' He smiled thinly. 'In any event, it's not our tunnels you should be worrying about. My folk have been hearing things from those Grungni-be-damned catacombs. Sounds like this storm of yours is already here, and raging beneath our feet.' He looked at Knossus. 'Then, that's why you're here, eh?'

'I am here to ensure that Glymmsforge stands,' Knossus said. 'Whatever comes, the city will weather it. That is my oath, Grom Juddsson. What about you?'

The duardin sat back and tugged at his beard. He looked away, frowning. 'This is our ground, now. We'll hold it, come fire or foe.'

'We shall do it together,' Knossus said. Juddsson glanced at him and, after a moment, nodded tersely. Balthas watched the exchange admiringly. He'd seen similar confrontations several times over the course of the week. He was forced to admit that Knossus was skilled in the art of politesse. Without him playing peacemaker, the city's defenders might well have done Nagash's work for him.

'If the enemy comes, why should we have to do anything, save sit behind these walls and pepper them with silver shot?' the Ironsides sergeant grunted. 'I was under the impression this city was impregnable.'

'No city is impregnable,' Orius said. 'Some are simply more difficult to get into than others.' He glanced at Lynos, who nodded with some reluctance.

'It's true. The city has been besieged before. Our walls are high and thick, but the dead are relentless and do not tire. They will come again and again, until they succeed or we destroy them to the last corpse and banish the last spirit.'

'This city possesses some defence against the dead other than walls,' Balthas said, gesturing to the map. 'I noticed the great channels of silver that circumnavigate the districts, and the purple salt that fills it.' The channels were marked on the map, and they formed a precise circle of many lines, stretching across the city and encompassing each district in turn. Despite its seemingly continuous nature, the circle was broken in twelve places. 'What do these points mark?'

'The Twelve Saints,' Knossus said, as he laid a hand flat against the map. 'The mausoleum gates they are interred within form the extremities of a star of protection about the city. They are at once our strongest points and our weakest. Only the most powerful of spirits can endure the celestial energies radiating from those sacred bones.' He frowned. 'If they are to truly take the city, they would need to destroy as many as they can and breach the wards keeping Glymmsforge sacrosanct.'

'If they're smart, they'll focus only on a handful,' Lynos said. 'Three, maybe four. Once they've forced a wedge in our defences, they could flood the city.'

Knossus nodded. 'Yes. The question before us is which ones?'

'We cannot defend them all.' Balthas studied the map. 'We lack the numbers.' He indicated the concentric walls. 'Perhaps we should pull back to the inner walls. Conduct a defence in depth, rather than a more conventional stratagem.'

'Is he insulting us?' Orius murmured to Lynos, loud enough for Balthas to hear.

'Not intentionally, I suspect,' Lynos said.

Balthas frowned. 'This city has defences, does it not? Runnel networks to pour blessed lead down on the enemy, and more besides. Evacuate the outer city, close the portcullises and use the time to reinforce the inner walls.'

'We'd be sacrificing a third of the city,' Orius said.

'To save the rest,' Balthas said. 'Surely that is an acceptable trade?'

'And what of those who live there? We cannot evacuate them all on short notice,' Varo Tyrmane said. The mortal did not sound opposed to the idea, so much as curious. 'Their deaths will only add to the enemy's numbers.'

'We could begin the evacuation now,' Balthas said.

'And we'd have a full-scale panic on our hands a few hours later,' the Silver Company captain said. 'The citizenry are on edge. Attacks by the dead have been on the increase for days. If it starts to look like we're abandoning half the city, the situation will become untenable.'

Balthas shook his head in annoyance. He thought of the necromancer's words. What did a lunatic like that know that they didn't? 'It is already untenable. The enemy *is* coming. We cannot simply do nothing and hope for victory. Even high walls and sacred circles can only do so much...' He trailed off and looked at the map again. 'But they do enough.'

'Brother – what is it?' Knossus asked.

'We have been asking the wrong question,' Balthas said, leaning towards the map, trying to see what it didn't show. 'Too focused on the where and when, but not the why.'

Knossus looked at him. 'What do you mean, brother?'

'If this city is inviolate, why bother attacking? Nagash is not some blood-mad warlord, seeking to impress the Ruinous Powers. He never does anything without purpose. If the dead are mustering, then there is a flaw in our defences. One we are not seeing.' Balthas turned. A murmur swept through the others, at this. Knossus looked at the map.

'I hope you are wrong, brother. But I fear that you are not.'

CHAPTER FIFTEEN

THE FALL OF FORT ALENSTAHDT

FORT ALENSTAHDT, THE GREAT LYRIAN ROAD

Juvius Thrawl wrapped his scarf about his face and flung the door to the station office open. Purple sand, cast into the air by the wind, scraped against his exposed flesh as he hurried towards the walls. The portly scribe had an armful of scrolls and records, several of which he dropped as he navigated the cramped courtyard of Fort Alenstahdt.

Made from blocks of sandstone and imported timber, the fort was shaped roughly like a star, with sloping walls and a wide courtyard, dotted with long, timber-frame structures. The station office was one of these, while the others were mostly used as barracks and storehouses. An immense well-house rose from the centre of the courtyard, and was connected to the walls by gantries of rope and wood. Great, tottering stacks of crates, barrels and sacks lined the walls, and groups of Thrawl's fellow scribes moved among them, recording the contents or preparing them to be transported to Glymmsforge.

From its position, Fort Alenstahdt stood watch over the Great Lyrian Road, a flat serpent of raised stone that stretched across the Zircona Desert from Glymmsforge. It was dotted by duardin-made oases and trading enclaves like the fort, garrisoned by whoever the merchant families of Glymmsforge could pay to do the work. Often, that meant one of the smaller clans of fyreslayers or otherwise uncontracted bands of Freeguild mercenaries.

The fort was a way station, situated amid a nexus of ancient trade routes stretching across the Zircona Desert. Those routes had been set by the great fortress-wagons of the Zirc nomads, which forever trundled across the deserts of the underworld, carrying the tribes from one oasis to the next. The nomads traded shadeglass and other oddities culled from the sands for iron and silver, both of which were in high demand by the desert tribes.

Thrawl sidestepped a pair of scribes arguing with a duardin trader. The duardin thumped a meaty fist into his palm, his tone becoming bellicose. His bodyguards fingered their axes and glared silently at the Freeguild soldiers lounging nearby, watching the proceedings with rude amusement.

The men wore what could laughingly be called a uniform – voluminous breeches of varying shades, tucked into knee-high boots, heavy leather coats made from the hide of some large species of reptile and reinforced caps of the same, hidden beneath the floppy, wide-brimmed hats that seemed to serve only to hide their grinning, scarred faces.

Both wore bandoliers heavy with powder, shot and an assortment of knives, axes and various implements of murder. Their hair and moustaches were long, and intricately braided. Both carried the long-barrelled handguns prized by the members of their company.

The Leatherbacks were a gun company, from the fenlands that stretched across the south of Ghur. As far as Thrawl was concerned, to call them disreputable was to do a disservice to the term. They were all but barbarians, with manners that put orruks to shame. Worse, they were all related, in ways too complex for an outsider to sort out. Thrawl had spent most of his time at the fort navigating a web of internecine alliances, blood feuds and grudges that had the local duardin nodding in appreciation.

But they were hardy warriors, capable of enduring the blistering days and freezing nights without complaint. They had little fear of the deadwalkers that roamed the dunes, and often trapped the hungry corpses in cages to use for target practice. And if they were a bit rough with the Zirc nomads who came to trade, so much the better as far as their employers were concerned.

One of the pair watching the argument lifted his handgun in the general direction of the duardin and sighted down the barrel. The other scratched his throat meaningfully, as the trader's bodyguards tensed. Thrawl wasn't concerned. The duardin knew better than to cause a scene, and the Leatherbacks were too lazy to actually start a fight.

Thrawl nodded to the one aiming his weapon. 'Where's Poppa?' he called out, fighting to be heard over the argument.

'Parapet,' the soldier grunted, hiking a thumb over his shoulder. His accent was atrocious, and he spoke with a pronounced drawl. Then, that wasn't surprising, given where he and his fellows came from. He lowered his weapon and gave it a fond pat.

Those Leatherbacks that weren't lucky enough to own such a weapon had to make do with a glaive or a halberd, until someone better equipped died and they could 'inherit' a handgun. In his time at the fort, Thrawl had seen no less than three duels fought over such abandoned weapons. The duels were theoretically fought only to first blood, but said blood usually wound up spurting from somewhere vital. The Leatherbacks would just as cheerfully murder their own kin as they would the enemy, if it meant getting their hands on a gun.

Thrawl started towards the parapet, but cursed as he trod on the tail of a dog – one of a dozen curs that seemed to have followed the Leatherbacks from their last duty. The big, yellow brute yelped and turned, teeth bared. Thrawl, used to such displays by now, fumbled loose a scroll and smacked the mongrel on the snout. It blinked and backed off, growling. Thrawl swept past, before it recovered its courage. More of the beasts lay in the shadows beneath the parapets, hiding from the wind. Several barked lazily as he climbed the crude wooden steps up to the top of the wall, and the enclosed parapet above.

Poppa Chown was waiting on him, at the top. The mountainous commander of the Leatherbacks was silver-haired, twice the height of his tallest warrior and heavy with fat and muscle. Even his scars had scars. His clothes had been altered to fit his massive frame, and gave him a tatterdemalion aspect beneath his battered coat. He sat on an iron stool in front of a firing slit, his rifle between his knees. It was half again as long as a handgun, with a narrow barrel that scraped the roof of the parapet and a reinforced stock that Thrawl knew was heavy enough to crush a deadwalker's skull.

His men bustled about him, keeping watch on the road and the desert that stretched out to the horizon on either side. Chown glanced around as Thrawl entered the parapet. 'Ho, children – look. The scribe has come to visit.' Chown spoke around a mouthful of the brownish herb he incessantly chewed, and he punctuated his welcome with a gobbet of spittle that narrowly missed Thrawl's boot. 'Say hello to the scribe, pups.'

Nearby warriors shouted obscenities or made rude gestures. Thrawl ignored them. 'I need your pay records,' he said, without preamble.

Chown turned with a grunt and squinted at him. 'Why?'

'To ensure that they align with my copies.'

'They do.'

'Even so, I wish to make sure.'

Chown smiled, showing off brown teeth. 'Don't you trust Poppa?' He gestured expansively, and his men laughed knowingly. Chown's title was informal but accurate. He was the patriarch of a wide-ranging clan, as well as its captain. He was father, master and commander, and his men loved and hated him in equal measure.

'I don't trust my own father, let alone you,' Thrawl said bluntly.

Chown gave a bellow of laughter and slapped his knee. 'And nor should you,' he growled cheerfully. 'We're cheating you.'

'I know.'

'Then you don't need the books.' Chown made to turn back. Thrawl stepped up beside him.

'I need them if I want to see how much you're cheating my employers by.'

Chown glanced up at him and grinned. 'Intending to skim off the difference and fatten your own purse, eh?'

'Obviously.' Thrawl looked out through the gun-slit. He could see the great wagon-fortresses of the Zirc nomads moving across the horizon, trying to outrace the storm everyone knew was coming but no one was talking about. Behind the hulking conveyances, Thrawl could see the purple glare on the horizon. It was brighter than it had been yesterday.

He shivered, suddenly cold. He fumbled a sigmarite amulet out from within his robes and rubbed it with his thumb. It was just a cheap thing, made from lead. His mother had given it to him before his departure, thinking it would protect him from the horrors of Shyish. Its weight was comforting, when the shadows of this realm pressed too close.

'The desert is on fire,' Chown said, idly. He reached into his coat and pulled out a pouch of tanned leather. He extracted a handful of leaves from the pouch before offering it to Thrawl as he stuffed the leaves into his mouth. Thrawl waved the pouch away, faintly disgusted by the musky odour emanating from it.

'It's getting closer, then,' Thrawl said, softly. They'd felt the realm shake, and the packs of deadwalkers roaming the desert had become more focused. Worse were the reports from the nomads, of the things they'd seen and heard, out in the wastes.

'Death always does.'

Thrawl frowned. 'Is that meant to be reassuring?'

Chown chewed thoughtfully for a moment, then shrugged.

Thrawl sighed. This hadn't been his first choice of posting, but it had been the only one available. Men and women who could read and write were in high demand on the frontier. Someone had to keep proper records, to keep barbarians like Chown from bankrupting Azyrite merchants. And to keep said merchants honest when it came time to pay their taxes.

Besides records, Thrawl had amused himself with writing a concise history of Fort Alenstahdt. He fancied his *Dispatches from Zircona* might one day be read alongside such volumes as Herst's *History of Greater Lyria*, Tertoma's *Forty Days in the Writhing Weald* and Guillepe Barco's infamous *The Klaxus Wars: An Eyewitness Account.*

At the moment, he was stuck on the chapter concerning the recent earth-tremors and the increased deadwalker activity.

Accounts he'd gathered from passing traders and pilgrims made it seem as if every tomb and grave had disgorged its contents. It all seemed so… impossible. But that word had little meaning on the frontier. He sighed again. 'I hate the desert. I hate Shyish.'

Chown grunted. 'You should put in for a change of post, scribe.'

Thrawl snorted. 'And do you have a recommendation, then?'

'The Black Marsh Barony, scribe – good place. That's where we're from. A place for men. Not like this desert. Only bones in the desert.' Chown leaned over and spat a mouthful of whatever he'd been chewing, hitting a dog that lay nearby. The beast yelped and whirled to its feet, snapping at the air in confusion. The men laughed. Chown wiped his lips and grinned. 'Sand gets everywhere. Scrape a man to his stilts.'

'Then why are you here?' Thrawl asked.

Chown rubbed his thumb and forefinger together. 'We go where the money is, friend.' He frowned. 'And where our creditors aren't.'

Thrawl laughed. 'You must have a lot of creditors, to wind up out here.' Few Freeguild companies sought frontier duty – it was alternately boring and dangerous work, with little chance of filling the coffers. Most preferred to bivouac behind high walls, and patrol civilised streets, rather than chance the wilds.

Chown shrugged. 'Powder and shot is expensive. And we don't like cities.' He stiffened and gestured to one of his men. 'Buzos, bring Poppa his spyglass, there's a lad.' Buzos hurried over, holding a heavy spyglass made from brass and gold. Its shell was scuffed and tarnished, but the lenses were almost perfect.

Thrawl blinked. 'Why does that have the Glymm crest on it?'

Chown shrugged again. 'It's a mystery. Hush now, scribe.

Something is happening out there. The Zirc are sounding their prayer-horns.'

Thrawl strained, listening for the familiar, winding call of the horns. The Zirc rarely sounded them and usually only just before a sandstorm. They worshipped the storm-winds, and some said that the nomads followed them across the desert. He squinted, trying to see what was going on. The wind had risen to a harsh shriek, and his eardrums ached.

'The soul-winds are screaming,' Chown grunted. 'The dead are angry.'

'When are they not?'

'In Ghur, we know how to treat the dead-that-are-not.' Chown drew a line across his throat. 'The stake, the sword, the fire. Simple. But here... not so simple. The dead are different here.' He handed Thrawl the spyglass. 'Look, scribe.'

Thrawl's mouth was dry as he looked through the spyglass. Chown was right. There was a storm on the horizon. But not of sand or rain.

Instead, a howling gale of spectral green energy was racing across the dunes towards them. He thought he glimpsed horsemen there among the roiling tide, and worse things besides. He stared, unable to tear his eyes away. Unable to speak.

'No, not simple at all,' Chown said.

The nighthaunt host sped across the burning sands like the evening tide. Cackling chainrasps led the way. Their clawed, skeletal limbs emerged from tattered grave-shrouds, and their fleshless countenances gnawed mindlessly at the air as they spilled towards the trundling wagon-fortresses. A volley of flaming arrows raced to meet them.

'Idiotic savages,' Malendrek said, watching as the arrows fell harmlessly among his hosts. 'However far they flee, they cannot escape us.' The Knight of Shrouds sat atop his skeletal steed, his flickering gaze locked on the line of towering, wooden conveyances. 'Perhaps they prefer to die tired,' Pharus said. He stood near the Knight of Shrouds, his sword planted point-first before him, his gauntlets resting atop the pommel, watching the assault. 'Well-rested or exhausted, they will perish all the same,' Malendrek croaked, not looking at him. 'All living things must die. My nighthaunts will rip the lives from these nomads. Their souls are our tithe to the Undying King, whose will we enact with this joyful slaughter.'

The first of the chainrasps reached the rearmost wagon. They clawed at the wood, their talons steaming as they encountered the sigils of protection carved there. The Zirc had enough experience with the dead to know how best to hold them at bay. But this was no ordinary attack – the chainrasps were not simply feral spirits, but an army. They would find a way in, eventually.

'They must be punished for their defiance,' Malendrek continued, hauling back on his steed's rotting reins and causing it to rear. 'Retribution must be had.'

Pharus did not reply. Malendrek wasn't really talking to him. Since departing Nagashizzar, he had come to realise that the Knight of Shrouds liked to hear himself talk. Malendrek waxed philosophical, when he wasn't uttering bitter denunciations of individuals Pharus was not familiar with.

But despite being obviously mad, Malendrek was smart. He had a keen strategic mind, beneath all the ranting. As they moved across the desert, following the trade roads, the army of the dead had added to its ranks. They had collected the inhabitants of mining encampments and oases. Souls were harvested from cooling bodies and added to the nighthaunt ranks, while the carcasses were later dragged stumbling in the army's wake. An efficient use of materials, in Pharus' opinion.

But the deadwalkers were slow and the deathrattle even slower. They would take days to reach the walls of Glymmsforge. Only the nighthaunts had the speed to strike the city before the gap in its defences was discovered. Which it would be, eventually.

Another volley arced from the upper levels of the rearmost wagon-fortress. Pharus watched the arrows fall, a part of him calculating the trajectories. The second volley did no more harm than the first. The Zirc were not unprepared. They would have other, more effective means of defence in readiness.

He turned, studying the sloped walls of the fort beyond the wagons. The Zirc had led them right to it. It was a crude thing. A muddle of harsh lines, interrupting the serenity of the desert.

As has ever been the way of Azyr.

Pharus nodded. Sigmar's influence was spread in stone and starlight. Where his armies marched, cities sprouted in their wake and grew fat and strong on the resources of the realms.

The folk of Azyr are ticks, buried into the flesh of worlds.

Pharus nodded again, unable to deny it. The folk of Azyr felled forests, flattened mountains, emptied seas – all in the name of Sigmar. Gods other than him were cast aside and forgotten by fickle mortals, seeking stifling safety within walls of celestine.

They will do the same to Shyish, if they are not stopped. The living are ever hungry, ever greedy, the voice inside him murmured. *They are not fit caretakers for existence. Only the dead can uphold the foundations of existence. Only in the arms of death, can the realms know true peace. Until all are one in Nagash...*

'And Nagash is all,' Pharus said. He could see why the Zirc had led them this way. A ruthlessly pragmatic folk, these nomads. The fort was close enough to divide their pursuers' attentions.

The Knight of Shrouds was already casting baleful glares in the direction of the sandstone walls, and muttering to himself.

The living were greedy. But so too were some among the dead.

The fort must be taken. No word can escape, no warning.

Pharus uprooted his sword and looked at Malendrek. 'With your permission, I shall deal with the fort,' he said. 'I shall cast stone from stone and drive the souls within into the arms of the hungry dead.'

Malendrek looked down at him. 'You still stink of Azyr,' he said, idly. 'I can taste the storm on your soul, Pharus Thaum. You wear the raiment of a deathlord, but you will never truly be one. Your hubris knows no bounds.'

Pharus met the burning gaze without hesitation. There was no fear in him, and he knew, in some secret part of his soul, that Malendrek was just another pawn.

Just as you are.

'I am but a weapon in the hands of the Undying King,' Pharus said. 'Let me gather the tithe, Knight of Shrouds. Let me do as Nagash made me to do.'

Malendrek turned away. 'Do as you will, little soul. I have the business of death to be about.' He urged his steed forwards, and its hooves left burning impressions in the sand as it galloped after the Zirc wagons.

Pharus turned to find Dohl hovering behind him. 'We are ready to greet our new brothers and sisters in death,' the guardian of souls rasped. 'But give the command, and we shall welcome them into our ranks, Lord Pharus.' He raised his lantern, and the dead of the Grand Oubliette and a dozen oases roiled around him, screaming and howling. At Pharus' nod, Dohl thrust his lantern forwards, and the hordes of chainrasps rushed towards the distant walls of the fort with an eager roar.

Pharus lifted his blade. He felt strangely eager – here then was the first test of his new self. The enemy before him served the same master who had abandoned him. Would they see the truth, as he had? Or would they merely fall and be added to the horde now surging past him? Inside him, something laughed.

It does not matter. Nagash is all, and all are one in him.

'Come, my sweet lord, why do you dawdle? There is justice to be done.' Rocha drifted past him, trailing pale, blood-stained fingers across his armour. 'And heads to be lopped.' She gave a cackle and sprang into the air, joining the mad rush. Pharus glanced at Dohl, who gave a dolorous sigh.

'She is but a tool, my lord – blunt yet effective,' he said, as he followed after his flock, surrounded by a knot of moaning, whimpering spirits. Pharus felt a lurch within him as the lantern's glow passed beyond him. He wanted more than anything in that moment to bask once more in that eerie radiance.

But there is blood to be spilled. The Great Work must be done.

'Follow, Fellgrip,' he said, not looking at the hunched jailer. It had not left his side since they had departed Nagashizzar. Like a faithful hound, it had become his shadow. Even so, he felt an uneasiness at its proximity. The chainrasps and other spectres that made up his forces refused to get any closer to Fellgrip than they had to, as if afraid that it might seek to return them to the prison they had so recently been roused from.

Pharus launched himself at the heavy wooden gates of the fort, sword held low. They stank of holy unguents and blessed waters, and he felt his form solidifying and his rush slowing. The storm of chainrasps swirled about him, like a flock of confused birds.

Their defences are weak. Pathetic. You are the storm. You are death. None may gainsay you. Strike. Strike!

His sword snapped out, the shadeglass blade passing easily

through the thick wood. As the splintered sections of the gate crashed aside, his army roiled past him, filling the courtyard beyond like a malevolent cloud. He saw mortals run, fleeing for the dubious safety of the buildings. Handguns roared, as a line of Freeguild soldiers in leather coats and wide-brimmed hats fired a volley. Chainrasps shrieked as silver shot burned through them. Their rush dissolved, as the hurtling spirits shot away in all directions, seeking easier prey. The handgunners stepped back, already reloading. A second line stepped forwards.

Pharus strode towards them, dust swirling about him. He could hear screaming. Men and women and… children. He paused. Something was burning, and a woman was screaming, and a child… Elya? No, that wasn't her name. He looked down at the sword in his hand, not recognising it for a moment. 'Elya,' he said, groping for an answer.

She is safe now. As all true children of Shyish will be safe. But these are different. Outsiders, brought to this realm to fight and die in Sigmar's name.

Anger flowed through him, bright and cold. 'Would you die here, in the name of a tyrant?' His voice, hollow and harsh, scraped across the stones of the fort. 'Or would you live out your full span in service to him to whom all that lives must eventually kneel?'

As if in reply, the handgunners fired. Pharus raced through the storm of shot, Fellgrip trailing in his wake. He lashed out, smashing guns and bones. He was not quite solid, but his blade was, and its edge was sharp. He saw Fellgrip swing his heavy chains about, staving in ribs and crushing skulls. As men fell to these clubbing blows, the spark of their life was drawn into the chains and trapped there.

Chainrasps joined Pharus in his attack, as the gun-line

disintegrated. They plucked struggling warriors from the ground and dragged them into the air, where they were torn apart, screaming. 'Kneel, fools,' he thundered. 'Accept death, and be one with Nagash – Nagash is all, and all are one in him.' His words rang out over the battlefield, but few paid them any attention.

He saw snarling dogs bite at the chainrasps, and men bearing silver glaives pin a struggling phantom to the side of a wagon. A horned spectre swung a wide scythe, sweeping a trio of warriors from their feet. A duardin, clad in the finery of a trader, hacked about him with a rune-inscribed hand-axe, as his bodyguards were pulled apart by the cackling gheists.

Balls of silver and lead punched into the back of his armour, as Freeguild soldiers fired a ragged volley down from the parapet above. He felt slivers of pain echo through him as he whirled, his face stretching in an inhuman snarl. He launched himself at them, his blade sweeping out. A soldier screamed and fell away, and Pharus felt a surge of strength wind through him. The blade ate lives, adding their span to his own and warming the cold within him for a few moments. He twisted, angling his blade towards another mortal.

More silver shot struck him, tearing ragged holes in his substance. He screamed in frustration and flowed towards the foe. Why could they not see that he was trying to help them? Why did they resist? His sword licked out, separating a head from shoulders. The soldiers on the wall fell back, some reloading, others thrusting glaives and halberds uselessly at the chainrasps swarming over the walls. A bellicose giant towered among the men, swinging a rifle like a club, exhorting them to greater efforts.

There. The leader. Without him, the others would break. They would retreat, and die in the doing. Pharus raced towards the giant. 'Kneel, mortal – seek forgiveness in the arms of death,' he roared. 'Only Nagash can save you now.'

'Poppa does not kneel, rag-a-bones,' the giant bellowed. He reversed the rifle as Pharus drew close, and fired. A spray of silver and iron ripped across Pharus, pock-marking his war-plate and stinging his eyes. He shrieked and rose up, clawing at his face. He felt the stock of the rifle crash against his armour and lashed out with his sword. The giant roared and slammed into him, as if seeking to tackle him.

'Fool,' Pharus snarled, 'I have no neck to wring, no limbs to break – I am beyond the weaknesses of flesh.' He caught at the giant's unshaven throat and flung him from the parapet. The warrior crashed down with a groan, somehow still holding on to his weapon.

Pharus stepped off the parapet and stalked down through the air towards his opponent. He could smell the stink of the man's injuries – the sharp tang of spilled blood and broken bone. Death was close. Death was here. Pharus raised his blade over the injured warrior. 'Rejoice, mortal – death spreads its wings above you.'

He slashed down. The giant interposed his weapon at the last moment, but the shadeglass blade continued its downward stroke unimpeded. It passed through his broad chest. The giant stiffened. A cloud of blood erupted from his open mouth. For a moment, he clutched awkwardly at the slick edge of the blade, and Pharus thought he might succeed in extracting it. Then, with a sigh, he sagged back.

Dogs began to howl throughout the fort, and nearby soldiers wailed. Shots plucked at Pharus as he wrenched his sword free. He turned. A mind-chilling smoke billowed from Dohl's lantern, to float over the battlefield. Wherever it passed, the souls of the newly fallen were wrenched screaming from their bloody bodies, to rise and join the ranks of the dead.

The soldiers were retreating in confusion, seeking the protection of outbuildings and stables. The most organised knot of them was steadily falling back towards what could only be the fort's chapel, along with the surviving civilians. The structure shone like a beacon, its every stone limned with azure light to his altered sight. He wanted to tear it apart and bury it in the sand, but knew that to cross its threshold would cause him more pain than any silver shot or blade.

Pharus hesitated. Perhaps it was best to leave it.

What is pain, to one already dead? Every life in the fort is owed to Nagash.

He started after the retreating Freeguild, his sword twitching in his grip. As he closed in, a shot ricocheted off his helm, distracting him. He spun, blade licking out. His attacker stumbled back with a yelp, just out of reach. Not a soldier. By his robes, Pharus judged him a scribe. A smoking pistol, its barrel etched with duardin runes, thumped to the ground as the little man scrambled to his feet. He thrust a hand into his robes, clawing for something as Pharus closed in on him.

Pharus raised his blade, and the scribe snatched a medallion from his robes. As he brought it into the open, it blazed forth with a blue radiance. 'Back,' the little man screeched, thrusting the sigil towards him. Pharus flinched away, unable to bear the sight of it.

'That will not stay my hand, mortal. Not for long.'

'Long enough,' the little man said.

Pharus glanced at him and then turned. He could see the last of the Freeguild survivors hurrying towards the chapel, despite the chainrasps harrying them. 'You are brave,' he said, flexing his hand. The sword thrummed in his grip, eager to taste the life of the little man. 'Do you think Sigmar will take you to his bosom, when I strike you down?'

'I… I don't know,' the little man said. 'But I'm not afraid to find out.'

'In Helstone, hubris was a crime.' Rocha rose up behind the little man. Before Pharus could stop her, her axe swept out, removing the man's head. His body sank down, the hated symbol falling from his limp hand. The executioner stared down at the body, jaw working soundlessly. She looked at Pharus. 'So was hesitation.'

Pharus extended his sword towards her. 'Remember who you serve, executioner.' He felt something stir in him – anger? Sadness? He could not tell, and told himself that he did not care. He again caught a glimpse of something, lurking in the facets of his blade – watching him, judging. A great eye, like an amethyst star, burned into his own.

'The same king as you, Pharus Thaum.' Rocha grinned, baring broken teeth. He wondered if she too could see what passed through the facets of his blade. Her expression of glee faded as the spirits clinging to her pulled her away, towards the next bloody deed. She laughed wildly and raised her axe in gaunt hands. Pharus watched her go, and then turned back to the chapel.

As he did so, he caught sight of the scribe's sigil, lying forgotten on the ground. He flicked it away, out of sight, with the tip of his blade. Then, filled only with cold and hunger, he started towards the chapel, to cast stone from stone, as he'd sworn.

To do as Nagash had made him to do.

CHAPTER SIXTEEN

GRAND TEMPESTUS

FREE CITY OF GLYMMSFORGE

'The desert burns,' Knossus said, staring at the horizon. He looked at Balthas. 'The enemy is close at hand. Can you feel it?'

Balthas nodded. The temperature had dipped precipitously over the past day. The heavy braziers set at intervals along the eastern wall struggled to hold the cold at bay. Flames snapped and whipped in the wind that moaned across the ramparts.

He gazed along the wall's length. The great cannons of the Ironweld were arrayed in batteries as far as the eye could see. Glymmsforge's arsenal was the largest in Shyish, and growing by the year. But all the powder and shot in the realm would not be enough to stop what he suspected was coming.

Still looking at the cannons, he asked, 'Any word from the fort?' Fort Alenstahdt had fallen silent as the fires on the horizon grew brighter. Galen Sleekwing, Prosecutor-Prime of the Anvils of the Heldenhammer's Angelos Chamber, had demanded the right to send out patrols of Prosecutors, but Knossus had refrained. There were things abroad in the dark skies that no warrior, no matter how skilled, could face and survive.

'None. Not for three days. If anyone is alive out there, they have other things to worry about.' Knossus leaned against his staff, looking surprisingly weary. Balthas could tell that the responsibility was wearing on him. They possessed superhuman vitality, but even it had its limits. And the city was under siege, even if there was no enemy in sight yet. The dead rose in greater numbers than ever before, despite the usual precautions.

In the past day, drowned corpses had surfaced in the Glass Mere to attack the villages that clustered along the shore-wall, and the effluvia of an abattoir in the tannery quarter had congealed into something monstrous and hungry. Each day brought new horrors, necessitating some form of intervention. Which further distracted from the efforts of the city's defenders to prepare themselves for the attack that was almost certainly coming.

Out among the dunes, Balthas heard the cry of a jackal. The eerie sound rose and quavered out. As if in reply, the howling of dogs rose over the city. The soldiers on the wall glanced at one another nervously. Balthas could see the fear that tinged their auras. He sent a whisper of power through his staff, so that its glow blossomed suddenly, washing across the wall. The fear in those nearest to him eased.

'Compassion, brother?' Knossus asked.

'Pragmatism. Fear sharpens the senses, but too much can overwhelm them.' Balthas looked up at the dark sky. He couldn't see the stars. A flicker of unease gripped him, but he said nothing of it. 'They must be alert.'

'As must we.' Knossus looked out over the desert. 'Death draws closer with every breath we take. It feels as if the underworld itself is closing in about us. As if Nagash has us in his fist.' He sighed. 'I thought I had seen my darkest days already, but this feels unsettlingly familiar.'

'Have you found the weakness in the city's wards yet?'

'No. But I am drawing close.' Knossus gestured to the north. 'There is a tang in the air, there – a musty note beneath everything. It is there, I think.'

'We must seal it, then, and swiftly,' Balthas said. 'While it exists, the city is weakened. Its defences are incomplete.'

Knossus blocked Balthas' path with his staff. 'I will deal with it. There is something else that you must do. The Grand Tempestus.'

Balthas paused. 'I was under the impression that it was protected.'

'It is. By you.' Knossus smiled. 'Sigmar sent you here for this purpose, brother. Defending the city's walls is my responsibility. You will defend its heart. I have already sent word to Calys Eltain, placing her under your command.'

Balthas bowed his head. 'My… thanks, brother.'

'You will not be alone. The Grand Tempestus sits amid the main artery of the city – I have despatched forces to hold the surrounding streets. They will be of some help to you.'

'Mortals?' Balthas said, doubtfully.

'Lynos and Orius are needed elsewhere. It will be up to us to hold the enemy on the walls. Hopefully, you will not see a single spectre or walking corpse.'

Balthas looked back towards the desert and the witch-light glow dancing on the horizon. He did not share Knossus' seeming confidence. Whatever was coming, it would take more than walls and mystic wards to stop it.

But he did not voice his concerns. Instead, he simply turned away. 'I hope you are right, brother. And Sigmar help us if you are not.'

Calys Eltain descended the steps of the Grand Tempestus, leading her cohort of warriors into the wide plaza that stretched before it. The cathedral rose up above and around her, an imposing edifice of celestine and marble that always smelled of ozone and rain. A massive statue of Sigmar the Liberator stood over the main doors, hammer raised to smash the chains of the oppressed. More statues, these of saints, Azyrite and otherwise, lined either side of the colossal, slabbed steps. Some were of Stormcasts but most were of mortal humans – men and women, sages and warrior-priests, great warriors and healers.

It had begun to rain, diffusing the glow of the storm-lanterns hung from the high posts at the bottom of the steps. The circumference of the plaza was interrupted by twelve streets, each demarcated by a high archway of stone that stretched between the buildings to either side. Freeguild troops in the uniform of the Glymmsmen marched through one of the archways, their voices raised in conversation or song.

Calys stopped at the bottom of the steps and looked up. She could not see the stars. The sky resembled a black wound. She frowned, uneasy. Beside her, the gryph-hound, Grip, chirped softly. Calys looked down, watching as the mortal soldiers filed into the plaza. Some had begun to unlimber artillery pieces, while others were banging on the doors of nearby shops and dwellings.

The order had come down from Lord-Arcanum Knossus that the Grand Tempestus was to be reinforced and made ready. She knew that the other temples in the city would be seeing similar activity, as would many of the larger buildings and gatehouses.

By dawn, the city would be a chain of interlinked, if somewhat makeshift, fortresses, ready to repel an enemy that shouldn't even be able to get past the outer walls.

'He is late,' one of her warriors said. He was behind her, spread out with the others along the bottom step. There were eleven of them. Twelve counting herself. One for each entrance to the Grand Tempestus. 'He could not even do us the courtesy of being here on time, this lord-arcanum.'

'Stop grousing, Tamacus,' Calys said, more harshly than she'd intended.

'It is not seemly. This duty is ours.' Tamacus half drew his blade and thrust it back into its sheath with a rattle.

'Your duty is to obey me,' Calys said. She looked back at him. 'And mine is to obey him. That is the way of it.'

Tamacus bowed his head. Calys stared at him for a moment longer, just to ensure he understood. Then she turned back. As she did so, she heard the familiar screech of a gryph-charger. Her new commander had arrived.

The Stormcasts trooping into the plaza wore the black of the Anvils of the Heldenhammer, which was something of a relief – at least these were from the same Stormhost. The lord-arcanum climbed from his gryph-charger's back, and his Knight-Incantor joined him. 'Calys Eltain – step forth,' the lord-arcanum said. He had a softer voice than she'd been expecting – like thunder, but far away. A distant rumble rather than the bone-rattling voice of Knossus Heavensen.

Calys stepped forwards, her helmet beneath her arm. The rain ran down her face, but she ignored it. She met his cool gaze without flinching. 'I am Calys Eltain, lord-arcanum.'

'I am Lord-Arcanum Balthas Arum, called by some the Grave Warden. You are under my command now. Is this amenable to you?'

'If it were not, would it matter?' The question came to her lips before she could consider it. 'You are here now.' She studied him. He was taller than she was – not massive, but simply tall. If he'd been mortal, she might have called him lanky, but clad in armour as he was, that was more due to how he held himself. But there was a power to him. The air crackled about him, as if there were a storm in the offing.

'I am. You are observant.'

Calys blinked, startled by his sardonic tone. Before she could reply, he went on. 'You were from Ghur,' Balthas said, looking through her. She hesitated.

'I have no memory of my mortal life.'

'Nevertheless, I see the threads of amber running through you. Mingled with purple and blue. More than most. Born in one realm and died in another. You were forged recently, then. After the realmgates were secured.' He looked away. 'You have come far, for one so young.'

'I seek only to do my duty,' she said, stung by his tone.

'As do I.' He looked back at her. 'I do not seek to take this responsibility from you. I only seek to do as I have been commanded.' He gestured towards the Grand Tempestus. 'You will guard the doors, as you have been ordered. I will see to the outside. Between us, we shall protect the Ten Thousand Tombs from the enemy.'

She hesitated, but only for a moment. He was offering a compromise, of sorts. She nodded. 'As you say, lord-arcanum.'

'Good. See to your duties, then, Liberator-Prime. And I will see to mine.' He turned away, and she knew that she had been dismissed. She gestured curtly, and Tamacus and the others began to climb the stairs once more.

She studied Balthas for a moment longer, and then followed. Whatever else, she would do her duty.

* * *

The deathlords met in a circle of witch-light, a day's march from Glymmsforge.

Skulls wreathed in eerie green flame hovered attentively around them, bound by the magics of Crelis Arul. The mistress of the deadwalkers had caught up with the nighthaunt vanguard a few days after the fall of Fort Alenstahdt. Her horde stumbled through the sands to either side of them – a flood of tattered meat and twitching limbs, moving unceasingly towards the city in the distance.

Nearby, the silent legions of Grand Prince Yaros awaited their orders. Unlike the shambling deadwalkers, they could be trusted to reach the walls in good time and thus were held back. Despite Malendrek's claims to the contrary, the deathrattle warriors were the solid core of the army making for Glymmsforge. It would be up to them to hold whatever ground the nighthaunts and deadwalkers took.

Pharus' own host was close to hand. He could feel the warmth of Dohl's lantern and hear the constant, impatient murmur of the chainrasps. The guardian of souls had awakened the dead as they travelled the desert paths, and now the broken spirits of those claimed by the Zircona served him alongside those twisted phantoms culled from the Great Oubliette.

Despite his impatience, Malendrek had halted their rush across the desert to wait for the other deathlords to catch up. He was no fool, whatever else, and Pharus had not complained – something told him that he would need every advantage to accomplish the task before him. Now, he maintained his silence, watching as Malendrek laid out his strategy.

'There is a hole in their defences,' Malendrek said. 'I know this because I created it – it was the price Nagash demanded, and I paid it gladly. It is the bleeding wound in Glymmsforge's side. We must capitalise on it.' A pale talon clenched into a knotty fist. 'I will lead the assault. My forces will flood the city and disrupt the enemy. You will follow, consolidating on our gains.'

'And leave you to reap the lion's share of the glory,' Grand Prince Yaros said. The wight king gestured with his axe. 'Perhaps I should lead the assault. My legions are unbreakable. We have weathered the storms of Azyr before.' It was more a boast than a demand. Neither Yaros nor Arul seemed inclined to challenge Malendrek – but they seized every opportunity to prick his ego.

Malendrek whirled on the skeletal warrior, his gaze pure balefire. 'I am in command. Nagash has commanded it thus, and all must obey.'

'We would not think of doing otherwise, O Knight of Shrouds. Your nighthaunts shall spearhead the assault, and cast open the gates for those of us who must stride on solid feet.' Crelis Arul stood flanked by her wolves. Their rotting jaws were wet with effluvia, and their eyes squirmed with maggots. She stroked their fraying manes idly as she spoke. 'We are content to follow at our leisure and make war on your leavings.'

Malendrek turned his fiery gaze on the Lady of All Flesh. 'Carrion does as it must,' he said, dropping his hand to the hilt of his blade. 'The honour of the vanguard is mine. Thus spoke Nagash, and his will cannot be denied.'

Pharus drifted forwards. 'No. It cannot. And thus, I shall accompany you.'

'What?' Malendrek peered at him. 'Is it the little spirit, then? Still here, little spirit? I thought you lost to the desert wind, by now.'

'I am not so easily swayed as that,' Pharus said. Malendrek had done his best to ignore Pharus after the fall of the fort. Together, they had reaped hundreds of souls, but the Knight of Shrouds saw only those he had taken personally. 'And my own task is equal to yours, Knight of Shrouds. There is something in the city I must claim in our lord's name. The sooner I do it, the sooner victory is ours.'

'You are nothing next to me,' Malendrek snarled. His sword sprang from its sheath. Pharus interposed his own at the last moment. Their blades locked with a screech, like that of enraged beasts. Pharus felt a wave of cold pass through him, and for a moment, it seemed as if the desert were alive with the sound of jackals howling.

As they strained against one another, the howling grew louder and louder, until Pharus could hear nothing else. Amethyst sparks spilled from between their swords, and in the polished shadeglass length of his blade, he caught the briefest glimpse of a skeletal countenance – not his own, but Arkhan. Or perhaps Nagash.

With a snarling cry, he tore his weapon free of Malendrek's and retreated. All at once, the jackals fell silent. 'If I am nothing, it is only because Nagash has willed it so,' he said, sheathing his sword without flourish. 'If you are something, it is only because he wishes it. Or do you set yourself higher than our lord and master?'

Malendrek eyed him balefully. 'Nagash is all,' he said, after a moment.

'And all are one in Nagash,' Pharus replied.

The Knight of Shrouds seemed to fold in on himself, wrapping shadow and spite about his lean frame. 'If you wish to walk into the eye of the storm with me, little spirit – so be it. But the glory of the assault will be mine. You will content yourself with opening the gates. Then you may lose yourself as you wish.' He turned away, muttering to himself. Pharus stepped out of the circle of witch-light, one hand on his blade. He did not expect Malendrek to attack him again, but there was no sense taking chances.

Out among the dunes, he heard the lonely cry of a solitary jackal, and wondered if it was a warning of some sort. Perhaps it was simply a reminder that all things passed and had their end. Even deathlords.

He climbed a dune, the soft amethyst sands barely disturbed by the chill breeze of his passing. His feet did not sink into the sand, did not press it flat or make any indentation. There was no sign that he had passed that way at all. A part of him – small and distant – felt sadness at the thought. It was as if he were nothing more than a dark dream, set loose from the confines of a sleeper's head.

A sea of ragged tents spread out below him. The dead did not make camp, save when it amused them to do so. Yaros' deathrattle had raised the tents scattered about the dunes in a parody of military discipline. Fleshless menials, indentured in death as they had been in life, moved among the tents, hard at their unceasing labours. They followed ancient routines, gathering buckets of sand from long dry wells and butchered non-existent game animals. Nearby, deathrattle soldiers erected field defences that would see no use – had seen no use in decades.

These slaves of the Grand Prince ignored him. He suspected that they could not perceive him. Or that if they did, he appeared much differently. He passed among them, unnoticed and unhindered.

It was rare that he was alone, since leaving Nagashizzar. Dohl hovered ever at his elbow, drowning out his doubts with the glow of his lantern. And if it was not Dohl, it was Fellgrip or Rocha. He could not say which of the three he found more distasteful. They were no more his warriors than he was

Malendrek's. They were loyal to Nagash alone. As he was. As he must be. To be otherwise was unthinkable.

He turned back the way they had come and saw the black radiance on the horizon there. A watchful flame, burning in the night. It would grow, in time, until it ate the stars themselves, and turned the sands of all deserts to glass. And he would be a part of it.

Pharus felt no joy at the thought. No fear. Only a dim satisfaction. The way a blade might feel, could it feel, when it was wielded with true skill. He tore his gaze from that dark glow and looked out over the dunes, towards the city on the opposite horizon. Satisfaction faded, replaced by anticipation as he watched the shuffling columns of the dead advance endlessly across the moonlit sands.

He stared at the city. Until recently, he might have stood on those walls and stared out at the dead as they massed for their assault. 'Reflections and shadows,' he murmured, flexing a gauntlet. He could not feel the weight of his armour. He'd found that to be the most disconcerting thing about being dead. War-plate should have weight – solidity. But his felt no more substantial than cobwebs.

Only the sword had weight. Too much, for its size. It had grown heavier, the farther they travelled from the Nadir. As if it had become more real, somehow. Or perhaps he had become less so. The thought was not a comforting one. Now, he felt content – felt whole – only in the glow of Dohl's lantern.

He was sure now that he had once borne a similar artefact. A thing infused with the false light of Azyr. Sometimes, he found himself reaching vainly for it, as the memories fluttered vainly at the edges of his perception. It was as if some part of him were attempting to remind himself of what he had once been. That longing was akin to a wound that would not heal, and only added to the agonies he felt. He had been a part of something, and now was not. And that absence made him angry.

That was the one thing that all of the dead had in common – anger. Anger at the pain they had suffered, at the glories denied them or the promises broken. A righteous anger, shared by the lowest cadaver and Nagash himself. Anger at the living. Anger at the realms themselves, for their defiance of the inevitable.

As the anger rose so too did the cold and the hunger. One fed the other, and he wanted to shriek aloud, to join his voice to that of the feral gheists that prowled the dunes. To scream in rage for an eternity, until all else was silence.

'It is beautiful, is it not?'

Pharus turned. Crelis Arul stood behind him, accompanied by her wolves. They snarled at him, flashing broken fangs. He gestured with his sword. 'If they attack, I will slay them,' he rasped.

'They are no more alive than you are, little spirit.' She stepped forwards to join him, ignoring his blade. 'It is beautiful. So much life, and death. I can hear them, the harvested, in their houses of stone, crying out to us. Can you hear them?'

Pharus peered at her, and then at the city. 'I hear voices on the wind. In the sand.'

'Innumerable souls drift about us, unseen and unheard save to those who stand upon the border between life and death.' Arul cocked her head, as if listening. 'They say that we are in Lyria – where the dead are given succour and strength through the celebration of their mortal deeds. There are a thousand or more underworlds in Shyish, you know. They rest within one another, like pearls in an oyster. We are a realm of nested secrets – peel back one layer and a new one presents itself.'

She took hold of the flesh of her arm and stripped it back, revealing bloody bone beneath. There were words and sigils in an unfamiliar tongue carved into the bone. 'See? Secrets.' She patted the torn flesh back into place.

Pharus sheathed his blade and looked away. 'If there are spirits here, why do they not serve Nagash?' He was almost offended by the thought. Death was the end of all lies, of all defiance – so how could such a thing be?

Arul laughed. 'Nagash is god of justice. And these souls have earned their reward. Why would he bend them to his will, when there are more fitting tools to hand?' She tapped a crumbling finger against his chest-plate. 'If we are cruel, it is because we must be. Because it is required that we be so. Did Arkhan not teach you that?'

'I do not yet know what the Mortarch of Sacrament has taught me. Perhaps nothing. Perhaps everything. A lesson's worth is judged in the field.' The words came unbidden to his lips. They were from his other life. He heard a voice, and a name – Lynos. He bowed his head. He was cold and empty. His sword shuddered in its sheath. It, too, was hungry.

Arul watched him, her eyes gleaming behind her veil. 'Cruel,' she repeated, 'because we must be. Nagash has stripped you of warmth and joy, so that you might be a better weapon. As you have stripped the life from others, so that they might join us and see the beauty that awaits them, on this side.'

'I can hear something else,' Pharus said. He touched his sword. 'It echoes, with every swing of this blade – a single voice, calling out of the deep places. Urging me on.' He looked at her. 'Do you hear it as well?' Then, after a moment's hesitation, he added, 'What does it say to you?'

'If you were wiser, you would not ask that question.' She looked towards the distant city. 'We all hear it, and it tells us all different things. It whispers to us in our own voice, but it is his.' She turned to him. 'You know this.'

'Arkhan said that the Undying King would always be with me.'

Arul nodded. 'As he is with all of us.' She tapped her arm, where the ripped flesh had sloughed back together. 'Inside us. Watching through our eyes, listening with our ears. We are him, and he is us.' She folded her hands, as if in prayer. 'As all things will be, in time.'

'Yes.'

Pharus heard a sound, as of waves crashing against the shore, and an unnatural wind kicked up, casting the sand about in all directions. He looked up. Shrieking chainrasps were hurtling towards the city on a wave of eldritch energy. Among them were scythe-wielding wraiths and heralds of disaster, tolling deadly bells. Malendrek was at their head with his host of spectral riders, riding high, like foam on a cresting wave.

Pharus knew at once that Malendrek was seeking to claim the glory for himself. That need drove the Knight of Shrouds. Arul clucked her tongue. 'So impatient, that one.'

Pharus did not reply. Instead, he sped back, to where he'd left Dohl and the others. If Malendrek intended to enter the city tonight, then Pharus would be right there with him.

As Nagash had commanded, so must it be.

The deathstorm had begun.

CHAPTER SEVENTEEN

DEATHSTORM

The wind whipped along the spires and buttresses of the northern mausoleum gate and set the lamps to flickering, when Lieutenant Vale got word that the lord-arcanum was on his way. He didn't know what that meant, but rolled out his men for inspection. With the rest of Third Company being deployed elsewhere, that left his section in sole charge of the northern mausoleum gate. There were enough warm bodies to man the walls – just. The city's forces were stretched thin everywhere.

The men came with much grumbling and the clatter of kit being hastily pulled on. None of them wanted to be outside their gatehouse-barracks on a night like this, and he didn't blame them. The nights were getting longer, and there was a purple fire on the horizon. Bad omens clustered thick, wherever you looked. And worst of all – it was raining.

'Get in line, get in line,' he hollered, as he splashed through the mud. A hundred men or more could comfortably line up single file in the courtyard.

Wide avenues of cobblestones ran through the courtyard, stretching from the pair of massive portcullises that were set into the high walls between the largest bastions. Once, those avenues had been crowded by columns of refugees, traders and pilgrims. Now, they were empty of everything save the overturned carts and makeshift barricades Captain Fosko had ordered set up before his departure. Storm-lanterns hung from nearby posts and support beams, casting a watery blue light over the proceedings. 'Boots on, breeches up, you jack-a-ninnies,' he shouted, slapping his gauntlets against his thigh as he strode down the line.

'I'm not sure that I'm drunk enough for this,' Sergeant Gomes said, upending his flask. Vale glanced at the squat figure of his second in command. 'Stow the flask, Gomes,' Vale said, but quietly. 'Kurst is coming this way. I'll never hear the end of it if he sees you with a flask pressed to your lips.' The warrior-priest was his section's disapproving shadow, assigned to them by Captain-General Varo Tyrmane himself, the better to keep his men's blades blessed and their souls relatively intact.

'Oh joy, the Vulture shows his beak,' Gomes muttered. Vale frowned, but didn't chastise his sergeant. Kurst did resemble a carrion-bird, and an ugly one at that; a thin, gangling man, clad in loose black robes and out-sized black armour, with baroque decorations of stylised bones and scythes. He was bald, save for a fringe of lank, colourless hair that spilled down the back of his scrawny neck. His face was pinched in a permanent expression of disapproval, and he thumped the head of his warhammer into his palm repeatedly as he stalked the line of assembled soldiers.

'I've always wondered where they dug him up – he must be sixty turns of the wheel if he's a day,' Gomes said. 'You can practically smell the grave-mould on him.'

'A man like that doesn't get older – just nastier,' Vale said. 'And that's not grave-mould. I've heard he doesn't bathe. Says it weakens the ligaments.'

Gomes chuckled. 'One good smack and he'd go to dust, ligaments or no.'

'Feel free. But not when I'm around.'

Gomes gave a gap-toothed grin. 'Worried about your prospects, lieutenant?'

'Not just mine,' Vale said. 'I– Hsst. They're here.'

The Stormcasts arrived, the lord-arcanum at their head. Knossus Heavensen made for an impressive figure, sitting astride his massive gryph-charger. Vale had grown up around Stormcasts, but he felt himself somewhat awestruck by the gold-clad warriors of the Sacrosanct Chamber as they marched into the courtyard.

Gomes took another surreptitious slug from his flask. 'They say he's really young Knossian Glymm, come again to defend the city he saved from Vaslbad the Unrelenting.'

'He's a Stormcast. They were all once someone else. Now be quiet.' Vale swallowed and stepped forwards, one hand on the hilt of the blade sheathed at his side. He caught sight of Kurst, doing the same. The warrior-priest stared at the Stormcasts with almost feverish intensity. As if they were living saints, or gods made flesh. He cleared his throat. 'Welcome, lord-arcanum. Would you like to inspect the troops?'

He realised how inane the question was, even as it left his lips. The lord-arcanum looked down at him, gold helm running with rivulets of rain. Then he looked around. Vale knew he was taking in the state of the courtyard. Vale closed his eyes, silently cursing himself for not ordering the men to make things ready for inspection.

'I stood here, once before,' Knossus said, his voice echoing through the courtyard. 'It seemed larger, then.' He looked down at Vale. 'You are in command?'

'Lieutenant Holman Vale, my lord. Third Company.' Vale gave the traditional salute – two thumps and a wave – and tried to stand as straight as possible. 'I have the honour of warding this place.'

'Do you know who is interred here, Lieutenant Vale?'

'I… I'm afraid not, my lord. Before my time, rather.' Vale glanced around and saw Kurst nearby. He gestured hastily, and the warrior-priest smirked.

'Orthanc Duln, the Hero of Sawback,' Kurst murmured helpfully. Vale grimaced. He had no idea who that was, or even where Sawback was. Ghur? It sounded Ghurdish. Vale looked up at Knossus and smiled weakly.

'There we have it – Orton…'

'Orthanc Duln,' Kurst corrected.

Vale shot him a glare. 'Right, yes, sorry, Orthanc Duln.'

Knossus chuckled, and the sound nearly turned Vale's bowels to water. 'Your youth excuses you, lieutenant. So long as you do your duty, it is no sin. The Celestial Saints are remembered by Sigmar and we who serve as his hand, and that is all that matters.' He slid from the saddle with a crash of sigmarite. Even on the ground, he loomed head and shoulders over Vale.

'Why – ah – to what do we owe the honour of your presence?'

'There is a problem.'

Vale froze, wondering if they'd found out about the pilfered wages. Or worse. There was no telling what Gomes got up to in his free time. He'd heard rumours of extortion, and local shopkeepers paying protection, to keep non-existent deadwalkers at bay. 'P-problem?'

'A weakness in our defences.' Knossus turned, studying the arcanogram carved into the street. A flicker of relief passed through Vale. They didn't know about the money, then. Then he realised what the lord-arcanum was saying.

'Oh. Ah.' Vale glanced up at the walls. 'Has something happened?'

'A long time ago, I fear,' Knossus said. He extended his staff and gently pushed Vale back a step. 'My warriors and I shall join the defence of this place. See to your men, lieutenant. The enemy is coming, even now.'

Vale felt a cold slither of fear and turned away. Kurst followed him. 'Is he right?' Vale asked. Kurst snorted.

'You only have to stand atop the wall to see that much. The eldritch glow on the horizon grows closer with every passing night. The winds wail, carrying the groans of deadwalkers. Listen, fool – hear them?'

Vale stopped. He'd never thought about it before, but Kurst was right. He'd been hearing the sound for days without knowing what it was – a dull, somnolent groaning. Like the rumble of distant thunder. He shuddered and ran a hand through his hair, trying to think. Gomes stumped towards him. 'Should I dismiss the lads?'

'Yes, but double the watch.'

Gomes blinked. 'They won't like that.'

'I don't give a damn,' Vale snapped. 'You heard him – they all heard him – something is wrong.' He swallowed. 'The wall won't hold.'

'Then we shall be the wall,' Kurst said. He thumped his hammer into his palm. 'We shall build it with steel and silver, or, failing that, with our bodies.'

Vale shared a look with Gomes. 'Right. Yes. Obviously.' He turned away, watching as the Stormcasts set up some sort of massive ballistae, near the entrance to the courtyard, where the two portcullis pathways intersected. Others, carrying heavy crossbows, were climbing up to the parapets, to join the mortal soldiers on duty there.

'What is he doing?' Gomes muttered.

Vale looked and saw Knossus gesturing ritualistically over the section of the arcanogram that ran through the gatehouse. Motes of corposant bristled about his hand as he moved it back and forth over the silver runnels. Light danced across the purple sands, and the air flickered with something like a heat mirage.

Ghostly images wafted into being about the lord-arcanum. Vale saw a stooped figure – an older man, worn sharp by life and heavily scarred, wearing the uniform of a Glymmsman – raise a breacher-spade over the sands and thrust it down.

Gomes cursed softly. 'I know that face. That's Vorgen Malendrek. The Hero of the Southern Gate…'

Vale looked at him in confusion. 'Who?'

'Before your time, lad,' Kurst said, flatly. 'Captain of Fifth Company. Or he was. He warded the southernmost gate during Vaslbad's attack on the city, and held Undst Keep against the Slender Knight.'

'Why haven't I heard of him?'

'He survived, didn't he?' Gomes said, grinning. 'Nobody likes it when heroes survive.' He leaned over and spat. 'But he vanished not long ago. Everyone thought he'd been taken in the night by a gheist.' He peered at the image. 'What is he doing with that spade?'

The image flickered eerily, as the breacher-spade came down

again and again. Kurst hissed. 'The blessed salts – he's digging them out!'

Vale stared at the image in horror. 'If the salts are gone…'

From the wall, he heard the winding call of a war-horn. He jerked around, eyes wide. The horn blared again, the echo of its warning shuddering through the rain. The image of Vorgen Malendrek vanished, as the lord-arcanum looked up. Vale heard shouts and cries of alarm. A man hurried to the edge of a parapet. 'Deadwalkers, sir! Thousands of them.'

Vale felt his stomach fall into his boots. Mouth dry, he looked at the lord-arcanum. The Stormcast nodded, and Vale was suddenly glad for his presence.

'It begins,' Knossus said.

The gutters of the Gloaming were overflowing with rainwater when Elya arrived. It had started slow, but the bottom had fallen out of the clouds somewhere between Fish Lane and Scratchjack Alley. Now alarm bells rang from the high places of the slums, warning the inhabitants that the city was under attack, or soon would be. The clamour of desperate shopkeepers hammering boards over doors and windows mingled with the sounds of looting, and the cries of those with nowhere to go. Weapons rattled in the dark, and horses whickered in growing nervousness.

Black Walkers stood on every corner, ringing their own bells and calling out the names of gods who were no longer listening, if they ever had in the first place. Flagellants wandered the streets, lashing themselves and screaming pious maledictions at those who gave way before them. The Glymmsmen were nowhere in sight, and it was left to local roughs and bravos to take charge. This they did with brutal efficiency. Streets were barricaded with whatever was to hand. Those seeking the dubious safety of these ramparts were stripped of what little of value they had, and put to work reinforcing the barricades.

Elya fought her way through a crowded street, liberally applying her elbows and feet, trying to reach the rickety exterior stairs that led up to the rooms she shared with her father. A man cursed as she stamped on his instep, and hopped back. She darted through the opening and winnowed swiftly through the forest of legs. Hands grabbed at her, for what reasons she couldn't say, but none managed to catch her.

The slums weren't safe anymore. They were never safe, really, but even less so now. The cats had told her what was coming, what they could feel on the air. Like a storm in the offing, and not one they could survive out in the open.

When storms came, cats sought high, dry places. There was only one place like that, in easy distance. As she started up the stairs, she glanced west and saw the dome of the Grand Tempestus rise over the city. Even at night, through the pall of rain, it was visible. Others would be heading there, looking for refuge. She had to hurry.

Things shattered on the street, hurled from the rooftops by roof-runners or vandals. She heard singing from one of the rooms as she passed by an open window. A sad song, slow and maudlin. There was smoke on the wind – something was burning, even in the downpour. A fire had raged through part of the Gloaming the day before. Deadwalkers, people had said. And the Leechbane. But no one knew for sure.

Elya didn't want to know. One brush with the Leechbane was enough. She reached her window. The doors of their rooms had been boarded over since the night her mother had died. The window was the only way in and out. She paused and glanced back.

Someone was screaming, somewhere close by. A long, drawn-out wail of denial that sounded barely human. And maybe it wasn't. She shivered and slunk over the sill.

'Halha, I'm back,' she said, softly. She caught a glint of silver, and saw her guest standing close to the window, tense, blade in hand. The trader woman's yellow robes had been discarded and replaced by dark ones, to better hide her identity. Her gold had been scattered in Elya's secret caches throughout the Gloaming, in payment for allowing her a place to hide. After checking to see whether or not she'd been bitten, obviously.

Halha relaxed as she recognised Elya. 'You weren't gone very long,' she said. She had a curious, lilting accent, like most folk from Gravewild. As if they were half-singing, all the time.

'Is he…?' Elya whispered, glancing towards the cot.

'Asleep,' Halha said. She sheathed her dagger. 'Still asleep. He moaned a few times, but did not stir otherwise.' She glanced towards the window. 'What is going on? Those bells – what do they mean?'

'The city is under attack,' Elya said. She looked around. There was nothing worth taking. 'We must go.'

'Go? Go where?'

'The Grand Tempestus,' Elya said. 'We will be safe there.'

Halha looked doubtful. 'I do not think anywhere in this city is safe.' The woman looked away, her eyes wet. 'We should not have come here. But Takha insisted. Said we'd be safer in a city than on the road.'

Elya took a bowl of water from the floor and poured it over her father. Duvak sat upright, spluttering. He stank of ale and cheaper intoxicants, and the water she'd dumped on him was as close to a bath as he'd had in a week. He blinked blearily at her. Then at Halha. 'Who's she?' he slurred.

'Up, father. The bells are ringing.'

'I don't care. Let me sleep, girl. I'm tired.' He made to flop back down, and Elya caught at him.

'You're always tired. Get up. They say the dead are at the walls.'

Duvak grunted. 'I don't care.' He pushed her back.

Elya shoved him. 'Get up, get up!' She glanced at Halha. 'Help me.'

Halha hesitated, and then drew her knife. She leaned over Duvak and pricked his throat with her blade. 'Up, fool. Or die here.'

Duvak blinked up at her, befuddled. 'Who are you?' But he responded to Elya's prodding and rolled out of his sodden bedding. 'What's going on?' he asked, looked towards the window. He was still dressed in his lamplighter's gear – badly dyed black-and-mauve clothes, with a leather harness for his wicks and oils. The harness was empty. He hadn't bothered to resupply after his last shift.

'We have to go, father. The dead are coming.'

He looked towards the door. 'But your mother… She's not back yet, is she?'

Elya paused. She ignored the look Halha gave her and instead, with an ease born of long practice, said, 'She's waiting for us at the Grand Tempestus. We need to go, or she'll worry.'

Duvak hesitated. Then, he nodded. 'Yes. She'll worry. Don't want her to worry.' She knew from his tone that he didn't believe what he was saying. He'd remembered, if only a bit. He always remembered, eventually.

She took his hand and looked at Halha. 'Come. We have to hurry.'

Balthas stood on the steps of the Grand Tempestus, watching impatiently as the Glymmsmen readied the plaza for war.

The echoes of the battle-horns still shuddered through the air. Beside him stood the mortal commander.

Captain Fosko, commander of the Glymmsmen's Third Company, was old, as mortals judged such things. His uniform was shiny with wear in places, and his armour was dull. But it was well taken care of, as was the sword on his hip. His fingers tapped against the skull-pommel of the blade, and the palm of his free hand scraped over his shaven pate, back and forth. The sound of it grew irritating after a few moments, and Balthas said, 'Must you?'

Fosko started, as if surprised that Balthas could speak. 'What?'

'That noise irks me.'

Fosko stared at him, and then looked at his hand. 'My apologies, my lord. I was lost in thought. It won't happen again.'

'You may continue to think. Simply cease rubbing your head.'

Fosko gave a snort of laughter. 'Was that a joke?' He peered up at Balthas. 'I wasn't aware your sort could make jokes, my lord.'

Balthas looked down at him. 'Humour is a skill like any other. One may learn it, if one is of a mind to do so.' He looked back out over the plaza. 'That said, it wasn't a joke.'

Fosko nodded. 'You are unhappy, my lord.'

'And you are observant.'

Fosko shrugged. 'Not hard to see. You radiate your displeasure like a storm cloud. Is this not as glorious a battle as you were promised?'

Balthas pondered the question for a moment. He was not particularly displeased. Annoyed, perhaps, by the situation – it was not ideal, having to defend such a place, with so many mortals underfoot. The Glymmsmen could be put to better use elsewhere. 'There are no glorious battles. Glory is accrued in the aftermath and doled out by poets and historians.'

Fosko shook his head. 'Then why are you here?'

'For the same reason you are, I imagine.'

'I am defending my home. The city I was born in.' Fosko reached up as if to rub his head, but stopped. 'I remember my grandfather telling me stories of when the first walls went up. When every night was a war against things that would drain a strong man's blood, or stop your heart with a gesture.' He leaned over and hawked a wad of phlegm onto the stones at his feet. 'It's better now than it was. But here we are again, with the dead at our throats.'

'If it bothers you, why stay?' Knossus had tried to explain, in his heavy-handed way, but Balthas still didn't understand. It made no sense to him. What was a place like this, next to Sigmaron, or even Azyrheim? No real history, no wisdom, sat in this place. The only things of any value here were the catacombs below, and that was debatable.

Fosko looked out over the plaza, as his warriors worked to fortify it. 'This place is more than markings on a map. This city is birthplaces and burial grounds. It is where I fell in love with my wife, and where my son was born. It is where my friends lived and died, where my grandfather fought a duel for my grandmother's hand, in the streets of the Lyrian Souk. It is the sum of us, and all that we are. I would no more abandon it than I would betray it.'

Balthas looked at the old man. 'Is it worth dying for? New memories can be made elsewhere. New stories told.'

'Only someone with no memories would ask that.' The old soldier gestured apologetically. 'Forgive me. I meant no disrespect.'

'And yet you gave it.'

Fosko laughed. 'Yes.'

After a moment, Balthas laughed as well. 'How much do you know of us, captain?'

'I've been around your kind since I was a child. I watched from under a table as my father and the other guild captains conferred with the Gravewalker on military matters. And when my father lost his skull to a Bloodbound axe, it was one of your host who brought it back to us, so that it might be enshrined in the family mausoleum.' He gestured to Balthas' war-plate. 'That black armour you wear is as much a holy symbol to us as the High Star.'

Balthas nodded. 'You were right when you said I had no memories. I am a city, built on secrets. Much like this one. Instead of catacombs, I have a life I cannot recall. Once, I might have lived in a place like this, and I might even have felt as you do. Even so, I do not understand it. Maybe it is beyond me.' He leaned against his staff. 'That is not easy for me to admit. I have seen things no mortal can conceive of. I have walked in the fiery heart of a star and endured the chill of the firmament. But I would not die for those reminiscences.'

Fosko squinted up at the sky. 'Maybe those are the wrong sort of memories.'

Balthas looked at him for a moment. 'Perhaps.'

They stood in newly companionable silence, watching the preparations. The Freeguild soldiers moved with impressive speed. Bucket brigades doused the barricades in water taken from the Glass Mere and blessed by the priests who moved through the ranks. Handgunners took up position at the entrances to the plaza, their weapons loaded with silver, salt and iron. Swordsmen rubbed holy oils into their blades, and softly sang hymns that had been old when the city was young.

Nearby, Grom Juddsson and his clan warriors had broken open casks of some dark duardin spirit, and were upending them. The warriors of the Riven Clans were the other unnecessary mortal defenders assigned to the plaza – they would hold the western edge, while the Freeguild held the east. Other kin-bands of duardin from the Clans were scattered throughout the city, defending the holdings of their particular clan.

The duardin drank until their beards were dripping, and the smell of their libations hung on the wet air, bitterly pungent. Balthas watched in disapproval as two heavily armoured duardin crashed into one another, heads lowered. As they slumped, Juddsson and the others cheered and toasted them. Fosko chuckled.

'Rowdy, aren't they?'

'I thought duardin only toasted victory.'

Fosko snorted. 'They do. The Riven Clans have never lost a battle. Or so they claim. They toast to their impending victory, so that it might be written in stone.' He turned away. 'Here they come.'

Balthas followed his gaze. He saw the soldiers making way for a tide of humanity. 'What is this? Reinforcements?'

Fosko laughed. 'Ha! No. Not enough room in the inner wards for everyone in the city, especially these days. Some have to make do the best they can.' Then, more loudly, 'Make way for them, make way!' He waved a hand, and soldiers scrambled out of the path of the fearful citizenry. They moved towards the temple steps in a great mass. Some were praying, others talking among themselves. Men and women and children. Old and young. The adults in evidence were more the former.

'Anyone with an able body is on the walls, or heading that way,' Fosko said. 'That leaves the gaffers and grannies to herd the children to safety. Such as it is.' He spat.

'We are here,' Balthas said after a moment's hesitation. 'We will protect them.'

'And who'll protect us while we're doing that?'

Balthas hiked a thumb at the statue of Sigmar. 'Him.'

Fosko glanced back and frowned. 'You might have something there.' He hesitated. 'Have you ever…? I mean…' He fell silent, looking uncertain.

'I have,' Balthas said, quietly. 'It was he who sent me here.' He looked down at the mortal. 'He would be proud of you, I think.'

Fosko's face tightened. He turned away. 'I do my duty,' he said, his voice harsh. 'Always have. Always will.' He pointed and bellowed suddenly. 'You, there – leave the bloody cart! No room for that in the temple. Idiot.' He whistled. 'Horst! Damael! Add that cart to the wall.'

A shamefaced carter hurried up the steps, leaving an overburdened cart at the bottom. Two of Fosko's soldiers toppled it, scattering its contents as they manhandled it towards the barricades. Fosko shook his head, looking at the detritus strewn across the ground. 'Fool. Risking his life for a few valuables.'

'Weren't you the one just telling me about dying for memories?'

'Things aren't memories. Things can be replaced.' Fosko grunted. 'Family and home is worth dying for. A cart full of badly made glassware and stolen silks is not.'

'I shall keep that in mind.'

Fosko laughed. And Balthas followed suit, a moment later. But the moment was interrupted by the blare of a horn, from somewhere on the rooftops around the plaza. Fosko cursed. 'That's torn it. They've sighted the foe – finish up those barricades, fools! We'll have deadwalkers on us before you know it!' He stepped down from the steps, bellowing orders. Balthas left him to it.

He opened his senses, testing the aetheric winds. They were strong here – stronger than they ought to have been. He wondered whether that was due to the surge in wild magics. But with them came something else – a spiritual murk, as if the realm itself had been struck by some malaise. He could see it in the tight faces of the mortals hurrying past him – a bone-deep fear. Primal and gnawing.

Something was coming. Something more dangerous than any nighthaunt or shambling deadwalker. Whatever it was, it was the reason he had been sent here. He was as certain of that as he was his own name.

He glanced back at the face of the temple and the great statue of Sigmar the Liberator. The sculptor had crafted the God-King's face with a determined snarl, and he seemed on the verge of exhaustion as he raised Ghal Maraz to shatter the chains of the souls cowering below him.

Balthas studied Sigmar's face for a moment longer. Then he turned and whistled. Quicksilver rose to his feet and padded towards his master, grumbling softly in eagerness. Balthas hauled himself into the saddle. As he did so, he saw Miska striding towards him.

'I heard the horns,' she said.

'The enemy draws close,' Balthas said, hauling on Quicksilver's reins. He gestured with his staff, as the rest of his subordinates gathered around. 'Porthas, stand ready for my call. Mara, take your Sequitors to the steps. Usher the mortals to safety. Quintus, you and your Castigators will support Porthas. Gellius, Faunus – set up the celestar ballista on the portico. Wait for my signal. Swiftly now!'

His officers moved quickly, calling out to their cohorts.

Balthas nodded, pleased by the display of discipline. He was confident that they would do as he'd ordered. Their discipline was the rock upon which the dead would break.

'I will stand with Porthas,' Miska said, making to follow the Sequitors.

'No,' Balthas said. 'I will do that. Take Helios and his Evocators and fortify the temple. We will need to fall back and I want you waiting. Seek out the Liberator-Prime, Calys Eltain. I want her warriors ready.'

'You think Fosko and the duardin will fail.'

'Can you feel it? That blotch on the aether.' He looked down at her. 'Something is coming. Something beyond the reach of shot and pike.' He shook his head. 'This is the foe we were made to fight. It is outside their experience.'

She frowned. Her hand fell to the spirit-bottles hanging from her belt. 'Yes.'

'We must be ready for the inevitable. We will cover their retreat, when the time comes.' He turned, scanning the sky. It had gone ominously dark. Not the dark of a storm, or of the night, but something else. There was a sourness on the air, clinging to everything, and it was only growing stronger.

Miska started up the steps, calling out to Helios as she went. Balthas watched her go, and then turned back to the approaching enemy. He urged Quicksilver forwards, and the gryph-charger bounded down the steps, squalling in readiness. Freeguild warriors made way for the lord-arcanum, eyeing both him and his steed with nervousness. Fosko was waiting for him at the outer edge of the temple plaza. The captain turned, eyebrow raised.

'Come to stand with us, then?'

'Yes,' Balthas said, looking down at him.

'Just you?'

'I am enough.' He could see the wheels turning in Fosko's

head. The old soldier was no fool – he and his men were expendable, so long as the temple remained inviolate. Balthas wondered whether he would protest. But, after a moment, Fosko simply nodded.

'Let's hope so.'

Miska found Calys Eltain standing watch above the nave. The Liberator-Prime stood on the balcony, arms crossed, her helm hanging from her belt. Her face was set and stiff, as if she wished she were anywhere else. Then, given how Balthas had treated her, that was understandable. The lord-arcanum was off-putting, even at the best of times.

The Knight-Incantor strode to join the other Stormcast, pausing only to allow a priest to hurry past. Calys glanced at her. 'I heard the horns. The enemy has entered the city.'

'As was expected,' Miska said. 'My warriors and I will fortify this place, to prevent the enemy from entering easily.' She could see Helios and the others spreading out below. They would perform the necessary rites to render the twelve entrances of the temple inviolate against fell spirits and shambling corpses.

'It is made of stone and hardened timber. What more can be done?'

'Much, if you know how.' Miska looked up at the glass dome of the roof. Golden sigils marked each pane of glass in the dome. Designed to draw the radiance of Azyr down to comfort the worshippers within its walls, the whole structure thrummed with divine power. She hoped it would be enough. 'Your warriors?'

'One at each entrance, save for the main. They will hold, whatever comes.'

'And the main?'

Calys looked at her. 'It is mine. It is my duty to hold this place. To keep the enemy from discovering what is hidden beneath us.'

'That is our goal as well.'

'I have never heard of you, or your chamber. And now, here, two of your sort, come to reinforce us. First Knossus, and now this Balthas.' Calys looked down, into the nave below and the people flooding the aisle. 'Almost as if the God-King were waiting for an excuse to unleash you.'

'That you have never heard of us does not mean we have been hiding,' Miska said. 'We have taken the field a total of fifteen times, since I was first called to Sigmar's side. Fifteen campaigns in the mortal realms, none so long as I might wish. Balthas is brutally efficient when he puts his mind to it.'

'You say that as if it's a bad thing.'

Miska didn't reply. She looked at the statue which loomed over the interior of the temple – Sigmar the Liberator, holding the realms on his back, his foot crushing the skull of a vaguely amorphous daemonic shape. Miska wasn't certain just which of the Ruinous Powers it was supposed to be – perhaps all of them. 'We are not soldiers by nature, not like you, though we are no less warriors. Our discipline has taken us down a different path.' She held up her hand and let crackling strands of aether dance in her palm. 'We seek not the foe in the open field, but a more insidious opponent – one we have not successfully defeated.'

'Dathus – Lord-Relictor Dathus – mentioned something about that. He said that you of the Sacrosanct Chambers wage war on the Anvil of Apotheosis itself.' Calys shook her head. 'I was not certain what he meant.'

Miska hesitated. The problems with the reforging process were not a secret. But neither was it spoken of openly. Before she could reply, Calys went on. 'They say that you witness the reforging.'

'I have that honour.'

'Have you – I mean…' She hesitated. She looked down, watching the refugees crowd into the temple. 'I did not know him well. I did not know him at all. But he saved me. You understand?'

Miska did. The bonds between the warriors of Azyr were as strong as sigmarite. She would die for any warrior under her command, and they would do the same for her. 'What was his name?'

'Pharus. Pharus Thaum. He was our lord-castellant.' Calys looked at her. 'He saved me. He died, saving me.' She looked down and, for the first time, Miska noticed the gryph-hound laying at Calys' feet. The beast looked up at her and yawned.

'I know that name,' Miska said, after a moment. 'The secrets of the reforging process are ever-changing, like the aether itself. No two spirits are the same, and thus no two reforgings are alike.'

'Then he has been…' Calys trailed off.

Miska looked away. 'Pharus burned like a star – he burned too brightly and was consumed by his own strength. That is what happened to him.'

'Then he is dead twice-over, because of me.' Calys leaned against the stone rail of the balcony. It crumbled in her grip.

'No.' Miska caught her by the shoulder. 'We are forged from memories and starlight, Calys Eltain. Both are volatile. They can consume us, as easily as they comfort us.' She decided not to mention that Thaum's soul might be loose somewhere in Shyish. 'Pharus fought and died, as a son of Azyr. We should all be so lucky, when our time comes.'

Calys turned away from her. 'I hope so,' she said, staring at the statue of Sigmar. 'I pray it is so.'

From outside, the horn blew again. Miska looked up. Dark clouds were visible through the glass dome, blotting out the stars. She felt the aether stir, and a cold sensation slid through her. She looked at Calys. 'The enemy are here.'

Calys drew her warblade. 'Good.'

Pharus ran across the sands towards the northern gatehouse, an army of ghosts at his back. He was moving faster than any mortal man, swept along in the wake of Malendrek's fury. The Knight of Shrouds had given the call to war, and the nighthaunts answered. They sped through the shuffling ranks of deadwalkers, rising up and past them in a hurricane of grey-green energy.

'Faster, faster,' Rocha shrilled from nearby. The executioner was almost a blur of darkness, her gore-streaked features pulled tight with unholy anticipation. 'There is justice to be meted out, and a tithe owed – faster!'

Pharus kept up with her easily, Fellgrip hurtling in his wake, chains rattling. He could hear Dohl's sonorous voice somewhere behind them, exhorting the multitude of spirits to greater speeds. They were a wave, crashing towards the distant shore – thousands of spirits, driven by one will. Pharus felt it fill him, and for a moment, he felt neither the cold nor the hunger, only a sense of fulfilment. As if the hand of his lord and master were upon his shoulder, as if it were Nagash's voice, rather than Dohl's, urging them on.

But the closer they got to the walls of the city, the brighter it became, until it was akin to staring into the heart of a roaring fire. The light pained and confused him, and drove the chain-rasps about him into a wailing frenzy. It was as if the city were encased in a dome of light, and he could see no way through.

He staggered, slowing, limbs smoking. It was as if he'd run

into a solid wall of heat. A chainrasp came apart with a despairing shriek. Another fluttered away, its tattered form alight with blue flames.

A great wail rose up, as the nighthaunts hurled themselves at the light, seeking to blot it out with their forms. As they struck it, thunder echoed through Pharus, and he saw streaks of lightning pass through the dead. Memories flickered – Sigmar had protected the city. Had set the dead to oppose the dead. Twelve saints and a circle of blessed salt.

'We must dim the light,' Dohl bellowed, from behind him. 'Overwhelm it!' His lantern blazed, and more and more of the lesser spectres streaked towards the city. But they would not be able to pierce the barrier.

And yet, there was a gap. A pinhole in the light. Pharus stared, trying to see past the glare. He spied Malendrek riding hard for the gap, his deathly riders spread out behind him. They pulled the rest of the nighthaunt horde in their wake. Pharus drew his blade and hurtled in pursuit. 'There,' he roared. 'Follow the Knight of Shrouds!'

He felt the winds of Shyish billow about him, lending him speed. There was a sound in his head – a triumphant shriek, rising from far away. The sword shuddered in his grip as the hateful azure light swelled to either side of him, blotting out the desert and even the gheists which surrounded him.

He heard the clangour of great bells, and smelled again the smoke of his dying place. He felt the cruel heat of his remaking and knew that this was the same power. Once, it might have warmed him. Now, it burned him, and might burn him away to nothing, were it not for Nagash. The hilt of his sword grew hot in his hands as he trudged forwards, determined to follow Malendrek through the light.

The heat grew unbearable, and he felt himself become

thin and weightless. As if, at any moment, he would be consumed. Dimly, he heard the scream of gheists and the rumble of thunder. Malendrek's voice boomed out ahead of him. 'You will all be remade in darkness,' the Knight of Shrouds shrieked.

Pharus felt a wrenching within him, and then he was through. Past the light, smoke rising from his armour and from his sword. He stood in a courtyard – familiar, but only just. The air was thick with the stink of Azyr, and the sweeter smell of mortal fear and blood. Thunder boomed, and he staggered back, throwing up a hand to shield his gaze as lightning washed across the stones.

He turned, seeking Malendrek. He saw the Knight of Shrouds locked in battle with a golden-armoured Stormcast lord, mounted on a screeching gryph-charger. Dark blade crashed against lightning-wreathed staff, as armoured warriors and mortal soldiers struggled against growing numbers of nighthaunts. The gheists slid through the walls of the gatehouse as if it were no more substantial than water. Some burst into flame as they breached the walls, but most endured and launched themselves gladly at the living.

Pharus took a step towards the duel, wondering if he ought to aid Malendrek. Something murmured within him, and he turned, spying the gate. It crackled with azure energy as well, but not so potent as that which banded the city. The light kept out nighthaunts, but the gates and the walls held out everything else.

He raced towards the heavy portcullis, blade held low. He had destroyed the gates of Fort Alenstahdt; he saw no reason he couldn't do it again. But as he made to strike them, bolts of crackling energy slammed into the ground around him from above. He looked up to see a trio of Stormcasts on the parapet, levelling heavy crossbows. One fired, and he swept his blade out, bisecting the mace-like bolt.

The resulting explosion knocked him backwards. Aetheric energies clawed at his substance, and he howled in pain. As he forced himself to his feet, he heard the clatter of sigmarite from behind him. He whirled, barely managing to interpose his blade between himself and a blow that might have sent his spirit shrieking back to Nagashizzar. Three Stormcasts, wielding shields and heavy mauls, closed in on him. He parried a blow, only to be knocked sprawling by another explosive volley from above. The three Stormcasts converged on him as he rose, trying to keep him away from the gate.

He cast about, seeking some sign of Fellgrip or Dohl. Where were they? Had they not made it past the light, as he had? A maul slammed down, and he twitched aside. Corposant flared, and he felt it burn. Snarling in frustration, he slashed out, and a Stormcast sagged back, body reduced to crackling motes of energy.

Pharus heard a scream from above and risked a glance. One of the Stormcast archers plummeted to the ground, body coming apart in strands of lightning. He saw Rocha chop through the sternum of another, her axe parting sigmarite in a burst of amethyst heat. She tore her weapon free and drifted down to stand between him and his opponents.

'Attend to the gate, knight. Let an executioner ply her trade.' Rocha raised her axe in challenge. 'Come then, iron-souls. Come and let me judge you.'

The first warrior lunged, maul snapping out. Rocha twisted aside, as weightless as a shadow. Her axe drew black sparks from the warrior's shield, and the force of her blow drove him back several steps.

'You, who took my betrothed from me, on our dying day,

and then again when the Undying King might have returned him to me,' Rocha howled as he strode towards the portcullis. Her words beat on the air like the tolling of a funerary bell. 'He was mine, promised and owed, and *you took him!*'

Pharus turned, leaving her to it. He slashed his blade across the silver chains that connected the portcullis to the ground, parting the metal like paper. Lightning flashed, and crawled across him. He could feel a weight press down upon him from all directions, and heard a voice murmuring on the air – prayers or imprecations, he could not tell which. There was a saint entombed somewhere in these stones, a corpse infused with the lie of Azyr's strength.

He drove his sword into the wood of the gate and grasped the portcullis. It was marked with protective sigils, and his hands smoked and steamed as he took hold of it. With a hiss of effort, he began to force it up. Blue flame spilled across his armour as he did so. A lesser spectre would have been destroyed utterly. Even one like Dohl or Rocha would have been consumed. But Pharus was not like them. He had felt the fires of Azyr before, and persisted. As he would persist now. The flames spread, licking at his substance.

He turned, catching the edges of the portcullis on his shoulders, forcing it above his head. He could hear the mechanisms that controlled it shattering somewhere above him, and cries of panic from the mortals set to guard it. Sparks rained down, as pulleys snapped and chains spilled from their alcoves to puddle on the ground.

He left the ground, rising, pushing, forcing it up and up, so that the stones of the gateway cracked and burst. Below, he saw Rocha push the Stormcasts back, step by step, with the fury of her assault. Her voice echoed over the screech of bending metal. 'You took him and clad him in silver so that he did not know me, and I will have justice.' She spat the words at them, as if they were arrows. 'I will take what I am owed in blood, until he is returned to me. My prince of the Fourth Circle...'

A Stormcast lunged for her, and she spun with a shriek, her jaw unhinging like that of a serpent. Her axe crashed down, splitting the warrior's shield and removing the arm that it was strapped to. The Stormcast staggered back, but had no time to fall before the axe licked out and removed his other arm. He slumped back against a support beam, blood pumping into the dirt. His companion darted towards the executioner, deceptively swift despite his bulk. His maul crashed down with a snarl of radiant energies, and Rocha shrieked in pain.

Pharus hesitated. Some spark of the man he had been urged him to go to her aid. A warrior aided his comrades.

But you are not a warrior. You are a tool. Tools perform their function, and nothing more.

Yes. Rocha's function was to fight for him – to perish once more, for him. And his was to crack the city wide, so that it might feel the full fury of Nagash.

With a howl of his own, he forced the portcullis up and wrenched it forwards. Stone shattered, and the twisted remnants of the portcullis were ripped from the gateway, to slam down into the courtyard below. Still burning, Pharus dropped and caught the hilt of his blade. He tore it loose in a burst of splinters, spun and slashed out.

The shadeglass blade cut easily through the thick wood, and the gates came apart with a mournful groan. They crashed away in a cloud of dust. The reverberations echoed through the courtyard. He dropped to one knee, his form smouldering. A moment later, the first of the deadwalkers emerged from the cloud and shambled past him. Then another and another.

He heard cries of alarm from the mortals and shouts from the Stormcasts, as this new threat confronted them. Pharus rose to his feet, an island of shadow amid a sea of dead flesh. A sea that would drown Glymmsforge and even Azyr, in time.

Thus, Nagash has commanded.

'Thus it will be done,' Pharus intoned.

Then, hand on his sword, he followed the rest of the dead to war.

CHAPTER EIGHTEEN

GRAVEWALKERS

It had all gone very wrong, very quickly, Vale thought.

Gomes was dead, torn apart by cackling gheists. Most of his men were dead. Those that weren't had fallen back from the courtyard, leaving the enemy to the Stormcasts. Now they took cover in shattered storefronts and behind overturned carts of the streets past the gate, watching as powers beyond them clashed. Vale sat, his back to a stone wall, his sigmarite sigil clutched in his hands, whispering every prayer he knew. It was only one, really, but he wasn't certain of the words, so he tried several versions.

He'd been too young to serve during Vaslbad's assault on the city, but he'd fought deadwalkers before. They were dangerous, but you could put them down with steel and fire, if you were careful. But this was something else. Something worse. Gheists crawled along the rooftops and circled in the air like birds of prey. They reached through stone and wood as if it weren't there, and could pluck out a man's heart in a trice. Honest steel did nothing, and silver wasn't much better.

Vale heard a shout and saw the black-armoured form of the Vulture lurch into motion. The warrior-priest's hammer snapped out in a looping blow, and a gheist fell away. The spirit crumbled to dust and tatters. Kurst stomped forwards through its drifting remains, his croaking voice raised in a battle-hymn.

'Up – up, you sons of Sigmar,' the warrior-priest snarled, as he smashed another gheist aside. 'Up, you gentle princes of Azyr! There is work to be done. Fasten your hands to the plough, and turn the soil – cast the dead back, and bury them deep! Up, you cowards and fools, up and look to the stars – there is courage there, if there be none in your gizzards!'

He reached down and jerked Vale to his feet. 'Draw your sword, captain, or I'll crack your skull here and now. Time to put in honest effort for your pay.'

Vale shoved the priest away and drew his sword. He didn't quite extend it between them. 'I'm no coward, but what good is steel against these things?'

'It is better than the alternative,' Kurst said. 'And it'll do well enough against those.' He pointed his warhammer at the inner gateway, where a line of Stormcasts had locked their shields against a flood of groaning deadwalkers. The corpses clawed at the armoured warriors, pressing them back through sheer numbers. 'Get the men up, Vale – we're needed.'

Vale swallowed and nodded. The Vulture was right. The northern mausoleum gate was his responsibility. Whatever else, he didn't intend to make a bad showing – he had his prospects to consider. He turned and, in what he hoped was a suitably heroic tone, shouted, 'Men of the Third – on your feet! Sigmar's chosen require aid.'

'Let someone else help them, then,' a soldier shouted back.

'Unfortunately for you, Herk, we're the only poor bastards around,' Vale snarled, grabbing the dissenter and dragging him out of hiding. 'Our only choices are to fight or die. And I don't plan on dying anytime soon. Now get moving, or I'll send you to Elder Bones myself!' He shoved Herk into the street and looked around. 'That goes for all of you. Up, or I'll give you to the Vulture – up!'

The men closest to him rose, if reluctantly. There was no time to see if it was all of them, and there was nothing he could do about it if it wasn't. 'Get moving,' he shouted. Vale let the Vulture lead the way, allowing room for the warrior priest's huge hammer. A Stormcast glanced back as they approached, and Vale saluted.

'You handle the gheists, my lord. We'll handle the corpses–'

Vale's bravado disintegrated along with the Stormcast. The warrior crumbled to flashing sparks of azure light as Vale watched, wide-eyed. A sword – as black as night and shining like wet glass – retracted, and a grotesque, iron helm appeared. Eyes like balls of balefire met his, and Vale stepped back, trying to scream but unable to find his voice.

The warrior, wrapped in black iron and grave-shroud, turned, almost lazily, and cut down another Stormcast. Lightning flashed, but didn't go far. Something hunched and horrid cast rusty chains about the warrior's soul, ensnaring it. Vale thought he heard the trapped soul scream in horror and despair.

'Blasphemy,' Kurst roared, striking at the hunched thing. His blow caught it on its warped helm, and it spun, smashing at him with its chains. Howling spirits rushed at the priest, obscuring him from view, though Vale could hear him cursing. More spirits boiled through the gateway, followed by shambling deadwalkers. The gheists hurtled away, streaking through the streets to either side of him. His relief was short-lived, as the deadwalkers lurched towards the line of Freeguild soldiers, groping blindly.

'Hold – hold fast,' Vale stuttered to his men, hacking at a deadwalker. His soul felt like ice in him, as he watched the dark warrior slay another Stormcast. How could such a thing be fought? How could it be faced?

He shook himself, trying to concentrate on the threat he could fight, rather than the one he couldn't. The deadwalkers were just as deadly as the gheists, and they were more interested in him than the spirits seemed to be, at the moment. He could hear the screams of the men on the walls, and still in the courtyard. They wouldn't last long, even with the Stormcasts there. 'Hold them back,' he shouted, chopping a deadwalker off its feet. Its icy fingers tore strips from his sleeves and left rotten smears on his breastplate.

More gheists streaked overhead, their wails digging into his eardrums. Dozens of them, then a hundred. Until the sky was all but blotted out by rotting, tattered shapes. There was a sound like bird wings flapping against the wind, as they kept coming. They passed through the walls as if they weren't there, and squirmed into the buildings on the other side of the street. He heard screams, but ignored them. The street was a tangle of confusion. More and more deadwalkers were pushing out into the street beyond the gatehouse. There were bodies slipping and falling all around him, men dying, corpses twitching and lurching. He ignored it all. The only thing that mattered was the dead thing in front of him. 'Keep fighting,' he screamed, trying to spot the Vulture.

A man beside him yelled as a deadwalker bore him to the ground, jaws champing. Vale kicked the corpse in the head and bisected its skull when it turned on him. 'Get up, Doula.' He hauled the soldier to his feet.

'We can't hold them,' Doula gasped. 'There's too many.' Vale shoved Doula towards the others – pitifully few of them now.

'Fall back, all of you. Fall back! We'll regroup at the lych-gate. Regroup…'

Something grabbed him, and he screamed. 'Shut it, boy,' the Vulture rasped. The old man looked like death warmed over, and his armour was coated with hoar frost, but he'd survived his brush with the nighthaunts. 'Call them back. Got to hold the line. Got to–'

He grunted. Vale looked down. The tip of a blade jutted from between the plates of the old man's armour. It was retracted with a wrench of metal. A gust of frosty breath emerged from his lips as he sagged against Vale. A tall figure, dressed in archaic war-plate and bearing a staff with a lantern atop it, looked down at him. The flame of the lantern burned with an ugly light that threatened to sap the strength from Vale's limbs.

'Have you heard the voice of Nagash, little mortal? Can you feel his hand upon your shoulder?' the nighthaunt intoned, its voice shuddering through Vale. 'Shall I speak of what awaits you, at the end of the last, long night? Would you hear the voice of Omphalo Dohl?'

Vale shoved Kurst's dead weight aside and turned to run. A Stormcast staggered across his path, clutching at his neck, lightning bleeding between his fingers. The warrior collapsed to his knees, losing cohesion. The hunched thing, wrapped in its chains, swooped down like a bird of prey, pouncing on the warrior's soul as it jetted upwards.

Before it could capture its prey, however, a streak of lightning cut across its path, driving it back. Vale turned and saw a gryph-charger rear up over him, its talons dragging a gheist from the air. From its back, Lord-Arcanum Knossus roared out an incantation, and another gheist was reduced to a cloud of ashes. 'Back, grave-maggots. Back, shadows! This city belongs to the living.'

Vale ducked as gheists shot past him, towards Knossus. Lightning seared the air, immolating spectres and deadwalkers alike. Something caught his leg. He raised his sword, before he realised it was Kurst. The old priest was still alive, somehow. 'Thank Sigmar,' Vale began, as he reached down. The old man groaned and caught at him. His eyes were empty and white, like the belly of a fish. His grip tightened, and Vale stumbled. Kurst fumbled for his throat, jaws wide – impossibly wide.

'No!' Vale hacked at the dead man's neck, nearly severing his head. From all sides, more dead hands clutched at him. He turned, slashing his sword out, lopping off fingers and tearing wounds in the bodies of his former subordinates. As he fought his way clear, towards Doula and the few remaining survivors, he saw the dark, shroud-clad warrior stride away through the carnage, followed by the hunched thing and the lantern-bearing nightmare.

'Fall back,' Vale shouted, as he hurried towards his men. 'The northern gate is lost. Fall back!'

'What about the lord-arcanum?' Doula asked, face pale.

Vale tossed a glance towards the gatehouse, where the fighting still raged. He could hear the snarl of lightning and the screech of a gryph-charger. But the dead were pouring through, and they were too few to stop them.

'Sigmar help him,' Vale said, turning away. 'Sigmar help us all.'

Lord-Celestant Lynos swept his runeblade out and sent a deadwalker's head tumbling away. The dead were pouring into the city. Gheists and spectres swirled through the streets, shrieking and cackling. Worse, those who died in their attacks were invariably drawn to their feet and set against those who'd failed to save them.

All along the city's central artery, the Anvils of the Heldenhammer fought to protect the citizens still fleeing from the outer districts, towards the presumed safety of the inner. A tide of panicked humanity flooded the wide street, pushing and shoving, as a horde of deadwalkers harried them on all sides. Lynos could hear the thunder of artillery, as the great cannon batteries of the Ironweld fired at something outside the city.

'Lock shields and hold,' Lynos bellowed. 'Form a corridor – every mortal life preserved is one less walking corpse we must face later.' Shields locked together at his command, and two walls of black sigmarite suddenly lined either side of the avenue. Judicators took up positions behind the bulwark of Liberators, their bows humming.

'Pragmatic as ever, my lord,' Varo Tyrmane called from close by. The captain-general of the Glymmsmen sat astride a night-black destrier, surrounded by his black-clad bodyguards. The heavily armoured mortals carried great, two-handed blades, edged with silver and blessed by the Grand Theogonist. More soldiers in the uniform of the Glymmsmen were attempting to control the crowd, and keep the evacuation as orderly as possible.

'What news, Tyrmane? Are your warriors holding?' Lynos shouted, hefting a deadwalker with his blade and hurling it aside. 'I hope you haven't come to tell me that you're calling for a retreat already.'

'No retreat, my lord. The Glymmsmen will hold, until the lord-arcanum commands otherwise. I merely came to provide aid in the evacuation efforts. My men here can protect the civilians, if yours can keep the deadwalkers penned at the other end of the avenue.'

'We can,' Lynos said. He lifted his hammer and signalled to the closest cohort of Liberators. The Liberator-Prime raised his own weapon in acknowledgement, before slamming it against the rim of his shield in precise fashion. The cohort stepped out of line as one, raising their shields and pressing the shuffling dead back. This action was repeated along the line, as each cohort advanced in turn, forcing the deadwalkers back. Judicators trotted in their wake, loosing volley after volley at the rear ranks of the dead.

At their best, Stormcasts functioned with mechanical precision. Each cohort fought in synch with the others. Unfortunately, the dead were equally disciplined, in their own way. Not like a mechanism, but like a single organism. A single mind, peering through a thousand eyes and reaching with a thousand hands.

But that mind could be distracted. Lynos glanced towards the cohort of Decimators who acted as his bodyguard. He clashed his weapons together, catching their leader's attention. 'Ocarius, dispersed formation. Time to fight as heroes and earn the songs the mortals sing about you, brother.'

'Finally – I've been waiting for this,' Ocarius growled. 'Up, axe-men – there is a forest of hands and teeth in need of clearing.'

Lynos fell in step with Ocarius and led the wedge of Decimators through the shield wall. They crashed into the seething masses of the dead and set to work. Great axes flickered out in a sharp rhythm, hacking through legs, spines and shoulders, as the Decimators steadily advanced and spread out, each warrior carving his own path through the dead. And the deadwalkers responded in kind, turning on this new threat and away from the shield wall.

By dispersing themselves, they lessened the pressure on the

shield wall, allowing the cohorts that made it up to focus on isolating and despatching the thickest knots of deadwalkers. Thus was the strength of a horde turned back on itself. At least temporarily.

He heard a shout of warning from above and turned to see a pack of dead beasts – wolves, or perhaps jackals – loping towards him. He dropped to one knee and brought his hammer down on the street, rupturing the cobbles. Lightning sawed through the cracks in the surface of the street, and a cleansing flame enveloped the pack of rotting curs. Lynos looked up as the winged form of a Stormcast Prosecutor swooped low overhead. 'My thanks for the warning, Sleekwing,' he called out.

Galen Sleekwing dropped from the air, his twin hammers snapping out to send deadwalkers tumbling. He spun, moving smoothly, clearing space with his crackling wings. The feathers could slice through flesh and bone as easily as any blade. Above, Sleekwing's warriors sped across the avenue, sending hammers of aetheric energy whirling into the packed masses of the dead. The Prosecutor-Prime fought his way towards Lynos, until they stood back-to-back. 'That's not the only warning I bring, my lord,' he said. 'The northern mausoleum gate has fallen. Lord-Arcanum Knossus is pulling back.'

Lynos hesitated. 'Orius?'

'Holding the eastern mausoleum gate, still. There's only one breach, but the dead are assaulting everywhere along the wall. The arcanogram does little to hold back deadwalkers, especially in these numbers. It's as if the desert has vomited up every corpse buried beneath the sand. Even Vaslbad's army wasn't this big.'

'One breach is all they need.' He turned, scanning the avenue. 'But there's more to it. The deadwalkers are a distraction – meant to keep us occupied.' He looked up.

The nighthaunts streaming through the skies weren't attacking, not in any concentrated manner. Most of them seemed intent on going somewhere. Worse, up the street, towards the outer walls, he could see more deadwalkers, shambling not towards the battle, but the heart of the city. 'Where are they going?' Sleekwing said.

'The Grand Tempestus,' Lynos said.

'Back! Fall back, if you value your lives – this foe is beyond you,' Balthas roared. Mortal soldiers streamed past him, retreating to the Grand Tempestus. He was a voice of authority, and they obeyed quickly. Deadwalkers clambered over or through the barricades, their moans rising and mingling with the shrieks of the nighthaunts who hurtled in all directions through the rain-swept air.

The dead had come upon them suddenly. First the nighthaunts, pouring through Glymmsforge's high canyons of stone like a flock of hungry crows. Then, following more slowly, the deadwalkers. Most were sun-blasted, sand-scoured carrion. Others were fresher, wearing torn uniforms, the blood still wet on the wounds that had slain them.

The nighthaunts slipped through barricades and even shields as if they weren't there, killing with abandon. The Freeguild soldiers were little match for the spectres, especially in such numbers. Those on the rooftops had died first, plucked into the dark sky and dashed to the cobbles below. Or, worse, they simply vanished – leaving behind only their screams of agony. Even the duardin weren't immune.

Balthas glanced west, where the warriors of the Riven Clans faced the dead from behind high shields, with shot and thunder. The duardin had formed three squares of wide, rectangular shields wrought to resemble the faces of dragons. Drakeguns bellowed through specially designed slots in the mouth of each 'dragon', filling the air with fire and silver. As nighthaunts swooped down from above, warriors waiting behind the gunners hefted rune-embossed shields, creating a makeshift roof over the gromril square.

But for every weak spirit that scrabbled ineffectually at the raised shields, a cackling spectre reached down and tore at the warriors beneath. Already, the outermost squares were buckling as the duardin were forced to defend themselves against the chainrasps and chatter-gheists that slithered across the cobbles, beneath the arc of their guns.

A war-horn echoed from within the centre square, and the duardin began to retreat. Unlike many of his folk, Juddsson was no fool – he wouldn't waste lives on a losing proposition. The duardin would retreat up the steps of the Grand Tempestus and reform on the portico, as the Freeguild were already doing.

Balthas thumped Quicksilver's flanks, and the gryph-charger darted through the field of silver corpses, carrying them to where Fosko led the rearguard in holding back the dead. The old officer was shouting curses as he plied his blade like a butcher's cleaver. 'Hold them back, you worthless sacks of cats' meat,' he shouted hoarsely. 'First man to take a step back without my order gets my steel in his belly.'

Spears of Aqshian flamewood thrust into the horde, as Glymmsmen braced massive pavise shields against the wall of rotting meat that pressed against them. The spears shattered skulls and snapped spines, dropping twitching deadwalkers to the cobbles. Fosko and those soldiers not wielding spears finished off those corpses that were still moving. It was efficient, if brutal, but the sheer number of the enemy was beginning to tell. As Balthas drew close, a soldier was dragged screaming through the shield wall and torn apart by the groaning corpses.

What was left of him began to twitch almost instantly. Soon, it would rise and join the charnel legion.

Balthas could taste the necromantic energies permeating the throng, like a sourness at the back of his throat. It had become a war of attrition, and only one side was replenishing its forces. The Freeguild and the duardin were leaving too many bodies behind as they fell back. The mortals had become a hindrance, rather than a help.

Even so, they had helped him to gauge the strength of the enemy. This was no sortie, no random herd of corpses, but an all-out attack. And that meant the enemy he had been sent here to fight was upon them. 'Pull them back, Fosko,' he snarled, jerking on Quicksilver's reins. 'You've done your duty – now let me do mine.'

He thrust his staff up and gave the signal. From the portico came a roar as the celestar ballista sounded its fury. Streaks of blue-white energy arced over the heads of the retreating mortals, and where they landed, chain-explosions of arcane energy ripped through corpse and gheist alike. As Gellius swung the ballista around, taking full advantage of its wide field of fire, Faunus readied bolts for loading. Balthas knew from experience that they could manage an impressive rate of fire, even by the standards of the Conclave of the Thunderbolt.

In the momentary lull that followed, he urged Quicksilver forwards, into the mass of dead flesh. The gryph-charger shrieked as he bore a corpse down and snapped its spine. Overhead, the nighthaunts roiled, some swooping towards the lord-arcanum, screaming. Balthas raised his staff and called down the wrath of the storm.

Lightning fell from the sky to leap from spectre to gheist, rending the bodiless spirits asunder. As falling ash mixed with the rain, Balthas swept his staff out, crushing a deadwalker's skull. As it fell, he murmured a transmutive incantation and transformed the flesh and bone of the deadwalkers around him to purest silver.

He turned in his saddle and spotted Fosko and his remaining men falling back, past the first battle-line of Sequitors. Porthas moved to cover their retreat in his own inimitable fashion. The Sequitor-Prime roared and swung his greatmace out, casting deadwalkers into the air. 'Come then, come and set yourselves in the path of the storm. See what it profits you!' He bellowed an order, and his warriors fell in behind him, creating a wedge of sigmarite, with Porthas as its point. He strode into the melee, greatmace swinging.

With every thunderous impact, deadwalkers were reduced to drifting cinders. Nighthaunts swooped towards him, wailing. Porthas set his feet and swung. A gheist exploded into rags of smoky effluvia, banished from the Mortal Realms. 'Shields up,' Porthas snarled. With a rattle, soulshields were angled to protect the Sequitors from the nighthaunts trying to pounce on them from above. Ghostly weapons bounced harmlessly from the shields, and the nighthaunts retreated in disarray.

As they fell back, Quintus shouted, and his Castigators fired. Aetheric energies burst upwards, as the bolts slammed into the ground beneath the nighthaunts. Several of the spectres were disincorporated by the blazing energies.

Balthas turned Quicksilver back towards the Grand Tempestus. 'Porthas – cover the Glymmsmen's retreat,' he shouted, as the gryph-charger leapt over the heads of the Sequitors. 'Mara, advance ten paces and set shields – hold until Porthas is clear.' He galloped towards the temple, trusting in his subordinates to do as he'd ordered. They would clear back the deadwalkers and nighthaunts, before retreating themselves.

The surviving Glymmsmen were reforming near the steps.

Fosko was shouting orders, gathering his soldiers into defensive squares. Nearby the duardin survivors had done much the same, warding their kin as they retreated up to the portico. Their shield wall was more precise, but Balthas could sense their agitation. He urged Quicksilver towards them, ignoring their glares and discomfited grumbling. 'What is it?' he demanded, without preamble. 'Something is amiss.'

'Our thane is injured,' one of the duardin growled. 'One of those spirits damn near plucked his heart from his chest.'

Balthas slid from Quicksilver's back. 'Take me to him.'

The duardin grunted and led Balthas through the shield wall, to where several duardin crouched over another, clad in rich robes and silver-plated gromril armour. Balthas recognised Grom Juddsson, though the duardin looked the worse for wear. His flesh was pale, almost translucent in places, and his breathing laboured. He clutched at his chest, and his eyes were squeezed shut.

Balthas sank down beside him. His storm-sight showed him the extent of the injuries done to the burly duardin. They weren't merely physical. Whatever sort of spirit had attacked him, it had left traces of itself on his soul – a sort of spiritual frostbite. If not treated, it could eat a mortal hollow in a few days, or even hours.

'Which one are you, then?' Juddsson gasped. 'Hard to tell with those helmets.'

'Balthas.'

'I don't know you.' Juddsson arched his back and grunted in pain. 'Feels like there are rats in my chest, trying to claw their way out,' he growled.

'I can help you with that. But it will hurt.'

'It already hurts.'

'It will get worse.'

Juddsson's grin wasn't quite a rictus, but close. 'Manling magic?' he gasped. The other duardin murmured in distaste and glowered at Balthas.

'Of a sort.'

Juddsson laughed harshly and lay back. 'Do it. I'll not die on my back, from wounds I can't even see.'

Balthas placed his palm on Juddsson's chest and murmured an incantation. The aether contracted around him. The air sparked and writhed, as thin rivulets of corposant ran down his staff and along his arms into the chest of the wounded duardin. Juddsson bucked. 'Hold him down,' Balthas snapped.

Two duardin dropped down, gripping their leader as he writhed. Balthas kept his hand in place for another moment, until the lightning seemed to illuminate the duardin from within. Then he ripped his hand clear, drawing the flickering energies out. A puff of blackness burst from Juddsson's lips as he went limp.

'You killed him,' a duardin growled, lifting his weapon. Others followed suit.

Balthas ignored the implied threat and rose to his feet. 'He's not dead. And he'll stay that way if you get him into the temple. In fact, all of you fall back. You can do nothing more here. Go.' He hauled himself back onto Quicksilver, as the duardin slid Juddsson onto a shield and carried him up the steps. The last few ranks of their warriors followed, after a final volley with their drakeguns at the approaching deadwalkers. Balthas signalled to Fosko. 'Fall back with the duardin into the Grand Tempestus,' he called out. 'We shall hold here.'

Fosko shook his head. 'This is our duty as well,' he shouted back. He flinched as the celestar ballista roared again, and streaks of blue fire pierced the air.

'And it is my duty to deny the enemy resources. Your men

will only add to the enemy's numbers. Fall back. This is our war, now.' Balthas spoke flatly and forcefully.

Fosko grimaced, but nodded.

Balthas turned back to the plaza. Porthas and Mara's cohorts backed towards the steps, shields facing the foe. Quintus and his Castigators were arranging themselves into a volley-line. They fired bolts into the nighthaunts that drew too close, scattering them before they could mass.

'More of them than I've ever seen,' the Castigator-Prime said, as Balthas drew close. 'It's as if they're all being drawn here by something, my lord. And the aether – it's twitching.'

'Something is drawing near. This attack is but the preamble.'

Quintus hefted his greatbow and tracked a skull-faced gheist as it raced down towards the Sequitors. He waited until almost the last moment before firing. The gheist was ripped apart, and the resulting snarl of lightning played across the battle-line, reducing several deadwalkers to ambulatory torches. 'Let it come. We will despatch it, whatever it is.'

'Your confidence is appreciated,' Balthas said. He stiffened, as the aether spasmed and tensed. Quicksilver squalled, disturbed. He twisted around in his saddle, searching. Nighthaunts clustered thickly about one end of the plaza, as if awaiting something or someone. More and more of them were gathering on the rooftops and in the shadows. These were not mere chainrasps, but spectral stalkers and reapers, strong with the stuff of death.

'It's an army,' Mara called out, as she and Porthas hurried towards him. Their cohorts stood arrayed before the steps in a solid wall of sigmarite, facing the shuffling mass of deadwalkers that was slowly approaching. 'Two armies, if you count the deadwalkers.'

'The corpses are a distraction,' Porthas said, glancing back.

'Keeping us occupied, until something worse arrives.' He tensed. Balthas felt it as well. They all did. Like a cold wind, wailing through the hollows of their souls.

Balthas straightened in his saddle. 'You are right. And I think that it has.'

Pharus strode over the bodies of mortals he might once have fought alongside in life. Indeed, he had fought alongside them. They and their fathers, and their fathers' fathers. How many years had he spent enslaved by the tyranny of the cold stars? How much blood had he spilled in the defence of a lie?

He stepped into the plaza, surrounded by ravenous gheists. They clutched at him, like fearful penitents seeking comfort. But he had none to give them. Contrary to his former assumptions, the dead were not silent. Indeed, they were a riot of noise. The spirits floating in his wake murmured and whispered to themselves and each other without ceasing. They had only grown louder after the living had retreated. Like hungry animals, denied a taste of meat.

He glared up at the Grand Tempestus, looming over the plaza, picking out the weak points in the ancient walls with instinctive ease. It was a solid edifice, and warded against his kind, but there was a way in. There was always a way in. He had learned that much, in his former life. But there were other obstacles to consider.

A wall of fire – or something as good as – separated him from his goal. It blazed cobalt, and he found it hard to look at for long. There were warriors in the flames. Stormcasts, but not any he was familiar with. Like the ones they'd fought in the northern gatehouse. 'They wait for us,' he intoned, with a certain amount of satisfaction.

'They defy us,' Rocha said, at his elbow. She ran a bloodless thumb along the edge of her axe, her features twisting from glee to grimace as the floating skulls of her victims caught at her hair, or the noose about her neck, gibbering recriminations. 'They seek to stop the inevitable. Hubris. They will be judged and found wanting.'

Pharus glanced at her but said nothing. Once, he might have challenged such certainty. Now, he cared only that she make good on that promise. She existed only to make good on it. As he existed only to do as Nagash willed.

He looked down. The bodies of dead Freeguild soldiers lay at his feet. 'Awaken them, Dohl. Draw them up. We will need an army to overwhelm them.'

'What Sigmar has abandoned, we shall remake,' Dohl murmured, from behind him. As the light of his lantern washed across the broken bodies, they began to twitch and moan. Something like mist seeped upwards from them, and things that might have been faces or limbs twisted within it. 'Thus the light of Nagashizzar calls to the wicked and draws them from their undeserved rest, so that they might shed their sins in honest labour.'

'Were they wicked, then?' Pharus asked. But he knew the answer. There was evil in even the most innocent of men. A kernel of darkness that might flourish, given time. Soldiers might be worse than most – or better than some.

Dohl gave a sad laugh. 'If the light calls, what is wicked in them will answer.' Misty, stretched shapes, like shrouds caught on a breeze, rose around him as he floated after Pharus. Newborn gheists rose from the bodies, whimpering and howling. Soon, the corpses would join their other halves, stumbling mindlessly in the wake of their own tormented souls. 'They seek refuge on sacred ground,' Dohl continued. 'Can you feel it? The heat of Azyr rises from those cursed stones. I cannot bear it.'

'You will bear it. You must. They cannot be allowed to hold us at bay. The way into the catacombs is below the cathedral. We must open the path and soon.'

'Impatience is a vice of the living,' Dohl said, studying the cathedral with almost mocking solemnity. 'You would do well to cast such things aside. What is time to such as we?' He looked at Pharus, his eyes glowing dully within his helm.

Pharus stared at him. 'What?'

'Time is a part of eternity, and eternity is a slave of time. Each moment drips into the next with a dim monotony, and eternity stretches across epochs.' Dohl studied him with ghastly eyes. 'For the living, there is no difference between moment and epoch. They are like beasts of burden, bowed beneath a weight they do not understand.'

Pharus shook his head. 'But the dead know different, do they?'

'We perceive the weight for what it is. We see, and in seeing, understand. And in understanding, we are driven painfully sane.' Dohl looked up at his lantern. 'The light of truth burns away all the comforts of madness, leaving the stark face of the thing, stripped bare of illusion.' He bowed his head. 'To be dead – truly dead – is a glorious thing. It is given to us to bear witness to the clockwork of infinity. You should rejoice.'

'I feel no joy.'

Dohl looked at him. 'You will, in time. Not that pale sensation that afflicts the living, but the true joy. The joy of knowing your ultimate place, without doubt or fear. This is the truth of the Corpse Geometries. The black formulae, which encompass all things.'

Pharus twitched, annoyed by the creature's apparent need to spout philosophical musings at every opportunity. What did such mutterings matter to such as them? But he said nothing. Let Dohl blather. Let them all chatter and weep and whisper as much as they liked, so long as they fulfilled their purpose.

A horn blew suddenly, echoing out over the cathedral grounds. The nighthaunts began to shriek and wail in agitation. The stones reverberated with the force and fury of the sound. As the echoes faded, Pharus heard the crash of boots on cobbles. A moment later, a battle-line of Stormcasts marched out from between the buildings on the opposite side of the plaza.

His hand fell to the hilt of his sword, and he could hear the sands shifting in the hourglass. And something else, as well… A rattle of bones and the slow, stentorian chuckle of a god on his throne.

A volley of crackling arrows arced over the heads of the newly arrived Stormcasts, and struck many of the milling cadavers that crowded the plaza. Bodies fell for a second time, blackened and smoking. But others pressed forwards over them, lurching now in the direction of the newcomers.

'Fellgrip. Attend me,' Pharus croaked. He looked at Rocha, who floated nearby. 'You as well. Their leader is mine. Carve me a path, executioner.'

Rocha grinned, displaying her broken teeth. 'It would be my honour, sweet lord.' She launched herself towards the approaching Stormcasts with a wild shriek. A clamouring of chainrasps followed her, until the air was choked with them.

Pharus looked back at Dohl. 'Continue your ministrations, Dohl. Call up more souls. Keep the rest of our foes hemmed in. They wish to defend that temple, let them. But do not let them come to the aid of the Gravewalker.'

Dohl inclined his head. 'As you will it, my lord.' His gaze flickered strangely, and Pharus hesitated. Was there amusement there, in the dead man's voice? He turned away, drawing his blade. The sands raced through the hourglass as he swept the sword out and flung himself towards the enemy.

The wave of nighthaunts crashed over the Stormcasts, shrieking and howling. Some among these spirits bore heavy scythes, or rang great bells and wailed hymns extolling Nagash's eternal glory. Sigmarite shields held against the sweeping blows of the scythes, but only for a few moments before the blessed metal parted, and the rust-streaked blades bit into the warriors behind.

Rocha led the reapers in their harvest, her great single-bladed axe rising and falling in mighty arcs. She was laughing, as she fought, but Pharus could make out the tears of blood streaking her countenance. Crackling arrows hissed towards her, only to shudder to pieces as the disembodied, chattering skulls of her victims interposed themselves.

The Stormcasts' shield wall bowed, as the nighthaunts spilled over it, and past. Pharus followed more slowly, watching as chainrasps pulled down a struggling warrior and thrust their crude weapons through the gaps in his war-plate. That he might once have known the warrior's name gave him little pause as he gestured to Fellgrip. 'Take him.'

The jailer gave an eager hiss as it flung itself on the dying warrior. Heavy chains slammed down. The Liberator's helm crumpled as Fellgrip finished what the chainrasps had begun. As the warrior's soul erupted upwards, Fellgrip swept its chains out, ensnaring the lighting before it could escape.

Pharus had seen to it that Fellgrip collected as many Azyrite souls as possible since they'd breached the gate. The jailer's chains shook with imprisoned souls, and Pharus could hear them screaming, if he bothered to listen.

They scream only because they do not understand. They do

not see. But they will come to do so, as you have done. All are one in Nagash.

'Nagash is all,' he rasped, as his sword licked out and danced across the back of a Liberator's neck, killing her instantly. 'All are Nagash.' He whirled, chopping through the upraised arm of the warrior behind him. The Stormcast sagged back, and Pharus thrust his blade through one of the eye-slits of the wounded warrior's helm.

Yes. Free them, Pharus. Help them escape the cage Sigmar has built around them.

'I will help them,' he snarled, tearing his sword free. As he left the soul to Fellgrip, a heavy blow caught him on the side of the head. His helmet was torn free in a burst of celestial radiance, and he wavered where he stood. Snarling, he turned and slashed at his attacker. Their swords connected with a harsh scrape, and Pharus saw his opponent for the first time – the lord-celestant of the enemy forces.

Their eyes locked. The shadow of half-forgotten memories fell over him. In his mind's eye, he saw a hard face, worn to sharp edges by a century of duty. Another slave of the stars, bound in chains of light. One who had once been as close as a brother. A name floated just out of reach, and he snarled in frustration. He knew this warrior – so why could he not remember his name?

All useless things are discarded. What purpose does such a little memory serve?

Pharus hesitated. He felt a hand clap against his shoulder. He heard a great, bellowing laugh – rare, that, for Lynos – *was that his name?* – almost never laughed. He felt the weight of his lantern, shining with all the glory of–

Their blades sprang apart with a screech of steel. He dodged a wild sweep of his opponent's hammer and backed away. He bent and reclaimed his fallen helm. As he placed it over his head, he felt his doubts recede.

He lunged, blade raised.

CHAPTER NINETEEN

BROKEN SOULS

Elya climbed through the stone canopy of the Grand Tempestus. As she climbed, she listened with half an ear to the babble of panicked humanity rising from below. Her father was somewhere among them, trying to crawl into a bottle. Maybe his last.

She'd left Halha with him. The trader seemed eager for something to occupy her time and was keeping Duvak from making a mess of things, or getting into a fight. Normally, that responsibility was Elya's, but it was hard to sit and do nothing but watch her father pickle himself and talk about people who weren't there anymore.

People were screaming and crying. The air throbbed with tension, and the sounds of battle from outside were only making things worse. She'd had to climb to get away from it. There were many people, in too small a space, despite the fact that the nave of the temple was as wide as a city boulevard, and almost as long.

She paused, watching as soldiers took up positions among the pillars and statues. Their commander shouted hoarsely, directing them with his blade. The duardin she saw were more subdued, but they readied their shields, making improvised bulwarks between the centre of the temple and the main doors.

Elya watched for a time, and then continued to pick her way across the stone carvings, as light as the cats that watched her progress from above and around her. They were scattered throughout the temple, seeking someplace safe and warm to wait out the storm.

Above her, a cat hissed suddenly. She froze as something passed across the face of a nearby window. A shape that wasn't a shape. She could hear the nicksoul gibbering as it slithered across the glass, scrabbling ineffectually at it, for the glass was blessed and it couldn't get in. It sounded like the mad men who sat on the corners and talked to people who'd died in the last siege. Just words, words, words and none of them making any sense.

Curious, she crept towards the window. It was one of hundreds, set into the base of the roof, below the immense glass dome that looked down on the nave. The windows were small circles of stained glass, meant to let in coloured shafts of light. Now, they were all covered in frost, so thickly that she thought it a wonder that they didn't crack.

The glass bled cold, and her breath frosted the air. The thing on the other side grimaced at the sight of her and began to twist itself in knots. It had maggots where its eyes ought to have been, and its teeth were nothing but sharp splinters.

But it had been a person, once. A man, she thought. No, a boy. It spoke to her, too fast and sounding like it couldn't catch its breath. The words tumbled over one another, and she couldn't make sense of them. It pressed broken fingers to the glass, and hoar frost spread wherever it touched. She hesitated, and then reached out, placing her fingers against the glass. It was so cold it burned.

The nicksoul stopped talking. It stared at her with its squirming gaze, and she could almost feel those maggots gnawing at her own eyes. She blinked and looked away. It hissed, not like a cat, but like a Mere-eel – a wet, guttural sound. '*He is coming*,' it rasped. '*He knows you, and he is coming.*'

A cat climbed up onto her shoulder and growled, tail lashing. The nicksoul jerked back, as if it'd been stung. Elya turned, something telling her to look up. The dome overhead was dark, and things that might have been stars flickered in that darkness.

But they weren't stars.

Stars did not scream.

'They're flocking like crows,' Mara growled, pointing her maul towards the dome at the top of the Grand Tempestus. 'Should we do something?'

'And what more would you have us do, Sequitor-Prime?' Balthas said, flatly. 'Turn from the enemy in front of us, to face another?' He glanced back at the temple and shook his head. 'Besides, if Miska and the others have done as I commanded, the nighthaunts will not be able to enter the temple – not easily, at least.'

'Small comfort to those within,' Mara said, turning back to the battle before them. She ducked her head as a deadwalker slammed against her shield. She braced herself and swept her maul beneath the rim of her shield, shattering the corpse's legs. As it fell, she stamped on its skull, putting an end to its struggles. But there were more behind it. There were always more. So many that they threatened to swamp the battle-line.

'I do not care about their comfort. Only that they survive.' Balthas thrust his staff forwards, and unleashed a crackling bolt into the corpses clambering at the Sequitors' shield wall. 'And that we survive.'

'Better odds of that now that the Gravewalker has arrived,' Mara said. She indicated the other side of the plaza, where Lynos Gravewalker's warriors had emerged, to launch their own attack. Balthas had seen his plan immediately. The lord-celestant had intended to catch the dead between their chambers and scatter them.

But that was proving more difficult than Balthas had hoped. For every deadwalker that fell, half a dozen spectres seemed to take its place, hurling themselves against the shields of the Stormcasts. Lynos' lines were beginning to falter as their momentum stalled. Unlike the rotten corpses that packed the plaza, the nighthaunts were calculating foes. They had a dark animus of their own, though they were as enslaved to the will of their creator as the deadwalkers were.

With his storm-sight, Balthas could see the faint glow of the souls they had once been, before the winds of Shyish had inundated them, twisting them all out of sorts. Flickering embers of amber, of jade and even azure were caught in a tangled shroud of amethyst – so dark it was almost black. Trapped by the magics of the ones who had drawn them up from their deaths. The sight of those magics made his skull ache, and he longed to unravel those black skeins.

Threaded amongst this heaving shroud were crackling striations of cerulean – the soulfire of the newly arrived warriors. Balthas winced as he watched a jagged bolt of lightning slash upwards. The mage-warriors of the Sacrosanct Chambers could weather such an assault, thanks to their mystic training. He often forgot that other Stormcasts lacked that training. They were at a disadvantage when it came to combating the aethereal hosts of Nagash.

But there was something else there. Something that taunted the edges of his storm-sight. He felt it on the wind, like the refrain of a half-forgotten song. It pulled at his attentions, distracting him from the battle. The blotch on the aether – it crashed against his senses, demanding that he face it. And suddenly, he knew what it was.

He could feel it now, at the edge of his perceptions. Like a storm that had turned back on itself. Somewhere, in the confusion, the soul of Pharus Thaum awaited him.

Decision made, Balthas raised his staff. 'Porthas, Mara,' he shouted. 'Lock shields and advance. They present their flank – let us bloody it, and show them why we were chosen to bear the mantle of Sigmar's wrath.'

'As you will it,' Porthas growled. 'Shields up, brothers and sisters.' At his command, his Sequitors moved forwards one pace, shoving back the deadwalkers before them.

Balthas swung his staff out, indicating the deadwalkers. 'Quintus, clear the path.'

On the steps of the temple, the Castigators fired their greatbows over the heads of the Sequitors. A chain of crackling energy washed through the deadwalkers' ranks, and the Sequitors bulled forwards, into the teeth of it. The aetheric energy washed harmlessly over their war-plate as they forced burning deadwalkers aside, trampling those that fell.

Slowly, in disciplined fashion, the Sequitors dressed their ranks, falling into a wedge. Porthas led the way, a half-step ahead of the others, his greatmace whirling. Balthas followed, after signalling to Gellius and Faunus. The two engineers swung their ballista around and fired into the ranks of the dead that stood between the Gravewalkers and the warriors of the Sacrosanct Chamber, clearing the path.

'Advance. Let nothing stay you. Not even death.' Balthas gripped his staff tightly, and overhead, thunder rumbled. Somewhere ahead of him, something was waiting. And he intended to meet it.

Pharus felt the hint of something familiar – a scent, a sound, something else – brush across his consciousness, but flicked it aside. His sword crashed against that of the lord-celestant, and the facets of shadeglass flared amethyst. They spun in a wide circle, trading blows. His opponent was skilled, but Pharus had passed beyond skill.

'I know you, I think,' he said hesitantly, as they broke apart. 'I know your voice, your gaze…' The battle surged around them, and lightning snapped at the skies. More souls lost. 'You are as I was, aren't you? A slave. A pawn.'

'Silence, grave-maggot,' the lord-celestant rumbled. 'The dead *will not* speak.'

Their blades crashed together again, and Pharus forced his opponent back a half-step. The lord-celestant grunted in shock. 'Sigmar aid me,' he growled.

Sigmar does not listen. Sigmar cares nothing for him, or you.

Pharus forced the lord-celestant back another step, the words ringing in his head. 'Sigmar cares nothing for you.'

'Lies!' Their blades crashed together again. The battle around them seemed to slide into the distance.

You are condemned, so that he might play the conqueror once again.

'How many times have you died? How many times have you seen warriors perish and return, lessened?' Pharus snarled the words, hurling them like javelins, the voice beating in his brain, as the lord-celestant reeled back.

'You know nothing, spectre,' the lord-celestant said. 'You are a hollow thing, made in the image of a hollow god.' Pharus hesitated, staring into his opponent's eyes. He wanted to tear them out and deny the contempt they held.

He is blind, the voice said. *Blinded by the light of Azyr, as they all are. They see only the light, not what it hides.*

'He uses you up, burning away memory and soul,' Pharus said. 'What will remain of you, in the end?' Hatred swelled up, subsuming uncertainty. 'You will be nothing,' he said. 'A husk, clad in black.'

'And what are you?' the lord-celestant spat.

'I am a thing of purpose,' Pharus said. 'And I will have justice.' The Stormcast hesitated. Pharus battered aside his blade, just for an instant, and swept his sword out, quickly. The black blade chewed through sigmarite, ripping and tearing the armour plates with fell strength. It darted, adder-quick, to pierce the flesh within. The lord-celestant groaned and sank back, blue lightning snarling around the edges of the wound.

Pharus reversed his blade and lifted it in both hands, ready to plunge it down into the lord-celestant. To finish him. But he hesitated. 'No. You'll not escape that way. I'll make you see the truth. And then we will fight beside one another.'

One thrust will be enough to hold him. Trap him. Quickly!

'Fellgrip – attend me! I have a task for you, jailer.'

The Spirit Torment drifted forwards, chains rattling like laughter. The lord-celestant struggled to rise, but Pharus set a foot on his chest and pinned him in place. He raised his blade high, for the killing thrust. 'You will see what I have seen and you will join me. There is no other choice.'

'There is always a choice, creature,' a voice thundered behind him. 'Even in the blackest shadow, there is a speck of light.'

Pharus turned and saw an immense, silvery, feathered shape bulling towards him. Chainrasps scattered like leaves in a wind as the gryph-charger bounded through their ranks. Lightning crackled about the head of the rider's staff. Something in Pharus flinched back from that blue radiance, as he turned to face this new opponent. The rider wore the black and gold of the Anvils of the Heldenhammer, but his war-plate was more ornate than that of Lynos – even so, he was familiar, somehow. As if they had faced one another before. The rider bellowed a single word, and a chain of lightning spat from the head of his staff.

It struck a chainrasp and leapt from phantasm to phantasm, causing the lesser spirits to spasm and jerk in seeming agony. They squalled like injured beasts as the celestial energies played about the links of their chains, and tore their aethereal forms to rags and tatters. The gryph-charger loped through their dispersing remains. It crashed into Pharus and knocked him sprawling.

Pharus made to clamber to his feet, armour creaking. The gryph-charger reared up over him, shrieking angrily. Its claws slammed down, tearing through his war-plate. Amethyst lightning sparked out through the ruptures, and the beast twisted aside with a yowl of pain. Pharus slashed out, driving the beast back. His blade bit into its flank, and a heavy hoof hammered into his hip, staggering him.

The rider twisted about and drove the ferrule of his staff down, into the side of Pharus' head. Pharus reeled, his spirit shuddering within his war-plate. Azure lightning crackled, and pain exploded within him. The gryph-charger turned, lashing out with hooves and claws. Chainrasps swirled about steed and rider like angry hornets.

Pharus retreated, trying to escape the terrible radiance bleeding off the rider. Images crashed through his head, insistent and painful. He saw the newcomer standing before him, shouting his name, and the awful, yawning tunnel of stars overhead. He felt the play of lightning – as hot and as agonising as the real thing – and the sudden lurch, as he fell upwards and away, caught in a cosmic wind. He shook his head, hoping to clear it.

Ignore him. He is nothing.

He saw the wounded lord-celestant clambering to his feet, as a phalanx of Liberators broke through the chainrasps and formed up about their wounded lord. He snarled in frustration and tried to side-step the gryph-charger. His prey would not escape him. 'Rocha – aid me, executioner!' he called out.

'A pleasure, my sweet lord,' Rocha shrilled, as she hurtled past, overhead. Her great axe licked out, cracking against the rider's staff. The souls of those she'd slain clambered over her opponent, clawing at him. The gryph-charger squalled, as its rider hauled on the reins and turned to face Rocha.

With his opponent distracted, Pharus launched himself at the Liberators, and his sword purred as it chopped through sigmarite shields. He felt strong as he cut them down. Their lightning washed through him, and the cerulean sparks became amethyst as they played across his war-plate.

Yes. Free them. Collect the tithe. Claim their souls in the name of the Undying King.

The Stormcasts fought valiantly, but he cast them aside with ease. Strength flooded him, and in the facets of his blade, he saw the reflected unlight of the black sun. It was as if Nagash stood at his shoulder, whispering into his ear.

Rejoice, for you are nothing more than a blade in the Undying King's hand, and his foes shall fall before you, like wheat before the reaper's scythe.

The last Liberator sank to one knee and was battered aside. Then, there was nothing between him and his quarry. Pharus gave the lord-celestant no chance to speak. He lunged, sword held low, and drove it through his opponent's midsection. The force of the blow carried them both, and the Stormcast slammed into the base of one of the statues that lined the plaza like silent observers. Pharus leaned forwards, driving the blade in deeper, until it bit into the stone.

Yes. Take him.

'Surrender,' he said, his voice a hoarse croak.

'N-no,' the lord-celestant gasped, clutching at him. His helmet had been knocked from him by the force of the impact, and his bare features sent distracting moths of memory fluttering across Pharus' mind's eye. His eyes still blazed, but more weakly now than before.

'Yes. You will see the truth, as I have.' Pharus made to twist his blade, to finish his task, but hesitated. Something in him raged, slamming against the bars of its cage. 'The truth,' he said again. Then, more softly, 'Do you know what it is?'

There is only one truth, Pharus Thaum. There is only one end, to your path.

'S-Sigmar,' the dying warrior said. Pharus wondered if the lord-celestant was answering his question, or merely pleading with the one who had sent him here to perish.

Pharus twisted the blade and put an end to his quarry's struggles.

'No. Not Sigmar. There is only one truth, and it is Nagash.'

Balthas felt, rather than saw, Lynos' demise. As he twisted in his saddle, he saw a crackling coil of lightning streak skywards, only to be drawn, with a scream of tortured energies, into the chains of the crooked, hunched spirit he'd noticed earlier.

'No,' he said, shocked to his core by the sight. He'd known it was possible to trap a Stormcast's soul, but to see it happen… For a moment, he sat frozen. Then he heard Porthas shout a warning and felt his opponent's axe grate against his back. The chipped blade tore through his cloak and drew sparks from his back-plate.

The force of the blow knocked him from the saddle, and as he struck the ground, his staff rolled from his grip. The ghostly executioner rose up over him, cackling wildly, lifting its axe in both hands. 'Come, Fellgrip,' it shrieked. 'Here is another soul for you.' The axe hissed down.

A greatmace blocked the blow. Porthas slammed his shoulder into the nighthaunt, knocking it aside. 'No,' the Sequitor-Prime rumbled. 'No more souls.' He turned, whirling his greatmace up, and brought it down on the plaza. Lightning erupted from the cobbles, driving back the swarming gheists, if only for a moment. Balthas took the opportunity to get back to his feet.

Around them, the battle had devolved into confusion. Nighthaunts crawled over Stormcasts, pulling them down or slowing them long enough for the deadwalkers to do so. Lightning burst upwards again and again, as more warriors fell.

Worse, more deadwalkers were pouring into the plaza. Where they were coming from, Balthas didn't know, but they were closing in on the Castigators on the temple steps, despite the impressive rate of fire produced by Quintus' warriors.

As he snatched up his staff, he caught sight of the dark-clad spirit who'd killed Lynos. The armour it – he – wore was baroque and tattered, hanging off a body and limbs that were barely there. The blade in his hand was black, and gleamed like glass.

As if sensing his attentions, the creature turned to meet his gaze. The world seemed to slow and dim. The crash of lightning became a drawn-out rasp, and the screams of the dying and the dead merged into a great roar. Balthas was unable to look away as the creature began to stride towards him, moving normally despite the slowed nature of everything around them. Balthas could hear the rattle of tattered armour and the crackle of the purple lightning that seethed beneath it. 'I know you,' the creature said. Its voice boomed like thunder, drowning out all other sound.

That voice was familiar – painfully so. Balthas had heard it before, in the Chamber of the Broken World, echoing in his head as it did now. He had known the moment was coming, but there had been no way to truly prepare for the shock of it.

The thing before him was a blight on the aether – a storm, caged in shadows. The wrongness of it made his senses ache. It flickered eerily, moving out of synch with the world around it. It was a thing that should not be, the essence of one god enslaved by another. Within the confines of its monstrous helm, its features bled and shifted – first human, then a bare skull, then something in between.

'I know you,' it – *he* – said again.

Balthas raised his hand, and tried to draw the lightning to it. 'And I know you, Thaum,' he said, as weak energies flickered about his gauntlets. 'I name thee Pharus Thaum, and bid thee–'

'Silence,' Thaum hissed, suddenly in front of him. His face stretched and wrinkled like canvas, lightning-scarred bone peeking through ravaged flesh. It was like a too-small mask, pulled over something horrid. Balthas took a step back as their eyes locked, and he saw…

Screaming, Thaum fell and fell and fell…

A child's face, a girl… Elya…

A God of Death, tearing him asunder and remaking him…

A tide of fell spirits, sweeping up towards the Shimmergate, towards Azyr…

Thaum shrilled in pain and twisted away, breaking contact. 'You,' he rasped. 'You hurt me before. You tried to make me something else – tried to take who I was…'

'No, I tried to help you – Sigmar tried to–'

'I said be silent.' Thaum spun, sword raised. The black blade slashed down, slowly, so slowly, but as inevitable as nightfall. In its facets, Balthas thought he saw a skeletal face, leering at him, its eye sockets blazing amethyst. And that face was reflected in Thaum's own – no longer that of a man, but a skull, stretched and warped as if something were growing within it. And he knew then what his failure meant.

'No!'

Porthas struck Balthas, slamming him aside, breaking the spell. As Balthas fell, he saw the blade part Porthas' helm like paper. The Sequitor-Prime toppled away, body shattering into starlight and lightning. The crooked spirit – the jailer-thing – swooped on the rising soul, chains clanking.

Enraged, Balthas instinctively caught hold of the aether and drew it taut. 'You shall not have him,' he roared. He slammed his fists down and lightning exploded upwards, driving back the spirits that pressed close all about him and sending the jailer-thing fleeing, its twisted form alight. Thaum too staggered back, shrieking in pain as the lightning tore at him.

Balthas rose and swept out his hand, ignoring the pain of the storm as it raged through him. Lightning punched Thaum backwards, sending the creature rattling across the plaza. Before he could pursue, a blow caught him across the back, knocking him to one knee. He heard the familiar cackle of the axe-wielding spectre, as it swept about him like a serpent readying itself to strike.

The axe came down, nearly taking his head off. He lunged awkwardly to the side, moving swiftly, trying to put some distance between them, so that he could employ his magics. He caught sight of his staff and shoved a deadwalker aside as he made to reach it. He whistled sharply, hoping that Quicksilver was still alive and able to hear him.

The spectre pursued him, the ghostly skulls swirling about it gibbering and muttering. 'I know you,' the spectre hissed. 'One like you took my prince from me – drew him up and bound him in star-iron. Made a false king of him and set treacherous thoughts in his head. Theft. Treachery. By these crimes, and a thousand others, have you been judged. And the sentence – death!'

Balthas turned and interposed his staff. He caught the blade of the axe as it descended, and the storm surged through him, cascading across the weapon and up into its ghostly wielder. The spectre screamed, not in triumph this time, but agony.

A moment later, the axe exploded into white-hot shards. The spectre flew backwards, form blurring and rippling as the celestial energies coursed through it. The creature plummeted to the street, its smoky form shredded and coming apart. It clutched at itself in agony, as the broken shards of lesser spirits clustered about it. These parasitic phantoms shot towards him as he approached.

He heard a screech, and Quicksilver pounced on one of the phantoms, the aetheric energies curling about his beak and talons allowing him to pull the dead thing apart as if it were living prey. Balthas stepped past the gryph-charger, closing in on his would-be executioner. The spectre tried to rise, its form tattered and fading. 'I will not... where is he... where is my prince?' it shrilled, lunging at him, ragged claws extended. 'Tell me!'

Balthas thrust his staff out, like a spear. The nighthaunt shuddered as the end of the staff punched through its chest. It clutched at him, and in that moment, the madness seemed to clear from its eyes. 'Tarsem,' it whispered. Balthas sent a pulse of aetheric energy through the staff and the nighthaunt came apart with a small, sad sigh.

Dead hands clutched at him as he pulled himself into the saddle, and tore at Quicksilver's fur and feathers. The gryph-charger snarled and lashed out, crushing the deadwalkers. But more pressed forwards. Lightning erupted upwards across the plaza, as Stormcasts were pulled down by the dead.

'They die as slaves. They will be reborn as something better.'

Balthas twisted in his saddle, as the words stung his ears. Pharus Thaum approached slowly, surrounded by chainrasps. Despite the din of battle, he could hear the ghostly warrior's words clearly. Smoke rose from Thaum's armour, but the creature seemed otherwise unharmed.

'As you will be reborn. As I was.'

'This is not rebirth,' Balthas spat. 'This is a mockery.'

Thaum laughed, and for a moment, it was as if another voice, deeper and greater, echoed him. 'It is justice. In death, I was redeemed. My eyes were opened to the truth of things. I see now that I fought in service of a lie. In service to a false king. And I have returned to cast down his works, and salt the earth.'

'And I will stop you.'

'You cannot stop the inevitable,' Thaum roared. He surged towards Balthas, blade raised. Balthas lifted his staff, and light blazed outwards. The air contracted and suddenly gleamed gold as a wall rose up, separating them. Thaum's blade struck the conjured wall, cracking it, but Balthas had bought himself a few moments.

He cast his voice into the air, knowing the aether would carry it to the ear of every Stormcast. 'Sequitors – fall back to the Grand Tempestus. All others – draw the enemy off, fall back into the surrounding streets. The battle will not be won here. I will buy you the time you need to disengage, but move swiftly.'

As he spoke, Balthas caught at the aether, his anger at the deaths of Lynos and Porthas – at his own failure – giving him focus. His fingers bent, and the air grew hot. He spat a single word, in the Igneous dialect of Aqshy. It reverberated through the thickening atmosphere. The rain around him turned to steam as he raised his staff.

Then, as one, every deadwalker in sight burst into flame. Not the orange fire of Aqshy, but the cobalt blaze of Azyr – a cleansing flame, rather than a devouring one. The fires of the stars themselves, focused through his will. As the azure conflagration blazed upwards, consuming and purifying, the nighthaunts drew back. The ragged spectres fled before the threat of the fire, and those that were too slow or too weak were immolated along with the deadwalkers.

The golden wall dissipated, as Thaum finally broke through it. He roared in pain as the blue flames swirled up around him and set him alight. His form wavered and he quickly retreated, with a last, parting glare at his tormentor. It would take more than flames to slay such a spirit, Balthas knew. Perhaps it would take more power than he possessed.

'But it will be done, regardless,' he growled. Just not here, he knew. Not now.

There was no salvaging this fight – the formulas of battle had irreparably broken down. A new strategy was called for.

As he urged Quicksilver back towards the Grand Tempestus, he flung out his staff, drawing the currents of aether to him. Where Quicksilver ran, the dead burst into cleansing flame in his wake, creating a corridor of purifying flame for the Sequitors to follow through.

Nearing the steps, he saw Quintus' Castigators falling back

towards the portico, as nighthaunts swirled about them. More gheists had fallen on the celestar ballista, and Gellius and Faunus were struggling to keep the weapon intact and firing. A hunched reaper drove its scythe blade through Faunus, and was consumed in the engineer's apotheosis. Gellius roared a curse and lashed out with his maul, destroying another spirit, even as his partner's soul was ripped upwards, back to Azyr.

'Quintus – pull back,' Balthas said, trusting in the aether to carry his words. 'We are coming.' The Castigators fired another volley and began to stream up the steps, smashing aside nighthaunts with blasts of cerulean force.

As Quicksilver reached the steps, the heavy doors to the temple were flung wide and Miska led Helios and his Evocators out onto the portico. The Knight-Incantor tore one of the spirit-bottles from her hip and sent it hurtling towards a knot of gheists. It struck the stones and exploded, releasing a frenzied storm-spirit. A crackling cloud of lightning zigzagged through the nighthaunts, reducing them to burnt particles, before at last escaping into the aether.

Helios and his warriors advanced across the portico at a stately pace, leaving crackling footprints of lightning in their wake. Celestial energies crawled across their armour, leaping out to cascade across the Castigators who retreated past them. Nighthaunts swooped towards the newcomers, cackling and screaming. The Evocators moved as one, creating an interwoven net of blows that reduced the howling chainrasps to sizzling ash. Lightning sawed out in a devouring fury from between their weapons, to lick through the air before contracting back.

Wherever the nighthaunts went, the lightning was there, reaching out to entangle and burn them, before retreating between the blades and staves of the Evocators. As this crackling display held the gheists' attentions, Mara led the remaining Sequitors onto the portico and through the doors of the Grand Tempestus, followed closely by Gellius, his ballista across his shoulders.

Balthas galloped past Helios, calling out as he did so, 'Efficiently done. Now fall back.' The Evocators fell in behind him and followed him through the great double doors. Balthas hauled on the reins, turning Quicksilver about in time to see Miska stride after Helios. She slammed her staff down, and the doors slammed shut behind her with a rolling boom. She nodded.

'The Grand Tempestus is sealed, lord-arcanum. No spirit will enter.'

Balthas was about to reply, when a sound echoed through the entry hall. The harsh scrape of many dead hands, clawing at the doors. The light of the storm-lanterns seemed to dim as the sound grew louder, and was joined by a piercing susurrus of babbling voices.

Miska stared at the doors for a moment. Then looked back at Balthas. 'They will not enter easily, at least,' she amended.

'For the moment, that will be enough,' Balthas said. 'It will have to be.'

Pharus stared at the doors of the Grand Tempestus, idly tracing the scorch marks on his war-plate. 'Balthas Arum,' he said. He did not know why he knew the name, but he did. Something in him laughed as he said it, as if at an old joke, now mostly forgotten. 'Balthas… Arum…' The name sounded wrong, somehow. As if it were a lie.

What is a Stormcast but a lie made flesh? A false promise, given substance by hollow faith. Stolen souls, caged and warped into new shapes by a trickster god. And who tried to do the same to others, in a parody of their deceitful master…

Again, the sour laughter came and this time, it rose through him and escaped his lips unbidden. He laughed low, loud and long, glorying in the certainty which gripped him.

Yes, you see now. You have bested them. They are naught but shadows.

'They are but shadows,' he said. He was close, now, and nothing – not his former brothers, not this Balthas Arum – would keep him from fulfilling his purpose.

'It is good to see you so pleased, Pharus. I feared you would find no joy in your purpose, as happens to so many who are bent to the great wheel.'

Pharus turned. 'My Lady of All Flesh,' he said, bowing. 'What news?'

'Glymmsforge burns,' Crelis Arul said, with some satisfaction. She rested atop her palanquin, her wolves growling softly as they gnawed on something wet and red. 'Malendrek wages the war he has dreamed of, and Yaros ensures that he is free to do so. As I have ensured that you are able to fulfil your desires.' She gestured to the remaining deadwalkers, as they pounded at the doors of the Grand Tempestus. 'Have they served you well?'

'They performed their function satisfactorily.'

She pressed her hands together. 'Oh, excellent. It makes my heart sing, to hear you say that.' She turned, as if scenting the wind. 'As it sings to hear the call of butchered meat. I can feel them waking up... My children. They see with new eyes, and hunt with new hunger. I must go and gather them.' She stroked a wolf's skull and looked down at Pharus. 'Will you accompany me, oh knight?'

'I will not,' Pharus said. He knelt beside the spot where the lord-celestant had perished. He could hear the warrior's soul howling as it rattled in Fellgrip's chains. Soon, his brother would know the same peace he did. So why did that thought bother him so? He pushed it aside, as the voice in him whispered in satisfaction. 'My duty is here, in this place. This is why I was remade.'

Arul laughed softly. 'Is it, now? How wonderful to have such a clarity of purpose.'

Pharus glanced up at her. 'And do you not? Does dead flesh not beseech you to raise it up, as the souls of the living call to me and ask for their freedom?'

'I think you were a thing of singular purpose, even before Nagash reshaped you. But we shall speak more on it, later. Once the city is ours, and the Shimmergate shakes with the tread of a million corpses.' She gestured, and her palanquin turned away. 'Fight well, Pharus Thaum. Our master stands at your shoulder, and you would do well not to disappoint him.'

Rest assured, you shall not. So long as you perform your function.

'I will not fail.' Pharus watched her depart, and then looked back at the Grand Tempestus. It called to him. Not the temple itself, but what lay beneath it. He looked down and picked up a Stormcast helmet, laying smouldering upon the stones. He looked at its stern features, seeking something familiar. Had he known the one who wore it? Would he know their face, if he saw it again?

'What now, my lord?' Dohl asked, drifting towards him. As ever, the guardian of souls was trailed by a flock of chainrasps, all murmuring and twitching in the light of Dohl's lantern. Pharus felt his growing unease fade.

'Let Malendrek rip the city's belly open. We go for the jugular.' Pharus stared into the scowling countenance of the mask. Sigmar's face. 'He makes us wear his face,' he said. 'As if we are but pieces of him, shed from the whole.' He cast the helmet aside.

Nagash and Sigmar. Apotheosis and dissolution.

The sun and its shadow, the voice murmured.

'The God-King seeks to blind you, to make you see as he sees,' Dohl said, as he drifted alongside Pharus. 'To convince enough souls of a lie is to make it the truth. But we stand firm. Nagash is all, and all are one in Nagash. He is the absolute, and the end. He is justice in an unjust universe.' Dohl lifted his lantern, and chainrasps gathered about him, seeking the hollow comfort of his light. 'He is vengeance for the innocent and punishment for the guilty. In Nagash, order is restored, and the madness of existence broken to the wheel of fate.' Dohl's voice rose to a sibilant groan, echoing over the shattered courtyard.

Nearby nighthaunts joined their voices to his, until a solid wave of mournful noise washed over the temple. Pharus swept his sword out in silent command. Nighthaunts drifted towards the temple, singly and in groups. If there was a weakness, they would find it. One gap, one chink – that was all Pharus needed.

He glanced down at what was left of Rocha's axe, lying scattered across the plaza nearby. It still smouldered from the lightning. He felt no regret over the spirit's fate. That had been her purpose, and there was nothing more to it. When a piece of the mechanism broke, it was stripped out, without sentiment. As he would be, if he failed.

But he would not fail. Nagash commanded that the Ten Thousand Tombs be opened, and Pharus would do so, whatever or whoever sought to bar his path. 'As Nagash wills,' he said, softly, 'so must it be.'

CHAPTER TWENTY

REFUGE

Inside the Grand Tempestus, all was quiet.

Few people spoke, beyond muffled prayers or the coughing of the injured. The Glymmsmen and duardin tended their wounded, while keeping wary eyes on the visible entrances. The citizens had gathered in bunches throughout the nave, or against the walls. Some moved aside as Balthas led Quicksilver down the nave, away from the main doors.

His warriors split up into smaller cohorts composed of Sequitors and Castigators, towards the twelve entry-points. Helios and his Evocators sat in a watchful line before the main doorway, their weapons across their knees and corposant dancing across their armour. Gellius had set his ballista up on the altar – shaped like a massive, twelve-pointed star – where he had a clear view of the entirety of the nave and the main entry hall.

Calys Eltain's Liberators still held their posts, at the doorways.

He saw no reason to pull them from that duty – twelve warriors more or less would make little difference. They would act as alarms, just in case the wards were breached and the dead managed to get inside. When he said as much, Miska frowned. 'She – they – deserve better than that, I think.'

Balthas didn't look at her. 'We all do.'

'Especially the mortals.' Miska looked around. Her face was set in a frown. 'I suspect you used Fosko and Juddsson to absorb the brunt of the enemy – to gauge their strength. We should have pulled them back from the beginning. I knew that and said nothing. Too many died that need not have.'

'You disapprove of my strategy?'

'You are lord-arcanum.'

'I am. And I saw fit to preserve my troops for as long as possible.' Balthas sighed and looked at her. 'The mortals had their duty, as we have ours. Now we must concentrate on what comes next.' He gestured to Fosko, and the Freeguilder trotted over, followed closely by Juddsson. The duardin thane was pale and moved slowly, but seemed to be on the mend. 'Status?' Balthas asked, without preamble.

'Most of my men are walking wounded,' Fosko said, bluntly.

'Bitten?'

Fosko grimaced. 'No, thank Sigmar. But we're checking, even so. If we find one… we'll deal with it, quietly.' He looked as if he wanted to spit, but refrained. 'I left the best part of my command out there, lord-arcanum. The dead were on us too quick – we're used to dealing with single nighthaunts, or just a handful. Never seen this many in one place.' He swallowed. 'Never wanted to.'

Juddsson nodded grimly. 'We weren't prepared. Too many manling promises of impenetrable walls lulled us. And now we're trapped.'

'Feel free to leave,' Fosko said.

'You'd like that, wouldn't you?' Juddsson sneered.

'No. You would have to open the doors,' Balthas said. 'That would not be ideal. We are not trapped,' he said, after a moment. 'This place is sturdy. It can be defended, if not easily.'

'A siege might last days, or weeks. If we're cut off from the rest of the city…' Fosko let the thought hang, unfinished. 'We should ask Obol about supplies. See what the Azyrites have been hoarding in this oversized chapel of theirs.'

Balthas turned, scanning the crowd of mortals. Priests in robes of blue and gold wandered through the crowd, speaking softly to those who huddled weeping, or sternly to those whose faith seemed lacking. The one in charge was a portly man, with a cavernous scar disfiguring one side of his round features. It ran across his eye, which gleamed white in its ravaged socket, and up over the crown of his bald head. He wore gold-plated armour over his robes, but cradled a battered, utilitarian-looking mattock in the crook of his arm. He was speaking to an elderly couple as Balthas approached, the others in tow.

'Lector Obol,' Balthas said, pitching his voice low.

Obol turned, his good eye widening slightly. Balthas knew a little about him, from Fosko. One of several priests – or lectors, as the Church of Sigmar called them – sent by the Grand Theogonist from Azyr to oversee the spiritual welfare of the citizens of Glymmsforge, both Azyrite and otherwise. A former war-priest, Obol now spent most of his time seeing to the upkeep of the Grand Tempestus. Obol bowed as low as he was able, given his bulk. 'My lord. You honour me – honour us – with your presence.'

Obol glanced at Fosko and smiled. 'Glad to see you survived, you old wastrel.' His smile faded. 'Can't say I expect we'll all be so lucky, if this keeps up, though.'

'Supplies,' Balthas said. Obol blinked.

'Some stores, in case of disaster,' he said, after a moment. 'Not enough for this lot, though. Even depending on whether you eat.' He looked at Balthas, eye narrowed. 'Forgive my impertinence, lord, but… do you?'

'We do. But we do not need to, save rarely.'

'Shame,' Obol said. He patted his belly. 'Sigmar knows best, I suppose, but a good meal sets the world to rights, I've found.'

'Often, by the looks of you,' Juddsson grunted. The duardin sat heavily on a nearby bench. Obol laughed.

'And have you ever turned down a meal, thane?'

Juddsson squinted at him and rubbed his chest as if it pained him. 'What sort of fool does that?' He turned. 'I remember installing a well. So there's water, at least.'

Balthas looked down at him. 'You built this place?'

Juddsson gestured dismissively. 'Why do you think I wanted to be the one to defend it? Took me months to get the capstones set properly. I wasn't going to just sit back and let a bunch of walking corpses infest it.' He stroked his beard. 'We could always use the tunnels, if need be.'

Fosko frowned. 'The catacombs would be worse than staying up here. Besides, I'd heard they'd sealed them off.'

'Not the catacombs,' Juddsson said. 'There are tunnels running throughout the city. We of the Riven Clans dug most of them. If we could get down there, we might stand a chance.'

'And go where?' Obol said. 'The city is under siege. The dead are everywhere. At least here, we know they can't get in. Sigmar would not allow it.'

Juddsson fell silent. Balthas looked up, at the high dome overhead. It was covered in a heaving shroud of gheists and hoar frost. 'Sigmar might not allow it, but he is not the only god present here, today, I fear,' he said. Obol paled and made the sign of the twin-tailed comet.

'Then it is true, what they say… Nagash moves against Azyr?'

Balthas looked at him. 'Who is this "they" everyone refers to?' He held up a hand. 'Never mind. Yes. I want an accounting of supplies. You will provide it.' Obol bowed awkwardly and hurried away, calling for several of the junior priests to accompany him. Balthas turned to Fosko. 'This place must be fortified. I want the entry halls blocked off, if possible. It won't stop the nighthaunts, but the deadwalkers are a different story.'

Fosko frowned. 'We're staying, then?'

'For the moment,' Balthas said. Fosko nodded and turned to rejoin his men. When he'd gone, Juddsson laughed harshly.

'Busy work, is it?'

'What do you mean?'

Juddsson tapped the side of his head. 'I'm no fool. This place was never meant to be a fortress, whatever manlings think. And it won't keep the dead out for long, blessings or no. So you're thinking of something else. Fosko doesn't see it yet, but he will.' He peered towards his own warriors. They had erected their heavy shields into a bulwark and were priming their drakeguns. One of them began to sing, softly at first, and then more loudly. Other duardin joined in, their deep voices echoing through the nave.

Balthas watched, perturbed. 'What are they doing?'

'Singing,' Juddsson growled. 'Did you think we did not know how?'

Balthas hesitated. 'I knew. I have simply never heard it.'

'Few have, outside the clan-halls. Our songs are not for the ears of the unwrought. Today, we make an exception.'

'Is it a dirge?'

Juddsson looked at him. 'Of course not. Why would you think that?'

Balthas didn't reply. Juddsson snorted and heaved himself upright, and made as if to stand. Balthas moved to help him, but Juddsson waved him off. 'The day I need help to stand is the day I no longer deserve to do so.'

Juddsson limped towards his warriors, one hand pressed to his chest. In moments, his voice joined theirs, rising in song. Balthas watched them sing for a moment. He glanced up at the windows, where ghostly faces were pressed to the glass, wailing silently. He imagined the nighthaunts clinging to the outside of the cathedral and felt faintly nauseated.

'They will not get in,' Miska said, after a moment. She had stood silent, while he conversed with the others, keeping her thoughts to herself. Now he looked at her, wanting her opinion. He felt uncertain… something he was not used to.

'Are you sure of that?'

'Aren't you?'

'Once, I might have been. But now… that thing – that creature leading the dead – was Thaum. I saw it. Felt it.' Balthas sagged back, onto the bench Juddsson had vacated. He wanted to take off his helm, but didn't. It would be a sign of weakness, and he needed to be strong. Strong enough to make right what he had allowed to go wrong. 'It – he – killed Lynos. His own lord-celestant. And Porthas.'

'He almost killed you as well,' Miska said.

'Something has happened to him. He has been altered somehow. His soul is tainted. The light of Azyr is trapped in a shroud of darkness.' Balthas shook his head. 'Only a god could do such a thing.'

'Nagash.'

He nodded. 'He has captured the soul of a Stormcast before.

More than once. Indeed, for some years, we thought it was his driving obsession. But never before has he managed something like this. I am forced to wonder – if he has the capability now, are any of us safe?'

'Sigmar would not allow it.'

'We must pray that it is so.' Balthas bent forwards. 'I saw into his mind – what was left of his mind.' He grimaced. 'It was like… a nest of maggots, making a hollow carcass dance. It is him, but he is just a mask for the thing inside. And I saw its plan.'

'The Ten Thousand Tombs,' Miska said, anticipating him.

'A place of censure. A moment of black time, stretched across roots of stone and left to fester.' Balthas closed his eyes, trying to forget the feeling of being in Thaum's head. 'There are ten thousand souls imprisoned below us. Fell souls – warlords and sorcerers, tyrants and failed heroes. More potent than the spirits commonly hurled against us, and left imprisoned here by the will of the Undying King.'

'Why would he do such a thing?' Miska asked. 'I have always wondered. Surely such souls might have been more useful on the battlefield, rather than chained here in the dark.'

'Unless even Nagash feared they might prove too hard to control,' Balthas said. 'That he seeks them now should give us all pause.' He looked at her. 'Where is Calys Eltain? I must speak with her.'

'She is at her post.' Miska looked down at him. 'Are you going to tell me why?'

'We know where they are going. Why else would Nagash send Pharus Thaum back to Glymmsforge, save to open the vaults he once defended? And to get there, they will tear this temple down, stone by stone. It is not safe here. We cannot defend this place for long. We will be overwhelmed long before Knossus is able to reinforce us. The only safety is down.'

'The catacombs?'

'We cannot make our stand here. They will overwhelm us sooner or later. So we must withdraw to face them on more optimal ground. There are reinforcements below.'

'If we cease our prayers, they will rush in.'

'Then someone must stay.'

'A death sentence.' She did not sound angry. Balthas nodded. 'Yes.'

'Volunteers?'

'One will be enough.'

'And you have one in mind?'

Balthas was silent. Miska smiled faintly. 'Go – speak to Eltain. I will tell him.' She turned away. Balthas raised his hand. Dropped it.

'Thank you, Knight-Incantor.'

'It is my duty, lord-arcanum.'

He watched her go and then let his gaze drift across the interior of the temple. Even now, preoccupied as he was, he couldn't help but calculate the geometries of the place. It was such a small thing – plain and pale next to the glories of Sigmaron. As Glymmsforge paled next to Azyrheim. But both were groping towards that glory, in their own way.

That, in the end, was the difference between gods. Where Nagash forced everything into the same shape – his own – Sigmar sought to raise his people up. To serve Sigmar was to forever reach for the stars above. To serve Nagash was to never notice the stars at all.

His eyes found the reliquary that rested at the opposite end of the nave from the main doors. It was the largest chamber in the temple, built to house the bones of the faithful, and now a hundred or more citizens of Glymmsforge crowded within its embrace. Innumerable skulls, marked by the symbol of the

High Star, peered down at the gathered mortals. Longer bones had been laid beneath the skulls, and thousands of phalanges hung from the ceiling.

The reliquary radiated a peace utterly at odds with the dead things outside. Here, a soul could find true rest, safe from the machinations of the Undying King. A shame that such peace would soon be disrupted. Another necessary sacrifice.

It seemed to him as if there were too many of those, of late.

Perhaps Miska and Tyros were right. He was easily distracted. He had not steeped himself in blood, the way others had. He had always thought himself possessed of a higher purpose – not just a warrior, but a seeker of hidden truths.

But what was the truth, here? The only one he saw was that he had failed, and his failure had compounded itself in ways he had never imagined. There was no telling what Thaum had done, or would do, if he was not released from Nagash's control. He leaned his head against his staff, seeking equilibrium.

He stared at the bones, at the ranks and rows of sainted dead lining the reliquary, and wondered where they were now. Lyria was but one underworld among millions. He could feel spirits here, watching. They existed outside the awareness of all but the most sensitive of mortals, and those possessing a spark of the divine. The truly dead, those who had passed beyond even the reach of gods, into spheres unknown and unknowing.

Only a rare few in the realms were so lucky as to travel on to that undiscovered country at the moment of their death. Many souls were trapped in the weft and weave of the realms, drawn into the aether that permeated everything. Sometimes they escaped, but other times, they simply... sat. Waiting for one god or another to collect them, or for the winds of magic to cast them back into physical form, through rebirth or reincarnation.

He knew this as surely as he knew that the war being fought

in the realms was not just a battle over physical territory, but a war for souls. The souls of all those who had been or ever would be. Even those souls already claimed by another.

He closed his eyes, listening to the wails emanating from beyond the walls of the temple. He felt suddenly weary, and his grip tightened about his staff. Corposant flared softly, dancing in tune to his simmering frustration. He had failed. Twice now, he had faced Pharus Thaum, and twice he had failed to contain him. Twice he had failed to prevent the repercussions of the rogue soul's rampage. The third time would be the last. He did not know how he knew this, only that it was as certain as the stars above. As constant as the firmament.

As this understanding filled him, so too did warmth, driving back the edges of fatigue and bringing with it clarity. He could see the way ahead clearly now. He was on the correct path. The battle could not be won here. But elsewhere, it might be possible. Like a hunter, he had to find the proper ground.

He could almost feel Sigmar's hand on his shoulder. Magic, sorcery, aetherworking, whatever you called it, it was all about ritual. About the meeting of craft and circumstance, the right words, the right gesture, at the right time. Too early or too late, and the spell would not work. Like a hunter, taking aim at his prey. Release the arrow too soon, and the prey escaped. The time had not been right, before. But it would be. He just had to recognise the moment, and… let his arrow fly.

'You look tired. I didn't think your sort could get tired.'

Balthas turned. Juddsson stood nearby. 'We can,' Balthas said. 'But I am not. Have you finished singing, then?'

Juddsson grunted and tugged on his beard. 'Yes, for the moment.' He sniffed. 'We're in the *krut*, and no two ways about it.'

'Yes, but I might have a solution. Come with me.'

Juddsson grinned. 'I knew you were a clever one. The moment I saw you, I said to myself – Grom, there's a clever sort of manling.'

Balthas frowned. 'Let us hope you are proven correct.'

He and Juddsson found Calys standing near the main doors, her gaze fixed. She spun as she registered their presence, her blade springing up. Balthas didn't hesitate. 'Your dutifulness does you credit, Liberator-Prime.'

She nodded tersely and turned her attentions back to the doors. 'As you say, lord-arcanum.' Balthas could feel her dislike of him, and he smiled. Eltain was not practised in hiding her feelings.

'The Ten Thousand Tombs,' he said. 'You were one of those who guarded it?'

'I was sent down only recently,' she said doubtfully.

'Can you find your way into it?'

'I barely found my way out – let alone back in – unaided. The ruins change shape constantly. Pharus did something. He created false walls and streets to nowhere, to confuse intruders.'

'Pharus did nothing. We built those things.' Juddsson frowned. 'Granted, he came up with the idea and drew the plans, but it was duardin hands that piled those stones. And duardin minds that improved on his human cleverness.' He packed so much condescension into the final word that Balthas felt vaguely insulted on the former lord-castellant's behalf.

He looked down at the duardin. 'Then you, or one of your clansmen, can lead us.'

Juddsson laughed harshly, and then winced. He clutched at his chest. 'No, manling. That place was built to isolate itself. Things move at random. Walls switch places, floors dip, paths bend back on themselves.' He shook his head. 'We know our business. Pharus didn't want anyone getting in there without his permission, so we made sure of it. Only the warriors assigned to protect the tombs know the way in and out.' He frowned and looked at Calys. 'Most of them, anyway.'

'And Elya,' Calys said, idly.

Both Juddsson and Balthas looked at her. 'Who?' Balthas asked.

'The child. The girl. Pharus said that she kept managing to get in, and he didn't know how.' She shrugged. 'If I hadn't seen it myself, I wouldn't have believed him.'

Balthas shook his head. 'A child?'

'She's shrewd.'

Balthas frowned. The rudiments of a plan were beginning to form. 'Let us hope so.' He looked at Juddsson. 'The tunnels below – the ones you mentioned before, with Fosko and Obol – do all of them lead in the same direction?'

Juddsson saw what he was getting at immediately. 'No, some lead elsewhere in the city. We can reach our clan halls, even.' He squinted, looking around. 'Slow going, with these. Especially if we have to fight.'

'You won't have to. The dead aren't interested in slaughter. At least not these.' Balthas looked back at the windows, above the main doors. Pale, distorted faces screamed in silence there. 'They'll follow us.'

'How can you be sure?'

Balthas looked down at him. Juddsson grunted and made a gesture of surrender. 'Fine. You know your business.' He tugged on his beard, frowning. 'I'll just go make the preparations, then, shall I?' He stumped away, still pulling on his beard.

'What is going on? What are you planning?' Calys said, deference tossed aside.

Balthas studied the doors. 'We must leave this place.'

'I have orders to ensure that nothing gets past these doors.'

'And you would perish in the doing so, your soul to be claimed by phantasmal jailers.' Balthas gestured dismissively. 'An inefficient use of resources. Once we get into the catacombs, you will be needed.'

Calys shook her head in confusion. 'Go down – but we can't...'

'We can.'

Calys eyes widened slightly. 'Elya. You mean to use her.'

'You said she managed to find her way below. We need a guide.'

Calys frowned. 'She's a child. It would not be safe.'

Balthas looked at her. 'Yes, and there is nowhere safer in this city than with us.' He paused. 'If we do not do this, the dead will surely break open the Ten Thousand Tombs. You will fail in your duty, Liberator-Prime. We both will.'

She stared at him for a moment. Then nodded. 'Come. I will take you to her.'

They made their way back to the reliquary, where the air stirred with the echoing hush of prayer. Many of the mortals had wrapped themselves in cloaks and blankets, passed out by the priests who moved among them. Some huddled in the corners, staring at nothing. Others spoke quietly among themselves. This ceased, as Balthas and Calys appeared. A priestess hurried towards them, but Balthas waved her aside. 'Where is the child?' he asked.

The priestess hesitated. Balthas realised that specificity was called for – there were many children in the reliquary. 'The girl,' he said. The priestess looked around helplessly.

'Elya,' Calys called, softly.

'Here,' a small voice called out. Calys started towards the back of the reliquary. Balthas followed. They found the child – a girl of perhaps ten seasons – sitting beside a lanky man, sleeping fitfully. A young woman sat near them, and she started at their appearance. Elya whispered to her, and then settled back beside her father.

Balthas could smell the fear that permeated him. His mind, slumbering as it was, was an open book to Balthas' storm-sight and all but impossible to ignore. Scattered memories flashed across his perceptions. The man – Elya's father – lived in a stew of recrimination and terror. Something had broken him, in ways too difficult to repair.

'Duvak,' Calys said. Balthas looked at her. She pulled off her helmet and hung it from her belt. 'His name is Duvak. Duvak Eltos. He is her father. A lamplighter.'

'He is broken.'

'One does not preclude the other,' Calys said, looking down at the man. There was something in her gaze that made Balthas look away. He looked at the girl. Elya was dark and scrawny. An urchin – an orphan, for all that she still had a parent. She met his gaze without flinching. He was struck, in that moment, by the thought that this was the child he'd seen in Thaum's memories. He did not question it – something deep in him told him it was true. But what did it mean?

'Do you have a face?' she asked.

'Yes.' Balthas tapped his helm and sat down beside her. 'This is it.'

'Father says that we're fated to die. Will I have a face like that, after I die?'

He studied her for a moment, trying to find the words. He suspected that even as a mortal, he had not understood children. 'Fate is another word for certainty. And the only certain thing in any realm is that nothing is certain. Not even death.'

'The cats don't believe in death. They say it's just a longer sort of dream.' Elya looked up. Balthas followed her gaze. Half a dozen felines lay nonchalantly among the stacked bones, or paced across the floor, tails twitching.

One, a brute with a scarred lip, leapt up into the girl's lap. It glared balefully at Balthas for long moments, then turned away with a disdainful twitch of its ears. Elya smiled and scratched the animal. 'I think he's the king,' she whispered.

'I wasn't aware that cats had such a thing.'

She frowned. 'Or maybe he's a marquis.'

'Maybe. Despite the folktales, cats have no king. Only a queen. And a queen may have many toms, but a tom only one queen.' He scratched the animal under the chin. 'Your mother was from Ghur, wasn't she? I can see the skeins of amber running through your blood.'

Elya shrugged with childish inscrutability. Balthas nodded as if she'd replied, and glanced at Calys. She was still watching Duvak sleep. He wondered what was going through her mind. 'Did you know that there were once many gods? As many gods as there were people, for every tribe and clan had their god. They were the gods of small things – of rivers and trees and fair winds. Death gods, as well.'

Elya looked at him, interested now. 'What happened to them?'

'Oh, their stories had many different endings. Some weren't really gods at all, in the end – just monsters. Others became as beasts, and lost sight of all that they had been. A few, like the King of Broken Constellations, were killed, while others, like Yahm, old god of the rivers, were defeated and imprisoned by those who came after.' Balthas leaned forwards. 'But some… escaped. They slipped between the cracks in the realms, where even the Ruinous Powers dare not go. One of those gods was the mother of all cats.'

Elya frowned. 'Not all cats.'

'The first ones, at least. She left her children in every realm. Some were big, some small. Some weren't really cats at all.' He glanced at Quicksilver, who lay nearby, beak resting atop his crossed forepaws, and then at Elya. 'But all gods leave a little of themselves behind, when they go. An echo, a whisper.'

'A ghost,' Elya said.

Balthas nodded. 'If you like. Not all of those echoes take a familiar form. And maybe the new queen of the cats isn't a cat at all. Or maybe it's just a story.' He hesitated for a moment, considering why Sigmar had seen fit to place this girl in his path. Not just to guide him, but for some other reason, perhaps. He hoped so. He held out his hand. 'I need your aid, Elya. I must get into the catacombs, and swiftly. I do not have the time to do so by the normal routes. Can you help me?'

She hesitated. 'Something is coming, isn't it? Not just the nicksouls.'

'Yes. But we can stop it. If you help me.' He turned, suddenly aware that every cat in the room was watching him. Armoured though he was, he could not help but feel almost like a mouse, in that moment. If Elya noticed, she gave no sign.

Before she could reply, Duvak screamed. He'd awoken at some point and was now wailing like an animal, trying to scuttle away from Calys, who reached out as if to comfort him. Balthas caught her wrist. 'Leave him,' he said, more harshly than he'd intended. Calys jerked her hand free and turned away, pulling on her helmet as she did so. Duvak had pressed himself against the wall of the reliquary, and was muttering a name, over and over again. The young woman Balthas had noticed earlier went to him, murmuring gently.

Balthas stood. He glanced up again, at the cats watching him. Watching it all.

Elya looked up at him, her expression unreadable. 'I'll help,' she said.

Pharus stretched out his hand towards the doors and felt heat envelop it. The Grand Tempestus was covered in wards much like those that had protected the city. But only the prayers of those within were keeping them from being overwhelmed by the sheer number of nighthaunts clawing at the structure. Given enough time, the gheists could overcome such lesser defences. Especially with Dohl urging them to greater frenzy.

Throughout the city, Dohl's fellow lantern-bearers were doing much the same. The air throbbed with the agonies of Glymmsforge. Malendrek had wounded the city. Now it was up to Pharus to finish the deed.

Idly, he wondered what the Knight of Shrouds' final fate would be. As far as he knew, Malendrek still fought somewhere in the city, locked in battle with the golden-armoured Stormcasts. Perhaps he would be destroyed. Or perhaps Glymmsforge would fall, and he would be named Mortarch, to join Arkhan and the others.

Either way, Pharus found that he cared little. Malendrek was a hollow thing, and his petty ambitions paled beside Pharus' sense of purpose. He drew his hand back and studied the smoking gauntlet. The pain was lost in the cold that gripped him. The satisfaction of battle had faded, leaving him empty once more. Leaving him craving the lives he could sense within the temple. Lives he could not claim. Not yet.

Screams drew his attention above, where a gheist hurled itself away from the temple, its ragged shape crumbling to fiery splinters of ash as it was overcome by the wards. 'More where that came from, my lord,' a nearby dreadwarden croaked. The creature still wore the remnants of a roadwarden's armour over its cadaverous form. In life, it had hunted brigands and outlaws. Now, in death, it acted as their overseer.

It raised its staff, surmounted by a ghastly candelabra made from the hand of a hanged man. The candle-flames dancing atop the tip of each finger flared, and chainrasps drifted towards the gale of howling spirits that enshrouded the Grand Tempestus. 'Always more,' the dreadwarden continued. 'No end to them, my lord. No use in them, save this. As Nagash wills, so must it be.'

'As Nagash wills,' Pharus said, turning his back on the creature. He had no interest in speaking to such lowly gheists. Unlike Dohl, or Rocha, their minds were circular tracks, broken only by memories of their mortal lives. Even Fellgrip was more companionable, for all its silence. The jailer floated at his elbow, its chains shimmering with caged lightning.

He could hear the cries of the souls trapped within those links, and wondered what it was like. Were they aware of where they were? Or was their pain that of an animal – senseless and maddening? The thought brought with it only the barest tremor of regret. But pain was the price of truth. Such was the will of Nagash. And as Nagash willed, so must it be. He turned his attentions back to the Grand Tempestus, watching as wave after wave of nighthaunts attacked the outside of the temple, watching as the temple and those within stubbornly refused to bow to the inevitable.

The realms suffered from an excess of will. That was a cosmic truth. Too many souls, too much will, too many lives running counter to the black geometries which guided all things. Nagash sought only to curb this excess, to ensure the continued persistence of the realms. Death was the reaper, and the realms were his fields – overgrown and thick with vermin. Now he plied the scythe, to put right all that had gone wrong.

Was it right, that the grain resisted the bite of the reaper's blade? Why do it? Pharus thought that he once must have known the answer, but could not call it to mind now. He touched his head, feeling the weight of his helm. It constricted him, in some manner. As the armour caged him, so too did the helmet cage his thoughts. Made him think in orderly lines. He knew that now, but felt no urgency about it. Urgency – worry – these had no place in death's order. Acceptance of inevitability brought peace.

All things died, and in death was purpose. More purpose than any possessed in life. Purpose… The thought brought back memories of life, of days spent watching over the dead. He remembered the smell of dust and incense, of dry, brittle bones and damp stone. He remembered the sound of ten thousand dead souls, scrabbling at the walls of their tombs. How could he have heard that desperate sound and not felt some touch of pity? How could he not have known the magnitude of the crime he was committing?

The lie of Sigmar blinded you to the truth.

'But I can see clearly now,' he murmured. He knew what must be done, and how to do it. 'I will cast aside the silver chains and shatter the warded stones. I will free the dead.'

You will do all of this and more. You will drag down the cruel stars, and prove their promises false. Such is the will of Nagash.

'And his will must be done.' Pharus felt Dohl approach. The warmth of Dohl's lantern brought its own sort of clarity, different to that imposed by his war-plate.

'Do you feel it, my lord?' the guardian of souls intoned. 'The wards weaken.'

'Not quickly enough,' Pharus said.

'But soon. I–' Dohl turned. Pharus felt it as well. The wards were falling. As if the prayers of those within were faltering at last. The hateful light that enshrouded the temple bled away, like frost before the sun. There was a sound, as of the shattering of a thousand mirrors and a last flare of cerulean light. It spread outwards, driving his forces back, but only momentarily.

In the silence that followed, he drew his sword and echoed its hiss of eagerness. The time had come at last. The scythe would meet the grain, and there would come a great wailing. Then, only silence.

As Nagash commanded.

Helios knelt in the centre of the nave, head bowed.

He ignored the formless shapes darkening the windows, and the sounds that echoed through the archways. They would be inside soon, but he felt no fear. No worry. Only peace. This was but a single moment, in a vast sea of such.

Contrary to appearances, the Evocator-Prime was not praying. Prayer was for those in search of reassurance. Helios had no need of such comfort. He simply needed to prepare. He concentrated on the tempest sweeping over the city, and began to draw down some of its strength into himself. He would need it, for a time.

Just until he had passed this final test.

Fear of death was the first test of a Evocator, and the last. It stretched across the entirety of the warrior's span, akin to a shadow, cast over life. It could not be bested, only endured – acknowledging that was part of the test. He had learned that lesson, among others, atop the towers of the Sigmarabulum. Twelve weeks of meditation beneath the firmament, with only the stars for company and rain to quench his thirst.

Helios had seen that what once had seemed immense, was merely an arrangement of small things, all colliding in the cosmic current. The winds of Azyr blew where they would.

Uncounted worlds rolled on in the deep. Distant stars were born, and then died, before their first gleaming had ever reached his eyes. And all without regard for what he, or any other, endured. Life was an infinitesimal part of that great dance – it meant nothing to the stars or the winds. With that realisation had come a sense of tranquillity.

A warrior – a true warrior – must have courage. Not the courage of one fighting for hearth and home, or the courage of a beast at bay, but a true courage – to live life to the fullest, even knowing of its unimportance. The courage to lack certainty and yet persevere. Such was the courage a Evocator learned, atop their tower.

He had learned that death, while certain, was only a little thing. Barely a pause in the music of the spheres. It was not an end, for there was no true ending, merely one more moment among many. The stars shone forever in the black, whether one was there to see them, or not. Though, he was not so stoic as to deny that he would miss watching them.

Glass cracked, somewhere above him. He could hear the sound of the enemy – like a gale wind, tearing at the stones. The protections of Azyr were fading, the strength of Shyish rising. He stood, stormstaff in one hand, tempest blade in the other. The weapons felt light, lighter than ever before. As if he might wield them forever and never grow tired. Or, perhaps as if he had just picked them up, for the first time.

In the dark above, dead things moaned. Their whispers fell like snow. They recounted the sins of their pasts, attempting to frighten him. But he could not be frightened by mere memories. That was what they were, after all. Bad memories and bitter times.

Then, what was time but a circle of moments? Invariably, the same one came around again, if you lived long enough. It was not immortality. There was no such thing as immortality, for it implied a linear constancy. But time did not flow straight. It bunched and wavered, and finally bent back on itself. One moment, flowing into the next, like a river.

The lord-arcanum thought differently, he knew. For Balthas, the stars were finite. He thought in terms of epochs, of history. One millennium upon the next. Time was a mountain, for Balthas. The future rose ever up and away, while the past crumbled below you. Helios wondered if there was something in that. He shook his head. No. Perhaps not. Balthas saw the heavens, but not the stars which made them up.

Then, that was his duty. To see the grand design, in all its glory. But for a humble Evocator, the stars were enough. He cocked his head, listening to something clawing at the stones. A shard of glass fell from a window above. He watched it fall, watched the light play off the shards as they scattered across the floor.

Miska had not asked him to volunteer. It had not been necessary. When the Knight-Incantor had explained the plan, Helios had understood, instantly. The final instant, come around again at last. He had lived, once, and died, in a moment like this, though he could not recall it in any detail. And now, having lived, he would die again. Painfully, perhaps. But gloriously, in a manner befitting a warrior such as himself. Balthas was a generous lord, to bestow such a gift.

He smiled. There was a poem, at least, somewhere in the meandering. He set the tip of his blade against the stones and began to scratch out the first stanza. He was still writing when the first window fully gave way, and the dead poured in.

He wondered what they thought, as they saw the empty nave and felt the silence. Balthas had led the others below, while the dead slammed themselves uselessly against the outside of the temple. Now, hopefully, they were on their way. But he would buy them a few moments more, just to make sure.

Shrieking spirits raced towards him through a storm of glass. He swept his staff out and caught one a solid blow. It convulsed as lightning danced across the links of its chains, and was reduced to a charnel mist. He did not stop, but remained in motion – thrusting, slashing, spinning. A few moments, well spent. A dozen spirits, laid to rest. He stepped back, and resumed his composition.

A dull boom sounded from the main doors of the temple. Spirits clustered in the broken windows, murmuring and rattling their chains. Helios did not look up as the bravest of their number rushed at him. The poem claimed the entirety of his attentions. His staff lashed out, and a spirit was reduced to tatters. The others retreated. As he scratched words into stone, arcs of celestial energy flickered about him and danced along the lengths of his weapons.

Another boom, accompanied this time by a sizzle-scorch sound, as the mystic barriers gave way. And, at last, the sound of splintering wood. An eerie mist seeped through the archways, slithering about the pillars and coiling in the alcoves. Still, the Evocator-Prime did not look up. The poem was close to completion.

Heavy boots thudded against the stone. An incongruous sound, utterly at odds with the hissing, sand-scrape of the nighthaunts. A smell, like ionised metal mingled with rotting meat, invaded his senses. He paused. 'You are a new thing, under the sun.'

The figure stood before him, a black pillar amid the ghostly mist. He was thin, almost spindly, as if all that was not bone and muscle had been sheared away, leaving but a shadow in its place. The armour he wore drank in the light, as did the blade he held balanced across his shoulders.

'I am the truth,' the dead man intoned.

'How portentous. A moment… I have almost completed my poem.'

'Poem?' The dead man sounded bemused.

'It is important to finish what one begins. Don't you agree?'

Silence was the only reply. Helios scratched a final word and stepped back. 'There. Now, we can speak.' He planted his blade before him, his hand resting on the pommel as he tapped his shoulder with his staff. 'Tell me your name, spirit, so that I might recount it, in moments to come.'

'I am Thaum. And once, I was as you are.'

'Oh, I doubt that. There is no one like me.'

'Regardless, you are here, and your soul is forfeit.' Thaum gestured, and a spectre, wreathed in chains and padlocks, drifted forwards. 'You will be made to see, as I have seen. Falsehood will be burned from you, by the radiance of the black sun.'

'All things are possible.' Helios studied the spirit, noting the amethyst light that bled from its padlocks. 'But we have not come to that moment, yet.'

'It is inevitable.' Thaum stepped closer, his black eyes empty of anything save purpose. Helios nodded.

'And yet, here I stand.'

'Not for long.' Thaum thrust his blade out, and the nighthaunts swept forwards in a howling typhoon. Helios sprang to meet them, moving swiftly. With every gesture, lightning arced out to ripsaw through the legion of spirits. It was rare that Helios could fight to the fullest, for the energies within him were as dangerous to his fellow Stormcasts as they were to the enemy. But here, now, in this moment, he was free to do so.

Chains struck the floor or tore divots from the pillars as the fight moved through the temple. Helios allowed the nighthaunts to drive him where they would, for he had no strategy beyond holding their attentions. He swept staff and blade out, catching unwary spirits in chains of his own – ones made from lightning.

Still, they pursued him, flooding through the temple in a wave of tattered shadows. Distorted faces grimaced and yowled, as clammy hands fumbled at him or rusty chains drew sparks from his war-plate. For every one he destroyed, two more took its place. Spiked clubs and ruined swords bit at him as he spun and twisted, staying out of reach.

He could feel their madness clawing at him, a tangible chill that made his limbs heavy and his head reel. A miasmatic frost clung to the plates of his armour. But the lightning within him carried him on, if not so fast or so sure.

Slowed, he found himself being driven back towards a semi-circle of drifting shapes. He heard the thump of rawhide drums and glimpsed the leer of bestial skulls within ragged cowls. The nighthaunts, wielding long, black glaives, began to close in on him as their lesser kin continued to harry and hamper him.

They had been wearing him down. Inevitable, as their master had said. The drifting spectres drew near, and he was forced to turn and parry a blow that would've split his heart. His tempest blade swept out, and a ragged cloak folded over as the gheist was torn apart. More blades thrust towards him, and he was forced to retreat.

Everywhere he looked, the dead looked back. He spun and lashed out, his storm staff passing through several grisly visages with little resistance. Lightning sparked out, dancing through their ranks. He turned, spinning his staff. The tempest built within him. But he would not release it for just any spirit. Not when he had gone to the trouble of weaving a trap of his own. They had harried him, and he had allowed it, knowing that they would drive him ever closer to – ah. And there it was.

The jailer-spirit, in its screaming chains, descended on him as he fought, seemingly oblivious to its approach. Miska had told him all about the creature – about what Balthas had seen. The souls of his brothers were caught up in its chains, condemned to an unknown fate. The Knight-Incantor hadn't known if destroying the creature would be enough to free them, but Helios saw no harm in trying.

He waited until it was within reach, then turned, letting his staff slide through his hand, so that the tip slammed into the bestial helmet. The creature squalled and swung its chains at him. He ducked aside and twisted his staff, catching the links. A flip of his wrist further tangled them about the length of the staff, and he could feel the soul within calling out for release. Before the spirit could rip itself free, he lunged, striking it in the head again. As he did so, he let the tempest loose.

Chains of crackling energy lashed out from him, ensnaring the jailer-spirit. Some of it raced along the creature's own chains, setting the rusty links alight with cobalt flame. The light swelled about him, washing away the shadows and momentarily driving back the dead. Helios felt his staff grow hot as he struck again and again, until it punched through the creature and struck the floor. The jailer-spirit gave an ear-splitting screech as celestial lightning ripsawed through it.

Helios released his stormstaff an instant before it splintered, consumed by the energies racing through it. The explosion hurled him backwards into a pillar. The stone cracked, and he tumbled to the floor. As his staff broke apart, so too did the jailer-spirit, which burned with a purifying radiance. Its chains melted into molten slag. Helios heard the imprisoned souls sing out as they were freed, and lightning speared upwards from the burning links, shattering the great dome above and casting a rain of glass down onto the spirits below.

As the reverberations faded, Helios rose to his feet, bits of glass sliding from him. He tried to take in a breath, and his ribs creaked painfully. His neck and shoulders ached, where he'd struck the pillar. His armour was scorched and dented by the fury of the tempest he'd unleashed. Besides the pain, he felt wrung out – empty. But satisfied. A final bit of good, before the end. Not enough, never enough, but some.

'You will pay for that,' Thaum said, in the silence that followed. He emerged slowly through the gathering ranks of the dead, sword-tip carving black trails in the stones at his feet. 'Your soul will scream in agony, before you are remade in the image of he whom you defy.'

'To speak and act are one and the same. Nothing will prevent me from doing as I have said.' Helios swept his tempest blade up, and gripped the hilt with both hands. 'Can the same be said of you?' He drew the blade back and readied himself. 'Come. Let us see.'

Thaum roared, mouth distending abnormally, and charged. Helios stepped forwards.

When the moment came around at last, he was ready.

CHAPTER TWENTY-ONE

DESCENT

Thunder rumbled above.

Balthas paused, listening. Helios had done as promised. He had bought them time enough, and now Juddsson and his warriors were leading Fosko, Obol and the others to the halls of the Riven Clans. Whether there was safety there or not, Balthas could not say. Regardless, the mortals were well out of what came next.

'Helios has returned to the stars,' Miska said, from beside him. He looked at her and reached up to ruffle Quicksilver's feathery mane.

'He held them longer than I calculated.'

'He did not return to Azyr alone. Can you feel it?'

Balthas nodded. The aether seemed lighter somehow. As if a burden had been lifted from the realm. He looked around. The tunnel sloped sharply downwards and was narrow enough that the Stormcasts could only move through it three abreast. The shadows were pushed back by the flickering glow of their staves, and the glimmer of corposant that clung to the arms and armour of the warriors following in their wake.

Built by duardin engineers, the tunnel was dry and sturdy, with heavy bracers of stone holding the crushing earth at bay. It twisted and turned back in on itself in ways that made sense only to the duardin, but always going down. Several times they came to crossways, and had to wait for Elya to come back and lead them into the correct passage. Smaller tunnels split off from the main, at intervals, but most had been sealed recently – bricked up or otherwise blocked off, and marked with runes of protection and warding.

Despite those runes, even here there were spirits. Balthas could see the dutiful echoes of long-dead duardin, working as they had in life, shoring up the stone and smoothing the floors. He'd read, once, that the duardin afterlife was very much just a continuation of life – the reward for a life of honour and hard labour was to live that life over, forever.

There was a pleasing sensibility to that. Then, Balthas could look forward to much the same – an eternity of war, waged beneath the stars. If he were lucky. He thought of Pharus and flinched away from the implication.

'The child has vanished again,' Miska said. Elya ranged far ahead of them, moving more quickly than the column of Stormcasts she led into the underworld.

'Can you see any cats?'

'A few.' Eyes gleamed in the dark, the creatures crouched in nooks and crannies, or slunk along the bracers. The soft pad of cat-feet, beneath the grinding tread of the Anvils of the Heldenhammer.

'Then she is close.' Balthas was confident that the girl was leading them in the right direction. There was something about the child – an ineffable quality that bemused and intrigued him. The story he'd told her had just been a story. One more folktale culled from his decades of study. That did not mean it wasn't the truth.

The mortals of the realms worshipped many gods, some old, some new, some real, some false. Who was to say that there hadn't been a god of cats, who did as cats often do and slunk into some small crack in the universe to wait out catastrophe?

Quicksilver grunted, and Balthas glanced back to see Calys making her way towards him, the gryph-hound, Grip, padding in her wake. She had been bringing up the rear, after having sent the rest of her cohort with the mortals. He knew what she wanted, even before she spoke. 'We're close,' she said. 'I can feel the vibration in the stones.'

'Good. Any signs of pursuit?'

'Not yet. We'll know as soon as it happens. Juddsson and Fosko left a surprise for them – they hid their remaining stores of powder and silver shot in the reliquary, ready to explode if the passage is opened.'

Balthas grunted. 'That will do little to deter them.'

Miska turned. 'Perhaps we should consider doing the same ourselves. A few warriors might hold this passage, for a time.'

'But not long enough to do any good. Besides which, they won't come this way. Pharus knows the secret route, hidden in the reliquary. He will attempt to force that one.'

'Then why are we here, rather than there?' Calys said.

'To get ahead of them, if possible. There are reinforcements below. Lord-Relictor Dathus, and those forces under his command. If we can join our forces to theirs, while Pharus is still trying to find his way through his own labyrinth, we might stand a chance of bringing him to open battle.' He looked at her. 'Without him, without a central, driving will, the nighthaunts will scatter.' He looked up. 'The battle for the city will continue. But the horde which follows us will take no further part in it… and the Ten Thousand Tombs will remain sealed.'

'And you will get to face him head on, once more,' Miska said.

Before Balthas could reply, a cat yowled. He looked up and spotted the same scar-lipped feline that seemed to shadow Elya wherever she went. He looked ahead and saw the child seated atop a bracer, waiting on them. 'It's here,' she said, as she dropped to the ground, light as one of her four-legged companions.

'Where?' Balthas looked past her. The tunnel continued on, its end swallowed in darkness. He wondered if it were a false seeming of some sort.

'Here.' She pointed down, at a rusty, iron grate set into the floor. Balthas had noticed many such grates since their descent, set every few thousand paces. Presumably these were to prevent flooding, in the case of the Glass Mere's rise. What marked this one as different, he couldn't say.

'Why this one? Why not the others?'

Elya looked up at him. 'Got to go this way, otherwise you can't follow me.' She looked down, into the dark. 'You're too big to go down the other ones.'

'How long will it take?'

She shrugged. 'You're not very fast,' she said doubtfully.

'We're fast enough.' Balthas pulled his staff to him and murmured a single word. A ball of corposant bloomed atop the staff. He plucked it free and dropped it through the grate. The light split into two, and two into four, until a dozen will o' the wisps danced in the dark below. 'And now we can see where we are going.'

A slope – steep and twisting, like a mountain path – descended away from the grate, and into the dark. Balthas could hear a steady crash, as of waves, rising from somewhere out of sight. He murmured a few words and waved his hand over the grate, and the rusty iron became red dust, which sifted away as if it had never been.

'Come,' he said. 'It is time we see what it is that Nagash so desires.'

Close. He was so close, he could feel it.

'Rip it open,' Pharus snarled. He slashed his sword out, shattering the holy bones that hid what he sought. The circular stone slab was as almost as large as the wall that held it. It slanted downwards all but imperceptibly. Marked along its circumference were celestial sigils that stung his gaze and forced him to turn away.

Wherever he looked, the skulls of saints grinned mockingly at him. He longed to drag them back and raise them up, but the symbol of the High Star carved into them prevented it. To show them that peace was an illusion, save in Nagash. That the dead, as ever, had been denied their true place by the living. As those below had been denied.

Can you hear them, Pharus Thaum? They are calling to you, out of the black.

'Yes,' he said. He could hear them. Demanding their freedom, pleading for forgiveness for their crimes against the Undying King. An eager army, ready to do battle with the stars themselves. That was what he had been sent to acquire, and he would do so, whatever the cost.

Even if it means your own destruction.

Pharus stopped for a moment, confused. That had almost sounded like a question. His helm seemed to contract about his head, as if to squeeze such thoughts away. He stepped back, head aching, as the few remaining deadwalkers pressed forwards, unhampered by the sigils. Broken fingers gripped the edges of the stone, as sun-dried muscle and ligament strained. A deadwalker tore its arms loose and stumbled back, jaw working. Pharus removed its head and shoved it aside. If it could not move stone, it had no use. 'Use the bones,' he croaked, not watching. 'Lever it out of place.'

Broken femurs and arm bones belonging to the fallen deadwalkers were stabbed into what little gap there was. Rusty blades joined them, as the deadwalkers employed the weapons they might have wielded in life. Slowly, the great slab began to move. Somewhere, unseen levers tripped, and gears began to turn. All it required was a strong enough hand to start the process.

'I remember opening it once before – my own two hands, then, and those of others… Briaeus…' he murmured. A name without a face. He shook the memory aside. It did not matter.

'You have more than two hands now. You have a thousand of them.' Dohl said, from where he waited just outside of the reliquary. 'The hands of every dead thing here are yours, my lord, as yours are Nagash's. All are one in him, and he is all.'

'Yes,' Pharus said, stroking the hourglass pommel of his blade. The sands hissed, sifting away. They never seemed to run out. He bowed his head. His helm felt heavy, suddenly. The weight of his armour threatened to drag him down. This place – the air closed around him like stone. It was worse since the death of the Stormcast who'd despatched Fellgrip.

He glanced back at the spot where the body had come apart in an explosion of lightning. The stones, pillars and walls were burnt black. The interior of the temple stank of celestial fire, and many of the weaker chainrasps had been consumed in the warrior's death throes.

Like the others, he had not understood the gift Pharus had offered him. And now he had returned to the tyrant's embrace. Angry now, he turned back. The slab was moving, but the deadwalkers continued to heave at it. The rest of them waited to descend. The first wave, to reveal any ambushes or traps.

There was a sound – sharp and rough.

He registered the spark a moment after it occurred. A piece of flint, trapped beneath the slab, scraped by the movement. A spark dancing across a mound of powder. Fire streaked along beneath the piled bones, cutting strange patterns beneath them. He turned, following it, dredging his memory. He had seen this before, what was it? What was–

The explosion followed a moment later. The reliquary was full of fire, and a whistling thicket of silver shot. Deadwalkers fell, burning. Nearby chainrasps squealed and fled. Pharus held his ground, ignoring the flames that swept up around him, seeking to consume him, though he had neither flesh nor bone. He roared in rage and snatched his sword from its sheath. He slashed down, striking the slab, again and again.

Chunks of stone fell away, cleaved raggedly from the whole by his blows. When enough of it was gone, he cast out a hand and shoved the remains of the slab aside, bending the unseen mechanisms out of joint. Flames roared past him, into the passage beyond. Burning deadwalkers stumbled past. A moment later, the nighthaunts flooded into the passageway, their screams and howls echoing from the stones.

'The strength of Nagash cannot be denied,' Dohl murmured. As he urged the nighthaunts into the reliquary, their presence snuffed the flames, drawing the heat from the air almost instantly.

Pharus did not reply. He stared into the passage, listening to the grinding of stone, once so familiar and now so strange.

Dohl drew close, the light of his lantern washing over Pharus. 'Do you hear them, my lord? Lost souls, calling to you out of lightless gulfs. They know you are here. Jailer-turned-redeemer. They welcome you. Do you hear them?'

Pharus did. Ten thousand voices, calling up out of the dark. Calling for him.

'Come,' he said. 'The inevitable awaits.'

Balthas led the way, the remains of his Chamber marching in his wake. There were barely thirty of them left. But enough to do what must be done.

Quicksilver paced beside him, Elya sitting in the saddle. She looked tiny, there, even with the cats that clung beside her. More felines ran underfoot. At times, there seemed to be dozens of them, or only a handful.

The slope was uneven. More than once, a Stormcast nearly lost their footing, sending a cascade of loose stone tumbling down into the gulf below. Every time, they would stop until the echoes of clattering stone faded. Then, they would proceed once more.

Balthas could hear the steady, grinding rumble of stone scraping against stone. Dust hung thick on the air. It sifted down from above in ribbon-like waves, and cascaded across the Stormcasts' armour. Occasional flashes of light rose from below, reflected from innumerable mirrored surfaces to bounce along the curve of the slope.

It was like an orrery. But within that orrery was contained a smaller puzzle box of shifting lines and sliding squares. Everything was in motion, if slowly. He could feel the aether sliding with it – the blessings and protections of Azyr, marking the sphere of tombs. Even without seeing them, he could feel the arcanograms that Pharus had engineered. As the shape of the catacombs shifted, so too did the arcanograms. From barrier to funnel to trap and back again.

'He was clever,' Miska said, from just behind him.

'He still is,' Balthas said. 'That is the problem.'

The slope widened ahead of them, and in the light, Balthas could make out the crude apertures of tombs and crypts, built into the walls. These were all sealed, with stone and silver chain, and he could see mystic wards glowing like phosphorescent fungi.

The ground beneath their feet trembled now, and an almost solid curtain of dust wafted down through the air. Elya leaned forwards. 'We have to wait,' she said, shouting to be heard over the rumbling that pressed in on them from all sides. Balthas raised his staff, and the column of Stormcasts crashed to a halt. The path ahead had come to an abrupt end. The crypt faces were broken and had collapsed into slumped piles that tapered off over the edge of the sudden aperture. Balthas peered down.

From where he stood, the catacombs below resembled the apex of a vast, almost spherical, column composed of intertwining tiers of streets and avenues. The column was trapped in a web of stone pathways and bridges, which stretched in all directions. The tiers shifted independently of one another, sliding up or to the side, or else sinking down as another rose in their place.

The whole thing was a work of genius. Balthas wondered what Pharus had been in his mortal life – just another warrior, or something more? Had Sigmar imbued him with the creativity needed to conceive of such a thing, or had it always resided within him? And how much of it was left to him now? Had Nagash left him that genius, or had the Undying King cast it aside, as something useless?

He suspected the latter. Pharus had seemed a clockwork

thing, to him. A hollow shell, driven by an unnatural force. A puppet of soul-stuff. He heard someone approach. Calys Eltain. 'Something you wish to say, Liberator-Prime?'

He felt her hesitate. Her aura was in upheaval. Her soul was tangled in knots of confusion. 'We should not be down here,' she said, after a moment. It was not the question she wanted to ask, he thought. But he decided to answer it anyway.

'Have you never wondered why the God-King set watch on these tombs, rather than destroy them?' Balthas asked, not looking at her. 'All of this could have been avoided, had he simply obliterated them, and all that lies within. It is well within his power to do so.'

'I had not considered it. That he commands is enough.'

'No. It is not,' Balthas snapped. 'Nor does he expect it to be so.' He turned swiftly, and she backed up a step. 'Sigmar encourages questions, Liberator-Prime. He encourages thought, as well as deed. Our enemies are not merely things of flesh and bone, but malign abstractions, requiring weapons beyond these we hold in our hands. To win the war ahead of us, we must consider all aspects of the thing, not merely the thing itself. Think. Why would he not dispose of those souls held here?'

Calys frowned. 'He has some use for them.'

Balthas nodded. 'Exactly. The dead are as clay for the gods. Souls can be reforged. Even those tainted in some way. We know this. Take for instance Tornus the Hero, who stands pre-eminent among the ranks of the Redeemed. Once, a foul thing, a pustule of Chaos – now one of the Huntsmen of Azyr.' He leaned close. 'There are others among our ranks whose souls were first claimed not by Chaos, but by Nagash – confined to skeletal husks or reduced to maddened spirits, and yet they too were remade into servants of Azyr.'

He looked away. 'Ten thousand dead are interred in this well of souls. Ten thousand warriors who might one day serve to turn the tide of the war we wage. Perhaps they too will wear the heraldry of the Anvils of Heldenhammer, in time, as we do. Or perhaps not. But the potential is there. And our need is great.'

'So we are here… for potential?'

'For hope. For a better day.' Balthas straightened. 'For the chance to repair what is broken and remake what is destroyed. That is why I hunt through ancient tomes and scour musty pages… seeking some sign of hope. Some promise that all that has been, might be again.' He set his staff. 'If we are tools, we are employed in great purpose. I take comfort in that.' A bridge of stone appeared out of the darkness to the left, slowly swinging towards the edge of the path. It crashed into place, the vibrations running up through his legs.

He heard the creak of unseen locking mechanisms, and dust spewed from the small gap between edge and bridge. He lifted his staff. 'Come. Time is fleeting.'

He led the way across, moving swiftly, aware that the bridge could break away to continue its circuit at any time. As soon as the last Sequitor set foot on the path beyond, the bridge broke away and sank out of sight, accompanied by the clank of chains and gears. The path ahead dipped sharply, descending in a slope towards a circuitous walkway below. Crypts and mausoleums tottered over the path, supported by angled pillars and struts. The route split and wandered in a hundred directions, winding among the houses of the dead.

Balthas gestured for Calys to join him. 'Do you recognise this place?'

The Liberator-Prime shook her head. 'I recognise some of the tombs, but the last time I saw them they were elsewhere.' She looked at Elya. The girl pointed straight ahead.

'Follow the silences, it's easier.'

Balthas grunted. 'Where is the main entrance?'

Elya turned, squinting. She pointed north, away from the slope. 'That way, I think.'

'If she's right, then that'll be part of the Avenue of Souls,' Calys said. 'It stretches from the main entrance and runs along the circumference of the pit holding the Ten Thousand Tombs.' She reached down and stroked Grip's narrow skull, ruffling the beast's feathers. 'There are dozens of false paths stretching off from it, though. It's as easy for the living to become lost as the dead.'

Balthas looked at Elya. 'Can you lead us safely along it?'

She nodded, frowning. 'I think so. It's easier when I don't have to think about it.'

With the girl's guidance, they made their way down among the tombs. Several times, the path ahead shook and sank out of sight, or bent in an unexpected direction as the ground shifted. Mirrored slabs had been placed at odd angles, distorting the light and making paths appear where there were none. Only Balthas' floating wisps of corposant enabled him to identify these tricks. More than once, the Stormcasts found themselves walking into a cul-de-sac that moments later split away to reveal a new course. A mortal would have become hopelessly lost in the ever-shifting necropolis.

As they passed through the stone canyons, the doors of some vaults rattled. Chains clinked and dolorous voices called out of the dark. The dead did not sleep easy. 'It is louder than it was,' Calys said. 'It is as if they are waiting for something.'

'They are, and it is on our heels,' Balthas said. He moved ahead of the column, peering into the darkness with his storm-sight. He could see hundreds of unquiet souls, clawing at the walls of the crypts around them. Hungry corpses thrashed in the gibbet cages that hung overhead, and shadow-shapes skittered out of sight. Eerie moans drifted among the crypts, following the Stormcasts as they made their descent.

When they reached the bottom of the slope, the path spread like the fingers of a hand. Immense crypts and burial vaults hugged the sides of the path, and leaned awkwardly, casting long shadows. The Avenue of Souls wound through this thicket of stone – not a rough path, but cobbled and slabbed in pale stone. It reminded Balthas of a spinal column, stretching as it did throughout the catacombs.

Balthas called a halt. He could hear bells ringing, in the distance, as his subordinates gathered about him. 'One of the bell towers,' Calys said. 'There are twelve of them, one at every major thoroughfare on the avenue. They only ring when there is danger…' Her hand dropped to her blade. Around them, Sequitors took up position, creating a wide square about the rest of the Sacrosanct Chamber. They locked shields and sank to one knee, waiting for orders. Castigators took up positions behind them, greatbows at the ready.

'The enemy is coming. We got ahead of them, but only just. We must decide now – make our stand, or press on.' Balthas looked around. The Avenue of Souls rose upwards to the north and the heart of the catacombs. Tombs jutted at wrong angles, and seemed to be collapsing with infinite slowness all about them. Everything was in motion, constantly. He could feel the path shifting beneath his feet.

'A good place for an ambush,' Mara said, looking around. The Sequitor-Prime removed her helm, revealing close-cropped hair. Dark eyes narrowed as she took in their surroundings with a veteran's attention to detail. 'They might not expect it.'

Quintus grunted. 'And they might ambush the ambushers.' The Castigator-Prime shook his head. 'This is unstable ground. Bad for making a stand.'

'Not if we're careful,' Gellius said. The engineer frowned, like a craftsman facing a stubborn bit of wood. 'We can hold them here, with a few warriors. Not forever, but long enough to slow them down, my lord. Give you time to reach the heart of this labyrinth, if that is your plan.' He peered down the avenue, towards the sound of the bells, and then looked at Balthas. 'The stone here is weak – too much movement. A few blasts, and down it'll come, every crypt and brace.' He grinned. 'If Sigmar is with us, I'll bury the lot of them.'

'Not alone you won't,' Mara said. 'I will take half of my cohort, and a third of Quintus', if he's willing.' She glanced at Quintus, who, after a moment, nodded. She looked back at Balthas. 'The rest, and the survivors of Porthas', will be enough to make a stand with you, my lord. We will bloody them for you.' She looked at him. 'It is the pragmatic choice, my lord. Efficient.'

Balthas looked down at her. He barely knew her. Mara, like Quintus and the others, was almost a cipher to him. He had never made the effort to know them, not really. And now, who they were was to be lost. They would not survive, and what emerged from the Anvil of Apotheosis would be a different person.

'Yes,' he said, after a moment. He glanced at Calys. 'You will take command of the remaining Sequitors.' It was not a request. She nodded, after a brief hesitation.

'As you will, lord-arcanum.'

Balthas paused. Knossus would have had a speech for a moment like this, he was certain. But he had no words. He looked at Mara and Gellius. 'Sigmar go with you, sister. And you as well, Gellius.'

Gellius smiled. 'He always has, my lord. Today shouldn't be any different.'

* * *

Calys did not look back, as they left Mara, Gellius and the others behind. The dark seemed to press in from all sides, and somewhere bells were ringing plaintively. It had not felt so stifling before, and Calys wondered what might be awakening in the depths. And what might be awaiting them, when they finally arrived.

She glanced at Elya, still sitting atop Balthas' steed. She tried not to think about the danger the girl was in, and wished she'd sent the child with the others, into the duardin tunnels. Then, perhaps Elya wouldn't be any safer with her father.

She frowned, thinking about the way Duvak had screamed at the sight of her. Balthas was right – something in the lamplighter was broken. He barely functioned, beyond the rote mundanity of his job. Elya didn't seem to mind, but it was hard to tell. The girl was as difficult to read as the cats who followed her.

A different thought intruded as she watched them. Something she'd heard and dismissed, if briefly. She'd wanted to ask Balthas earlier, but her courage had failed her. But now, watching Balthas striding alongside Elya, the desire to know was renewed. She turned, searching for the one she might ask about it.

'What did you mean, when you said that the lord-arcanum would get to face Pharus again?' she murmured, as she fell into step beside Miska, where she strode at the head of the column, her gaze sweeping their surroundings warily.

The Knight-Incantor stiffened. She did not look at Calys. 'I misspoke.'

'Did you? How do the dead know how to get down here? I assumed they would follow us, but Balthas seems to believe differently. And he said Pharus' name as well, then. You said his soul was lost, Knight-Incantor. What did you mean by that?'

Miska bowed her head. 'I meant what I said, Liberator-Prime. He is lost.'

'Then how can Balthas face him?'

Miska looked at her. 'Do you truly wish to know?'

Calys hesitated. She wanted to say yes, but couldn't bring the word to her lips. Something in the Knight-Incantor's tone sent a chill through her. She had been taught that to become one with Azyr, as all Stormcasts were, was something irrevocable. Stormcast souls could be lost, or even destroyed, but never changed. If that were not true…

She looked down at her hands, disturbed by the implication. 'Can he be returned to us?' she asked, finally. 'Can he be made… what he was?'

Miska sighed. 'No.'

'Are you so sure?' It came out as an accusation. Miska glanced at her, a sharp smile on her features. Calys stepped back, suddenly ashamed. The look in the other Stormcast's eyes was as hard and as cold as the winds of the Borealis Mountains.

'If I were not, I would not be who I am, sister. And perhaps I would be happier for it.' Miska looked away. 'We would all be happier for it, I think. But we are who we are, and we are needed, sadly.'

Calys shook her head. 'Why did you not tell me?'

'And what purpose would that serve?' Miska smiled – not cold now, but sad. 'Our purpose – the things we must do on occasion – they are whispered of among some of our brethren. None wish to believe, but all fear it nonetheless. As they should.'

Calys looked away. 'You speak so plainly of it, sister.'

Miska shrugged. 'It is no longer a whisper. Instead it is a roar. Sigmar cast aside the veil of secrecy, and now our existence, our purpose, is known.' She looked ahead, to where Balthas walked beside his steed and Elya. 'Balthas came here because of Pharus. He feels that he failed and seeks to redeem himself – and Pharus, as well. So you see, you are not alone in your guilt, misplaced as it is.'

Calys frowned, studying the lord-arcanum. She wondered if she had misjudged him. She nodded at Miska and moved to catch up with Balthas. He glanced at her as she drew near. 'Lord-arcanum, I–' she began. She was interrupted by the gryph-charger. The animal reared with a shriek, as crackling arrows hummed out of the shadows and thudded into the avenue before him. Light flared in the dark. 'Hold,' a deep voice called out, from somewhere above. 'Announce yourselves.'

'Dathus,' Calys shouted, recognising the voice. 'It's me, lord-relictor. I come bringing aid.' She stepped forwards, arms raised.

'Calys?' The light grew brighter, revealing the figure of the lord-relictor, standing atop a broken stairway. Retributors moved into view, through the crypts. Dathus looked battered, as though he'd been fighting his own war down in the dark. His mortis armour was dented and scorched, and a wide crack ran through the left eye of his skull helm. The Retributors who accompanied him looked much the same. 'What are you doing here?'

'We are here to help,' Balthas said.

Dathus started. Then, he bowed his head. 'Lord-arcanum.' He straightened and hurried down the steps. 'Calys, what is going on?'

'The dead have entered the city, brother. Worse, they have entered the catacombs. We mean to intercept them, before…' Calys trailed off. Dathus' eyes widened within his helm.

'If that's so, how did you find your way down here to warn us?' Then, more urgently, 'Is there a gap in our defences?'

'The child, Elya, led us…' Balthas began. Calys turned. Elya was no longer sitting atop Quicksilver. Neither were there any cats visible. 'She's gone,' Balthas said.

'Gone?' Calys turned, searching, her voice rising. A cold surge that might have been fear swept through her. A raw sensation, and one she was not used to. 'Where is she?' She made as if to go back, but Miska reached out to stop her.

'She slipped away a few moments ago.'

'You saw her go?' Calys demanded.

'She went back.'

'Back? Back where? How could you let her go? She's just a child!' Calys shook off Miska's hand. 'I must find her.' She started back the way they'd come. 'I made an oath.'

'And does that oath outweigh your duty?' Dathus said, sharply. 'That child knows these catacombs better even than Pharus did. If she is hiding, not even the dead will find her.'

Calys whirled, denial springing to her lips. But before she could voice it, she heard the bells. They were ringing somewhere to the south. And beneath their clamour, the groaning of the dead. Not the pathetic things, trapped in their tombs, but the feral dead. Nighthaunts and nicksouls. Balthas caught her arm, and she looked at him.

'There is no time,' Balthas said.

'She is in danger,' Calys said, hoarsely. 'I told Pharus – I swore to him that I would protect her. I cannot…' Her words trailed away. 'I swore to him,' she said.

Balthas stared at her a moment, as if searching for something. Then, with a sigh, he released her. 'Go,' he said, softly. 'And Sigmar go with you, sister.'

Pharus stared into the dying priest's face, seeking some sign that the mortal understood. That in these final moments, he'd grasped the truth Pharus had brought him. That there was no salvation in Azyr, only in death.

But the priest simply died. And then… nothing. Pharus

shook the body. He looked at Dohl, hovering nearby, the light of his lantern illuminating the slaughterhouse interior of the bell tower. The priests had put up a desperate fight, but prayers and silver alone were little match for nighthaunts. 'Where is he?' Pharus croaked. 'Draw his gheist from him.'

'Alas, my lord, I cannot. This place is warded with filthy starlight. It has poisoned the air and the soil. We can free those dead things already trapped here, but we cannot draw up the newly fallen. They are imprisoned.' Dohl leaned close. 'But that will change, once you have freed the ten thousand. This place will belong to Nagash once more, and the fallen will rise at your command.'

At the command of Nagash.

Pharus let the body fall. 'At his command, you mean.'

Dohl bowed his head. 'Of course, my lord. As you say.'

Pharus turned and grasped the hilt of his blade, where it jutted from between the shoulder blades of another priest. The sword resisted for a moment, before it allowed him to retrieve it. There was no blood, clinging to the edge, as if the facets of the blade had absorbed them. He stared into the facets, seeking a sign that all would be as Dohl had sworn. But he saw nothing save amethyst motes, swirling in the black.

Listen.

He paused, listening. From all around him rose voices, crying out for release. Some were unbearably close, while others seemed impossibly far away.

They call to you. Listen – hear the prisoners cry out for their liberator.

He did not sheath the blade. He would need it again soon enough. Above, the bells were still ringing, though all the priests were dead. Whether they were ringing in joy or sorrow, he did not know. Perhaps both. Joy of what was to come, sorrow at the loss of what had been. To be dead was to be trapped eternally between the two.

To be dead is to serve Nagash. Nothing more. Nagash is all.

'And all are one in Nagash,' he murmured. Outside of the bell tower, his nighthaunts were busy clawing at the crypts and tombs, opening those only protected by the weakest of wards. His army would grow, even if they could not draw up the spirits of those they had slain. 'Get them moving,' he said. 'We must reach the tombs.'

Dohl began to speak, but Pharus ignored his exhortations. He drifted out of the shadow of the bell tower. The air trembled as the ground shifted. The patch that the bell tower stood on felt as if it was sliding out of position, and the path ahead vanished amid a sudden profusion of stone crypts and slabs. But he was not confused. He counted silently, and the path changed again, revealing itself.

This place has no secrets from you. That is why only you could do this.

The bell towers were one of the secrets to navigating the catacombs. Their position was fixed. In fact, most of the catacombs were physically fixed in place. But they gave the appearance of moving, thanks to carefully placed mirrors and illusory backdrops. Silvered chains rose from the dust as a section of stone slid out of place, blocking the route to a section of the nearby necropolis. Nighthaunts retreated, wailing disconsolately.

Pharus watched, trying to banish the voice that whispered urgently, just below the surface of his thoughts. It was the price he paid for remembering the way through this maze, but it was becoming harder to ignore, the further he travelled into the catacombs.

You will ignore it. Your purpose is set. Inevitable.

'Inevitable,' he said. He turned west and saw the catacombs

fall away in a sea of irregular tiers. Storm-lanterns burned in the dark, tiny pinpricks of azure light. Their presence disturbed the black, and he felt a twitch of anger, somewhere deep in him.

The light of Azyr, the voice hissed. *The light that bars the dead. You must snuff it.*

The sands in his sword's hourglass hissed, and he felt something in him draw him back around. Towards the heart of the labyrinth.

You will snuff it. You will douse the sun in shadow, and silence the stars.

First one step, then two. The need – the command – beat at his brain like the heat of a sun. Until he was striding along the avenue, followed by a storm of dead souls.

Dohl joined him. 'You seem eager, my lord.'

Flood the catacombs, the voice murmured. *Crack open all vaults, and set the prisoners free. Where death once ruled, let it rule again.*

'Send chainrasps to the east and the west, as we drive north,' Pharus said, not looking at the guardian of souls. 'I would not fight an organised enemy. Keep them looking in all directions at once.'

'A wise plan, a keen plan, my lord,' Dohl croaked. 'We shall fight not as an army, but as a force of nature – a flood, a fire…'

'A storm,' Pharus said. He was moving swiftly now, not running but flowing. Dohl kept pace, the light of his lantern growing brighter, until it was almost blinding. Wailing spirits surged in their wake, filling the air and scrabbling across the stones of the ground. Some flew like birds or slithered like snakes. Others stalked on shattered limbs, or dragged broken gallows in their wake. Regardless of their appearance, they all crashed together and hurtled on, in the wake of the lantern's light. Some of the eagerness that gripped Pharus held them as well, burning through them and driving them into new heights of frenzy.

They flowed in a wave of spectral energy across the avenue, and along the slope above and below. His followers passed through stone, and around the pillars with their glowing wards and between the lengths of silver chain stretched across the smaller paths. Bells had begun to ring, deeper in the catacombs, and he felt a flicker of satisfaction.

The flicker was snuffed, as something exploded in the midst of the chainrasp horde just behind him. The glare of lightning washed across him and broke the momentum of the advance. He turned, as smaller explosions swept across the slope above. Crypts tore loose from their foundations and slid down, gaining speed, until an avalanche of stone was rumbling down on the avenue.

CHAPTER TWENTY-TWO

THE WAR OF HEAVEN AND DEATH

'We should not have let her go alone,' Miska said. Calys had already vanished among the sliding corridors of mausoleums. She could hear the crash of Gellius' ballista and the all-consuming rumble of stone. Lightning flashed to the south, tearing holes in the dark. The dead were close. She reached down, touching the spirit-jars hanging from her belt, making sure they were close to hand. She looked at Balthas. He didn't reply. He stared back the way they'd come, as if entranced by the sounds of battle.

She turned to the lord-relictor, Dathus. 'Go. Muster who you can. Ring the bells, call every warrior, Stormcast or mortal. I fear they will be needed.'

'And what about you?'

'We came to defend this place. And that is what we will do. We will delay them. Give you the time you need. Go, brother!

Ring the bells! Sound the call to war. And leave us to do what we were made to do.'

Dathus hesitated. Then, he nodded and turned away, heading north. He barked an order, and his warriors followed him at a trot. They soon vanished into the gloom that shrouded the avenue, leaving behind only the echo of sigmarite ringing against stone. Satisfied, Miska turned back to Balthas.

'I was wrong,' Balthas said, so softly that she almost didn't hear him.

She looked at him. 'About what?'

Balthas caught hold of Quicksilver's saddle and hauled himself up. 'I thought I could choose the moment. But it chose me, instead. Chose us.' He looked down at her. 'I thought we were to meet them in the open, Shyish against Azyr, on the black rim of the world. There was a… a resonance to it. But instead, the moment comes upon us here, in the middle of a forest of crypts. The final clash comes, not over ancient tombs, but over a child's soul. Do you understand?'

He sounded so annoyed that she could not help but smile. 'I do. I wondered why you were so insistent on bringing her. And if you're asking my opinion, well, I would rather fight to preserve a single living soul than ten thousand dead ones.'

He gave a disgruntled sigh. 'I think I would as well.' Balthas straightened in his saddle. 'Gellius and Mara are buying us the time we need to get into position. The aether swims and surges. The foe will come this way. And we will meet them. Head to head, and soul to soul.' He lifted his staff. 'Castigators to the fore. Sequitors, make ready to advance. Miska…?'

'Aye, Grave Warden?'

'I want Pharus. Clear me a path.'

She nodded serenely. 'We shall provide you a fitting honour-guard.' She turned and signalled to the remaining Evocators.

They were gathered behind the Castigators, kneeling, their heads bowed. As they prayed, small sparks of lightning danced across them.

They rose at her gesture, and she joined them. Memories of a time half-forgotten rose. Of the rattle of shields and the call to war. The feeling of running across the taiga, beside a hundred others, racing to meet the enemy. It was a good feeling, that. She smiled.

'Come, brothers. Let us be as the storm wind, and wipe this place clean.'

Pharus stood unmoving as the broken crypts crashed around him, scattering the chainrasps. Another large explosion bit a chunk from the avenue, casting gheists back into the slide of the avalanche. Pharus followed the trajectory and swept his sword out, pointing. 'There – take them,' he howled.

He sprang up the incline, racing towards the spot he'd indicated. He could feel the heat of the magics that gathered there. Explosions gnawed at the crypts around him, but he avoided them with ease. He saw the ballista mounted atop the roof of a semi-collapsed crypt, and the other warriors below – Judicators, he thought. No. They weren't Judicators. These were something else. Reeking of magic.

He raced towards them, but a wall of shields interposed itself with a crash. The shields blazed with celestial light, forcing him to stop short. He stepped back, letting chainrasps flow past him. Some were consumed as they struck the shield wall. Others were torn asunder by the crackling mauls the Stormcasts wielded. But some got past. They crawled over the living warriors, seeking any gap in their war-plate.

He heard the clangour of funerary bells, as a flock of reapers swept through the air, down towards the warriors. The great scythes slashed down, cutting into ensorcelled war-plate in a burst of sparks. Stormcasts fell back, raising their shields to block this new attack. But one of them lunged forwards, out of the press, her maul swinging down.

Pharus avoided the blow, and it shattered part of a nearby statue with thunderclap force. His blade snaked out, scraping a scar across the face of her shield. She retreated. Pharus pursued, his blade held low. He did not waste words on her. The shield was suddenly limned in blue fire, and he shied back, momentarily blinded.

He heard the crackle of the maul as it looped towards him, and ducked away. The radiance of the weapon burned him as it passed by. Half-blind, he drove her back with a wide sweep of his blade. Light washed over him, clearing his eyes. He saw Dohl rise up behind her, and his tomb-blade sweep down. The warrior staggered, and Dohl finished her with a blow from his staff, crushing her skull. Her soul fled upwards with a roar.

'We are soon to overcome the enemy,' Dohl said. He swung his staff out, casting the glow of his lantern across the nearby crypts. The Stormcasts were still fighting, but wherever Dohl's lantern passed, the weakened stone of the tombs shattered, releasing the spirits trapped within. The organised shield wall had dissolved into struggling islands of cobalt light, slowly being swallowed up by the dark.

'Let us finish this,' Pharus began. Behind him, something hissed. He turned. There were dozens of cats perched among the tumbledown tombs and archways, glaring hatefully at him. 'Elya,' he said. The name tasted strange, on his lips. Why had he said it?

'What?' Dohl asked.

'Pharus?' a child's voice called out. The din of battle seemed to die away. The sword in his hand became heavier, threatening to drag him down. The sands sifting within the hourglass sounded like a nest of serpents. Past the cats, he caught sight of a small face, streaked with dirt. A child. A girl.

'Elya,' he said, again. Memories fluttered, moth-gentle, across his mind's eye. He hesitated. 'You are… Elya.' The words came out almost as a question. He took a step towards her. The cats hissed again, their eyes gleaming in the light of Dohl's lantern. She retreated, her eyes wide, face a pale oval.

She fears you. She is nothing. Ignore her.

'Leave her, my lord,' Dohl intoned. 'What is a child, save a morsel of fear?'

'Quiet,' Pharus snarled, turning to extend his sword towards Dohl. 'Quiet,' he said, to the voice. He turned back and reached out his hand. 'Elya? Is it you?' More memories, filling the empty caverns of his mind. 'Elya… come here.'

Silence, save for the hissing of cats. The child was gone. Fled. He lifted his blade. He was dead, and the dead had no fear, but even so, he felt a certain wariness. There was something at work here that he could not perceive, and it drove him to distraction. 'Dohl, cast your light. Find her.'

She is not important. Do not turn from your path.

'She is but one little life, my lord. Leave her, and she will be snuffed with the rest.'

'Find her!' Pharus lifted his blade, so that the tip rested where the hollow of Dohl's throat would have been, if he'd had one. 'Find her, or I will claim your lantern for my own.'

'My lord… the battle…'

Pharus turned without a word and sped in the direction he thought the child had gone. He did not know why. He could feel the cold and hunger returning, and his armour felt more like a cage than ever before. He had to fight it to move, even to lift his blade, but a voice deep in him – a different voice, this, to the other – spurred him on, telling him that he had to find her – he had to–

He stopped. Turned. His reflection glared at him from every direction. He had been led down a mirrored path, and everywhere he looked, a face he only dimly recognised looked back at him. He could see the skulls beneath their skin, and felt the amethyst heat of his own reflected gaze. And behind them, above them, in and out of them, something great and terrible crouched, its talons on his shoulders.

'What…?' He hesitated. The shadow behind him rose, its eyes blazing with cold fire.

Fool. Would you cast aside the chance at justice so quickly?

'I have cast nothing aside. The child is…'

Nothing. She is nothing. A memory. A useless thing, well discarded.

As the words echoed in the hollows of him, he saw something else. A light, shining through the gaps in his war-plate. Not amethyst, but azure. He felt the twisting bite of lightning inside him, and snarled, forcing it down.

'This place… It eats at me.'

Which is why you must not delay. Break the seals. Free the dead. Purify this place.

He reached out a skeletal hand, but his reflection did not mimic the gesture. Instead, it simply stared at him, as if in pity. The eyes – his eyes – blazed cerulean, and Pharus felt a flare of rage. He swept his blade from its sheath. The glass shattered, revealing a new path. He sheathed his sword.

'Come,' he said. 'This way.' He could hear the crackle of lightning, and the crash of sigmarite, echoing from elsewhere in the catacombs. The battle wasn't over yet. But it soon would be. Then, then he would… What? He paused, trying to think. Trying to push past the rush of memories…

...the dead were everywhere in the streets, everywhere he turned...

...his halberd swept down, chopping through a door as dead hands caught at him...

...Elya wailing as something from the grave clutched her to its bosom...

...he raised his lantern, and there was thunder...

'My lord,' Dohl began, from behind Pharus, drawing him from his memories. The light of the guardian's lantern washed across the mirrored slabs, doubling and redoubling in its intensity. 'There are greater matters, at hand. Fate cannot be denied. It is...'

'Inevitable,' Pharus said, not stopping. 'Then why do you fret so, guardian? What was it you told me – that such worries would pass?' He slashed out, shattering another mirror to his left. He paused, staring at the mirror in front of him. Whose face was that, staring back? 'If it is inevitable, then what I do here is of no matter.'

'You lose sight of your purpose.'

No. It had not been him. Not him as he was, or even as he had been, but who he had been before the gods had taken an interest in him. Was that whose voice cried out, somewhere inside him?

It does not matter. There is no truth in the past. Only in the present. The past and future are nothing more than false promises. Your course is set. Certain. Hold fast to your purpose.

'I will not be swayed from it,' he said. But the memories...

...thunder, and the screams of the dead, as Azyr caught them up...

...thief, the spirit shrieked as it burned, thief...

'I see everything,' he said, staring at the glass and what it held. Another him, burning in the flames of Nagashizzar. One quick stroke destroyed it. As it collapsed in a mass of winking shards, he saw the shape that had been crouched behind it. Shapes, rather. Cats sped away, scattering into the catacombs. And among them, their queen. 'Elya...' She did not stop.

He loped after the girl, driven by something he did not understand. Spirits howled in his wake, drawn to the hunt by the light of Dohl's lantern. Hunger warred with cold in him, and something else. A need greater than either. Around him, his reflection warped and stretched, as the thing that rode deep in his soul raged in fury.

Calys raced through the catacombs, moving as swiftly as she could. Grip ran alongside her, and they both followed a familiar shape – the scar-lipped cat that seemed to be wherever Elya was. The beast scampered through the crypts and ruins, moving swiftly. The cat had appeared, as if aware of who she sought, and Calys had followed it without thinking.

She could hear the thunder of battle all around her, but she ignored it. Balthas' warriors had their duty, and she had hers. She concentrated on the cat. Grip gave a sudden squall and put on a burst of speed, racing ahead. Calys followed. She heard Elya scream, and cried out. 'Elya!'

She turned, trying to follow the scream, but the labyrinth spun around her. Then, she caught sight of the light. An eerie glow, flickering among the tombs. She raced towards it, drawing her blade as she went. As she neared the light, she realised she was actually above it. She caught sight of Elya, climbing a statue.

Calys thudded across the half-sunken roof of a crypt and leapt. She slammed down near the statue. 'Elya,' she called out.

'Calys,' something said. Something that glowed with an eerie grey-green light.

Calys turned as the light washed over her, and saw something foul emerge from the dark, dragging its tomb-blade in its wake. 'Calys Eltain,' it said again, in a dull, harsh voice. 'I know you. I… remember you. This place… it is making me remember.' The thing straightened to its – his – full height. A thin, almost skeletal shape, clad in black-iron armour and ragged burial shrouds, its gaze bored into her. It's voice, distorted as it was, seemed familiar.

'You will not touch her,' Calys said to the creature, warblade extended. She glanced up and saw Elya scrambling to the top of the statue. She turned her attentions back to her foe. 'I will not let you.'

The dead thing laughed, a harsh croak of sound. 'Calys,' he rasped. 'I think we have been here before, you and I.' He tapped the side of his helm. 'Do you remember? Or did Sigmar take that from you?'

Calys hesitated. 'Remember what?'

'The night I killed you.'

She blinked in sudden, sickened recognition, as she saw the flicker of azure lightning in the dead man's gaze. 'Pharus?'

Pharus surged towards her, more swiftly than her eye could follow. Their blades connected with a crash, and she was driven back, into a half-toppled pillar, losing her shield in the process. Nighthaunts swirled up around them, like a swarm of angry night-wasps. But they did not come any closer, retreating as the watching cats hissed and spat. Something about the animals kept them at bay. She caught hold of her warblade with both hands.

'You're the one who died,' Calys said, trying to force him back. But he was strong. Too strong. The edge of the black blade pressed down towards her, despite her best efforts. Past his shoulder, she caught sight of Grip, crouched atop a crypt nearby. The gryph-hound was readying itself to leap, its eyes gleaming.

'Before that,' Pharus hissed, as his balefire gaze burned through her, down into her soul. 'I remember it all, now. I remember that night, and your daughter's screams, and I see you, not just this shell, but who you were before. I see the ghost of you, Calys Eltain. I see it, hiding in the false radiance of Azyr, and I will drag it out, into the true light. And you will thank me.' He glanced up at Elya, who stared down at them in horror. 'And you will thank me as well, child. You will be together again. You will have justice – both of you.'

'No!' Calys drew on the last of her strength, and twisted away from him. Their blades parted with a screech. As she stepped aside, he caught her a blow on the side, dropping her to the ground. Desperate, she rolled onto her back, interposing her blade as his descended. The blow rocked her, nearly tearing the warblade from her hands.

Grip leapt. The gryph-hound slammed into his back, claws scrabbling. The beast's beak snapped uselessly at Pharus' non-existent flesh. He staggered. 'Get off me, beast,' he snarled, with no sign of recognition. Grip held on, claws tearing strips from Pharus' armour. They reeled, and Pharus finally flung the animal aside. She was up again in a moment, feathers stiff, tail lashing, and lunged again.

Pharus' hand snapped out and caught hold of Grip's head. He turned and swung her into the base of the statue that Elya had sought refuge atop. There was a sharp crack, and Grip flopped down, still and silent. The animal was dead.

Pharus turned back to Calys. 'First the beast… now you.' He raised his sword, but stopped. He looked up at something. Calys risked a glance, and saw Elya staring down at them from the top of the statue, tears streaking her grimy features. Pharus seemed frozen. Uncertain. Instinct took over, and Calys drove her sword up, through the plates of his armour. Pharus roared and staggered back, ripping the blade out of her hands. She was on her feet in a moment. 'Run, Elya. Run and hide!'

Calys went for the hilt of her blade. She ducked under Pharus' wild slash and tore her weapon loose. Pharus howled, his face distending and twisting. They traded blows, reeling through the crypts. The air throbbed with the grinding of stone, and the landscape was beginning to shift. Pharus caught her with a savage blow and knocked her sprawling. She scrambled back as he advanced.

'You cannot escape death, Calys. Not forever.' He raised his blade. 'In the end, the dark always swallows the light.' But before his blade could fall, lightning snarled out, catching Pharus in its clutches. He screamed and staggered. A shadow fell over them both, as something snarled. Calys looked up, into the curved beak of a gryph-charger, crouched atop a sunken crypt. Balthas nodded to her.

'Up, sister. See to the child. Her part in this – and yours – is done.'

'You,' Pharus said, glaring up at the lord-arcanum. 'You. Again. Twice you have put yourself in my path.'

'As I will continue to do, until matters between us are settled to my satisfaction.' Balthas thumped his steed in the flanks, and the gryph-charger leapt with a scream. The beast crashed into Pharus, carrying him backwards. Calys scrambled to her feet as they disappeared into the tangle of shifting paths. A nighthaunt shrieked towards her and she ducked aside, racing towards the statue. She saw Elya crouching near Grip.

'She's dead,' Elya said, cradling the gryph-hound's head.

Calys reached for her, but spun as something lean and terrible rose up behind her. The hideous light emanating from the spectre's lantern washed across her, nearly driving the strength from her limbs. She sagged back, standing between it and Elya.

'Soon, you will join the beast,' the spectre intoned, raising the blade it held. 'Rejoice. Die and see the beautiful thing that awaits, past the edge of the final moment.'

'I have died once, creature. I do not intend to do so again!' Calys lashed out, aiming not at the nighthaunt, but at its lantern. Her warblade struck home, and a flare of necromantic energy raged out, knocking her backwards. Her blade shivered to fragments, and her arm went numb. The spectre wailed as its lantern exploded, and the staff crumbled away in its grip. The flame within the lantern licked hungrily at its arms, causing it to twist in agony as it reached for her, snarling and cursing.

But before it could lay hands on her, a lilting refrain pierced the cacophony of battle. The burning wraith turned, as pieces of it broke away and were drawn towards Miska, as she stepped into the open. The Knight-Incantor's song rose in volume and urgency, and the bottle she held began to glow with a soft light. Slowly, like oil spilling across water, the spectre was drawn into the bottle, its screams dwindling as it shrunk and twisted.

Miska sealed the bottle and peered at it. 'A strong one, this. Without your blade, I wouldn't have been able to trap him.' She looked at Calys. 'Where is Balthas?'

Calys pointed as lightning crashed and a gryph-charger screeched, somewhere out of sight. As she did so, a swarm of chainrasps shot towards them, emerging from the paths between tombs. The Knight-Incantor turned and sang a single note. The wind rose into a howling gale, and the semi-aethereal creatures were somehow swept back the way they'd come. She turned back. 'Up, sister. Gather the child. We have a battle to win.'

'What about Balthas?' Calys said, and bent. 'On my back,' she said, glancing at Elya. The girl swiftly complied.

'Balthas has his own battle to fight,' Miska said.

'Let us hope, for all our sakes, that he wins it.'

Quicksilver's lunge carried them through the necropolis. Already weakened tombs collapsed, throwing up clouds of dust and squalling spirits. Mirrors shattered and stone pathways were gouged up by the gryph-charger's elemental fury. Pharus Thaum howled as he was driven back, into a fallen pillar. The stone cracked as he struck it, and the aetheric energies that issued from the gryph-charger's claws set his armour aflame.

Roaring, he slammed the hilt of his blade against Quicksilver's skull, staggering the beast. As the animal reared, gheists swarmed over Balthas and his steed, striking at them with rusty weapons and splintered claws.

Quicksilver stumbled back, screeching. Nighthaunts clung to him, biting and tearing. Balthas sprang from the saddle moments before the gryph-charger fell. He landed hard, but scrambled to his feet as Pharus Thaum rushed towards him, sword held low. 'Madness,' the dead man said, his voice like sour thunder. 'Madness to pit yourself against the inevitable.'

'As Sigmar commands,' Balthas said. He raised his staff.

'Sigmar the liar,' Thaum spat. 'Sigmar the betrayer. I spent decades in the dark, protecting his city, his people, and then I was cast aside. As you will be cast aside when your use ends.'

'You were not cast aside,' Balthas said, avoiding the black blade. It tore through his cloak. He spat a word, and Pharus was driven back by a sudden celestial wind. 'The value of a thing is not simply in its immediate use, brother, but in its potential. No true craftsman disposes of his tools, whatever their condition. He repairs them, or else repurposes them.'

'And what if I do not wish another purpose?' Thaum snarled, advancing against the wind. 'What if I was satisfied to be as I was? What then?'

'Then blame the one who took that from you, not the one who sought to help.' Balthas extended his staff. 'This is not you, brother. You speak with the voice of another. A blacker will than your own drives you, as it drives those broken souls you command. I can hear its echo in every word that passes your dead lips.'

'My will is my own,' Thaum said. 'I was promised justice, and I will have it.' His blade licked out, and Balthas was forced to interpose his staff. The black sword chopped into it, and he was driven back a step.

'A lie.' Balthas braced himself. 'Once, maybe, but now – you are hollow. A mask, hiding the face of another. You are but the puppet of a will greater than your own.'

'We are both pawns together, then. It makes no difference. I will cast the stones of this city into the heavens and break free all those imprisoned below. Lyria will belong to Nagash once more, and all the souls that dwell within will know true peace. That is inevitable. That is justice.' His voice, once a hollow rasp, had deepened. The sound of it made the marrow in Balthas' bones curdle.

'That is not justice. That is oblivion.' Balthas twisted the blade aside and drove the end of his staff into the centre of Thaum's chest. Thaum reeled, and Balthas ripped his staff free and slammed it against the side of the nighthaunt's helm.

As the creature reeled, Balthas turned. The necropolis rocked as his warriors clashed with the dead. They had arrived too late to save Mara, but some of her cohort still fought, and now the two forces moved as one against the horde of spirits. With Pharus distracted, the creatures were little more than feral gheists – certainly not an organised threat.

Even so, gheists rose from the ground all around him, dripping upwards, their bodies distended like hot wax. Balthas slammed the ferrule of his staff down and scratched an arcanogram in the stone. The nighthaunts screamed as the stones they emerged from became threaded with silver. They sank out of sight, their twisted forms burning with a cleansing flame.

Pharus lunged through the flames. Blade met staff and they skidded back, smashing into a crypt. It collapsed with a rumble as they twisted away, weapons still locked. Balthas grunted as the amethyst lightning flickering beneath Pharus' armour licked across his own, charring away the ritual sigils marked there.

'Nagash has commanded,' Pharus snarled. 'So must it be.'

Balthas said nothing as they staggered in a macabre dance, neither willing to give ground. Fire swept out around them, first amethyst, then cobalt, setting the ancient stones alight. He felt strange, as if something inside him had torn loose and were burning, along with the stones. Every blow took a century to fall, every riposte, an epoch. But Balthas met his opponent blow for blow, and held him. Even as his arms grew numb and his head began to ache, filled as it was with thunder and heat. He could call to mind none of the magics he knew – instead his mind was full of lightning, and all he could see was fire. A hundred thousand fires, a million, more, all burning in the dark.

Nagash had set the realms aflame. What he had done could not be undone. What he had started could not be stopped. But Balthas knew they must try, even so. And as he fought, he knew that he had done this before, in another life, in another realm. He had set himself against the inevitable, and failed.

But he would not do so again.

Lightning burned through him, snarling outwards to engulf Thaum. For a moment, they were connected, as they had been in the Chamber of the Broken World. He saw all that had happened, all that Thaum had done, and knew that Thaum saw into his mind as well. For an instant, they saw one another with perfect, aching clarity.

The dead man staggered, smoke boiling from the gaps in his armour. And within the smoke, Balthas saw a light. Just a spark of cerulean, tiny and barely there at all. But it was a spark nonetheless, trapped in the hollows of Thaum's shell. An ember of the man he had been, waiting to be rekindled.

The moment had come.

Now, a voice rumbled.

Balthas stretched out his hand, his magics spearing out towards the spark of blue. But the moment stretched and warped out of sorts. The sands in the hourglass pommel of Thaum's blade ceased their flow. Time… stopped.

'You.'

A single word, followed by a laugh that curdled his soul. Unable to stop himself, Balthas looked up into a gargantuan rictus. A god was looking down at him. Not as one foe looked at another, but as a sage might study some unknown species of insect.

The cavern seemed suddenly small. The sounds of battle faded to a dim rustling, as if all sound and fury had been drained from the moment. Taller than any living man, clad in shrouds and bones, the Undying King loomed over his servant, eyes blazing with unlight. Thaum jerked and twitched like a marionette with tangled strings.

'You,' Nagash said again, as if savouring the word. 'I know you, little soul. I know your scent. You were mine, once, as Pharus Thaum was.' He leaned through the glare of lightning and fire, his witchfire gaze fixed on Balthas. It burned hot and cold at the same time, and Balthas felt something in him shrivel. This was no nighthaunt or daemon to be banished, but a god. He possessed no power that could match the immensity before him.

'Insult of insults, that he uses you to block my path,' Nagash continued. His voice was like some great, black bell, tolling out Balthas' final hour. 'I will crack open this black shell you wear and scoop out the spirit within. Shall I show you who you were, little soul? Shall I answer those questions I see burning in your mind?'

Balthas blinked sweat from his eyes. In the fires around him, he could see things. Faces. People. Places. Moments from a life that was no longer his – a voyage to a great city, and a flare of light as lead became gold. The whicker of a horse, and the flap of great wings. The pain of unintended betrayal, and the relief brought by redemption. He felt an ache inside himself, as if Nagash had reached into him and torn something loose. He closed his eyes to the swirl of broken memories, and felt what might have been a hand on his shoulder. A voice, as deep as the seas and as warm as the summer wind, spoke softly in his ear.

I told you I would be here, Balthas. Let me guide your aim.

'I have no questions,' Balthas said, through gritted teeth. A new strength flooded his limbs, dulling the pain. He felt something beyond strength, growing inside him. 'I am not who I was. The past is ash. And the future is yet to be written.'

'Yes. By dead hands. I will order a record made, so that in the silent aeons to come, I might read it and remember.' Purple flame caressed Balthas' form. His war-plate grew warm, almost painfully so. 'No,' Balthas said. The heat increased. He could smell his flesh burning. He wanted to scream, but he lacked the breath to do so. Lightning erupted from his flesh, savaging the air.

'No,' another voice echoed, and the sound boomed out,

shaking the stillness. Nearby flames darkened and then paled, becoming azure.

Nagash drew back, as if nonplussed by this turn of events. 'Who would stand between the Undying King and his prey?' he roared, shaking the cavern.

'Me, brother. Always me.'

The words echoed from Balthas before he realised he was speaking. He felt invigorated, suddenly. He pushed himself to his feet, lightning crawling across the edges of his armour. 'I stand against you here, and along every wall. I stand against you, as the day stands against night.'

The words – the voice – neither were his. Balthas felt as if something were inside him. As if he were no more than a mask that the speaker had chosen to wear in that moment. But he felt no fear. This moment – all that had happened – had been planned for. Sigmar had seen it, in the stars, and set the blocks to tumbling into place. What came next was a matter of gods, not men, whether dead or alive.

He had chosen his moment, and Sigmar would guide his aim.

'Without the night, there is no day,' Nagash said. He swept closer, and Thaum stumbled in his wake. 'Without death, no life. To stand against me is to stand against the law of all things. Are you so prideful, then?'

'No longer. Necessity guides my hand.' Out of the corner of his eye, Balthas saw something take shape around him. A vast form, greater than his own, and yet similar. Thaum made a harsh croak of recognition, and Balthas wondered what he saw.

Nagash seemed to swell, until his skeletal form filled Balthas' vision. 'Necessity. What would you know of such a thing? I *am* necessity. By my will alone shall the realms be preserved from the ravages of Chaos. When I have claimed all that I am owed, when all are one in death, I shall cast my spite into the teeth of the dark gods, and drag them from their petty thrones.'

'And then you will rule over a silent kingdom, until the last star is snuffed, and even death perishes at last.'

Nagash was silent. Sigmar sighed, and Balthas thought of a high wind, stripping the bark from trees. 'Can you even conceive of such a thing, brother? Or is your arrogance so ironclad that your own end is an impossibility to you?' The God-King extended his hand, and Balthas, unable to resist, followed suit. 'We were allies, once. Brothers in spirit, if not blood. We tamed these realms and set the foundations for what they would become.'

'You freed me,' Nagash said, simply. 'A debt was owed. It has been repaid in full.' He shook his monstrous skull in dismissal. 'Is this the moment where you speak of our similarities, God-King? Where you play the wronged innocent, and once more extend the hand of friendship?'

'No. That moment has come and gone.' The lightning roiled outwards, burning black knots into the nearby crypts. Nagash's towering shape wavered, the amethyst fires retreating before the fury of the storm. 'The War of Heaven and Death begins anew. But this time, I will not make the mistake of mercy.'

'I am stronger now than I was then, barbarian.'

'And I am wiser. Let us see which of those proves the greater advantage, brother.' Sigmar looked down. His eyes burned like dying stars, and in that look, Balthas saw what was to come next. He saw Thaum rising up before him, wreathed in amethyst flame. Nagash roared and Thaum hurtled forwards, raising his blade.

Balthas flung his hand out, and lightning roared down. Thaum screamed and lunged through the smoke of his own burning. Balthas interposed his staff at the last moment, and the two warriors stumbled back, their weapons locked together.

'End me, fool,' Thaum snarled, his voice small against the immensity of Nagash, which still loomed above. He sounded strange, as if some struggle Balthas could not see were occurring within him. Above, both gods stood, watching as their champions reeled. 'End me if you can. Or I shall surely end you.'

Balthas said nothing. His eyes sought the azure spark he had seen earlier. He saw it, flickering through a hole in Thaum's armour. A gouge made by the claws of a beast, perhaps, or a Liberator's warblade.

There, Sigmar whispered. *A bit of me, trapped in the dark. A bit of who he was, struggling against the shadows that bind him. Set it free, Balthas. Give him the peace he has been denied.*

Balthas, holding his staff with one hand, drove his other into the gap. He felt the heat of the spark, felt it respond to his presence. It flared, a mote of light, hidden in the darkest shadow. Thaum stiffened. Blue light seeped from his tattered shape, piercing his limbs and torso in thin streams. He twitched. 'I... remember,' he said, and his face softened.

'I am sorry,' Balthas said, softly. Hoarsely. And then, one last time, he called down the lightning. The spark blossomed as the lightning fed into it. It grew, spreading within Thaum's form. Azure cracks formed on his armour and intangible flesh, growing wider.

His phantom shape began to crumble like paper in a fire. His sword fell from his hands and shattered, black shards spilling across the ground. He staggered back, a man-shaped torch of cobalt.

Thaum tried to speak, as the black helm slipped from a head that was no more solid than a wisp of smoke. He threw back his head, and gave a final, desolate howl before the storm caged within him broke free at last. His form shivered apart with a clap of thunder.

The shock wave shook the entire catacombs. Chunks of stone fell from above, crashing down into the necropolis, and the crypts surrounding Balthas crumbled into broken rubble as the fury of the storm radiated outwards in a single, frenzied moment. It washed over the catacombs and surged through the ranks of the dead, immolating the nighthaunts in a burst of cerulean radiance.

Pharus Thaum was gone.

Nothing more than ash, trailing away through the ravaged air. Nagash's form wavered like smoke on the breeze. But as he faded, he spoke one final time. 'You served me once, Balthas Arum, in another turn of the wheel, as a world burned, and you will do so again. As all who live shall eventually serve me.'

Then, he too was gone.

Balthas sank to one knee, breathing heavily. He felt wrung out – hollow. Smoke rose from the joins of his war-plate, and he knew the flesh beneath was blistered and burnt. Damaged beyond the scope of the healing arts of Azyr, perhaps. What was left of Thaum's war-plate lay nearby, smouldering. Beneath the exhaustion, he felt a flicker of regret.

He had come to bring a rogue soul peace. And he had done so. But somehow, victory felt like defeat. The sounds of battle had faded, with Pharus' fall, with the lightning. He tried to push himself to his feet, but he couldn't force his limbs to bear his weight. Not yet. He looked within himself, seeking some sign of Sigmar's presence. But the God-King was gone. This battle was ended, but there were others requiring his attentions. The War of Heaven and Death had begun anew.

'Lord-arcanum – do you live?'

Calys Eltain made her way towards him, her free hand pressed to her side. Blood stained her war-plate. Miska and several Sequitors followed her, stepping warily through the blasted rubble. Miska led Quicksilver by the reins. Balthas felt a flicker of relief at the beast's survival. Wearily, he bent his head, until it was resting against his staff. 'That… is entirely a matter of perspective,' he croaked.

'He's gone again,' Elya said, clinging to Calys' back. Balthas did not meet her eyes.

'He's gone,' he repeated. He closed his eyes. Just for a moment. Then, he pushed himself erect. 'But the battle is not done. Glymmsforge is still under siege.' He looked at Calys. 'And the Ten Thousand Tombs still need defending.'

She met his gaze and nodded. Balthas turned to Miska. 'Gather whoever is still standing. Knossus is going to need us.'

'As you say, my lord,' she said, bowing her head. She hesitated. 'You did well, brother.' She turned away, shouting for the others. Balthas stroked Quicksilver's neck, as the brute butted him in the chest.

'Easy. We have work yet to do.' Balthas dragged himself into the saddle, his body protesting. He looked up. Nagash, like Sigmar, was gone, but Balthas could still hear his final taunt, could still feel it echoing through the dark places within him.

You served me once, in another turn of the wheel, as a world burned, and you will do so again…

Balthas shook his head. 'No,' he said, softly. 'Never.'

And as he urged Quicksilver into motion, he found that he almost believed it.

EPILOGUE

AS CERTAIN AS THE STARS

NAGASHIZZAR, THE SILENT CITY

The desert was still burning.

Arkhan knew it would be for some time. He stood atop the ruins of one of the black watchtowers which lined the outer districts of Nagashizzar. The spirits bound to it had been freed during the necroquake, and so he could stand in blissful silence for a time. His dread abyssal, Razarak, lay nearby, tail clattering as it sat and waited patiently for its master to finish his ruminations. The skull-faced beast hissed softly, and Arkhan nodded.

'The sky is beautiful, yes.'

The horizon was awash in purple light, and ash fell like snow. Nagashizzar shook with its master's rage. Whatever came next, in the battle for Glymmsforge, for Lyria or the other underworlds, Nagash would not be satisfied. Once more, Sigmar had thwarted him. The War of Heaven and Death would continue.

The Mortarch of Sacrament could not help but feel some

small satisfaction at the way things had gone. He had wagered heavily, and lost little. Nagash had no one to blame but himself. The Undying King's rage would fall on lesser champions, and Arkhan would stand blameless, and loyal, as ever.

The failure had revealed much that was of interest. The Ten Thousand Tombs yet remained waiting – Sigmar had not destroyed them. Perhaps he lacked the power. Or, more likely, the God-King saw them for what they were: a resource yet untapped. The thought sent a prickle of apprehension through Arkhan's bones. If Sigmar had at last realised what Nagash and the Ruinous Powers already knew – that mortal souls were the most valuable resource in all the realms – then the game had truly entered a new, more deadly phase.

Razarak shifted its weight and hissed in warning. This, plus a bat-like screech from above, alerted Arkhan to the arrival of an uninvited guest. He looked up and saw the feline shape of a second dread abyssal swoop towards the tower. Ashigaroth was as recognisable as its master, and about as trustworthy.

The beast slammed into the edge of the tower and perched there, amid the crumbling ramparts of stone. It shrieked challengingly at Razarak, who responded with a restrained yawn. Arkhan gestured surreptitiously, and his steed settled back, content to ignore the newcomer. Ashigaroth's rider dropped from the saddle with a rattle of armour and the clink of spurs. Arkhan turned away.

'I do not recall requesting your presence, Mannfred.'

'Your little toy failed, liche. As did your scheme. Neferata is probably laughing herself sick in whatever palace she's currently occupying.'

Mannfred von Carstein's voice plucked at Arkhan's awareness like the buzzing of a singularly annoying insect. He turned slightly, as the vampire sidled towards him, smirking. 'I felt

Nagash's shout of rage echo through my skull. Thought it wise to return and offer my services. Perhaps he'll send me after Glymmsforge next. Now that you've failed.'

'The battle for the city still rages, leech. Malendrek might yet attain the victory Nagash demands. The Knight of Shrouds could well be elevated to the station he so desires. A new Mortarch come among us.'

Mannfred snorted. 'Doubtful.'

Arkhan said nothing. Privately, he agreed. Malendrek was powerful, but a fool. He was a weapon crafted from need and regret, blind to his own shortcomings. Much like the one who had created him. He brushed the thought aside as quickly as it had occurred to him. 'The future is written. What will be, will be.'

'How very philosophical of you.'

'Perspective, not philosophy. The end is not in doubt. Only the speed with which it arrives.' Arkhan looked out over the desert. 'Though it is best that it does not do so too soon.'

'That almost sounds like you don't want it to end at all,' Mannfred said, slyly. 'Have you come around to my view at last, liche?'

'No. I merely wish it to arrive at its predestined time. Death has its place, as all things do. It is part of the cosmic balance – as certain as the stars shine in the heavens, death welcomes all things.'

Mannfred laughed. 'A measured response. Nagash would not approve, I think. Especially as it concerns the certainty of the stars.' He tapped his claws against the pommel of the basket-hilted sword sheathed at his waist. 'I am curious – how does this wish of yours align with your manipulations of Nagash's newest servant? What scheme was born at the crossing of those two threads, liche?'

'There was no scheme.'

Mannfred drew his blade with a flourish and let the edge kiss the underside of Arkhan's jawbone. Behind them, Razarak heaved itself to its feet with a rumbling snarl. Ashigaroth crouched, growling shrilly. Arkhan gestured for his steed to remain where it was. This was nothing more than a bit of play-acting on the vampire's part.

Mannfred leaned close. 'Do me the courtesy of assuming that I am not so blind as all that, Arkhan, my old friend. I knew you were up to something the moment you sent Neferata and I away. And so did she.'

'And yet she is not here.'

'She is better-mannered than I am. Rest assured, her spies in Nagashizzar and Glymmsforge both have reported all that occurred to her already. But I am here, and put the question to you as one equal to another. What were you up to, if not to seize the glory of conquering Glymmsforge for yourself?'

Arkhan sighed, a sound like wind whistling among gravestones. He reached up and pushed Mannfred's blade aside. 'My concerns are neither glory nor conquest. The universe is caught fast between two spheres of order. One, a sword. The other, a shield.' He thumped the ground with his staff. 'Shyish is the sword. Azyr, the shield. Thus has it always been. Thus must it always be.'

Mannfred frowned and sheathed his blade. 'Nagash does not agree.'

'No. But he *believes*. And that is all that matters. Between them, Azyr and Shyish held the Ruinous Powers at bay for centuries. Even when lesser gods fell by the wayside, the Lords of Death and Heaven stood firm. They are two parts of the same whole – beginning and ending. One cannot stand without the other. The realms cannot stand without either.'

Mannfred chuckled. 'I begin to see, now, I think. How clever you are.' He clapped his hands mockingly. 'You think to manipulate the gods into open conflict, so that they might – what? – become allies once more, once they've vented their divine furies? Lanced the holy boil?' He leered at Arkhan, teeth bared in a snarl of derision. 'And then what, eh? Will they turn their attentions to the true foe who besets us?'

Arkhan shook his head. 'I manipulate no one. Nagash would have done this regardless. But, as you said – there was opportunity in the madness. And so I seized it.' He paused. 'And for the first time in centuries, the Undying King and the God-King met face-to-face. And neither destroyed the other.'

'Clever, liche, clever, clever, clever. Risky, though. A gamble.'

'Yes.'

'And what if your gamble should fail?'

'Then silence shall fall over the realms, and Nagash shall stand alone.'

Mannfred frowned. 'An unpleasant thought. An eternity of stultifying darkness. Even the damnations of Chaos might be preferable to that.' He shivered suddenly, as if recalling an unpleasant memory. He looked at Arkhan. 'If you'd told me sooner, I might have aided you. Neferata would have too. It serves our interests, as well.'

Arkhan looked at Mannfred. 'If I had told you, you would have simply sought your own advantage. I required a tool fit for purpose, and fortune bestowed one upon me. A weapon of both Azyr and Shyish, but truly part of neither.'

'And now that that weapon is destroyed?'

'There will be others. A saying occurs to me, though I cannot recall where I might have heard it… Rival lions must drink from the same oasis.'

Mannfred threw back his head and laughed. 'Quaint, but apt.'

He turned back towards his steed, flinging the edge of his cloak over his shoulder with a flourish. 'Let us hope you are right, Arkhan. Let us also hope that Nagash realises it, before it is too late. For if this war continues, it will not be long before the Ruinous Powers seek to turn it to their advantage.' The vampire climbed into the saddle. 'And if that happens, we are all surely doomed.'

He thumped Ashigaroth in the flanks, and the dread abyssal leapt from the tower with a raucous cry. Arkhan watched them swoop away, towards the horizon.

'Yes. Let us hope,' he said. After a moment, he turned away to take his own leave. Nagash would call for him, soon. There were new plans to be made. New wars to wage.

The Undying King commanded, and his most loyal servant would obey.

As sure as death. As certain as the stars.

ABOUT THE AUTHOR

Josh Reynolds is the author of the Horror novella *The Beast in the Trenches*, featured in the portmanteau novel *The Wicked and the Damned*. He has also written the Horus Heresy Primarchs novel *Fulgrim: The Palatine Phoenix*, and two audio dramas featuring the Blackshields: *The False War* and *The Red Fief*. His Warhammer 40,000 work includes *Lukas the Trickster* and the Fabius Bile novels *Primogenitor* and *Clonelord*. He has written many stories set in the Age of Sigmar, including the novels *Shadespire: The Mirrored City, Soul Wars, Eight Lamentations: Spear of Shadows*, the Hallowed Knights novels *Plague Garden* and *Black Pyramid*, and *Nagash: The Undying King*. His tales of the Warhammer old world include *The Return of Nagash* and *The Lord of the End Times*, and two Gotrek & Felix novels. He lives and works in Sheffield.

YOUR NEXT READ

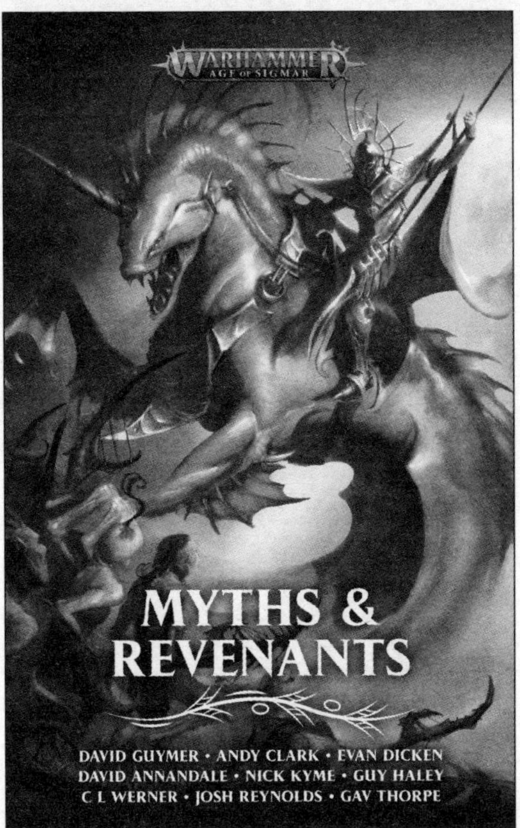